THE RED PEONY

BOOKS BY LIN YUTANG

KAIMING ENGLISH BOOKS (3 vols.)

KAIMING ENGLISH GRAMMAR

THE LITTLE CRITIC (2 vols.)

CONFUCIUS SAW NANCY
AND ESSAYS ABOUT NOTHING

A NUN OF TAISHAN

A HISTORY OF THE PRESS AND
PUBLIC OPINION IN CHINA

MY COUNTRY AND MY PEOPLE

THE IMPORTANCE OF LIVING

WISDOM OF CONFUCIUS

MOMENT IN PEKING

WITH LOVE AND IRONY

A LEAF IN THE STORM

WISDOM OF CHINA AND INDIA

BETWEEN TEARS AND LAUGHTER

THE VIGIL OF A NATION

THE GAY GENIUS

CHINATOWN FAMILY

WISDOM OF LAOTSE

ON THE WISDOM OF AMERICA

WIDOW, NUN AND COURTESAN

FAMOUS CHINESE SHORT STORIES

VERMILION GATE

LOOKING BEYOND

LADY WU

THE SECRET NAME

THE CHINESE WAY OF LIFE

FROM PAGAN TO CHRISTIAN

THE IMPORTANCE OF UNDERSTANDING

LIN YUTANG

THE RED PEONY

THE WORLD PUBLISHING COMPANY

CLEVELAND AND NEW YORK

PUBLISHED BY The World Publishing Company
2231 WEST 110TH STREET, CLEVELAND 2, OHIO

PUBLISHED SIMULTANEOUSLY IN CANADA BY
NELSON, FOSTER & SCOTT LTD.

Library of Congress Catalog Card Number: 61-12018

FIRST EDITION

The flower, half unfolding, half withholding,
Pauses in quivering hesitation,
Hanging a smile upon her dreamy lips
That none may know her love-essence within.

BOOK ONE

CHAPTER 1

At the last rites of Fei Tingyen, Chief Secretary of the Salt Tax Bureau in Kaoyu, April 23, 1891, the friends of the deceased came in to pay their respects; each bowed deeply three times before the black coffin, then tiptoed away—the men to one side, the women to the other. This was a makeshift affair, hastily arranged by some friends of the family, before the remains were shipped back to the deceased's home town for burial.

The day was uncomfortably hot and humid. Forty or fifty men, women, and children crowded about in the small yard of the house. It was an old, rented house, with ceilings made of exposed, unpainted beams. The friends, most of whom had never been invited there before, were surprised to find that Mr. and Mrs. Fei had lived so modestly, for Fei had come from a family of wealthy landlords in Kashing, down in the lake region below Shanghai. There was a touch of poetic disorder about the bare furnishings and books in the study, where some of the guests had congregated. Two latticed windows, with their original vermilion paint faded to dull, cracked pink, let in a barely adequate light, made even dimmer by the moving, whispering shadows of the guests. Some of the women noticed cobwebs around the corners of the windows, and decided that the young widow was not much of a housewife.

Many of Fei's colleagues had come out of curiosity to see the young widow, whom they had heard spoken of as a great beauty. She would be there today, they knew, standing beside the casket, responding to the bows of the guests.

The somber memorial service had made everyone feel uneasy. Something was not right. There was a bitter incongruity between the solemn funeral atmosphere and horrendous-looking casket, and the young widow's white face, half hidden by her peaked mourning cap. She was encased like a human sacrifice in that sharp-pointed cap of coarse white cotton, overlaid with burlap, and the bulky sackcloth of the same material. That white image of a half-moon, with the long, dark lashes, very straight nose, luscious lips, and well-modeled chin, gleamed in the darkness at the far end of the room, where a pair of large candles on the altar table flickered with lurid, satanical lights. Her bowed head seemed like a silent protest against the whole scheme of things. They understood the widow was only twenty-two. A widow of a scholar, or of a member of the rich upper classes, was, in the best moral tradition of the times, not ever supposed to remarry.

The men were overcome with sympathy for this pretty young woman, for the sacrifice of such youth and beauty. These men were chiefly members of the Salt Tax Bureau. Most of them were married, and had come with their wives for various motives of their own. Some had come as a matter of social obligation, some were deeply shocked by the suddenness with which the hand of Death had struck one of their own, in the midst of the raging cholera epidemic. The minor clerks (who had disliked their haughty, effervescent colleague), came because the Chief of Bureau had ordered them to contribute toward a handsome gift of money for the widow, to be presented in the name of the staff—money which they could ill afford, and which the rich family of the deceased did not need. One among them, who was expecting the arrival of his wife and family in a month, and had already rented a house, hoped to find a good brass bed and some redwood chairs; he knew that the widow was going away, and the furniture might be bought at a bargain.

Shueh, the Chief of Bureau, a tall man with sharp features, was especially proud that through his influence they had been able to secure a casket of such fine quality, at a time when the coffin shops were rapidly running out of stock. He wanted to have the personal satisfaction of watching everyone admire it; and so he had spread the word that the widow was a remarkably attractive woman. She had always kept very much to herself, and he was one of the few who had seen her before.

The Bureau had done its best for the widow, since none of her husband's family had appeared to help out. They had sent an old family servant to assist with the transportation of the remains; but Liensheng was half deaf, and utterly useless on this occasion, since he did not understand the Mandarin dialect spoken in the area.

Ceremony required that a relative of the deceased stand at one end of the casket and respond to the bows. Even a child would be acceptable. But Mrs. Fei had no children, so she herself stood behind the casket, like a lump of burlap-covered misery. From time to time the burlap shape stirred, as her legs shifted. You could see her heavy-lashed eyelids winking in deep preoccupation. Once in a while, she glanced up, seeing, yet not seeing the crowd before her, in a veiled look that was totally indifferent to the proceedings. Beads of perspiration glistened on her forehead. Her eyes were dry. She neither sniffed nor wailed aloud, as in good form she should have.

Many among those present had noticed this fact. How dare she not weep! Her total absence of tears or signs of grief at her husband's funeral was shocking, according to the rules of convention. She did nothing, except to bow as required, but this "nothing" was so palpable and visible that it was offensive to all well-mannered persons. It was like watching a lighted firecracker which did not go off.

Some of the men had withdrawn to the eastern room, which looked out on the front yard. With great relish they discussed what was going on.

"Imagine old Fei having such a pretty wife and going about whoring!" an elderly man remarked.

"Who can tell about these things? Did you see her eyes? Such deep, mobile, flashing eyes. 'Liquid temperament and floating pussy willows,' as we say. She certainly was not grieving for her husband."

"I saw them. What beauty and what passion in that pair of eyes! I bet you she is going to remarry."

"Shut up!" said another colleague, annoyed. "Who are we to judge? All right, there's a plague. I understand Tingyen had two elder brothers. Even if the old man wouldn't come himself, he should have sent one of the brothers, and not let the young woman handle all this by herself."

"Not even a snivel, or a sob or whimper," said a small, wizened man, in an oversized gown that covered his ankles.

"They shouldn't have put her through it. She can't go on like this, standing for hours," said a soft-spoken old man in his sixties, square jawed and wearing a pair of horn spectacles called "crystal glasses of Canton." He was Mr. Wang, the schoolteacher and a neighbor of the deceased. With his grayish mustache and tufts of sparse, yellowish beard he commanded the respect due a scholar of his venerable age. He held his two-foot-long tobacco pipe unlit, and seemed to fidget with it.

The Chief, Shueh, who spoke with a heavy Anhwei accent, interrupted. His black, heavy mustache moved sharply as he said, "I do not think there are many visitors today except our circle. If we do not talk, others won't. Above all, do not make an issue of it—whether she wails properly or not. As far as transportation is concerned, I have asked my nephew to help. No one shall say that the Bureau did not do its best."

A young man with a noncommittal face gave a small snort. "All right, there's the plague as you say." He directed his words to the schoolteacher. "His family shouldn't have been so scared. They should have sent one of his brothers along. A funeral is a funeral, after all."

"Of course, they will have the regular ceremonies in their home town. All they want is to transport the remains home.

But I can't help thinking that they might have shown some consideration for the widow. She is so young."

"How old is she?"

"Twenty-two," answered the schoolteacher.

"How long have they been married?"

"Only two or three years, my wife tells me. And it never looked like much of a honeymoon. Well, it's none of our business." The scholar closed the subject with a sense of delicacy.

The scholar's wife appeared at this juncture to whisper to her husband. She was a broad-faced woman in her fifties, with a long upper lip, and radiated serenity and good cheer wherever she appeared.

"If there are no more callers, we may inform Mrs. Fei to withdraw. It's almost noon now. It's no joke for a woman to stand for hours like this. And there is no one to take her place for a change. Have a heart, you gentlemen."

The scholar rose and approached the tall Chief of Bureau. "Mr. Shueh, this is not much of a ceremony, I know. I think it would be kind of us all to leave now, and not stay for the noodles. One doesn't have the heart to eat. Sympathy is in the heart. Chief, if you say the word, we'll all leave, and let Mrs. Fei rest."

Chief Shueh's roving eyes creased a little, which showed that, in spite of his notorious deals, he was not entirely unromantic where women were concerned.

"Of course," he said in a throaty voice. "You are perfectly right."

His re-entry to the central hall was taken as a signal. He did not speak; he winked. Everybody watched and understood. Liu, the nephew, who had been recording the gifts and callers' names, stood up from his desk near the door and closed his book. One by one, they approached the coffin to say farewell to the dead man; each bowed silently, and tiptoed toward the door with great solemnity.

Old Shueh took an extra minute loitering at the coffin, giving it a few taps with his knuckles to listen to its hard, firm thuds, and beamed with immense satisfaction.

"Such beautiful timber!" he murmured admiringly.

Young Mrs. Fei raised her head at this moment, perceptibly relieved, but with that same preoccupied look in her eyes.

When the guests had left, schoolteacher Wang remained. His wife had taken charge of the light lunch of a simple soup with noodles and white buns, and was staying to help with the formalities. Even though these business friends had left—friends chiefly associated with the Salt Tax Bureau—there were still sundry neighbors who had come to pay their respects and offer condolences, and the requirements of form must be observed strictly. White buns had to be sent to those who brought presents. Such details required a woman's attention.

Young Mrs. Fei was inwardly grateful. Mr. and Mrs. Wang were her neighbors living at the other end of the street, and Mrs. Fei, young and lonely, used to visit them and play with their children, of whom she was very fond. They had not been really close friends of either herself or her husband; but when she needed help, when catastrophe struck at her house, swift and unexpected, when she was left alone to handle the entire, complicated business and the social aspects of a funeral, this couple had suddenly come and extended that hand of sympathy and help which she so sorely needed.

"Thank you so much," she said to Mrs. Wang, simply and yet, rather distantly, when the latter had led her to her chamber. She said this without even looking at Mrs. Wang—in a voice young, resonant, but peculiarly soft, like a small jingling bell which had a hidden crack. She spoke very much as a child would have, without affectation and without demonstrativeness. Then, almost as an afterthought, she added, "I don't know how I could get through all this without you."

"Oh, but you are alone," replied Mrs. Wang. "It is the least a friend can do."

The simple thanks were accepted with an equal simplicity. The scholar's wife continued, "Now you lie down a little. I will go to the kitchen and fetch you some soup. Don't you worry about the distribution of presents. I'll see about it. And you will need all your strength for the voyage home."

She helped the widow take off the bundle of sackcloth. A charming, youthful, almost girlish figure in white emerged. Peony (which was her name) had successfully resisted the temptation to use powder and lipstick today—it might have caused a scandal—but the natural bloom of youth and her pursed cherry lips did not really require cosmetics. The older woman saw the beads of perspiration on her forehead and gave her a towel.

"It must have been stifling under that sackcloth," she said as she helped to wipe her forehead. "It is so unusually warm."

Two pearls of tears formed on the edge of the young woman's eyelids, poised there an instant, about to brim over. But she controlled herself.

It was after Mrs. Wang had left the room and she had thrown herself upon her bed that she really broke down crying. It was the first time that she had wept, and wept bitterly, since her husband died, and, in fact, since he had been struck down with the epidemic. If she had tried to cry those last few days, she would not have been able to find tears. Now a sluice gate had been opened and an irrepressible flood of hot, unsuspected tears burst out like spring freshets over a dam.

She lay thinking, not of her husband, but of herself, of her future, not yet sketched in, of her young life, yet to be lived. She had nothing to grieve for in her loveless marriage, which had been arranged by her parents against her wishes. Her life had been a series of frustrations, and that was not only because Fei Tingyen philandered openly with women, or that he was boorish and in a young, conceited way, habitually talked with a kind of swagger which she despised and which irritated her. Highly sensitive and passionate by nature, she knew what love could be, had experienced too bitterly the joys and pains of a hopeless romance, had known all the pangs and remorse of passion for a man who was taken away from her against her will. Chin Chu, her lover, was now married and had two children. But they had carried on and met secretly even after her marriage. She felt like a fly caught in a spider's web, in an entanglement which confused her mind and thinking. And now as her tears flowed from a deep and nameless source, there was an urgency about it, a longing for what she did not know. Nevertheless, she experienced an immense relief from the mere act of crying and felt better for it.

She had chuckled inwardly when all the women guests bemoaned the harsh fate of her having lost a husband while so young, with the prospect of lifelong widowhood. The women's thoughts were on their tongues; they all sympathized with her; they all said quite openly that such young widowhood was "difficult." (According to custom, they discussed a widow as they discussed a bride, in her hearing, because neither the widow nor the bride was supposed to talk back.)

The women's assumption was that she was going to pay the full price for Virtue. Virtue in widowhood had been codified and classified into two main well-defined categories; it should be a widow's aspiration to be one of two things—"Madame Chaste" (*chiehfu*) for lifelong widowhood, and "Madame Heroic" (*liehfu*) for those who chose to commit suicide against attempts to force them to remarry.

Peony had dismissed these thoughts with a chuckle. Her joy in living and her youthful instincts told her that it was all wrong. She was seeking, consciously, and this was backed by her reading, what was good and beautiful and satisfying in every man and woman's life, and she was far too intelligent to let the women's talk disturb her. Temperamental and of an impetuous nature, sensitive, noble, and craving for an ideal, she had small regard for what was accepted good form. If she happened to weep or wail aloud, it was because she wanted to.

Mrs. Wang was somewhat long in the kitchen. Coming in with a tray of hot steaming soup and some dish of an appetizing, pungent odor, she was surprised to find the young woman, her black hair loosened over her shoulders, bending over a bamboo-framed bookcase in most un-widowlike fashion, and looking for something.

"What are you doing?" chided Mrs. Wang. "Come on, you must eat something!"

As the young woman turned around, Mrs. Wang saw the keen excitement in her eyes. Peony's face flushed as if her innermost secrets had been exposed.

Mrs. Wang moved a chair. "Now sit down and eat!" Her tone was almost motherly. "I have fried some eggs with minced ham, and I am going to eat with you, and see that you eat."

Peony really smiled, pleasantly. She knew Mrs. Wang's way with her five children, and she was not surprised by the woman's kind solicitude.

In the midst of her eating, however, Mrs. Wang noticed Peony's red, swollen eyes and said, quite vehemently, "I wish those visitors could see you now."

"Why?" asked Peony, puzzled.

"You have really wept."

"And they would have approved, I know," snapped the young widow.

The vacuous look had returned, and Peony went on eating her eggs silently. No one could possibly know or understand why she had cried, lying in bed a moment ago. She wished that Mrs. Wang weren't there, so that she could be left alone with her own thoughts and the problems which vexed her mind. She wanted to make sure that the schoolteacher's wife did not see her love letters as she packed.

"What were you looking for when I came in?" Mrs. Wang said, to bridge the chasm of silence.

"Looking for our *fuchih*, the district history of Hangchow," she lied.

"Is that your home town?"

"Yes. I am from Yuyao county."

"I suppose after the hundred days are over, you'll want to go back and see your maiden family."

"I suppose so."

Mr. Wang tapped at the open door. He wanted some tea. He had finished his meal in the study and wanted to know how they were doing, and when his wife would be able to go home.

"You go home first. I want to keep Mrs. Fei company. She'll have all this packing to do."

To the scholar's surprise, the widow had stood up and asked him to come in. The scholar hesitated. He was of the elder generation and his wife was there, but all the same, his whole breeding was against his stepping into a neighboring woman's bedroom.

Peony saw the hesitation on his face and advanced toward the door. Addressing him respectfully as "Old Teacher Wang," she said, "I really must thank both you and your wife for all the help. I'll bring tea to the study, and ask you for some advice."

A minute later, the young widow appeared with a tray in hand and brought tea to the study. Mr. Wang stood up and said a courteous *pukantang* ("You shouldn't have done this").

Peony's manner was crisp, lively, so unbecoming a widow whose husband had died only a fortnight ago. Mr. Wang saw the youthful apparition before him and his heart twitched a little. A pretty young woman in her early twenties, condemned to a lifelong widowhood. So it was to be, he assumed. At least, this was accepted form among the widows of ranking scholars with government degrees. Widows of common people often remarried, but not the widows of *shiutsai* or *churen* (scholars with the equivalent, respectively, of B.A.'s or M.A.'s, in the imperial examinations) observing a code that Confucianists had imposed on their women.

At this moment, Old Teacher Wang found it somewhat difficult to visualize the young woman before him as a lifelong martyr to Virtue. She did not look it.

"Old Teacher, you have been so kind. You can give me advice on what to do. Tomorrow I will go home with Liensheng and escort the spirit casket home." (She used the euphemistic and literary word, *lingchiu*, for the casket.) "I shall wear the sackcloth, of course, as I go down to the boat. Is it necessary to wear it all the way?"

"This is a matter of the heart, Mrs. Fei. Certainly you should on embarkation and disembarkation, especially on disembarkation, when your parents will come to meet you." Surveying her from top to bottom, he said, "You shouldn't appear like this. I do think it necessary. You should wail all the way until the *lingchiu* is carried within your husband's house. Of course I know nothing about your parents-in-law, but normally they would expect it of you. There will be sisters-in-law and women neighbors, and they'll all be watching. You wouldn't want them to say things behind your back."

Old Teacher said all this fluently, expertly, like a professional guide at a temple or historic monument.

"And what is going to happen to me?"

"The probability is that your family will adopt a child to continue the altar fire of your husband. They always do this. They say it helps to keep a young widow's mind chaste and virtuous to have a child to look after. Mind you, I don't mean that young widowhood is easy, but it has to be *got through*. Did your husband have a government degree?"

"Not really. He paid for a *kungsheng* when the government was raising money for flood relief. It was the year before I married him. You know, a thousand dollars for a *shiutsai*, three for a *churen*, and I think five hundred for a *kungsheng*." (A *kungsheng* was not a degree, but a "fellowship" subsidized by the government.)

Old Teacher studied the young woman's face sharply, and uttered an "I see!"

"What do you mean?"

Old Teacher was on familiar ground. "It is like this. It is up to you, up to you entirely. I shouldn't be discussing this. But you have asked me. You want to know what to do. I say it is up to you. It would practically be unheard of for a *shiutsai's* widow to remarry. But a *kungsheng* is 'still in the running,' as we say. So much also depends on your husband's family. When they talk of adopting a baby for you, you know what they expect of you."

"Do you think it is right?"

"As I have said, it is a matter of the heart. Also, it depends upon what your parents-in-law are willing to provide for you."

"Don't you think a woman would prefer to have a baby of her own?"

The old schoolteacher was really embarrassed; his face flushed.

"I think you should discuss this problem with your own mother. She is still living, I presume?"

"Yes, in Hangchow."

"Well, then, don't bother your head about it. Go through the hundred days of mourning like a good daughter-in-law. Perhaps they will permit you to visit your mother for a rest. Hangchow is not far away. I hear you are from the clan of Liang of Hangchow. Have you ever heard of Liang Mengchia of Hangchow?"

Peony's face suddenly lit up. "Of course, you mean Liang *Hanlin*, the academician. As a matter of fact, we are related—cousins. We of the clan refer to him as 'our *hanlin*.' There is no other." Her evident pride was understandable. On the average, a clan might produce a *hanlin*, a Member of the Imperial Academy, in a hundred years. Such a degree was a feather in the cap of every clansman.

"He should be able to advise you."

"He hardly knows me. He is in Peking all the time. I saw him only once when he came back; I was a girl of ten or eleven."

"I thought you might know him. I saw on the shelf some published volumes of his essays."

Peony walked over to the shelf with her hip-swaying, lazy shuffle and, pointing to three volumes on the second shelf, said proudly, "There they are!"

Mr. Liu, the nephew of Chief Shueh, came in to inform Mrs. Fei that a boat had been engaged, ready to start down the Grand Canal the next morning, whenever she was ready. He would send someone to help with the luggage. To tell the truth, Liu was surprised to see the widow out of her sackcloth and talking so vivaciously with the schoolteacher.

The accidental mention of the "Imperial Academician" at Peking left a pleasant echo in Peony's mind. When she was at the impressionable age of eleven, the young Liang Mengchia, then twenty-seven, had returned to Hangchow after his crowning victory at the national championship in letters. He had laid a hand on her forehead and called her "brilliant"—a compliment which dominated the years of her girlhood. For a moment, images, memories, sounds, a particular garden tree in her home leaped out of the long forgotten past and jabbed at her tired nerves.

Mrs. Wang was truly wonderful. Although young Mrs. Fei had never confided in her, although she was going away tomorrow, and most probably would never return, she felt it her human duty to see the young woman through.

The packing was largely woman's work in this case. Peony was only to take her personal belongings along. The furniture, the heavy equipment of the household, was to be left behind; it would be sold or transported later.

Mrs. Wang helped by turning out would-be callers, sending for things needed, such as twine and locks, and buying an oilcloth for protection of the luggage. Now and then a word of encouragement, a smile, a touch on her shoulder made Peony feel that she was being treated like one of Mrs. Wang's own daughters. Yet when Peony, profoundly moved, offered her in all sincerity a jade brooch as a parting gift, Mrs. Wang felt offended.

"What do you think of me? I came to help because I thought you needed help. I came because I wanted to. Are you paying me for it?"

"No, but I am sincere. I *want* to give you this as a souvenir."

Mrs. Wang did not reply. The forceful way in which she put back the offered article and buried it in one of the receptacles in the trunk gave a touch of finality to her words.

Mrs. Wang's own boy had run over to ask when she would be home, and the mother replied, "Tell your second sister to prepare the supper without me. I'm staying over for supper with Mrs. Fei."

When candles were lit, the Old Teacher found that by a kind of unconscious volition he was back in the Fei house again. He remembered that when the young widow spoke of "our *hanlin*," the *hanlin* of her clan, there was an almost childish intensity in her voice, like a confession of faith. It reminded him of a little boy shouting proudly in the streets, "That top is mine!" He wanted to hear more about the Liang *Hanlin* from the widow.

After supper, they were having tea and plums in the eastern room. After some routine irrelevancies, they were soon back on the topic of what she was going to do about herself. She had come right to the point. She had already indicated that she would not care to raise an adopted baby but would prefer to have one of her own.

"If my parents-in-law want a child to continue the ancestral altar fire of my husband, any of his nephews will do. All that is necessary would be to take one of them and *kuochi*, in order to have him adopted as the legal heir of the deceased son."

The naïveté of her words really piqued the Old Teacher. "I see you are a kind of rebel," he commented.

"I stand rebuked," replied Peony. The highly polished phrase (*yen chung liao*), so unexpected, pleased the scholar.

"Old Teacher Wang," she said, "I am only a woman. You men scholars have thought it all out. The Sung scholars started this cult of widowhood. Confucius never started it. 'No widowers abroad, no lonely women at home'—wasn't this what he taught?"

The schoolteacher was somewhat taken aback, and stuttered. "Of course, it started with the Sung philosophers."

"Through the Hans and the Tangs, none of the Confucian scholars knew about *li*, Universal Reason," Peony was quick to reply. "Does this mean that the Sung scholars were right and Confucius himself was wrong? So you place Universal Reason over and against human nature. The Han and Tang scholars never did this. The *fulfillment* of human nature was really what the sages taught as the human ideal. Universal Reason and human nature were one. Now the *lishueh*, Sung Puritans, came along and started to repress human nature as sin. It's all Buddhism."

"Where did you learn all this?" The Old Teacher was truly surprised at this stream of heterodox outburst, especially coming from a young woman.

"Isn't it what our *hanlin* says?"

She pulled out a volume of Liang's essays, and showed him the passage which embodied such astounding thoughts—new even to the teacher himself. Wang had heard of Liang's national reputation, but had never read him.

Old Wang read on, fascinated by the ideas and style. He recited it, word by word, enjoying the sound of it, with a low mutter coming through his moving beard, shaking his head now and then in visible appreciation. Liang wrote with classic terseness almost in an archaic idiom, as if to make every word count, precise and weighted with thought, as few affected to do.

Peony's eyes followed the schoolteacher as he read.

"Well, what do you think?" she asked tensely, a gurgle of pride rising in her throat.

"Beautiful! Beautiful!"

"What do you say to his thoughts and ideas?" Peony pursued, unsatisfied.

"*I chia yen*, very original indeed! What can I say, as a village schoolmaster, about one of the foremost writers or our day? My opinion is not worth anything. But what a classic style he writes in! I like that part toward the end where he really tears apart the idea of the orthodox school, and says that the Neo-Confucianists stood to profit, by making themselves the 'spokesmen of heaven.' *Tai tien shing chiao*—what they say was almost the Word of God—'The Puritans deny themselves pleasure and love to see their women suffer, too.' That's where he is trenchant, powerful, devastating. He can get away with it. Nobody else could."

Peony gobbled up every word of this praise as if it were a tribute to herself.

"I adore our *hanlin*," she said. "I chuckle every time he calls the *lishueh* 'cold-pork eaters.'"

"You are lucky to have such an illustrious son of your clan. What does he look like?"

"A wide head bulging at the temples and a pair of scintillating, sparkling eyes. Oh, yes, I remember his soft white hands. It was so long ago."

"And you have not seen him again? Doesn't he come home for the ancestral sacrifices?"

"No. We never saw him again. I haven't seen him since I was a child. He's been in Peking, at the Imperial Court, all these years."

"Your people must have corresponded with him."

"Oh, we wouldn't dare. He is just a name to us."

Peony forgot how she was drawn into this conversation. She had not talked about Liang to her husband, or to anybody else, for years. Her face was flushed, the skin around her eyes was firm and smooth, and her eyes were distant. After a while she said, "The idea of my forgetting to pack these books! I had intended to have them sent for."

"Is all the packing done?"

"Almost. We just have to leave certain things and send for them later. I am bringing my personal things and the 'soft goods' of my husband. There won't be much room in the boat, half taken up with that casket."

Just before leaving, Mr. and Mrs. Wang said good-by and asked, "Won't you wail a little before the *lingchiu*, just for form's sake? The neighbors may talk." This wailing was usually done during the evening vigils for seven times seven days.

"Let them. I can't."

"But you'll have to when you are in your parents-in-laws' home."

"Oh, don't worry. I can pretend when there are others wailing with me."

When they were outside the door, Mrs. Wang said to her husband, "It makes my heart ache to see such a bitter fate for a young girl—to become a widow for life. And without a child, too!"

"Just you watch," her husband replied. "There is a little rebel. One day you'll hear of an explosion. She has a mind of her own."

"What were you talking about in the study?"

"Nothing that you'd understand."

CHAPTER 2

They had to pay an exorbitant fare for the boat on account of the unusual nature of the "cargo."

The boat they had hired to transport the casket was a small affair, not much more than thirty feet long on the outside. A bamboo matting, or rather two or three of them sliding into each other, bent like a tent over the middle of the boat, served as shelter against rain or sun. Mrs. Fei arrived in a sedan chair, and remained in it, her head lowered, her face partly covered by the cap of hemp, while the casket was being placed toward the bow. The coffin was draped in red, so that it would not be resented by people passing in other boats as bringing "bad luck." A strip of white cloth placed across the front of the casket bore characters giving the identity of the deceased. Bureau Chief Shueh and his nephew Liu were there helping.

Mr. and Mrs. Wang were also there, to stay with the widow till the last minute. When all was ready, the old servant and Mrs. Wang escorted her gingerly down the bank, across the shaky gangplank into the boat, where a space toward aft under the matting, spread with bedding and pillow, had been reserved for her to sit or lie down. The voyage would take perhaps ten days—across the Yangtse and then to the lake region around Soochow, via the Grand Canal.

As the gangplank was hauled away, she stood up to thank all those friends who had come to say good-by. All they could see was her half-covered face and tightly drawn lips showing from under the ceremonial mourning cap; she stood like a statue, silent as death.

The Grand Canal traffic was always crowded below Kaoyu,

on the way to Yangchow, a great center of luxury in those days. No more than forty or sixty feet across, varying a great deal from place to place according to the terrain, the imperial waterway was crowded with the traffic of sampans, dinghies, lorchas, and houseboats, some with elaborately carved and painted cabins, others bare and nondescript. The air resounded with the splashing of oars and knocking of punting poles, the thump of boatmen's bare feet upon the floor boards, the creak of bamboo matting, and the harsh scraping of wood as boat knocked against boat; it was a form of transportation as leisurely as it was comfortable. Passing through town after town, the scene was always lively, and jam-packed traffic was normal and expected; one got nowhere by trying to push forward and bypass others. Shops and homes stood on the banks; or where the banks were high, the houses and lofts were supported by piles drilled into the lower bank level. Buckets were let down from these lofts to haul in water from the Canal, and women, kneeling on the banks, beat their laundry on smooth flagstones. In summer, the banks echoed with the tap-tap-tap of washing clubs and the gabble and laughter of the women, their babies playing at their sides, or riding on their backs. Especially on moonlit nights, in spring or summer, the splatter and chatter increased as one came near a town, for women preferred the cool evenings in which to do their laundering. Young men, too, strolled along the banks, to watch either the moon, or the parade of female bottoms, as the women bent over their washing labors.

Out in the country, the Canal usually broadened, and the sails were hoisted to take advantage of the wind. As the boats slid between the green banks, the curving sails made silhouettes against the morning or evening sky. In the heat of the day, the boatmen, usually stripped to the waist, sat smoking their pipes, their queues tied up in a circle around their heads, their firm brown shoulders and backs and limbs shining in the sun.

As soon as the boat had started and the friends seeing her off had departed, Peony experienced a strange solitude and freedom; her voyage had finally begun. The fuss and hesitancies and last-minute decisions over what was to be packed in, or left out, were over. She felt a deep sense of finality, of at last being on the way to a new future and new problems, a sense of being utterly alone, of holding a mental mirror to her own soul, and of closing one chapter of her life and opening another. The future was vague and dark, not yet sketched in. She felt a strange new stirring inside her.

The spring breeze and the sight of the green country seemed to clear her head and she was able to breathe freely, to think in a mood of blissful solitude. She lay back on her pillow, staring at the matting close in front with an abstracted expression. She had thrown off the sackcloth and was in her tight-fitting white pajamas. At this moment, she certainly did not look like a widow in mourning. She was totally oblivious of the couple in charge of the boat and their daughter, a young woman with a bouncing apple face, an open smile, and a prominent, full bosom. Liensheng kept to himself at the bow of the boat; it did not matter to her, anyway. She had let her hair down, and her hands were cradling her knees in a kind of luxurious reverie over her unknown future. It would create a scandal if she left her husband's home too soon, she knew, and her own parents would object. But she knew that her fate was in her own hands, and she was not going to let anyone interfere. She lit a cigarette, gave a puff, and slid down into a reclining position, a posture which no conventional lady would assume in broad daylight without covering herself properly. Her eyes rested on a small diamond ring sparkling on her finger. Chin Chu had given it to her. She moved her hand about and watched the diamond catch the sunlight. Under her breath she mumbled Chin Chu's name.

The ring was given to her after they'd had a bitter argument. Chin Chu and she were both quick-tempered. They had had many lovers' quarrels and each time, love triumphed. The ring was a reminder of that triumph. She had forgotten what they had quarreled about, but there was such tenderness in his eyes when he brought her that gift—a look which made their differences of opinion seem entirely unimportant. That was Chin

Chu always. He had an instinct for buying her things she wanted—small feminine things, like Yangchow lipstick and a fine big-meshed Soochow hair net—presenting them to her with an utterly captivating look of tender adoration.

For once in her life, she was now truly alone and independent. No one who was not in love could know the infinite pleasure of being alone and free. Yet at the same time her heart was filled with an infinite sadness and longing, a sense of the tragedy of her life. She longed to see Chin Chu.

Perhaps the day after tomorrow she would be able to meet him at Chinkiang. She had sent a letter ahead and was sure that he would come. The very thought quickened her pulse. For Peony, to desire a thing was to have it already. Chin Chu was the reason for her wanting to break away from widowhood as quickly as she could. He was now living with his family in Soochow, but he had a grandmother and two aunts living in Hangchow, which was his ancestral home. Twice or three times a year, she would come home to visit her mother and, behind her husband's back, meet Chin Chu in hotels and on prearranged trips to Tienmushan, or Mokanshan. Once she met him at the home of her best friend, Paiwei. Both were driven by a power greater than themselves. Each meeting, the more frenzied for its being so hopeless, left them tormented with a longing and sadness for the time when they could meet again. Externally, each lived a normal life.

The boat glided along, its rhythmic creak of oars and the suck and swish of the water sending her deeper into reverie. Soon she would be free, and they would be able to meet as usual, two or three times a year perhaps, but what was she going to do with herself the rest of the time? Was it possible to carry this on forever? Her heart pounded as she thought of her dream—that they might belong to each other completely and she could have Chin Chu all to herself, with nobody else around to bother them. She knew she was being selfish, but Chin Chu loved her passionately, had no other wish than to marry her. She was his first and only love. Peony had no grudge against Mrs. Chin, whom she had seen with her children. Mrs.

Chin had a very slender, ordinary Soochow figure, and wasn't bad looking. If Chin Chu loved her as much as she loved him, why would he not have the courage and the determination to sacrifice everything for her? That was the question which bothered her.

She took out from her trunk a copy of the letter she had written to him as soon as she knew she would be leaving Kaoyu, and stared at her own words, as if in rereading them they might once again express the full intensity of her longing.

Dear Chin Chu:

My husband died a week ago. All social conventions to the contrary, I shall break free, no matter what it costs, to be near you. Are you not happy to hear this news? I am coming to Kashing and shall be passing Chinkiang on or about the 26th or 27th. Please come. I have so much to discuss with you and I must meet you and have your opinion at this crisis of my life. Leave word for me with the gate keeper of the Goldhill Temple so that I will know where we can meet.

I know that you and I shall be able to keep this a secret from all gossiping tongues, which don't concern me in the least, anyway. For my part, I am disposed to sacrifice everything to belong to you completely. I do not know what you will think of me. I do not want to wreck your happy home. I have no wish to hurt your wife. But what can we do, if we love each other madly?

I have gone over your situation, point by point, and fully appreciate your difficulty. I shall be willing to wait two or three years to be your wife, if I know that you love me as much as I love you. I shall be able to endure everything if I have your love.

At this moment of my life, I have to think of my future, our future. Sometimes I wish that you were with me now, every minute, and nothing and nobody should stand between us. I do not want our love to be a burden and a remorse to you. I am not prepared to give you up—not ever. I am ready to abandon everything, sacrifice everything, to be at your side. Will you be able to do as much for me?

I fully realize the dilemma we are in, and the love which enslaves both of us. But please understand clearly, I do not want to prejudice you. I do not want anything which does not spring from your own free and fervent will.

I do not know what to think. I know that you adore me, and I have thought and thought until my insides are tied into a hundred knots. Always the question remains: if we love each other so much, how can we live separated from each other? Do you love me enough to take this step?

Pardon me for this letter. Pardon me for this madness. Pardon me for loving you so much!!!

It is my exasperation and my deep longing for you which make me write like this.

Once more, I want you to remember I shall be free of all obligations in August, and shall be your wife whenever you say so, whenever you are free.

Please do not think evil of me, for all that I do is done out of my love for you.

I love you. I need you. I am dying to see you.

Yours always,
Peony

Only a year ago, Peony sadly recalled, she had made this voyage with her husband to his new post. A year ago, her husband Tingyen (the "Flame of the Court") had made good his boast that one day he would occupy a lucrative government post. Fei Senior had encouraged it. The grandfather had been a *shiutsai*, appointed magistrate in remote Kweichow. The family always thought of themselves as belonging to the "gentry," although a *shiutsai* was the lowest rank among scholars, and the post at the remote, poor, mountainous district of Kweichow was far from enviable. The grandfather hated the place and died there; but after his death, Kweichow became a family legend; to all the Kashing neighbors the family described it as a place of opulence and power and glory. Mrs. Fei Senior, Peony's mother-in-law, never tired of telling her friends of the day she was married as a magistrate's daughter-in-law, carried as a bride in the magistrate's own sedan chair of green velvet. One of the places where her grandchildren played hide-and-seek was the very same sedan chair, now covered with faded and frayed green velvet, standing in a corner of one of the corridors—a reminder of ancestral glory.

Fei Senior, the father-in-law, was once an accountant at a *taotai*'s (magistrate's) office when the *taotai* was imprisoned for falsifying tax and income accounts. According to the theory of responsibility in the government, the accountant received the greater part of the blame and he was disqualified from government service for life. He had laid aside a nest egg, however, and it was sufficient to buy property at Kashing and allow him to retire in comfort for life. And he had been doing well. His eldest son had become a wholesale merchant, buying up farm products such as tobacco, rapeseeds, and beans from farmers, and selling it at Hanchow or Soochow. His second son was now managing the farm. He had a total of seven grandchildren. He had a very respectable house, if not the wealthiest, among the many wealthy landlords of Kashing. He had wanted his third son, the "Flame of the Court," to burst into flame again and shine brilliantly and glorify his ancestors.

As a boy, Tingyen had never liked studying. He could never have passed the examinations and got a degree, the necessary qualification for entering government service as an official, and he didn't try. However, he had gone about moving up in the world in the right way. He had made friends with the right people, by contacts at wine feasts, by sharing common singsong girls with them, by being generous with friends who could one day do him a good turn, and also, it must be admitted, by a certain native gift for sociability. He had succeeded in securing a post as chief secretary at the Salt Tax Bureau of Kaoyu, rather a better break than he could have hoped for. Shueh, the Chief, was the uncle of the man whose friendship he had cultivated assiduously, and Kaoyu was, if not the fattest, one of the "fat" posts.

"I told you so," Tingyen had said to his wife when he announced his appointment. "You thought your husband was just whoring night after night. Now you will see. I'll be worth something in a year or two."

Peony was totally unimpressed.

"And now I have come home with this marvelous news. We are made! And you haven't even congratulated me!"

"Congratulate yourself!" was Peony's curt reply.

Tingyen was really bitter and disappointed. This was the "gay, vivacious" girl he had married. Well, you never knew a woman until you had married her.

Even that night, when he was happy and very amorous, she refused to sleep with him. The fact was, she loathed the very contact with this person, who by no choice of her own had become her husband.

There was a celebration before their departure—Mr. and Mrs. Fei Senior did not let the occasion slip by—a round of entertainments and dinners with theatrical shows lasting three days, to which all persons worth knowing in the district were invited. Considerations of cost were thrown to the winds. Even the old sedan chair was reupholstered and refurbished and put up for show. Old Mrs. Fei's eyes could not stay still for a minute; she could not be talking to one person without surveying the whole company of guests. She wanted to see that she was being seen. How she loved everybody!

During those dinners, Peony had managed to put on appropriate smiles and hated herself for it. ("Am I perhaps growing more mature?" she had asked herself.) The post of a secretary at a local tax bureau was, in a financial sense, nothing to laugh at, and yet, in another sense, nothing to celebrate, as far as official honors go; but it sounded like a good deal to the townspeople of Kashing. The shallower the puddle, the bigger the splash. The emptier the jar, the louder the clang. Besides, it was a *salt* tax bureau. The salt merchants of Yangchow were millionaires, everybody knew.

To be quite honest, the very thought of a job enforcing laws against millionaires made the father's head spin. If only his young son was worth his "salt"! His son did not have to go to the millionaires; they would come to him. Such things were openly discussed at the family dinner table, to Peony's great amazement.

Ten days later, the new "official" and his wife went up the

Grand Canal to his new post with a big send-off. The presents from friends alone amounted to three or four hundred dollars. The whole family had risen in the eyes of the people of Kashing and acquired class.

"And now you will see," said Tingyen with unquenchable enthusiasm, when they were alone. "I will show you."

"And if you go on whoring," replied his wife, "your future is unlimited and you may soon end up in Peking."

A veiled look had descended upon her face during that voyage a year ago. Nothing had seemed quite real. Her eyes hurt her, and she was afraid of intense sunlight. Even when she had headaches, she had difficulty in believing that her headaches were real. All that surrounded her, herself, her husband, this voyage up north to a new place, were things she could not understand or appreciate the meaning of. It seemed that human life consisted of eating, sleeping, and defecating, that the human body consisted essentially of one gullet and one defecator, like a fish or a goose, performing necessary, inevitable functions, with an extra bloody period for women—actions without purpose, movements and speeches without meaning, a body without a soul. What horrifying emptiness! Yet she was so young.

It was at Wukiang, near the entrance to the Taihu Lake, where she had got up enough energy to beg her husband to let the boat go by way of Mutu, so that she could take a good look at the famous lake of Taihu.

"What for?"

She could not answer. No one could answer that question. For what purpose should one take a look at a mere body of water?

She kept quiet and did not insist.

"I mean it is a misty, cloudy day," the husband made an effort to be pleasant. "The fog will be heavy on the lake. You will see nothing even if you go out."

"There are always pretty girls at Mutu. Don't you want to see the famous beauties of Soochow?"

Mutu was a famous flower and orchard region in the outskirts of Soochow.

"Now you are being wicked."

"No, I am not. You can look at the young women and I can look at the mist. It makes me feel as if I were floating somewhere, shrouded, alone and hidden in a region unknown."

To be fair, Tingyen gave up trying to understand his wife. Walking in a fog was to her like walking upon clouds, a luxurious, blessed state of mind typical of her, but difficult for others to understand.

"You are crazy," he said.

"Yes, I am."

But, after all, they did not go to Mutu.

She could not say whether her new life at Kaoyu was better or worse. She had insisted on bringing along the myna. She kept it in her bedroom and taught it many words and phrases, just to see how long, complicated sentences could be learned by rote, and parodied without understanding. She got intense pleasure out of identifying herself with that black bird and its ability to say things with apparent meaning, which neither she nor the bird really understood. The sentence which pleased Tingyen most was: *"Pour tea! The master has come home!"*

There was a boat incident after passing Yangchow, which was only a few miles from the great river Yangtse. During a particularly bad traffic jam a boatman had in the general confusion knocked down into the water the official oil-paper lantern of a traveling high official. The lantern bearing the clan name of the traveling official in one large red character served to identify the passenger for the benefit of the customs officers and police. When it was discovered that the boat belonged to an "official from Peking," there was great consternation. The boatman who was responsible came over and, kneeling down, offered to be punished or pay a fine. But nothing came of it. The official dismissed it with a laugh, and the boatman and people around him bowed and bowed and expressed their gratitude for his leniency, while shaking their heads in disbelief for getting away so easily. Peony saw the commotion and the broken, oblong lantern made of oil-silk spread over a bamboo frame, bobbing up and down in the water, with the big red letter giving the clan name mangled and illegible. She heard people say that it was an "official from Peking," but did not give it another thought.

When her boat reached the bank of the Yangtse, it followed a great bend circling around an island; as soon as they rounded the island and approached Chinkiang, she saw the golden roofs of the famous Goldhill Temple sparkling in the April sun, a fabulous creation of red pillars, painted girders, and glazed roofs.

How does one describe Peony's frenzied state of mind as she caught a glimpse of the glazed curved roofs of the Goldhill Temple, where she expected news of Chin Chu? How can one communicate the mixture of ecstasy and longing and infatuation which set her mind in such turmoil? Chin Chu was the embodiment of something good and beautiful, for which her whole feminine being yearned, despite all the barriers, all the conventions, and all the rules and preachments of society. Peony's enthusiasm, her idealism, and the keenness of her intelligence were centered on that first love which she could not, and would not, learn to forget. She enjoyed even the cruel pains of their separation; she cherished the tortured memories of their secret meetings. These memories were so real that they seemed to her the only things that had meaning in this life; they were more real than her routine, everyday life. Was not life itself just a passing show, without lasting meaning, and these memories and thoughts and feelings the real things of permanent meaning and significance?

Only her best girl friend Paiwei knew it all, her own sister Jasmine only part of it. When she first met him, Chin Chu was about her age, a *shiutsai* at eighteen. He had silky white hands, such as were common among men of Kiangsu-Chekiang, with dark eyebrows and a smile always playing about his lips. He was brilliant, young, handsome, and active. He was a writer, and she had always loved writers. The best essays at the civil service examinations were always published, or circulated by means of handwritten copies; they were studied carefully as

models by the other candidates. Peony had come into possession of one copy through her aunt, and fell in love with it.
Chin Chu had also heard her spoken of as a bright girl of the
Liang clan, whom the *hanlin* had singled out for praise. It was
love at first sight. They had exchanged correspondence and
arranged secret meetings, either in Paiwei's company or alone.
Then one day the thunderbolt struck. Chin Chu informed
Peony that his parents had arranged another match and
there was nothing he could do about it. Within six months
he was married to a girl of Soochow. (Many factors entered
into this arrangement by parents, but one thing was certain:
the young man's mother, knowing of their rendezvous, highly
disapproved of Peony.) She had gone to his wedding; it was like
witnessing her own execution, but she preferred to endure it
for some reason she could not explain to herself. She must see
it all. That explains, in part, at least, why her marriage was
doomed from the beginning. Mentally she compared everything that Fei was with everything that Chin Chu could be.
Occasionally her husband was surprised at the sudden, passionate violence of her embrace, and guessed that it was not
he she was kissing, but a mysterious person of whom she would
never speak.

CHAPTER 3

In those days, before the Tientsin–Pukow Railway was completed, Chinkiang was a great thriving river port. It stood at
the junction of the Yangtse and the Grand Canal running
north and south. Most canal boats stopped at Chinkiang for
rest and supplies, as it marked the end of the voyage in north
China and the beginning of the south. Many passengers
changed here for one of the more luxurious houseboats of
Kiangnan, with good cuisine and fine appointments in the
painted, latticed cabins. Many stopped here, too, after a long

voyage, to enjoy its wonderful public baths, its famous roasts and black vinegar, and its theatrical shows.

Peony did not have to give reasons for asking the boat to stop at Chinkiang, and she did not care. Of course she would visit the Goldhill Temple, and would want a good bath at a bath for women. It had suffocated her mind and spirit to be sleeping in such close proximity to the coffin for the last three days, day and night.

"We will stop here for a couple of days," she told the boatman's wife. "You may go up and do what you want to do. I need a rest, too, to stretch my legs." Turning to the family servant, she said, "Liensheng, you will stay and watch the coffin. Somebody must be in the boat all the time. If you have to go ashore, be sure that someone stays behind."

"Don't worry, no one will want to steal it."

"Go up," said the silver-voiced boatman's daughter. "Go up to the baths and have yourself pedicured to heaven."

"I am going to. I really want to," Peony replied airily. She had heard of Chinkiang pedicures and was going to try one, and besides, she really wanted to freshen up and look her best when she met Chin Chu.

She really had never traveled alone, had never enjoyed this absolute freedom which she had craved so much. The boatman's daughter had offered to accompany her as her guide, but she declined. She wanted no one to watch. How rare was the occasion when one could be truly alone and find the true center of one's own gravity, to recover an individuality free from the external influences of friends, relatives, and well-wishers. The boatman's wife was afraid that a young pretty girl like Peony might fall into the clutches of evil young men in a strange city and was solicitous for her. Peony laughed it off.

With a sense of adventure, she crossed the gangplank and went up the steep steps of the bank, wet with water carriers going up and down all day. Her hands swaying easily at her side, she blithely ran up the steps. Thanks to her rebellious nature and to the influence of the Shanghai and Christian missionaries on her family, she had not had her feet bound. She wore her dark gray, tight-fitting trousers, which she had always preferred to skirts. Skirts were for married ladies like herself, but that was a rule flouted by all women of the poorer working classes who had to climb hills or wade through streams or work in the fields. She turned to look at their boat below. Liensheng was looking up. She was not really trying to create the impression of a model widow, since her mind was already made up to leave her husband's family. She could not care less what the old servant would tell the family when he got home.

The road leveled up into a warren of pebble streets crowded with jostling men and women. Peony was soon lost in a street thick with hanging vertical shop signs. With her easy ways, she tapped a young stranger on the shoulder and asked him where she could find a bath. Since her girlhood days, she had learned to be at home with crowds, to gather where the crowd was thickest, to exchange talk with idlers at wine shops and tea shops, to hail any young man as *laoshiung, huochi, huopan* (old brother, mate, messmate) or any of those familiar words (equivalents of "Charley" or "Mac" in English). Her twenty-two years made no difference. Some of her gamin speech and habits remained; she would not call a person by his family name if she could call him by his first name. So it was always with an air of self-confidence that she mixed in a crowd of strangers.

The young man turned and saw with pleased surprise the pretty young girl asking for directions. It was late afternoon, and her bangs cast light curling shadows on her forehead. Her eyes were serious, but her smile was friendly.

"Why, it's just around the corner. I can show you the way." She found, as she well knew, that the young man was eager to oblige.

"Just tell me where it is, *laoshiung.*"

He pointed to a turn to the left, and said, "You go in that alley. There are two of them there."

She thanked the stranger. Following his directions, she came to a house decorated with glazed tile mosaics in white and blue.

Over it, a black wooden sign with faded gold characters spelled the name, "White Horse Bath."

The term "pedicured to heaven" used by the boatman's daughter was not an exaggeration. After entering a luxurious hot bath, aided by a woman attendant who scrubbed her back, Peony was ushered to a room with a rattan couch, where she was served one cup of *lungching* tea and made to rest. She covered herself up while an expert masseuse came in. The woman began by kneading and tapping her legs. Then, wrapping her fingers in an ordinary dry towel, the masseuse started to rub and tickle her toes, one by one, with the subtlest touch, until she wanted to go to sleep, lulled by a delicious sensation pulsing up and down her spine.

"Lady, you like it?" asked the masseuse.

Peony merely groaned. At moments, her toes shrank from the touch. She did not know just why the toes below the nails were so sensitive to pleasure and pain, but it required an expert, delicate touch to torture a toe into an instrument of pleasure resting on the borderline of pain.

"I shall not forget it," she said, and tipped the woman a dollar.

Completely refreshed, Peony felt her limbs supple and light as she stepped across the blue-and-white, mosaic-lined corridor into the late afternoon sunlight outside. Her pores were open in more senses than one, as she drank in the life of an unknown city. She experienced a sense of belonging, as she always did in a city crowd, where the artificially cultivated and enforced separation of men and women was unknown, except to the class which went about in sedan chairs and lived in large homes enclosed behind high walls. A working womanhood could not afford the luxury of seclusion. She was not unaware that men were but too ready to exchange a friendly word with her. Yet what personal charm she had, she was determined to reserve for the one man alone whom she was going to meet. She must hurry to the Goldhill Temple to get the news.

If she arrived with a palpitating heart, then she left, after loitering until sundown, in a spirit of deep chagrin. She had inquired both at the outer gate and the inner gate of the Temple to see if there was a letter for her. The old man in a rough gray cassock, neither a monk nor an ordinary priest, was totally indifferent, and gave absent-minded, perfunctory answers. She hung around talking with the fruit sellers, took a rapid tour of the Temple on the chance of finding Chin Chu in person, and came back once more to the gate. In answer to her repeated pressing inquiries, the gatekeeper threw an angry glance at her and replied that the place was not a post office. It seemed strange to her that a matter which concerned her so deeply could be of no importance to that old man. She was helpless. She had thought of the Goldhill Temple as the most unmistakable place, easiest to find, most impossible to confuse with other places.

It could be that her letter had not reached Chin Chu in time, or that he was away. If he had received it and could not come, he certainly would have sent word. The feeling of waiting in vain was familiar to her; she knew full well the uncertainty, the impatience, the alertness for every sign of his approach, from all the times she used to wait for him in their rendezvous at Hangchow. She stood leaning on the high stone balustrade outside the Temple grounds, peering over the housetops, ready with an excited smile if she should catch a glimpse of Chin Chu's figure. She was in no mood to enjoy the exciting beauty of the monastery in midriver or the cloud-covered hilltops in the distance, or the islands bathed in the twilight glow of orange and purple. All this conflicted with her tumultuous, urgent impatience within.

The next morning, she visited the Temple again, with increasing hope to see him or at least receive word from him. She had told the servant that she would not be back until nightfall. Hearing from Chin Chu was of urgent concern to her, for on him much of her plan for the future depended.

Having nothing to do, she wandered through the Temple alone and watched groups of tourists or believers come and go. The Goldhill Temple was built on successive levels and separated into different courts. One of the best-endowed temples, dating back a thousand years, it was graced with stone pavement, choice trees, and charming arbors which led to out-of-the-way courtyards that combined luxury with peace and seclusion. She even climbed to the Golden Turtle, the highest rock, and saw the Sunrise Cave.

After resting in the spacious reception room after lunch, she came out, determined not to go back until sundown. Chin Chu had never failed her at these appointments, and if he did, there had always been a good reason. Since her moving up to Kaoyu, she had not seen him for a whole year.

She loitered about the landing of the court, biting her lip in impatience. Then she noticed two guards coming out of a corner passageway. Their coats bore two white circles with the words *shienping* on them. They led the way for a gentleman visitor to the Temple. Obviously, he was a mandarin of great importance, as the guards' uniform indicated they were imperial policemen of Peking. The gentleman, of medium height and dressed in a gown of cream-colored silk, walked at a brisk pace, unlike the usual slow, measured gait of mandarins in formal court dress. He was accompanied by a very neatly dressed young monk, one of those assigned to receive honored visitors to the Temple.

They were about thirty yards apart. The monk seemed to want to take him to the reception hall, but the official indicated he would rather go on. As the latter glanced around the court his gaze rested for barely a second on her girlish figure. Peony's finger froze to her lip as she saw his face. He reminded her of someone, but who could he be? He probably had not seen her. He went and stood for a minute looking over the parapet at the opposite bank, nervously turning his head and contemplating a white British gunboat lying in midstream. His eyes swept up and down the river, as if he were deeply occupied with the topography of the place. Always that sharp, swift, sweeping kind of glance, that look of intense observation all around, like the glance of a scout surveying a landscape hidden with enemies. Then he turned and walked through the hexagonal gate, followed by the young monk and the metropolitan guards of

Peking. Peony saw his figure gradually disappearing down the long flight of stone steps until it was obscured by an overhanging branch of pine.

Where had she seen that peculiar, sweeping, sparkling glance before? She could not remember. His expression reminded her of a friend's face, a face she had known long ago, a face which she could not place at the moment—one of the myriad memories of her childhood stored away and buried, forgotten. Yet, why should she feel a peculiar stirring inside her? The grooves of memory refused to connect. Only a vague association of something pleasant remained.

The brief encounter with the official from Peking left her with a mixture of excited curiosity and frustration. She couldn't stop thinking about it.

The evening sun was low, splintering the river below with flecks of gold. Chin Chu still had not shown up. Nor was there any sign of a letter at the gate. She trailed with tired legs down the rugged steps, her mind a heaving confusion of doubts, fears, and dejection.

She had not gone far when a happy thought came to her: the official visitor from Peking at the Temple might be her clan cousin, Liang *Hanlin*. She guessed it by a feminine instinct that couldn't be analyzed.

With a quick breath, she retraced the steps and approached the gatekeeper. The old man interrupted before she could finish her question.

"Why, you are back again! I've told you. There are no messages for you."

"Please," she begged him, "tell me who the gentleman visitor was this afternoon, accompanied by two policemen in uniform?" She smiled at him imploringly.

The gatekeeper took his pipe from his lips, and said, raising an incredulous eye at the young woman, "A *hanlin* from Peking. What is it to you?"

"May I look at his card?"

"No. The receptionist has it."

Peony stood transfixed. She did not know why she trembled

so. From that moment on, she did not see the gatekeeper or the road she was walking on. She went down treading on clouds, her knees soft and yielding. The gentleman was not the Liang *Hanlin* as she had imagined him to be; it was like the recalling of a dream shape projected into material form, altered and different. From the glimpses of him at a distance, he was no longer fair and slim and young. He was a man about forty, with a slightly tanned face and of a heavier build than she had seen him a dozen years ago. What was he doing at Chinkiang? She regretted so much that she had missed the opportunity of going up and speaking to him. *He* would not remember *her*, of course. And now the oportunity was lost. She felt too ashamed to retrace her steps once more to go back and ask the receptionist where he was staying and where she could find him. Probably the receptionist would not know, either.

The next day she told the boatman that they would resume the journey. She expressed the wish to see the Taihu Lake; it had always been a dream of hers to see it, as she had a strong desire to see many other places she had read about.

"In that case," said the boatman, "we will go directly south at Tanyang and cross the lake from Ishing, instead of following the Grand Canal. It may take a couple of days more. But it's less crowded and more in the open. Some people like it."

"Then let's go by way of Ishing. I want to cross the lake."

On the third day, in the neighborhood of Liyang and Ishing, they were passing a beautiful country of rich fields, covered with rice saplings in different shades of light and dark green. Rivulets and tributaries converged into irregular bodies of water covered with fishing boats. The morning was quiet, the sky decked with white fleecy clouds. Except for a few hawks circling in the air, the birds had hidden themselves after the noisy twitterings of daybreak, like watchdogs taking a nap in midmorning. A stiff wind rose from the northeast, wrinkling the surface of the water in swift, moving patches across the lake.

Two boats, some hundred yards in front of them, were hoisting their sails, and Peony's own boat was starting to do the same. The lapping of water on the sides increased and the boat scudded along. They were making good speed and catching up on the two boats in front. These were bigger houseboats, built for leisurely movement rather than for speed, and the one behind was being towed by the one in front.

In a short while, her boat was overtaking them. Liensheng was standing up, and the boatman's family and Peony were watching the boats they were passing with glee. A small red flag with characters on it was fluttering on a pole on the first cabin boat. Now they were just a few feet apart. Two guards kneeling across the gunwale were shouting angrily.

"Are you crazy? What are you doing? Haven't you got eyes?"

Peony strained to look. Her heart leaped to her mouth when she thought she recognized the uniform of the guards. The characters on the red flag were too small to read. So it was the "official from Peking" again! She caught a glimpse of the legs of a passenger, inside, sitting in a low easy chair. As the distance between the boats widened, she could see a figure in a chair, his face hidden by something he was reading. She wouldn't be surprised if it were her cousin himself.

Peony had a bad night and woke up early, thinking of the incident of the previous day; she dozed off again when the boat started moving down a stretch of winding waterway the next morning. As they approached Ishing, the traffic got much busier.

Peony was suddenly wakened by screaming and shouting. She threw on her outer jacket and sat up. The guards of the official's boat were shouting for Peony's boat to draw up. Her boatman was aghast and rested his oar in confusion. On came the other boat from behind, moving toward them at full speed. A violent scrape sent her boat keeling to one side with a loud crack and a rattle. Peony almost fell to the floor. Their boat had been rammed on purpose.

Enraged, she stood up and demanded to know what was wrong.

"Don't you see the flag? Eyes glued with rice paste? Draw

alongside. We want to go ahead and not sit watching that blessed coffin of yours all the way."

"I never heard of such a thing!" Peony shouted back. She was furious. "This is an imperial waterway. Even the emperor himself cannot stop a person from carrying the remains . . . "

She suddenly stopped as she caught sight of the big red character, "Liang." She had no time to think before the *hanlin* appeared from his cabin. He cast a glance at the screaming woman and the guards and asked for an explanation of the disturbance.

"Your Excellency, this is a coffin boat," the guards explained. "We've seen it appear and disappear ahead of us for the last three days. We don't want your Excellency to have to trail behind a coffin boat all the way, so we asked them to drop back and allow us to move ahead."

"I didn't see it. What's wrong with somebody carrying the remains of a relative home?"

"But it's bad luck, and we thought you might not like it."

Peony's hand was upon her open mouth. She never lost her presence of mind in front of men, but now her anger turned into bewilderment. Liang saw the young woman on the verge of tears, her hair loosened over her shoulders, looking at him like a hypnotized bird staring at a snake.

Pointing to the guards, she said, "They rammed our boat on purpose." Her eyes were still blazing with excitement.

The official was exchanging words with the guards which she could not hear.

"Aren't you Liang *Hanlin* of Yuyao?" she asked, surprised at her own courage.

"Yes, I am. Who are you?"

She drew a quick, inward breath, and her voice betrayed a keen surprise of joy. "I am a Liang from Yuyao, your clan sister. You called me 'Sanmei,' Third Sister, when I was a child. You wouldn't remember me."

Liang Mengchia's face softened. His eyes glistened and his slightly tanned face broke into a smile as he said, "Oh, Sanmei, of course. I remember you so well. You were a bright little girl when I saw you last."

"You remember me?" Peony was amazed, and to her further surprise she saw him wave a hand to the guards and say to her with an inviting gesture, "Come over." The boat was being pushed forward and the guards were preparing to help her climb into the official's boat.

It was altogether incredible that he should remember her at all, and that she was asked to come over to his boat. She was still quivering inside when she saw him walk over to the center of the boat in his white socks and ask her to sit down. Liang Mengchia was, in fact, delighted at meeting a clan sister here to break the monotony of his voyage. An old woman in her fifties was standing by.

"I presume you are going south," Mengchia asked. "Where are you going?"

"To Kashing. I am bringing the remains of my husband home."

The mandarin looked at her penetratingly and said to the guards, "Have the other boat towed behind."

The guards, completely taken aback and somewhat cowed, lost no time in hooking up a towline. "Now we are certain to have that blessed thing with us all the way," one of them said. Soon a rope was thrown over, and the three boats fell into line as they started to move again.

The sergeant came up with a cup of tea and apologized, "We didn't know that madam was related." Again he explained to the master that they had only wanted to have the coffin boat draw up and follow behind.

Mengchia raised an eyebrow at the sergeant, and his lips curled into a smile. He seemed to be enjoying a private joke as he said slowly, "Now you have your wish. It is behind us. . . . And I like it that way."

He spoke with ease and then chuckled. "These people—" he said to Peony—"when they are traveling on an official boat, they think they represent the emperor himself. I don't know how many times I have reminded them not to give themselves airs."

He paused with a quiet look on Peony, and added in a warm, low voice, "I hope we didn't frighten you."

"Why, our boat almost keeled over. It came bang right from behind." Her eyes were bright with a youthful, impish humor.

"I am sorry. I apologize for them. You haven't had your breakfast, I am sure. Well, please join me."

Tingma, the woman servant, rushed aft to give orders. She was more than a woman servant; she had nursed Mengchia from his childhood, and had been his housekeeper for years, looking after the bachelor *hanlin* like a mother all these years in Peking.

Peony's heart was still palpitating with excitement.

"I saw you at Goldhill Temple, but you did not see me," she said, as if they had been friends for years. It was her way, frank and familiar with the men she met. "You really remember me?"

"Yes, I do indeed." Mengchia was intrigued by her voice, soft, yet with a youthful ring, and by her attitude of familiarity.

"*I saw you but you did not see me.*" It might have been presumptuous if she had not said it with such openhearted, childish candor. He had seen many pretty ladies of Peking, but had never felt quite the same fresh, warm, and artless enthusiasm in the few words she had said and the way in which she had said them. He remembered perfectly this girl with the extraordinary, bright eyes. Her quick and clear flow of words seemed like a confession: "I was eleven and you had returned a *hanlin* from Peking, and our clan was celebrating it and putting up that tablet of honor in our ancestral temple. You remember Uncle Sueipo?"

"Yes, I remember."

"Well, Uncle Sueipo introduced me to you, and you looked at me. How I adored you! You laid a hand upon my forehead and stroked it and called me 'brilliant.' It was the greatest moment of my life. Thereafter, everybody in the clan called me 'Sanmei' because you did. I grew up feeling the touch of your soft hand still upon my forehead. You don't know what you did to me. Then, when I could read, I read every one of your books, whether I understood it or not."

Mengchia felt both flattered and pleased. He seemed to have met a spirit akin to his own. There was no reserve, no false self-restraint in her.

"Just tell me how we are related," he asked.

"Well, Uncle Sueipo is a Su. He is my mother's brother. We live at Yungchinmen."

"Oh yes, of course. He married my mother's sister."

In the quick exchange of conversation, Peony learned that Liang Mengchia had been sent by Grand Councilor Chang Chih-tung to go down to Foochow and make a report on the new Naval Academy and Dockyard. Chang Chih-tung, one of the elder statesmen, was taking the lead in the awakened interest in Western learning, particularly in opening railways, mines, the Hanyehping Iron Works at Hankow, and the Naval Dockyard and Academy at Foochow. Mengchia was going to Hangchow first, and expected to be back in Peking before winter. She saw his graying temples and asked as a normal part of the conversation, "What is your venerable age?"

"Thirty-eight. And what is yours?" It was all according to good form.

"Twenty-two."

"I have lost track of all the townspeople. I have been away so long."

"How proud I shall be when I tell them that I've met our *hanlin* on the voyage and shared the same boat with him."

He talked slowly in a throaty, low, unperturbed voice, yet his eyes were quick with a reserve power, as if he understood everything before him. He was a man who had traveled a great deal and seen a great deal, but was always at peace with himself. Just a moment ago, when the guards were shouting and ranting, he was looking on with amusement. She knew from his writing that he looked at life from a special point of view, with a quiet humor, half ironical, but never cynical. From his books she had come to know all his pet prejudices and ideas, as one knows those of an intimate friend. She felt she understood him, as if she had known him for years.

Now she felt completely at ease. She shuffled lazily to the side of the boat and read the inscription on the small, rectangular red flag. It said: "By Imperial Order Fourth Rank, Special Adviser to Grand Councilor Chang. Special Commissioner on Foochow Naval Academy, Hanlin Liang of Yuyao."

She came back and congratulated him.

"Only Fourth Rank. Don't let it frighten you. All that stuff and nonsense."

"Why do you say that?"

"Because I know nothing about the navy, or gunboats. I am, as a matter of fact, quite a repairer of clocks—learned it from a Jesuit friend. The Viceroy"—Grand Councilor Chang Chih-tung was more commonly referred to as "Viceroy"—"sent me just because he wanted me to make sure that the Naval Academy was running smoothly, like a clock. Of course, I have read all the Jesuit publications and understand a few things about the steam engine. . . . I really can take a clock to pieces and repair it. I have some sort of a reputation as the only Chinese clock repairer in Peking."

"You are marvelous."

"Not marvelous. Just trying to understand. There are so many things made in the West that we haven't begun to learn and understand."

Mengchia saw Peony in an attitude most characteristic of her, an attitude of lassitude and languor—languor in her eyes and languor in her carriage. She threw her head back, just a little, whether standing or sitting, when she was alone, in an attitude of reflection and ease, her eyes dimming, happy and relaxed, drinking in the essence of things around her. He was to see her many times like this, as she sat at a precarious angle on the bow, turning her face upward, as if thinking and yet not thinking, taking in the smells of the breeze, the sounds of the mockingbird and the woodpecker, the sensation of the sun's warmth upon her face, breathing in existence itself. Though she stood erect, her gait suggested the shuffle of lazy feet and a relaxed mind, her neck arching forward, her arms falling easily by her sides, the fingers curling upward like the tip of a vine.

As the table was being set for lunch, Mengchia heard a half-suppressed screech of delight. He looked up from his reading and saw her slim figure, in white jacket and skirt, pointing a white arm with childish joy at something ahead.

"What is it?"

"The cormorants!" Her ringing voice dwelled over the words tenderly and trailed off in a loving, pleased gurgle. She turned a sharp profile against the blue waters, with her arm still outstretched, her locks fluffing over her forehead, a study in sheer childish vivacity and joy. He came over, less curious about the fishing birds than moved by the freshness of young delight that the scene had produced in her.

She had stood up, her eyes fixed intently on the scene ahead. Two fishermen, standing on separate rafts, were pounding the water with long poles, crying "Ho! Ho!" The rafts were coming from divergent angles and driving the fish toward the center. The black cormorants dived and plunged and each came up with a fish in its mouth, surrendering it to the fishermen. Having disgorged the fish, the birds rested on the rafts, shaking their beaks in proud satisfaction, and then plunged in again to exercise their natural inclination and skill. The birds swallowed the small fish, but a ring of soft-woven split bamboo on their necks forced them to let their masters have the big ones.

A strong, acrid smell from the birds wafted to the boat, as they were fairly close now. The fishermen continued to drive the fish with the "ho-ho's," striking the water from the farther side with their punts, while the birds filled the air with their flinty croaks. One of the birds had come up with a big one when at the same instant Peony, standing beside him, tugged at his arm, and gasped "Look!" She let her hand remain on his arm, as if she were truly his own sister. It was indecorous, but natural and innocent on her part.

Such a small gesture gave Mengchia a novel feeling of close and warm companionship with the young woman. He seemed at once to understand her unique character, confiding, familiar, and warm. Her eyes turned to see if he were enjoying it as much as she herself.

Liang Mengchia had a feeling that the clan sister he had
praised in her childhood had now grown up into a young
woman, magnificently frank and disorderly, unconventional in
the grand manner. He felt someone was breaking into the
privacy of his soul. As a confirmed bachelor, nearly forty, his
life had settled into a pattern of a regularized routine, centered
selfishly on his books, studies, and travels, pleasing to his own
tastes. The shock he received when Peony pressed her hand on
his arm and gazed into his eyes was like someone breaking into
his sequestered life and turning it upside down, like a powerful,
mysterious force entering into his being and rudely shaking him
up. Someone, fresh and gay and surprising, had invaded his
privacy, robbed him of his self-composure. It had happened very
suddenly and in an inexplicable manner.

Success had come easily to him; he had not courted fame,
but it had come to him, anyway. Perhaps at this time, a certain
barren mellowness had begun to pall. Except for a few close
friends and his work, nothing excited him very much. (He was
still ready to do battle royal for his ideas, whenever anyone challenged him on the corruption of Confucianism through Buddhist influence, or took up defense of the Cheng brothers, the
Neo-Confucianist philosophers.) Outside of this, he had never
cared for official rank and honor. Even when he was made a
hanlin, he thought of it merely as a title, conferred on him from
the outside; he knew that a writer must stand or fall with his
works, degree or no degree, and his real love was his studies.
And now he suddenly felt he had missed life. There was no
reason for it except his encountering the person and presence
and voice of Peony. He was quite upset and yet liked the
feeling.

CHAPTER 4

The boat had stopped at Ishing about sundown. With an excitement that was new to him, he said to her, "Let's celebrate
tonight."

"Why? Where? How?" she asked with open, wondering eyes.

"We'll go up and have supper at some small restaurant."

They went up the muddy tracks. The shore line where boats clustered together was always wet and slippery. Mengchia had given the guards leave, for he disliked nothing more than going with escorts, and liked nothing more than prowling about in strange cities on his own. The two of them strolled about the narrow cobbled streets and spent a long time at a store choosing a rustic-styled earthenware tea set. Ishing was famous for these charming tea sets of dull maroon unglazed clay outside, and glazed green inside.

At a small restaurant, they ordered fried shrimp, tiny, but delicious here at the lake region, and sesame cakes freshly baked from the oven, followed by a large carp smothered in a pungent sauce, with bean curd and *shiangku* mushrooms and garlic, to which Mengchia ordered a pinch of *wuchiapi* liquor added for aroma.

They were completely alone. Two oil lamps cast unsteady shadows upon the table and illuminated their faces with a soft glow. On a side table stood a large red candle a foot high, stuck into a pewter stand of the same height, made in the form of the decorative character for "longevity." The dim lights shone upon Peony's extremely straight nose and her quivering light brown pupils, as she stared at him with a kind of hypnotized look. She felt she was being carried along in a dream, finding herself in this situation of drinking alone with her adored cousin, a situation which she had never thought possible. Her eyes had a way of dimming out in a misty gaze when the world itself became dangerously like a somnolent half dream.

"What are you thinking of?" he asked.

She cast a quivering glance at him and said, "Just wondering. It's like a dream. I never thought I would be drinking with you face to face, as we are tonight. Oh, it's divine!"

In the course of the dinner, they talked of many things, of his work, of his writing, and of herself. Mengchia was a good talker, and had a store of amusing anecdotes to recall about his travels.

Of medium height, dark of complexion, his most characteristic feature was a head of shaggy hair, just beginning to turn
gray at the temples, and bushy, dark eyebrows. His retreating
hairline revealed a distinctive high forehead set above powerful,
sparkling eyes. The center of his soul was in these eyes, searching, brilliant—especially so when he was slightly drunk. The
skin around his eyes was smooth and shining, and his temples
were crisscrossed with veins.

Peony had read many of his essays on the Great Wall and
Inner Mongolia. He was recognized as an authority on the Great
Wall separating China from the north and could even talk the
Manchu and Mongolian languages, which made him especially
useful at court when the viceroy wanted information on the
northern regions.

He had made a solitary journey to cover all the dubious, con-
troversial points on the Great Wall. This had taken him from
Shanhaikuan on the China Sea to Inner Mongolia (Suiyuan,
Ningshia) on the extreme northwest. His writings caught some
of the antique, moss-covered historic flavor of the Great Wall
itself. The mere mention of the famous passes with their historic names, like Chuyungkuan, and the familiar knowledge of
ancient battles and incidents, made these sketches abstruse,
scholarly, and very impressive, equally so to those who knew
history and those who did not. Mengchia delighted in the
knowledge that most people did not know what he was talking
about. This was characteristic of him. His thoughts were his
own. The sense of isolation, of breaking the frontiers of thought,
of coming to direct, close grips with the problems of philosophy
and of life made him a unique, original writer of his generation,
brilliant, erratic or enigmatic, accused by the orthodox Neo-
Confucianists of being perverse and trying to be different. He
rapped his fingers at such opinions and enjoyed his isolation.

"Is it true that you went as far northwest as Ningshia on the
border of the Gobi Desert?"

"Yes. There are so many contradictory records about the
Great Wall. The Wall doubles and redoubles or breaks off

abruptly on the bank of the Yellow River, as in Ningshia. Once I drank mare's milk out of its udder."

"How?" she broke into an amused chuckle.

"I had lost my way, covering a small detour all alone." His voice grew enthusiastic. "It's an extraordinary experience to find yourself completely alone in this universe, with nothing behind you or in front of you, except a desert stretching out in complete silence. For five days I was lost in the desert mountains—nothing but rocks and sand. My wheat cakes had run out and nothing edible was in sight. No villages, no travelers, nothing. I was famished. I figured I had to go another day and night before I could return to the town. At the foot of the Great Wall I saw a mare tied to a rock. It must have belonged to some smuggler. But how do you eat a live mare? I stole silently up to the Wall and knocked her on the head with a rock. The mare staggered and fell and I finished her off. Then I crouched on the ground and drank her milk straight from her udder. It saved my life. I hung around the place. Since there was a mare, there must be an owner. I thought if I saw him I would pay him for it. But nobody came. I suddenly thought of the danger and went away as fast as I could."

The tale filled her with a sense of wonder. "You are very original," she said.

"No. I just want to know what I am talking about when I write. So many books, especially geographical works of the past covering mountains and rivers, just copy one another. I had to see the places, and got deeper and deeper into the subject. I have always wanted to do what I feel like doing, especially when nobody else has done it before."

"You have already done that. Most people do not do what they want to do, or can't. Or do not know what they want in life."

"If they want it badly enough, they can do it."

"I suppose so. If you desire a thing very much, you do it, providing you are willing to pay the price for it."

He steadied a glance upon her and said, "Tell me about yourself. What are you going to do?"

"I want to leave my husband's family and marry again." She knew he was against the cult of widowhood and spoke easily with disarming frankness.

"I was a bad wife to him, I know. He must have hated me. We did not understand each other, that was all. I didn't weep over his death. I couldn't and I wouldn't. . . . At home, too, I am the bad girl. From my childhood, I always had my own way. I am not like my sister."

"You have a sister?"

"Yes, three years younger. Her name is Jasmine. She is sweet, quiet, and submissive, while I am the rebel of the family. I went out with boys when I was fifteen, while my sister wouldn't even talk with strange boys at that age. We are just born differently. Everybody loves her, and thinks me crazy. It's the way I was born. I was a very ordinary child, ugly and in everybody's way."

"I don't believe it."

"Yes, I was a very common child—until you came and called me brilliant. It changed my life completely."

"How soon do you propose to leave your husband's family?"

"As soon as the hundred days are over. I don't want to bury myself in that small town. I am supposed to be in mourning for him, but in my heart I am not."

"I can see that."

Mengchia paused in thought. He had a fear that Peony might be taking the ideas of his books and carrying them out too literally.

"Of course no one can force you. But it will be painful for your husband's family—painful and disgraceful for them."

"Why, don't you approve?"

"I do. I only think they are not going to like it. And of course there will be a lot of talk and women's gossip and all that."

"Yes, 'women gossip and men goose-step,'" she replied readily. "That's what most men and women in this world are doing." As she said it, there was a memorable ring to the phrase; the men *huen* and the women *pai lungmenchen*. Mengchia was quite impressed. Here was a rebel.

"Somebody has got to try and risk social censure, don't you think? As you say, if a person wants to do a thing very badly, he can. This load of Confucianism is too much for us women. You men are sitting on top of it, we women under it."

Mengchia's eyes registered a quick surprise. He wished he had the courage to write a line like that.

"What were you saying? Say it again."

"I say the truth of Confucius is too much for us women. We can't bear it. It's all right for the men scholars to say that all literature must bear the truth. Truth is too heavy for women to bear."

Mengchia roared. He had never heard the phrase *tsai tao* (bear the truth) taken in that physical sense of a ship "bearing" or "carrying" cargo. He said with an appreciative look at her, "Say, if I were Chief Examiner and women could take the imperial examinations, certainly I ought to pass you with honors."

"Don't you think it is true?" With a sudden artlessness, she asked, "I am told you divorced your wife years ago. Tingma told me she has been taking care of you living alone all these years. Is that correct?"

Mengchia looked intently into her eyes and said, "It was so long ago. I got married at the age of twenty to a girl, a brainless, unbearable snob belonging to one of the richest families in Yuyao. I was a *churen*, then, young for the degree. I suppose I served a useful purpose to her and her family—in the same category and on a par with her jewels and her father's acres of land. A petty snob without anything to be snobbish about. It was a marriage of convenience. I don't see why I should be a 'convenience' to some woman so that she could parade herself as a *churen*'s wife. I never saw her or her family again."

"And you never married again?"

"No."

"Why?"

"I don't know. Perhaps I am a writer and a writer is always a selfish man. He cherishes his individuality too much to share it with another person. But perhaps because I did not meet the right girl."

Her practical woman's head was running ahead. "May I ask you a question?"

"I am listening."

"Will you help me? When will you be in Hangchow?"

"Why do you ask?"

"Because after the hundred days, I shall ask to go back to see my mother. Let me see you again. You can help me by giving me advice."

Mengchia crooked his fingers and made a mental calculation. He would be in Hangchow in a week. Then the journey to Foochow and back in a few months. It would be early autumn, in September, he thought. For a scholar requisitioned to study the Naval Service, he hated the sea; he would prefer not to go to Foochow by boat along the coast.

"I hate storms. I was once in a terrible storm on the Canton Sea," he said.

As they left the restaurant Mengchia felt that here was a woman whose spirit and thinking were akin to his own. They walked through the dark, cobbled alleys to the boat, her arm resting on his. More muddy lanes sloped gently toward the bank. Peony insisted on carrying the parcel of the tea set herself. As they came toward the slippery mud paths, she was holding the parcel in one hand and pressing down on his arm with the other. It was a moment of rediscovered youth for him. For a long time he had not felt that intoxication of folly and light-headedness. But all was permissible in the dark. He felt as if he were walking with a strange, enchanting spirit descended suddenly from nowhere, violently taking away from him that state of splendid isolation in which he had been living all these years. Love was a form of robbery, of someone not yourself stealing upon you to take up habitation in your own being and claiming possession of it.

That night, as he lay in the boat, he felt that something great and important had happened to him. He could not take his mind off her. He felt that everything about her was just right: her eyes, her voice, her hair, her keen enthusiasm and languid smile, her understanding and spirit fascinated him. No other woman had touched him so deeply. He was surprised at himself. In all his life he had never felt so inwardly integrated with a woman, one who so happily answered to his ideal. He had had an episode with a Manchu princess, a prince's wife, an excruciating romance from which he had extricated himself in time. Now Peony seemed to hover over his mind, extravagantly beautiful and alluring, free, intelligent, something of a rebel, independent-minded, dreamy, gay, and daringly unusual. He liked her and felt that he needed her forever—did he have to give a reason? What he dared not quite admit to himself was that, when he thought himself safe and secure from women's charms, he was now utterly shaken by her. It was like hearing the syncopation of a full orchestra, when the deepest notes are struck with fury, *appassionata*. He was astounded that the mere voice and look of a woman could throw a man's critical faculties into such confusion. Love itself is a grand disorder, an imbalance of mind, not subject to logical analysis.

He knew that he needed her now forever.

The first two days on the Taihu Lake were cloudy, and physically there was nothing to see. The Taihu was for all purposes like the ocean; on the horizon, the water merged with the grayish, shadowy forms of lumpy clouds. Their boats hugged the shore. Now and then the shape of a hilltop or a misty island loomed up before them from the vapory atmosphere. Mengchia noticed an expression of sadness in Peony's eyes and left her alone with her meditative silence.

On the third day, the sky cleared up. They had come to the east shore, which was covered with green foliage and thickly settled hamlets and busy towns. They were able to spend a day drinking tea made with the famous Hueishan spring water. Toward midday they went on to visit Kuangfu. In the bright sun, red temples nestled in the crooks of hilltops.

Steadily going south with a tail wind, they came to the promontory of Mutu, on the outskirts of Soochow, where lilacs and the white plum blossoms of May were in flower.

Peony recalled that this was the next to the last day of their voyage. They had disembarked at Mutu and were now resting at one of the many pavilions in that beach region, where fruit and flower trees extended for miles.

"This is one of the happiest days of my life," she murmured softly. The glow of the late afternoon sun came in from the lake, throwing a torrent of strange, soft light on the white blossoms and contrasting green leaves. The lake-born breeze gave to the fragrance of the flowers a tang of the sea. With her chin cupped in her hands at the tea table, she sat dreaming and emitting sighs of happiness. Mengchia had rarely seen a woman so rich in emotion.

"To live intensely like today is what I want. I thought of this as soon as I grew up. You cannot imagine the life I led at Kashing, supervising the kitchen, directing servants, saying correct things I did not mean, to people I did not care for." Her eyes were fixed on Mengchia. There was passion in her eyes, the fire and delicacy of one who could not be satisfied to goose-step or muddle through life. It made Mengchia feel that he, too, had perhaps missed living intensely.

But Mengchia's mind was preoccupied. There was a sudden moment of silence. She wet her finger with the tea and doodled on the black tea table. Slowly and in the most natural way, he captured her hand and covered it with his. Their eyes met, and they were silent. Words seemed to be shaping up on his lips and evaporated. He seemed to have plunged deep into his soul and come up with something which stuck in his throat.

"Sanmei," he said at last, his voice in a low quiver, "I don't know how to say this. I never felt like this before in my life." Their faces were close together, and she was listening, her eyes quivering, her lips drawn firmly together. "This cannot be. You are my cousin and a Liang, too. I am also a much older man. I have no right to disturb your young life. . . ."

Her hand squeezed his and she replied, "You are not old at all. You are marvelous."

"Tomorrow you will go back to Kashing and we are going to part." His words began to flow easily. "I have been thinking for the last three days since you came over to my boat. . . . I have no right to say this, but I never want to be apart from you again. Can you, will you, consider coming to Peking?"

She felt the whole force of what he was trying to say. She recovered from her shock, and answered, "I want the same, too. I want never to stop seeing you."

"I cannot offer you very much. All I know is that I need you. It is something within me. I do not think I can be happy again without you. I need you."

"Very much?"

"Very, very much."

"I have felt the same way about you, too. I am your Sanmei, and I adore you. I have felt so sad the last two days. I realize that you are much more than a man who has changed my life, much more than an admired cousin, much more than a friend. You are a mountain of different, wonderful things to me, all wonderful, all marvelous. But it is so sudden. You must give me time to think."

Her face was deeply serious. Her mind reverted to Chin Chu and the unresolved and unresolvable hopeless romance with him. She felt an infinite pain in her heart at this moment for him. Yet her sharp, feminine mind had seen it all in a flash, how Chin Chu could never marry her. She was very quick in her decision.

"I would love to go to Peking," she said.

"You will?"

She gave him a direct nod in silence.

An understanding was established between them. They were alone. Neither of them knew how or at what moment their hands came together and she found herself resting in his arms, feeling and responding to a tremendous pressure which expressed but lamely their mutual longing for each other. She turned her face toward him and he bent and kissed her mouth, passionately, ravishingly, as if he could never satisfy his hunger. Peony felt as if she were melting into a ball of inarticulate desire. Neither of them could say a word. It was a moment of truth, naked, inexorable, when any spoken words would have been an intrusion. She was sufficiently awake to smell the scent of lilac coming over the meadow. His fingers were smoothing her hair. She never wanted to have anything disturb this exquisite moment.

"You like the smell of lilacs?" she asked.

"I do. It is made for moments like this."

"I like violets, but I think I shall like lilacs now."

At last, she sat up.

"What will become of us?" Mengchia asked.

"What can become of us if we feel as we do? All my life I have been searching for this, for something which is significant and meaningful."

"I mean we are cousins of the same clan name. Yet I know that I want you. This I know. . . . "

"You have never felt like this before?"

"Never in my life. I have liked many women, but never this sense of complete belonging, of wanting you and needing you so much."

"Haven't you fallen in love before?"

"Physically I have known many women, but never felt this thirst, this need which comes from inside me—this feeling of someone who enters into the very fiber of my being, like you. . . . I suppose this is destiny, my meeting you on this voyage. Do you believe in destiny?"

"No," she replied in her quick, clear voice. "All that happens to us is the result of our own effort. I do not believe that an outside power controls the happenings in our lives."

"But what can we do?"

"I don't know."

"You are a Liang and I am a Liang. Society forbids our marrying. What if I find I cannot live without you?"

"I don't know. It's enough, isn't it? For me, the knowledge that you love me, though I may never see you again—this knowledge is enough. Though I live in a prison, my heart shall be free."

"But this shall not be. I cannot separate myself from you. I know I shall live only half a life, when you are not at my side."

"Then let us do as we like. I don't care what they say."

"Not in my position, with all the gossip and publicity. You are a Liang and I am a Liang. It is just against all tradition. And on top of this, your former husband died just a month ago. We will be excoriated by society."

"I don't care."

"And by our own clan."

"I don't care."

Her recklessness surprised him. Mengchia was a little giddy from the light of her deep, fathomless eyes, which seemed to survey the society of men and women with disdain, and to come from another planet than our own.

But the day was not without an accident. So fickle was the weather at this season that a mass of black clouds rose suddenly from the southeast, and a chilly gust of wind swept over the garden where they were sitting, sending the white petals flying high and low, presaging a coming shower. Thunder rolled in the distance, while in front of them the lake still shone in the afternoon sun like a pool of painted gold. They were sitting in an open pavilion, some fifty yards from shelter.

"Let's run for it," said Mengchia.

"What for?"

"We'll get wet here."

"Then let's get wet."

"You are impossible."

"I love the rain."

The shower came in huge drops pelting the roof and the leaves noisily in staccato notes. The slanting drops sprayed the inside of the pavilion, alternating with gusts of wind. Soon the benches and tables were drenched with a coat of spray. Mengchia saw that his companion was enjoying it immensely.

"It will soon be over," said Peony with a chuckle.

But the whistling shower became a steady patter. A thunderbolt crashed, drawing lurid lines of fire across the sky. Peony turned her nose up, closed her eyes, and murmured, "How divine! How I love the rain!" she said, opening her eyes. Mengchia watched her, tremendously amused. There was the same excitement in her voice as there had been when she said, on first catching sight of the lake, "How immense!"

There was no letup in the rain. He was afraid she might catch cold. In the distance, someone with an umbrella was coming at last. Mengchia recognized him as one of his guards.

"Here he comes."

But Peony was deliciously happy, laughing airly when the umbrella came.

"Here we go!" she said.

He had to assist her. The oil-paper umbrella was not much help as they picked their way across the rapidly forming puddles and the sodden grass. Thunder cracked as they were halfway to the temple.

"This is better than the sunset," she said, her voice drowned out by the flailing rain tip-tapping on the oil-paper.

"What did you say?"

"I say this is better than the sunset a while ago," Peony shouted against the downpour.

What a strange creature, thought Mengchia, feeling young again as he remembered his own boyhood, how he had felt exactly the same fun running in the rain—except that now he had grown up and had forgotten it. She hadn't. Where could he ever find such a wayward devil of a girl again?

Arriving in safety at the large temple, he felt rather foolish in the eyes of the guards. Their shoes and the lower part of their gowns were wet through. Her laughter had not yet completely subsided.

"You know what?" she said. "Mencius must have enjoyed running in the rain."

"How do you know?"

"I just feel it. He said a great man was simply one who had not lost the heart of a child."

By a strange irony, the rain stopped a few minutes after they had reached shelter at the temple. She noticed his bedraggled appearance and laughed. The guards had borrowed a towel from the temple and solicitously tried to rub off some of the moisture on his gown. The abbot, having learned at last who the distinguished visitor was, came out and asked them to rest in an inner room, while he poured hot tea for them.

"How Tingma will scold me when we get back!" he said.

"But that is part of the fun of traveling. Can't she understand that?"

"No, she can't."

"All my life, I've wanted to travel and visit places I read about in books, to climb high mountains until one reaches the abode of the gods a few feet above one's head, as Li Po says."

"How romantic! I believe you are a woman born with the soul of a man."

"Perhaps. Or perhaps a man with the body of a woman. What does it matter?"

"Nothing matters to a man who says nothing matters," Mengchia said.

When they reached the boat, they found the lanterns already lit.

Dinner was already laid out and waiting for them. But the old nurse was in a state of near collapse with her abnormal fear of thunder. She lay bundled up in her bedding, and got up only when reassured that the storm was over and they had returned. Then she forgot her own troubles and asked Peony to go into the cabin and change into dry clothing.

Mengchia was waiting outside. She seemed unusually long inside. After a while he heard the young woman's voice from across the partition, "You like Tai Tungyuan?"

Mengchia laughed, but gave no reply. Tingma tapped at the partition and said, "You must not keep him waiting too long. He must change, too."

"I shan't be a minute."

A minute later she emerged, saying emphatically, "Tai Tungyuan is my favorite. I saw a volume by him on your desk."

He felt that he had made enough of a fool of himself that afternoon. "We can discuss that when I have changed."

He noticed that she had not completely buttoned up her jacket. He hated her effrontery, yet thought he had discovered a unique, enigmatic spirit; she was like no one he had ever known. On entering the cabin he discovered that she had thrown her things pell-mell on the floor for Tingma to pick up. For a moment, he wished to heaven that there were more Puritanism on earth.

Tai Tungyuan was not a popular writer. He was for the scholar. When they sat down to dinner, Peony's lips pursed in sullenness, like a dog chided by its master. She would not say a word. To humor her, he began, "So you have read Tai Tungyuan. I am truly surprised."

Her face softened. "It was you who introduced me to Tai's ideas. You mentioned him in one of your essays as striking at the very root of Neo-Confuciansim. I had quite a time trying to find a copy of his work on Mencius. Wouldn't you say, as you do in your writing, that he leads us back to classical Confucianism?"

"Of course he does. The root of Neo-Confucianism of the Sung scholars is Buddhism—the Buddhist view of human desires as something to be suppressed or kept in control by piety. Imagine, the key word of the philosophy of Reason is *ching,* fear and reverence. You don't get away from this fundamental fact. The Neo-Confucianists were fighting for their survival against Buddhism by taking over Buddhist ideas themselves, of sin and desires of the flesh. Tai shows from his study of Mencius that there was no such necessary conflict between our instincts and Pure Reason itself, that human nature is good. That is the basic naturalism of Mencius."

He said all this and more. Neither was much interested in the food. Tingma was exasperated. She ordered the soup to be taken back and reheated. "Can't you two discuss this when you have eaten? All the dishes are getting cold. We must have the wine warmed up again. I thought it would do you good to have some warm wine after getting soaking wet in the rain."

After the wine, they sat in the bow. It was their last night together, for with luck they should be able to make Kashing the following day. The lake was bathed in clear moonlight and the nearby shores were covered with a thousand lights, for they were now in the densely populated lake district of Soochow, near Wukiang. Tomorrow they would enter the Grand Canal system once more.

Some two hundred yards away, a restaurant boat with lights and music was moving slowly, wrinkling the mirror surface of the lake, and cutting inky black lines which smoothed out again like quicksilver into bluish-white opalescence. From the distance came the splashing of oars on the water, and the sound of a flute, piercingly sad and moving, yet tranquil as the moon which had come out from behind the clouds.

Peony sat in the bow in silence, her head thrown back meditatively. He watched her and discovered that her eyes were moist with tears. There were many reasons for these tears—her future, Chin Chu, and perhaps its being their last night on the lake. He respected the privacy of her thoughts and did not want to pry.

"Why don't you say something?" he asked after a while.

"There is nothing to say. I only want to feel . . . to print the memory of this night on my mind. All words are inadequate, don't you think?"

"You are right. Then don't talk."

"What is the use of saying anything?" she commented languidly, the syllables of her small, bell-like voice falling upon the watery silence like marbles thrown into a jade bowl.

He saw the hunger and longing on her face. Then her mood passed. She wanted to be gay this night of all nights. Catching a clue from the distant music, she hummed softly a *kunchii* air from "Chang-O's Flight to the Moon," accompanying herself at the intervals, in default of a guitar, by a tra-la-la of dancing notes in the moon-drenched silence. Mengchia listened silently.

Neither of them said more than a few words that night, so eloquent was the silence between them, while the moon paced among the clouds, now sending out shafts from silver-edged clouds, like a half-concealed, diffident bride, now showing her full round face, suffusing the night with a soft, quivering luminosity designed to make lovers go mad. Mengchia retired, but Peony sat silently alone watching the moon until midnight. Now and then she looked back into the boat, and verified, from the light shining through the cracks of the partition, that he was still reading or writing. When she retired, Tingma was snoring soundly in her sleep.

The next morning Peony woke up with a headache. She had spent a restless night, aware that she would have to make an agonizing and unavoidable decision. All odds were against Chin Chu. In her letter she had told him she would be willing to wait two or three years to be his wife; but all along she had known it would be next to impossible for him to abandon his wife and family and social position. They had been meeting secretly for four years—four years of passion and longing and remorse which had led nowhere. Outside of a divorce, there was no solution; a girl from a good family simply could not accept the position of a concubine. Peony longed for a solution, for some relief from the hopelessness of the entanglement. Finally, she knew she would have to leave Chin Chu; it would hurt him deeply but it would hurt her, too. Yet she could see no other way. And now there was Mengchia. Mengchia was so outstanding in character and spirit. How could she ask for more in a man? She knew she loved him with all the impetuosity of a new love, but also with an understanding based on all she knew about him from her girlhood years. And she could not lie to herself: Peking opened up a whole new world, with the infinite attraction of the unknown.

It was the last day of her voyage. Peony's heart was heavy with the sense of impending separation. While Tingma was busy packing in the stern of the boat, she found an opportunity to be alone with Mengchia.

"Well, this is our last day together," she said sadly.

"We will see each other again soon," Mengchia said slowly, "if you haven't changed your mind. Have you considered carefully?"

"I have. I want to come to Peking with you."

"But do you think you can leave your husband's family so soon? I may be back in Hangchow at the end of August or the beginning of September. Now I have a reason for wanting to come back early."

"I'm sure I can leave. As the proverb says, you cannot keep a reluctant widow. I am ready to come with you now, if you tell me to."

"You amaze me," Mengchia said in an amused tone. "Is this what you call living intensely?"

"Yes."

"No, Peony. At least go through with the vigils and the hundred days. You'll stir up a lot of talk, even if you leave right after the three months are over. Anyway, since I won't be back until September, there's no need for you to leave earlier. I should advise you to arrange the break with your husband's family as amicably as possible. You can come with me to Peking as my cousin, and nobody will say anything."

She stretched out a hand to hold his. When they noticed Tingma approaching, their conversation changed abruptly.

"Where will you be stopping in Hangchow?" she asked.

"With my aunt, of course," he answered rather curtly.

"You must excuse me—I have to do some packing." She glanced at Mengchia and her eyes sparkled with tears. The old nurse saw it all.

After lunch she felt tired and sleepy and went to lie down in her own compartment.

"Why don't you go into my cabin?" Mengchia suggested. "You'll sleep better there."

"Don't you want to take a nap?"

"No. I am going on with the boat. I can sleep all I want to tonight."

When she was resting in the cabin, Tingma said to Mengchia, "Poor girl, she must be in a panic, thinking of her husband's family. I heard her sniffling in bed all night."

Mengchia was glum. He did not want to tell her about their new plans. Tingma would be only too happy to proffer her old-womanish advice and wisdom.

"What do you think of her?"

Tingma whispered, "Never saw a widow in mourning behaving the way she did. Whether you like it or not, I will tell you what I think. The way she sits! The way she stands! And she should have worn skirts for form's sake, even though we are on a boat. I never saw a more disorderly person. I was putting back some laundry in her trunk. You should have seen—everything just thrown in. And her toothbrush. It is splayed flat. I would have thrown it away long ago and bought a new one."

"I know you would. What's wrong with a splayed toothbrush?" He felt called upon to defend Peony.

Her old eyes glinted at him. "Mengchia," she said, "you don't know a woman. I do. You men judge a girl by her pretty looks. She is extraordinarily pretty, I grant that. But I pity the man who is going to be her husband."

Mengchia chuckled. "I think she is a very pretty and very intelligent girl." He felt drawn into a discussion despite himself.

"I know you like her. You can't fool me."

"I do. Why should I fool you?"

"Stubborn, that's what you are. Why don't you pick a nice girl and settle down? If your dear mother were living, *she* would have made a match for you. Remember, you are nearing forty and still have no seed. But you will never listen to me. . . . If you are going to settle down, don't pick a girl like that one. I don't know what you were talking about last night at dinner. No use stuffing a girl's head with books and ideas. You must choose a wife who can look after you. . . . "

" . . . and cook and wash and mend my clothing," rejoined Mengchia good-humoredly. "Oh, I forgot. Why don't I marry a restaurant and a laundry?"

"I have had enough of you. Stubborn, that's what you are."

Mengchia was used to her bullying ways. He stopped for a second and said to her, in a cajoling tone, "Tingma, you've been like a mother to me. The other night you were talking of retiring in Hangchow to live with your grandchildren. I don't blame you."

"Who doesn't want to retire in her old age and live in her home town?"

Mengchia said, "I have been thinking of it. This time when I go back, I will hire another housekeeper and marry a restaurant and a laundry. Don't worry about me. I'll be fed, and I'll be washed."

"That's gratitude for you! So you don't need me now, my Mengchia."

"I am speaking seriously. I shall never forget you. If you really want to, I will give you three hundred dollars. You can buy a farm and live in comfort."

They were nearing Kashing, where the canal closed in between houses on both banks. As the hour drew near, Peony could not contain herself and broke out into great sobs. It was very convenient, for her relatives would see the swollen eyes of a loving and dutiful widow.

On the gangplank, she turned her tearful eyes toward Mengchia and without saying good-by went up on the bank.

When she was gone, Mengchia went to his cabin for a rest. He found a note under a paperweight, giving her address, with one simple message in two words: "*Write me.*"

CHAPTER 5

Mengchia had returned to Hangchow at the beginning of September. He had made the trip to Foochow by river boat and then by horseback, passing through some of the most beautiful mountains he had ever seen. After finishing his business at the Naval Academy, it was already near the end of August. To reach Hangchow by September, as he had promised Peony, he had taken the ocean route—despite his aversion to the sea.

This day there was an undercurrent of great excitement in Peony's family. The young widow had returned from Kashing a week ago with her mother, who had gone personally to bring her back, at her daughter's request. Her mother had always been partial to Peony. She wanted to set her free of all obligations. She no more wished to see her daughter remain unhappy in the Fei home than did Peony herself. This had caused a great deal of bad feeling on the part of the Feis and considerable dismay to her own father. But the mother had fought and won and the final arrangements were made. Although Peony had brought back all her personal belongings, it had been agreed between the mother and the Fei family that, as far as outsiders were concerned, the widow was merely returning to her mother's home for a visit and a rest. At the send-off, none of the Fei relatives had appeared; her luggage was brought to the boat by a family servant.

The *hanlin* was stopping at Uncle Sueipo's home; tonight a dinner was being given by Uncle Sueipo, in honor of Mengchia's return. It was to be a family reunion and no outsiders were invited. It was Mengchia's wish to avoid public receptions and official dinners, which annoyed him considerably. The first thing he did upon arrival was to call on Peony's parents and see her. She had already told her parents that Mengchia had offered to let her go to Peking. The father was as much agitated over this news as he was annoyed over his daughter's refusal to remain a good widowed daughter-in-law with the Fei family, according to the best moral tradition. It did not look right and proper to him, and he suggested that if Peony were going to Peking, Jasmine should go, too. After all, he said, the *hanlin* was a lone bachelor and there was no other woman in the house. Jasmine had jumped at the idea. So there was a great deal of talk and excitement, and everyone expected that the subject would be brought up at the dinner.

Peony was intensely happy at this turning in her life. Although Mengchia had been formal and had not said much during the visit yesterday, she felt intoxicated to see him arrive at the beginning of September, just as he had promised. He had written her two passionate letters from Foochow, and she felt secure in the knowledge of his love.

"You ought to start getting dressed," Jasmine said in her usual quiet, level tone. "What are you so happy about?"

The weather was getting cooler, and Peony was trailing around in her slippers, holding a fly swatter, looking around for the last flies of the summer. In wild pursuit of a fly which had eluded her, she shouted exuberantly, "Because I am *free, free, free!* Do you know what that means to me?"

Ignoring her, Jasmine said, "What are you going to put on? I think it would be better that you dressed in white, for form's sake. You are supposed to be in mourning and we don't want others to talk."

"Do you think they will?"

"We're afraid the *hanlin* may think that you don't know the rules."

Peony chuckled. "He understands."

Just as she was about to wash and get ready for the dinner, Paiwei suddenly appeared.

"Paiwei!" Peony exclaimed with great excitement. They had not seen each other for over a year. Paiwei was her best friend, and had come down from Tunglu where she and her husband had a delightful mountain home. She had made this special journey just to see Peony.

Their eyes met and they surveyed each other with great interest. No two temperaments were more alike; there were no secrets between them. Peony adored her friend—with her spirit, her quick intelligence, her charming ways. She was happy that Paiwei had a husband like Joshui. In a way, Paiwei was more disorderly, more poetic and unconventional than Peony. It had been Peony's dream that she too should find a man who would understand her and approve of her and love her, as much as Joshui loved Paiwei.

Paiwei was thinner than Peony. She often changed her hair style. Now it was done in the fluffy pompadour affected by Chinese girls who had studied in Japan. She wore tight-fitting trousers, a fact which scandalized Peony's parents. Every respectable married woman of their class wore skirts. But Joshui had approved and liked the tight slacks.

Paiwei's voice was thin and soft. "So you are free! You devil!" Jasmine was quietly watching them.

"I am," replied Peony. "I am only supposed to be visiting Mother; but I am never going back. What you don't know is that I am going to Peking."

"Yes, and I am going, too," said Jasmine quietly.

Paiwei's eyes were wide open with surprise.

"Slowly, slowly. I can't take it all in."

"The Liang *Hanlin* is here, my cousin, you remember? We are going up to Peking with him."

Paiwei glanced at the happy sisters, and said, "I envy you. He will find you husbands, I am sure. When will you start?"

"We're not sure yet. We are going to dinner at Uncle Sue-ipo's. In fact, we have to leave soon."

Paiwei glanced at her and said, as she turned to leave, "Come on, I have to talk to you for five minutes."

The two of them walked out of the small gate. Jasmine was not surprised. She guessed that it had something to do with Chin Chu, but she would never ask.

When they were alone, Paiwei took her hand and they sauntered down the alleyway.

"Chin Chu is here. He wants me to let you know. What kind of a mess are you getting into? He said he wanted to see you tomorrow. I think he hinted that he was making arrangements to get transferred to Hangchow and come and live here. Are you going to see him?"

"Yes, of course. You must tell him that I am coming. To-morrow."

Peony's family had not turned up yet. The uncle's home was in the very center of the city, some ten minutes' walk from her home, surrounded by walls thirty feet high, called "fire walls" whose purpose was to break the spread of conflagration from neighboring houses. Many of the houses had this protection on account of the crowded streets and the density of the population.

Uncle Sueipo was a man of sixty, with a longish, full face graced with a yellowish beard. He was retired, enjoying his old age while his son had taken over the business at Kinwha. He was inordinately proud of his wife's nephew, the academician. Although he was a Su, he felt proud to be related.

"You must allow the clan to give you a welcome dinner. Last time you passed through Hangchow, they blamed me for not letting them know. After all, you don't come home often, and they are so proud of you."

"I think I will accept. I am not on official business here, and I would rather not go to any public receptions and just stay quietly with my family. Of course, there is Prince Yi, the *shünwu*, our Military Governor. He is an old friend and I must call on him tomorrow. As for my clansmen, I am glad to accept."

"I am glad. They are so sincere. Give us a few days for preparation. You don't have to rush back to Peking, do you?"

"No. How is business?"

"My son is looking after it. There are good years and bad years. But I have got enough to live on." He fingered his beard softly and happily.

At this moment Aunt Su came into the parlor. She had the high forehead and fine eyes of the Liangs. She was simply but elegantly dressed in a black gown without any jewels. She supported herself with a cane, and her body shook a little when she moved on her dainty, bound feet.

"They should be here now," she said, looking at the clock on the wall, and seated herself on a straight blackwood chair with a flat, hard, turquoise cushion.

"When are you going to see your mother's tomb?" she asked Mengchia. "I am so old; otherwise I would be glad to go with you. I haven't been there for three or four years."

"I intend to visit it soon," replied Mengchia.

"And you yourself," said the old aunt. "Filial piety does not lie in sacrifices. If you love your mother, you ought to be taking a *shifu*, a wife, and continue the altar fire. I have two grandchildren, and my future is assured. You really ought to be thinking about it seriously."

"I know, I know," replied Mengchia good-humoredly. "All the ladies of Peking have been telling me that. Have you women nothing else to talk about or think about? I have escaped their conspiracies—so far."

"Don't try to be smart." Aunt Su raised a white finger in warning. "You will regret it. Just why are you so scared of marriage? Are we all vampires thirsting for your blood?"

"Don't put it that way, Auntie. Viceroy Chang wanted to make a match for me. The unfortunate thing is, everybody wants to make a match for me with a prime minister's daughter, or anyway, with what they call a girl from a high-class family. I am an academician, so nothing but some rich family girl would be suitable for me. Always *menhu*—family status. I am sincerely scared. If there is one class of people I really cannot stand, it is the snobs—people who happen to marry rich, or have rich parents, and have never done a thing themselves, but put on airs anyway. There are undeserving poor, but I see just as many undeserving rich around."

Ren-Ren, the five-year-old grandson who was living with the grandmother, ran in excitedly to tell them that the guests had arrived. The young girls' voices were heard in the front courtyard. The boy ran out to join them again.

In came Mr. and Mrs. Liang, the parents, followed by Peony and Jasmine and the boy. Aunt Su stood up to welcome the mother and the girls. It was very informal. The father drifted toward a couch where the academician and the uncle were sitting. Jasmine had disappeared into the kitchen with the boy. Jasmine was Aunt Su's favorite, just as she was her father's. In the past years, owing to Peony's absence, she had had more chance to see the aunt. Aunt Su was greatly impressed with her sweet poise and quiet dignity. She had joked that since she had only sons she would like to consider Jasmine as her daughter. Jasmine went about Aunt Su's home as if it were own home.

Peony was sitting with Aunt Su and her mother. She was tense and preoccupied with the thought of meeting Chin Chu the next day.

Soon Jasmine came out, holding in her hands a big white bowl with a cover; Ren-Ren trotted beside her.

"You should let the servant do it," said the aunt.

"Come on. Let's eat," Jasmine announced. "It's steamed duck." It was all as informal as could be. The servant had come out, but Jasmine had made it her business to see that the right chairs and chopsticks were in place. Ren-Ren wouldn't leave her side, and got in her way constantly.

"Get seated . . . over there!" she chided the boy.

"I wish I had a daughter like Jasmine," said the aunt, when they had sat down.

"You have!" said Ren-Ren.

"Hush! Not so loud," admonished Jasmine, putting a finger over his mouth. It was clear that the boy was very much spoiled by the grandparents.

The aunt chuckled. "It is so good to have the young people around. You must be so happy to have Peony back," she said to the mother.

Jasmine was very busy attending to the food and the pouring of the wine. She was paler than Peony, with soft, doelike eyes. She resembled her sister in her pointed nose, well-modeled chin, and the general oval contour of her face; but while Jasmine was pretty, Peony was beautiful. Peony had a dreamier expression, and the sudden flashes of light in her eyes made her captivating and unforgettable.

"Of course," said the mother, "I am glad Peony is back. I had to promise not to say that she had left her mother-in-law's home for good. We will let people know about it gradually."

The father said to Mengchia, "My daughter is very unusual. I did not approve of this. But the women always win. Don't you think it looks bad to neighbors and others? She might have waited at least a year or so."

The father had served for years as an honest, dutiful, and trusted employee at a local bank. By careful thrift he had saved enough to buy a house of his own; he had sacrificed a great deal for his family, and wanted some show of respect from them. But now, with his daughters grown up, he found that Peony was constantly giving him problems.

His wife had gone to bring Peony back against his wishes. Then, when they had returned, Peony had shouted with glee, "Father, I am free!" and in the next breath announced that she was going with her cousin to Peking. Since childhood, Peony had always gone ahead and done what she wanted, whether he liked it or not. He was most anxious that the *hanlin* should not think that *he* had sanctioned Peony's erratic behavior, her flouting of the social conventions. Peony's eyes looked from her father to Mengchia. Her father's attitude, she could see, was most respectful; he was prepared to accept anything the great scholar said.

"Uncle," said Mengchia slowly to the father, "I do think you are right when you say that it might look bad to the neighbors. But if you are thinking whether it will make your daughter happy to remain tied to in-laws she does not love, then it is a different thing. I think her happiness is important. After all, a person has only one life to live."

"Of course, if you think so."

"I think Aunt told me yesterday that you have agreed not to let people know about it. And if people don't know, then they can't talk. So you have no cause to worry."

Peony suppressed a perceptible smile.

The mother must have been a pretty woman in her youth. She added, "The marriage was a mistake. Peony was very unhappy. Now that her husband is dead, I am not going to sacrifice my child's happiness to make the Feis happy."

Aunt Su looked at the father and mother and concealed a smile.

Much wine was drunk and Uncle Su proposed that they toast Mengchia. Everybody felt happy, and then the talk turned to the sisters going up to Peking. They all agreed that if Peony were determined to go, it would be better if both sisters went together.

Jasmine stood up, holding a cup. In her quiet but dignified way, she said slowly, "To Tako! What unexpected luck for me and my sister! I will put it this way: If you do not think us unworthy, you may accept us as your girl disciples."

Peony had so far been rather quiet. She stood up and joined her sister in the toast. In the family, Mengchia was called Tako, as "Brother Mengchia" was the regular form used by friends. "Tako," she said, "tell them about your work, or about Peking."

All were in a mood to listen.

"I don't know where to begin."

"About the court, or the Empress Dowager—or anything," said Jasmine.

Uncle Sueipo added his plea, "Tell us about the court."

Mengchia's veins stood out on his temples, but his face had not colored from the wine. Slowly he smiled and said:

"The court? It is lousy."

"What do you mean?" asked the aunt.

"It is a question of personalities. Take the Naval Academy at Foochow, for example. It's all crammed with relatives of this and that important personage from Peking. And the same is true of the general situation. I don't see how we are going to build a modern navy that way. When a war comes, our navy will not last thirty minutes." (Three years later, Mengchia's prediction, unfortunately, came true in the Sino-Japanese War of 1894. At Tientsin, the European Allies were to find one million pounds of ammunition, bought from Japanese, English, French, German, and Czech firms, entirely unusable for the guns. One gunboat was caught in battle with only two shells. The Empress Dowager was using the money appropriated for the navy to build herself the new "Summer Palace.")

"Ha!" he said, suddenly prompted to tell a great story. "You know when Yeh Mingchen fought the French, he made himself famous by his war motto:

I'll neither attack, nor defend, nor sue for peace;
Nor die, nor surrender, nor flee.

The 'six not's.' He should have been decorated for thinking up such an unbeatable couplet."

The whole family laughed.

"What about the Emperor?" asked Uncle Sueipo.

"I don't want anything said here to go outside these doors. He is wonderful. To us he is the Emperor, but in the Palace he is only the Empress Dowager's nephew. Emperor Meiji of Japan is more fortunate. He doesn't have such a benighted old aunt to hinder him. He and Prince Ito are brilliant men, and together they are completely modernizing their country."

"Tell us about Viceroy Chang Chih-tung and Li Hung-chang," asked the aunt.

"I am partial, of course, to my chief. At court, there is always the struggle of personalities. Both of them are great men. Unfortunately, Li Hung-chang is in eminence at present. You hear about these reforms—mines, railways, et cetera. Li has great financial stakes in all of them. The Chinese Steamship Navigation Company is the most notorious example."

"And Chang?"

"He is really great—a man with a vision. He thinks China must quickly learn from the West or perish. He is thinking of starting a movement called 'Strength Through Learning.' Those who can learn are strong, those who refuse to learn are old and must die."

"What do you do under the Viceroy?" asked Jasmine.

"Guest adviser, you know. I am not a part of his official staff, but do what I am called upon to do as a personal friend and guest in his house. The *muliao*, you know. I have no office hours, no definite duties. We discuss problems, policies when something turns up."

Liang Mengchia had once served as *muliao* to a general in the northwest. Chang Chih-tung saw a memorandum he had drafted to the throne for the general and was quite struck by it. He had heard of the story of the memorandum. The general had been suffering a series of crushing defeats at the hands of the rebels. He had written, "We always fought on, and always lost." Liang Mengchia took a brush and made a mark of inversion, making it read, "We always lost, and always fought on." Grand Councilor Chang "borrowed" Liang from the general and never returned him, nor intended to do so. There had been many such famous "guest advisers." When they were working with a governor, he fared well; when they left, the governor did badly. Apart from drafting memorandums to the throne, they helped study crises and problems and shape policies. Their work called for a fresh, quick intelligence, while the staff of the secretariat usually floundered in bureaucratic routine.

"Do you want to hear a good story about Shü Wenchang, the famous guest advisor?"

Everybody loved Shü Wenchang. He had become a kind of legend.

Mengchia went on: "Once the Governor of the Two Kiangs got himself into a mess. He had made a routine report concerning a murder committed during a theatrical show. Some expert at the Ministry of Rites discovered a very grave dereliction of duty on the part of the Governor. The date of the murder indicated that the theatrical show had been held during the period of national mourning for an empress, when public entertainments with music and song were forbidden throughout the country. The Governor could have lost his job for permitting it to happen under his jurisdiction. He consulted Shü. Shü thought a while and said with a smile, 'Your Excellency, are you willing to forfeit three months' salary?' He then explained, 'I suggest that you need only add one word to extricate yourself from this difficulty.' 'What is that?' asked the Governor. 'Put in the word *monkey*,' Shü replied. 'You should immediately write back that there was a copier's error in the report; the word *monkey* had been left out before the word *show* by mistake. You should explain that it was only during a monkey show that the murder was committed.' A monkey show consists merely of an itinerant entertainer who has one or two monkeys dressed in a red vest and a cap and trained to do a few tricks, and therefore is not a violation of the national mourning. The Governor followed his advice and got away with a fine of three months' salary for carelessness in documentary text."

Dinner over, they sat around in the parlor. Uncle Sueipo again brought up the question of the clan reception.

"I will see. The only official call I want to make is on Prince Yi, the Military Governor here. I used to know him in Peking. I am thinking of calling on him tomorrow."

Aunt Su said, "Are you sure all your clothes are ready for the visit?"

"Oh, it's only a personal call."

"Still I think you should put on formal dress when you call on him at his office."

"I suppose so. Is the laundry back?"

"I am afraid it isn't. I am sorry—I didn't know you were going to visit him so soon. I must see to it."

"You see, with Tingma gone, I am rather lost."

"Where is Tingma?" asked Peony.

"She has gone back to her farm. She wants to retire, now that she is back in Hangchow."

"She is not going with us to Peking?"

"No. She has spent enough time taking care of me all these years. I have given her three hundred dollars."

Aunt Su had left and Jasmine followed. Soon they returned with a gown and an overjacket (*makua*).

"Tako," said Jasmine. "Put it on. We want to see how you look as a mandarin."

Mengchia smiled. "See how well they take care of me!"

Aunt Su examined the blue silk gown and discovered it needed ironing.

"Look. There is a lost button under the armpit. I don't see that Tingma was such a good housekeeper."

"It's not her fault. I remember I lost the button while in Foochow. Never mind, with the overjacket on, nobody will notice it."

"What if the Military Governor asked you to *shuipien kuanyi*, feel at home, and you should take it off?" said Jasmine. "I could sew it on right now. A girl disciple should normally bring a gift to the master. Let me do this for you."

She went to borrow a needle and thread. While the talk went on, she sat in the dining room under the table lamp working on the button. The braid had to be made and the knot tied expertly, and then she had to iron the gown. It was twenty minutes before she came out and joined them.

"There it is—ready."

"This teaches you a lesson, Mengchia," said Aunt Su. "The idea of being a bachelor and living without a wife in the house!"

CHAPTER 6

Everything a young girl does may be explained by her primeval
instinct to find a satisfactory mate. Her dress, the care of her
hands, her music lessons, and her choice and direction of activi-
ties all have a purpose, the purpose of finding herself a husband.
Where marriage is arranged by parents, the workings of this
instinct go on, imperious, undismayed. Passion is the expression
of this instinct. Described often as blind, it is not. The mature
girl always knows perfectly well what she is doing when she falls
in love. Peony was no exception.

She could not explain to herself why her ardor for Chin Chu
had cooled when she finally realized the hopelessness of their
entanglement. All she knew for certain was that the day she
went to the appointment she did not seem to care so much as
she used to. She did not feel the intoxicating happiness welling
inside her, and her face showed it. It was true that before she
left Kaoyu her one great desire and longing was to see Chin
Chu again, to be by his side and discuss with him their future.
She had only one thought: to belong to him completely. For
this she was willing to sacrifice everything, as she wrote him, to
cut herself loose from all ties and obligations. She had wanted
to break with the Feis as soon as possible, so as to come to him.
It was her dream, and it was also his dream, she knew. Yet in
the course of the past few months, things had happened which
took away the wholehearted quality of that love, a love now
fringed with hesitancies and doubts. Her plans had already
changed.

She was surprised to find that this was, indeed, the case, when
she entered the hotel lobby and found Chin Chu waiting for her
with a keen, expectant, wholehearted smile. It was a hotel where
they had met many times and which they knew well.

"Oh, Chin Chu," she gasped softly.

He took her hand and they went up to his room. It was early.

She had left word with her sister that she was going to spend a day with Paiwei and might be home late. They had a whole day free to themselves and alone. The meeting had come at last —the moment which both of them had prayed for and waited for with such ardent intensity. On other occasions, they would have found themselves in each other's arms, embracing passionately. They kissed—yet the passionate quality was lacking and Chin Chu felt it.

Chin Chu looked at her with the same adoration, the same continual wonder and love, which to him had been like a miracle. He had got up early this morning and put flowers in the vase; he had thought out everything they might do, had planned every detail, so that their meeting might be perfect.

"Why didn't you come to Chinkiang? Did you get my letter?" she asked.

"I did. I was ill and could not come. In fact, I have been ill for a month. But I am all right now."

She looked at him lovingly, and found that indeed he had become much thinner. There were lines on his face which she had not seen before. He was not the same specimen of youth and health that he had been before. Of course, she knew it was temporary, but it saddened her to see the change.

He said to her, "I have a suggestion and don't know whether you'll like it. Let's take a trip to Kwanyin Cave, unless you'd rather stay in the hotel and talk instead of rushing about?"

"Certainly, I want to see the Kwanyin Cave. I have never seen it."She spoke in her quick, girlish, golden voice.

"Won't you be too tired?"

"No, Chin Chu," she smiled.

"Then we'll have to hurry and get started at once. I will go out and get a carriage." He suddenly raised his eyes to her and said, "My, you are beautiful! There is some walking to do. Are you sure you have on the right shoes?"

Today she had on her beige jacket and skirt—it was the closest thing she could wear to get away from the white of mourning without attracting too much notice. The suit was of a very rich material and emphasized her small waist.

"I am all right," she said.

She began to give her hair a few touches and looked at herself in the mirror.

"Is it all right?" she asked him for his approval.

"You are perfect."

But she was dissatisfied and began to adjust and raise her skirt an inch higher, at the same time taking it in at the waist by one button.

"Come, help me," she said.

He came close and buttoned it for her. Even with her jacket on, her extremely small waistline showed her firm hips to great advantage.

"You get yourself ready and wait downstairs. I am going to hire a carriage for the day."

Chin Chu came back with a carriage. Peony was just about to get in, when she remembered she had forgotten her purse, and ran upstairs again.

While Chin Chu was waiting, the hotel clerk informed him that he had received a notice for a registered letter at the post office. He decided he might as well take the carriage and pick it up now. But the post office, he discovered, was not yet open. When he returned, Peony was waiting on the sidewalk with her purse.

"Come on, get in." Chin Chu jumped down from the carriage to assist her. He missed her "lovers' " smile, but thought it was because he had gone off without telling her and had kept her waiting.

"At last," he said when they were seated side by side.

To his surprise, there was still no tender smile on her lips. It dampened his high spirits.

"What's the matter, Peony?" he asked. "Are you not well?"

"Nothing is the matter."

His hand pressed on her thigh. She did not repulse him, nor was she her usual ardent self. She leaned back, her head rolling with the movement of the carriage, but remained silent. Her mind was in a tumult of conflict and confusion. Down in her soul she cared for this man very deeply. Yet something had intervened. For those who believe in psychic influences, it would seem that they were under evil stars, that an invisible occult force was at work to separate the lovers. Later, Chin Chu consulted a fortuneteller as to why he had so inexplicably lost his love, and he was told that someone had cast a spell on her by incantation and black magic, that she was not to blame for what happened, and that she loved him and would come back to him.

There are many fine days in September in Hangchow. Their carriage had come out of the busy Hupin Square, rolled along the beautiful shore line of the West Lake, passed the Paiti Embankment which separated the main body of water from the Inner Lake, and then moved on toward the foothills. All the way, the mountainsides were glowing with reds and purples and all the rich colors of autumn. But Peony scarcely noticed. They held hands without saying anything.

"So you have left your mother-in-law's family and are free now," he said.

"I did it for you," she said briefly, and what she said was true.

"You don't seem to be so happy, as we ought to be. Why?"

"I don't know."

"I got your letter. It is a difficult dilemma for me. You see my wife's family and my family are connected by business ties. Her father and my father built the local bank together. That was why our marriage was arranged in the first place. I'll tell you what's been on my mind. I will have myself transferred to the Hangchow branch and come and live here. I know I can arrange it. At least, it will be easy for us to meet often. And if you are willing to wait a few years, things may change. Who knows? It may be unfair to ask you to do this . . . I know . . . "

She looked extremely sad and said, "It's no use." Her tone indicated that she did not approve of the idea of living as his mistress at all, even though it was, perhaps, only for a short time. "I may as well tell you—I am planning to leave the city and go to Peking with my sister. My cousin, the *hanlin*, is here on a visit, and has persuaded my parents to let us go and visit the national capital."

"For a visit only? How long? I am willing to wait."

"I don't know."

From the way she squeezed his hand and held it, he knew that she loved him deeply; but he had a premonition that Peony's feelings for him had changed, that a force was drawing them apart. This confused feeling weighed heavily upon his heart until their carriage had gone up into the hills.

It was a long ride. At last, the carriage drew up at a temple. After a light lunch of noodles and vegetarian ham (made from hardened bean curd), they came out for a little rest. He showed Peony the notice from the post office and said, "I wonder what it is? We must be back in the city before the post office is closed."

"It must be something important. Can we make it? Where is the letter sent from?"

"It doesn't say. The post office is closed at five. I am sure we can make it."

A bright sun was shining. The day was suddenly very hot, as often happens in early autumn. He sought a cool stone bench under the trees, and said, "Come on, sit down."

Of course she would sit down. They needed a little rest after lunch before going into the cave. But she shook her head and did not come near him, and walked away silently to be by herself. Was it their future that was disturbing her so? He could see only her feet under the carriage where several carriages were parked together. She stood still for a long time. Apparently she was leaning upon the carriage, buried deep in thought. When she came back, he saw that she had been crying. He kept quiet and did not ask questions.

A guide to the cave approached them with a couple of canes in his hand.

"Shall we go inside now?" Chin Chu asked. He had checked with the driver to make sure that they would have enough time to get back before the post office closed.

They went down the hill along the paths of red earth, covered with small bushes of grass and outcropping rocks. Each carried a cane for support. At the entrance, they halted for breath. The guide held the torches ready.

The small size of the entrance was deceptive; the cave was very deep, and twisted with long, cavernous passages. At their approach, a whir of dark, flapping shapes, accompanied by weak, high-pitched squeaks, made its way toward the entrance. There were swarms of bats, hundreds, perhaps thousands of them. All was dark inside. The guide lighted a torch, and gave another to Chin Chu. Slowly, they descended the steep steps. After a while, the ground flattened out. A roped handrail helped the tourists to follow the rough, crooked path. Now and then, they could see the light of a party fifty feet below them, shining up through sharply silhouetted holes in the rock formations. The steps, which were cut roughly out of the rocks, were wet with dripping water, and the air was cold. They came to a chamber, flanked by fluted pillars. The guide pointed with his torch to a rock formation that looked remarkably like a statue of the popular goddess Kwanyin, with her palms together; the strange rock was supported by a base resembling a lotus flower.

"You don't want to go any farther, do you?" asked Chin Chu. His voice made a hollow echo in the darkness.

"I think we'd better not, if we want to get to the post office in time."

He held her tightly by the waist, and they traced their way upward and back. Sometimes he would lead her and sometimes she would be leading him as they carefully climbed the treacherous paths. Their hands never parted for a second. He was intensely happy.

It seemed to Chin Chu that no more than ten minutes had passed before they saw the white light of the entrance. At last they stood outside, her arm linked tightly in his. For a moment they seemed like the lovers of old.

On their way back, they told the driver to hurry and make as good time as he could. Peony slouched down in her seat, her legs up, indifferent to how her skirt was arranged. He made her head rest on his shoulders, and he felt the fragrance of her hair and skin and the warmth of her body. Once more she withdrew into her silent mood. What she was thinking at the moment he did not know and did not want to ask. Sometimes she sat up a little, or shifted in the seat, as the carriage rolled from side to side. He wanted to kiss her, but she avoided turning her face toward him. She had never been so aloof, so unresponsive to him, before.

When they were back in the city, he thought first of sending her back to the hotel and getting the letter himself. But they had only about a quarter of an hour before the post office closed.

"Let's go to the post office first, shall we?"

She seemed completely exhausted, but said, "Perhaps." Her mind was clearly preoccupied.

Together, hand in hand, they went in. He produced the notice he had received and gave it to the clerk at the window. The man was either short-tempered or very anxious to go home. He took the little slip of paper and disappeared into another room, keeping them waiting a long time. At last, the letter was delivered to him.

"What is it?" she asked in a voice of deep concern, as he tore the letter open and read it.

"Oh, it's from my firm. They want me back on Friday. That's three days from today. I have to start day after tomorrow."

He was evidently upset by it. He had with much difficulty asked for a week's leave, but the leave was now cut short. He had to go back to Soochow.

"That means tomorrow will be our last day," he said in the carriage.

In the hotel room, she was silent. She had to tell him of her decision. But it was hard. She took a long time in the bath.

At last, she came out with nothing on and threw herself on the bed where he was lying. Every time he looked at her marvelous body, her full bosom, her lithe figure, he wondered afresh at her perfection. And she was prepared to give herself to him entirely. Yet there was no ardor on her lips. It seemed as if she had deliberately come to him to make a farewell of love.

They lay locked in each other's embrace. His hand roamed over her body slowly, lovingly, and she was yielding as if her whole body had dissolved in a mist of passion.

He pressed his mouth against hers and cried, "Oh, Peony, you'll never know how much I've longed for you." She nibbled at his lips, but said not a word.

"Come on, take me," she said.

"When will I see you again?" he asked.

"I really don't know."

It was the law of love that both lovers should abandon themselves completely and forget everything else in the consummation of their passion. He was not thinking particularly of anything, but her whole behavior since their meeting this morning had been strange. The thought weighed upon him heavily and he could do nothing.

They lay there in each other's arms, like a smoldering fire, unable either to burst into the flame of ecstasy, or quite snuff it out. It was as if the physical sensations were there but his mind was not, in spite of all the endearing contact of their limbs. Then she seized him passionately, and covered him with ravishing kisses, as if she were giving him a present of love so that he would never forget this moment, or simply because she was caught in the flood of an uncontrollable passion herself. She wanted him to remember this moment and every twist of her body and every gesture of her embrace. If he could believe in black magic, that an evil influence was working to separate them, it would make sense.

"You," she said, repeatedly. It was an invitation that he should consummate their union, should shatter her with the wild embrace she knew and loved so well.

Suddenly it was over. He forgot how they separated. He got up and washed, and came back to see her lying with her face buried deep in the pillow. He came and touched her gently. Her eyes were closed, and she was breathing regularly, as if she were asleep. But her eyelashes moved. A tear rolled down her cheek.

He bent and kissed her. His heart was ready to break. She opened her eyes and began to blink, still deep in thought. She wanted to say something, but how could she say it? She knew that her mind was made up, that she was determined to make a break. It was cutting her heart to pieces. Yet he clearly had indicated that he would never think of a divorce. How, she asked herself, was she to carry on with him, to meet him as his mistress, for months, for years? Her way was clear; there was no alternative.

Her silence and her tears puzzled him. She was his whole life. He had repeatedly said to her, and he still felt it now, that she was his all, his life, his soul. Whether she was with him or away from him, she was the thirst and the fulfillment of his soul. There was only one person, one Peony, in this world. There was no other.

Now she seemed exhausted and asleep. It was suffocatingly hot in the room. He took a fan and very gently fanned her, changing from one side to the other, almost like a mother fanning a child, so that she might enjoy a cool and peaceful sleep, while he devoured her sprawling body with his eyes. He took a corner of the sheet and covered her tenderly that she might not catch cold.

He must have spent half an hour like this, sitting on the edge of the bed, fanning her, watching her, protecting her as a mother would a sleeping child, and with the same infinity of love. Her eyes opened and she turned over, facing him.

"Why do you do this?" she asked.

"Because I love you."

"Didn't you take a nap?"

"No. It makes me happy just to be watching you."

Suddenly she sat up. He went to the desk and took out a cigarette, lit it, and gave it to her. She took it and blew a tremendous puff, like an aching sigh, glancing at him nervously.

"So tomorrow will be our last day," she said.

"So it seems. When can you come and see me?"

"Any time I am free."

"Say tomorrow night. We must have supper together."

"Good. I will excuse myself from my family, somehow or other."

"Why don't you come in the early afternoon so that we can talk?"

"I will see if I can."

She got up, settled herself at the desk, and started to write something. When he came near, she partly covered it with her hand. Puzzled, he left her alone. Then she went to the mirror and started combing her hair. She looked so beautiful that Chin Chu felt his heart twist inside him.

"I feel I want to go out—alone—now," she said. With a smile, she handed him the letter in an envelope and said, "Read it when I am gone."

He was completely taken by surprise. "What is it?" he shouted after her. "Please tell me."

"Read it," she said and, with a beautiful smile, went out.

He tore it open and read:

> Pardon me, Chin Chu. I could not bring myself to say this to you. I am going away to Peking. I am leaving you. There is no use fooling ourselves.
>
> I have loved you madly, blindly, as I have loved no other man. But the time has come for us to part. Try to forget me, your own Peony.
>
> I cannot lie to you. I love another man. Forgive me. I can no longer give you the wholehearted love that I've always had for you.
>
> I am profoundly sorrowful. I know you must feel the same.
>
> I will come tomorrow.
>
> > Yours in tears,
> > Peony

With a tremendous curse, he crumpled up the letter in his strong fist.

He felt completely unhinged, like one who had completely lost his bearings in this world. Something good, something beautiful had been destroyed and had left in its wake only fathomless darkness. He couldn't believe it. He knew that she loved him. If their love had not been so unique, so true, so good, he might have accepted it. Oh, no, not Peony whom he

loved so well, and after such a long and confident exchange
of feelings and perfect fondness for each other, after they had
found each other in this wide, wide world. Only an hour ago
they were walking hand in hand.

He read Peony's letter again and again, smoothing out the
crinkled paper. It was clear that she had meant to tell him this
all day. So it was true. Peony had changed.

He had been willing to fight and surmount any obstacle, that
they might eventually belong to each other completely. But
when Peony herself was the enemy and the cause of the break,
then there was nothing left to be angry about. He felt weightless and insubstantial, and without purpose, as if he had been
pushed backward into black space, floating down, down, down,
into the darkness which was the beginning of the world. He
was stripped defenseless.

Suddenly he lit a match and set fire to the letter. He watched
with glee as the flames ate into the paper. A thin feather of
black smoke curled into the air and gave off a hot, acrid smell.
He had brought along some of her last letters, as he always did
when traveling to get the feeling of being near her, including
the one she had sent to Chinkiang. He lighted these and threw
them into a metal receptacle. Then he remembered he had been
halfway through reading a long love story which held him
spellbound. That, too, had no meaning any more and he threw
it into the fire with the other papers. It did not burn well,
and he sat on the ground, tearing it page by page to feed the
fire until the iron basket was blackened and hot and black
pieces of burned paper flew up into the air. The room choked
with smoke. His hands and face were all smeared. He felt a
sensation of pleasure and relief. So should all love go up in
smoke! The smoke suffocated him. He opened the window. A
hotel waiter saw the smoke and called the staff. Some people
came and watched from across the court, but he stood before
the window and told them to go away, that it was all right and
not to worry. Then he carefully washed his face and hands
and went out.

It was long past the supper hour and the shops were closed;

only a few stalls and restaurants were lighted. He suddenly felt very lightheaded. The peddlers' cries, the stream of black smoke rising from the lamp of a seller of hot snacks, the faces of the men and children around—all had an appearance of unreality. Time seemed to have stopped. It was curious that in the midst of this he should remember one thing: that he must return to Soochow. He yearned to be back at his desk so that he could get hold of himself again.

Going back to the hotel, the dull pains in his belly that had made him ill a short while ago started again. He felt slightly feverish. No doctor had been able to tell him what was wrong. Anyway, it was not very painful and it did not matter.

At three o'clock the following afternoon, he heard a knock at the door.

"Who is it?"

"It's Peony."

He went to open the door. They stared at each other for a second, unsmiling.

"Come in," he said.

She walked in in her usual shuffling step and surveyed the room. All of a sudden, his madness for her returned. She was Peony, it was enough. He began to smile ruefully.

"I have come, as I promised. At five o'clock, though, I have an appointment," she added quickly.

"But we were going to have dinner together."

"I will come back. At what hour?"

"At eight."

Her eyes were looking at him steadily. All his love, his frenzy for her returned. No, he could not be angry with her, just because she was Peony.

"All right, Peony," he said. "I accept your terms. And I want to thank you for the happiness you have given me in the past years."

"Chin Chu," she said, with a heaviness in her voice, "all that I told you in the letter is true. I hope we can remain friends."

"But what happened? Have I offended you? Did I do anything I shouldn't have done? Have I changed?"

"No."

"Then why? why? why? You have changed. Why?"

"I don't know."

She was silent then, and as was her habit she threw herself on the bed and would not say a word.

He came and tried to kiss her.

She placed a finger on his mouth and said, "No."

"Don't you love me a little?"

She did not answer at once. But then, slowly and clearly, she said, "It's all or nothing."

His pride was hurt, and he did not insist. He longed to know whom she was in love with, but would not allow himself to ask.

"What did you do last night?" he asked.

"Oh, I went out with some of my girl friends. We went to a marine club on the lake. I didn't go home till half-past one. Some of us went out boating. The night was beautiful."

When she was talking of subjects not directly concerned with themselves, they were like good friends, exactly as before. He knew she had three or four girl friends, Mita and others; but he still didn't think that she was telling the truth.

"Whom are you going to meet at five?"

"Paiwei and Joshui."

"Oh, Paiwei! Always Paiwei!"

She half sat up. "Don't you believe me? She wants to invite me to go to her home at Tunglu."

In the years before her marriage, they had often gone to the theater at night, with Paiwei serving as a cover. He remembered the crazy night they had passed at Tunglu in the open, when Peony first gave herself to him with wild abandon. It was unforgettable, the high point of their love. He still had hope that some of the love Peony had for him had not entirely disappeared.

It was stiflingly hot, and she opened the top buttons of her gown. He misunderstood her, and thought it was an open suggestion. He came close to her and wanted to kiss her.

But she looked at him directly and said, "I have told you. I cannot."

He felt as if someone had hit him across the mouth.

"Then it is all over between us."

She was quiet. It was clear to him, and it was final. Something snapped within him. He pressed his belly on the spot where it hurt. A momentary contortion of pain showed on his face.

"What's the matter?" she asked, alarmed.

"It's nothing."

He felt no fury, no rage, but just a cold emptiness within.

He took out his wallet, and plucked out a snapshot of her which he had carried when away from home, and returned it to her. Next he took from it a lock of hair she had given him, which he had concealed in a paper wrapping.

"There," he said in a cold, unemotional tone.

She took it, with a grim glance at him.

"I have also burned your letters, the last ones you wrote."

Her eyes registered a note of pained surprise. "You *have!* How could you?" she chided.

"Why not?" he answered in a controlled voice.

"Will you see me again when I come back?"

"No. What for?"

She was stunned into silence. After a while, she said, without looking at him, "I thought that, even though we have stopped being lovers, you could still offer me a pure and disinterested friendship."

He flared up. "When was our friendship not pure and disinterested? How can you say that? I don't know what to think. Our dream has vanished. You have destroyed it. How could such a love as ours die out so casually, so easily? How could you? I believe you are not capable of a great love. I am inclined to think you are a flirt and a coquette."

"No, I am not . . . a coquette. Believe me," she protested, almost sweetly.

"Then tell me why."

"I can't explain it. Don't ask me to. I don't know. Believe me that I did not lie to you, that I did love you once."

"How can I believe in you any more!" His voice was tense and brittle. "I have no confidence in you at all."

It hurt her deeply. Her eyes misted and she looked away.

He softened in spite of himself and said, "You are still coming tonight?"

"Yes, of course. You don't understand me at all."

"Of course, I don't. But let's not talk about love any more. Tomorrow I shall get up early to go back to Soochow. . . . Oh, you exasperating, crazy, lovable Peony!"

In the next breath, his tone was normal and friendly again. He said softly, almost to himself, without reproach and without malice, "I have lost everything. Something in me has died. You have killed me, although I still seem to exist."

She almost made a half gesture to make up, to offer him a kiss, but he pretended not to see it. He lit a cigarette and puffed it and smiled at her, but it was a cold smile.

She picked herself up and went to the bathroom to freshen up. After a while she came out, threw a pale pink handkerchief at him, and said, "There."

He remembered he had asked for it. It was the traditional article for a souvenir between sweethearts.

"No. If you do not love me."

He left the pink handkerchief on the bed, untouched. She gathered her things, and biting her lower lip, walked out wearily.

When Peony was gone he was filled with a cold fury at himself and at Peony. Then remorse followed anger, and he was ashamed that he had spoken to her so harshly. He found that it was not true that he was finished with her, that he was indifferent. The very image of her biting her lip when she walked away hit him hard. His love did not die so easily as he had pretended. His whole body sagged into a straight chair, and he broke down completely. A violent surge of emotion swept through his entire body. In the next moment, he was sick of her caprices, her hardness, of his own weakness, of everything.

When she walked into the restaurant that night and he saw her white figure weaving its way through the room blocked with people his heart started to beat violently. He rose at once to meet her, and guided her to the table. She sat down, smoothed back a falling lock of hair, and appeared calm and silent, as if she were ready to take anything from him, as if she expected him to say something caustic or nasty, or coldly cynical. She glanced at him quickly. It was a glance not of anger, but of reproach.

"Thank you for coming," he said rather formally. His pride prevented him from showing either frustration or remorse. What he wanted to say, he had already said that afternoon.

The waiter, an old man with a balding head, came with the menu. He asked her what she wanted. Neither was in the mood for a festive farewell dinner. She picked roast lamb served with kumquats and onions, and a dish of deep-fried bean curd. He asked for a half bottle of *shaoshing*, for he knew that she always enjoyed a little drink with dinner, and added a dish of *Ningpo kali* (small black soft-shelled clams).

"You really love them," she said with a smile.

"And I know you don't," he responded with the same smile.

"I never care for shellfish."

He stretched a hand across the table and grasped hers. She looked up with a smile and they were friends once more.

"You have pardoned me?" he said.

"For what?"

"For speaking to you as I did this afternoon. We are friends?"

"Of course we are. None of your nonsense."

She was wearing a string of crystals which glittered in the soft light. Once more he felt proud of her, as he always did, conscious that other men in the room, including the waiters, were admiring her beauty and envying his luck for coming out with such a captivating, youthful beauty. Even the old waiter with a bald head sought an opportunity to say a few nice words when he brought the roast.

"I am sure you will like it," he said, lifting a gesturing hand. "We do it perfectly here. Nobody in Hangchow does it as well."

"A roast is a roast," she said, feeling quite at home with waiters as usual.

"Ah, no. It's a secret. It's not the roast but what goes into it before the roasting." He walked away, straightening his shoulders. Curious what the sight of a lovely young girl does to an old man.

They had wine first, and she picked herself a small kumquat. She closed her eyes and exclaimed softly, "Oh, it's divine! . . . Remember when we picked kumquats at Tunglu and ate them off the tree?"

"Oh, yes, at Tunglu. I remember."

Her glance slanted down toward him, as he hung his head. He remembered very well indeed how they had passed a night in the open near a mountain stream and then, the next morning, gone swimming in the nude. It was dangerous emotional ground and he quickly shut his mind off. He raised his head and said,

"Peony, I want to say something to you."

"Go ahead."

"You are going to Peking. I presume there will be lots of men at the capital. I want you to be very careful. I don't ever want to see you get hurt, or get into trouble."

"What do you mean?"

He said with infinite sadness, "I am dying a little. Slowly, bit by bit, I mean . . ."

"Don't talk like that, please."

"Never mind about me. That is not what I want to talk about."

"Then what?"

"You must protect yourself. The way we have lived together. Babies—you know what I mean."

"Oh, that!" she broke into a laugh. "Don't worry."

"But I am worried. You may be fond of a man. He may like you for a while. Then something happens and you are caught."

"You know I can handle myself."

She spoke with perfect confidence. They went into a discussion of different age-old methods of birth control. They had known each other so well that she went into very intimate details. She asked for a pencil and paper. He searched his pocket and found a small diary. They put their heads together and she began to make a little obscene sketch. Some waiters nearby were watching with amusement as she giggled.

The wine was finished and they asked for a little porridge to finish up with. On the whole, the dinner went off very well.

She looked at her watch.

"Oh, it's after half-past nine. I must be going."

He was flabbergasted.

She explained, "I have to meet someone at ten."

He could see that she was anxious to leave. "Oh, well, that's it," he thought to himself. This was their last night. She would be going away, and they might not see each other for years. She might have reserved the last night for him. But it did not seem to mean anything to her. Her love for him was dead. That was the cold, brutal, inescapable fact. "You are very anxious to part early," he thought, but he did not say it.

He rose reluctantly, realizing the full consequences of this parting. He swallowed hard, paid the bill, and they left.

It was pouring outside. They stood on the stoop, waiting for rickshaws.

"You will write me?" she asked.

"No."

"Shall I see you again?"

"No. I may not be here when you come."

There was a deep disappointment in her voice when she said, "Well, this is our farewell."

She turned her face up and gave him a quick kiss. The rickshaws came, and he saw her going up. Her face showed above the oilcloth, but he could not see whether she was smiling or crying.

Then, at the last moment, his infatuation overwhelmed him and his heart felt a violent twinge. He rushed up close to the half-closed rickshaw and stuttered, "Good luck to you!"

CHAPTER 7

The things we do live after us. Certain events pass, but their memories remain, stealing upon us unawares. Passion passes, but remorse is eternal. Both Chin Chu and Peony deluded themselves when they said good-by, thinking it was all finished between them, never to see each other again.

Her relations with Chin Chu held the key to Peony's life. It was destiny, some believe, that she should meet and then lose him, that he should be married to another woman. If she had been able to marry him as a young girl, there would be no story to write. No ballad would be sung about the "Red Peony." On the other hand, by cutting loose from him, she was doing something to her lover and to herself. Does man control Destiny, or does Destiny control us, to wreak her vengeance in a way unknown to the people involved?

Peony had not lied when she told Chin Chu that she had gone boating at night with Mita and the others. For the past two days, Mengchia had been occupied with various affairs, including a visit to Prince Yi, the present Emperor's cousin, a *peileh* by rank. The Prince, as Military Governor, had jurisdiction over the Two Kiangs (Chekiang and Kiangsu; that is, down below Hangchow and up north beyond Nanking). Once Mengchia's presence became known, invitations and requests poured in at the hotel where his secretary was staying. There were many requests for his calligraphy, and Chen Li, the secretary, came with an armful of special calligraphy paper. These he could not reject. Like all scholars, he traveled with a special high quality ink cake and personal seals for this purpose (the paper and brush he could always obtain on the spot); he had also with him a favorite collection of Sung lyrics which could come in handy. Otherwise he just wrote out of his head witty comments or poems, known as *tsiching*, or *ad hoc*, made on the spot, which were generally more appreciated. He told his secretary to decline the other interviews or invitations with polite excuses, while he hid himself in his aunt's home. There was one exception, an invitation from the Shiling Club, a club of local poets and writers.

The next day, Peony received a note brought by Ren-Ren, saying that the *hanlin* hoped to see her in the afternoon to talk over various matters. He would be going to visit his mother's grave on the Phoenix Hill, which was south of the city on the bank of the Tsientang, in fact, less than half an hour's walk from Peony's home. He would call for her on the way back, and they might have tea and refreshments at the Shiling Club, which commanded a superb view of the West Lake.

"You come along," Peony said to her sister.

"No. I am not included. He did not mention me," said Jasmine. "You go and find out when he proposes to leave for Peking, and what dresses we should bring along. And now, what are you going to wear?"

"Why, as usual," Peony replied, "my black pantaloons."

"How shocking!"

"He doesn't mind. I can't wear silk, anyway."

"I mean you should wear something more respectful, and not so casual. Won't he be offended? . . . I mean this matter of mourning."

"No, I know him."

If Peony had intended to be casual, she could not have succeeded better. The day was beautiful, dry, and brisk without being chilly. She had on an old, pale blue jacket and her black pantaloons, somewhat the worse for wear. Jasmine admired the extraordinary self-confidence with which she went out with the *hanlin*. She had a daring which Jasmine did not possess; she seemed to be able to take everything in her stride.

Their carriage drew up at the Shiling Club on the Paiti Embankment, fringed with graceful, browning willows on this bright autumn day. On its right was the famous Louwailou (Tower-Above-Tower) Restaurant; on its left, the residence of Yu Chüyuan, the poet and novelist. The Shiling Club was built on a steep slope with a sprinkling of cherry, apple, pear, and other choice trees. A long series of stone steps led to the top, so that standing on the terrace, one overlooked the restaurant. There were various rooms in the Club containing art objects. Scrolls of contemporary calligraphy hung on the walls.

Mengchia examined with great interest a five-foot-high scroll, on which the local poet, An Tonien, had written a couplet. He was quite struck by the poet's bold, rugged style. It was, as a matter of fact, not strictly a couplet, but contained two powerful lines of five words each:

> *The Tsientang embraces the Tienchu,*
> [And] *the Phoenix rides the Tsientang.*

It was one of those inevitable lines a writer stumbles upon when inspired, as if the lines had been there from eternity, and the poet had merely filched them from the outer darkness. The ten words described the composition and topography of the whole city of Hangchow now lying below them. It contained not one adjective, but only named the river and the two hills. The force of the two lines was concentrated on the two graphic verbs, *embraces* and *rides*.

"I doubt if I could better that," the *hanlin* said with an appreciative delight. "An Tonien was here when they gave me a dinner last night. That man has my respect."

"What is he like?"

"A very brilliant young poet, and quite a character—very vivacious and romantic. I like him. He is completely natural and has no airs about him."

They went out to the terrace where they were served tea. Out in the distance lay the broad Tsientang, flowing into the bay; the river curled in the late autumn afternoon like a band of silver. On their right, wisps of clouds rose from the Tienchu, now appearing as mauve-blue spots in the distant sky, while the Phoenix Hill nearby "rode the Tsientang," as the lines say. Below them slept the pool of bluish light of West Lake, reflecting the shadows of trees and villas on its colorful shore lines. Behind them was the Inner Lake and the Paosuta Pagoda, almost a thousand years old, where, according to a local legend, the White-Snake Spirit was kept subdued under its stone vaults. In the center of the Lake stood the Thrice-Mirrored Moon, like an enchanted isle, and immediately below them was the willow-covered shore line which went by the long name, "Listen-to-Orioles-Among-Willows." They could see the Thrice-Mirrored Moon now, the island appearing as a temple, in front of which were three pools on successive levels, enabling a visitor to see three moons at the same time reflected on these separate pools at night.

Peony slouched in her straight chair, with her legs outstretched in the half-frayed pantaloons and not-so-new shoes. Mengchia had told the waiter to leave the tea; he would pour it himself. The gentle hint was taken.

Peony's heart beat fast in wonder and admiration for this man. His brawny cheeks showed heavy lines in the sun—a man who was a scholar and yet not a scholar. As far as appearances went, he might be mistaken for a much-traveled sales agent. His manner was easy, informal, and, one might say, un-mandarin. He loved to tuck up his sleeves quite a few inches above his wrist, by turning the white inner jacket sleeves outside. Just now, as she was dreamily surveying the lake below with half-closed eyes, she was aware that he was looking at her.

"What are you thinking of?" he asked.

"Nothing at all. Just floating and happy. And you?" Her voice chirped in the fresh air like a sparrow.

"Just looking at you and wondering."

"Wondering at what?" She cast a side glance at him.

"At the miracle of our meeting. Why should you be taking the Ishing route as I did? I chose it because it was more in the open. . . ."

"And I went that way because I wanted to cross the lake from Ishing."

"We might never have met otherwise. . . . Peony, I want to say this. We will be living together as cousins. But you and I can never marry. You are sure that it will be all right with you?

I feel I have no right. . . . Yet I want you so much. We belong to each other, whether we can marry or not."

"Of course." She turned her face confidently toward him. "You mean everything to me, but I don't see what you see in me. I can't believe it myself. At times I thought I was dreaming when you were in Foochow—that the whole voyage had been only a dream. . . ."

"I will tell you one thing. You may think of me as a Peking official, but I have my own private dream. Two simple souls united in a simple home. I was looking at you a moment ago, and was sure that we belong to each other. I have always been scared of marriage—the endless in-laws, the social façade, the inane gossip. I would be hearing that Mr. Chang was married to the niece of the Minister of War, and Mr. Lee was the grand-nephew on his mother's side of the Military Governor of Kiangse. Naturally, I would become just a part of that picture. *Oh, the Liang* Hanlin, *isn't he the son-in-law of the Prime Minister?* or *He and the Tupan of Kansu married the Lee sisters.* You go round and round and forget where you are and what you are. This is what happened in my first marriage. But I have a private dream—a small family with a girl of my heart, someone like you by my side, simple, gay, with a heart full of love, and breathing defiance to the world. That's enough. I don't want anything else. You fit into that dream exactly. Dressed as you are. Just like that."

Peony cast an incredulous smile at him, and asked, "Like this?"

"Dress is all relative. You wouldn't appear like that at the Court of Peking. But you look superbly dressed for a desert island. . . . I don't think I have reason to be scared of you. . . ."

Peony chuckled. "You know my father is *nothing but* a bank clerk. Isn't it wonderful?"

"There is something more than this. I believe that when a person is born, his soul goes out in search of the other soul made for him. He may never find her. Or it may take ten, twenty years. The same is true of a girl. But when they meet, the recognition of that other counterpart of his soul is instantaneous, instinctive, without discussion, without reason, and mutual. They know that since they were born, they have been looking for each other. They merge and nothing can separate them again; they are tied by the strongest force in the universe. That's the kind of feeling you gave me when you put your arm on mine that day looking at the cormorants. It happened that fast."

She replied gently, "I don't know whether I deserve this or not, but I felt the same thing about you. It was a sweet feeling, a feeling of complete ease, as if we had known each other in previous incarnations. Maybe it is true."

"Of course it is true."

She went and leaned over the stone balustrade, overwhelmed once again at what had happened to her; Chin Chu intruded in her consciousness just enough to make her feel infinitely sad. Mengchia saw her pantalooned legs sprawling at an angle, her chin resting on her arm. She must have remained that way for five minutes, happy and sad at the same time. Then she heard him pushing back his chair and coming up behind her. She straightened up as he rested a hand upon her shoulder. She turned her head and said, "Isn't it marvelous, a moment like this? It cannot be recaptured again."

"No. Everything passes. Su Tungpo was standing here on this very spot a thousand years ago. If you read his poems carefully, you would know."

"Was Chaoyun with him then?"

"She was only a girl of about twelve or thirteen when they met on the West Lake. She was his true love, not his wife. How do you explain those things?"

"She was very much younger than he, I know."

"Yes, she accompanied him to his exile. But they belonged together. So they belonged. The best love poems he wrote were about her, the most exalted in tone, the most refined."

He was standing behind her. Suddenly he had an inspiration, as he gazed over her shoulder at the view in the distance. "I have a couplet for you," he said.

The clouds of Tienchu arise from your coiled locks,
And the Thrice-Mirrored Moon lies below your
*   gorgeous breast.*

Peony smiled at him, her eyes flashing warmly.

Later, when she repeated these lines to Paiwei, the latter remarked, "What a sensuous verse!"

Hand in hand, they walked back to their seats.

"When shall we start for Peking?"

"I don't know yet. I was discussing this with Uncle Sueipo last night. He was taken with the idea I suggested to him that I might be able to persuade Prince Yi to come to the clan dinner. I know he will if I ask him. Of course his presence will give a great honor to the clan. But we have to find out first when he will be free. As soon as the clan dinner is over, we'll be able to depart for Peking."

"Did you talk Manchu with the Prince? You really can speak Manchu, I hear."

"A little—enough to get along. . . . I want to go away for a little rest, a retreat somewhere. I have been thinking of Tienmushan, but the journey will be too hard for you."

"For me?"

"Who else? I have only you in mind. I mean a retreat where I can be alone with you, where we'll be unknown. Any suggestions?"

An idea suggested itself to her mind at once.

"Would you come if I invited you to Tunglu? That is the mountain home of my best friend, Paiwei, and her husband. I want you to meet her. She adores you already, even though she hasn't met you yet."

"I was thinking of a retreat where there would be nobody but us."

"We will be alone. . . . You were speaking a moment ago of a private dream of yours. A simple home of two simple souls, isolated from the world's hustle and bustle. She and Joshui live exactly such an enchanted life up in the mountains. I really think you would like it there. As for privacy, Paiwei and I have no secrets between us. I can do everything I like."

"You are very persuasive."

"You will go? . . . Then I must tell her. She will be overjoyed."

"From the way you talk about your friend, it almost seems that I will have to have her approval before you'll go to Peking with me."

"Don't talk like that. You will like her, I know."

CHAPTER 8

The autumn hillside was brilliant with red and gold on both sides of the river when they went up the Fuchunkiang. In this region of the south, vegetation was dense. Precipitous cliffs stood a hundred feet high on the banks. The river current was broad and deep, and the mountains were high, casting deep shadows which lent a deep emerald green to the water. The scenery was gratuitously beautiful. The entire region, where the vigorous Fuchunkiang and the Tienmukiang converged from Yenchow in the north, and Tunchi, Kinwha in the south, was land rich in soil and in commerce. The river boats carried traffic to the great capital of Hangchow. And here were no longer the barren hills of the north, but majestic uplands radiant with forest and bird song, stretching down hundreds of miles from the awesome, snow-capped peaks of Huangshan, or the Yellow Mountain, all the way back in Southern Anhwei. As the name "Fuchunkiang" indicates, the river was "rich in spring."

Mengchia and Peony shared the river boat with over a dozen passengers. Paiwei had left a day ahead to prepare their welcome. They felt truly alone on the river boat, Peony chattering all the way in the secure knowledge that nobody knew who they were —free and alone with this magic of the eternally fresh mountains and water, with hearts dedicated to a budding romance. She knew what was inevitable, what was going to happen that night.

The boat stopped at Tunglu where a few passengers were

getting off. It was a river port with a couple of cobbled streets. Joshui, in black astrakhan hat—Turkish style—was standing at the wharf to greet them and take them home. The tall hat increased the impression of his height. Locally, at the village on the river, he was well known. Thin, slender, and pale, he was handsome in a very distinguished way; his slight pallor and small, well-trimmed mustache made him attractive. Just why, it was difficult to explain, but he always fancied a broad, ample gown, unbuttoned at the neck, which hung down like a sack.

"Paiwei is waiting for you in the house. She is sorry she was not able to come down herself."

"It's good of you to come," said Mengchia.

Joshui had already secured coolies to carry their luggage up, and had engaged three sedan chairs.

"Can't we walk up?" asked Mengchia.

"It's quite a way—two miles."

Mengchia turned to Peony. "What do you think?"

"It is so beautiful. Why don't we walk up?"

"Why not do this?" suggested Joshui. "Let's get into the chairs, and we can get down for a walk whenever we want to. I have bought a pair of walking sticks, too."

"That will be fun," said Peony, grabbing a knotty, unpainted stick, which was cut from some wood in the local forests.

"It's good to see you so merry," commented Joshui, for she was blinking happily all around. Her face was radiant.

Several young chair carriers were fighting for a chance to carry her. "Come to mine!" "Take mine!" they shouted.

A mountain chair was a simple contrivance, merely a low rattan seat with a hanging board serving for a foot rest, and carried by two large bamboo poles tied below the chair arms. Peony stepped into one; then the chair was lifted and on they went. She saw Joshui's black hat bobbing up and down in front, while Mengchia brought up the rear.

Halfway up, she caught sight of the bright trailing plumage of a pheasant flitting into a wood. She turned around and pointed it out to Mengchia.

"Lady, be good! Lady, be still!" said her chair carriers. This was taken up by the other carriers. It was a point of great importance to them, when every ounce was felt on their shoulders.

"I am sorry. . . . Why don't we get down and relieve them a little? Why should I be carried when I feel like walking?"

Mengchia and Joshui felt the same way and readily agreed. The chairs drew up.

"That's a lady," said one of the carriers when she got down.

She was easy and familiar with the carriers. "Am I too heavy for you?"

"Not at all, lady. Any time you want to ride again, tell us. It will be a pleasure."

They had all come down and stood for a moment surveying the neighboring peaks. The carriers were wiping their perspiration with the black towels they each carried. The oldest man was panting.

"Take it easy, old uncle," said Mengchia. "How far is it from here?"

"We have gone two thirds of the way. It's just twenty minutes from here."

The track zigzagged up through a grove of dogwood and maples for a distance. Here and there their path was crossed by outcroppings of tree roots and rocks. Luckily, the red earth was dry and the walking easy. The three of them went on, followed by the chair carriers behind. Joshui paid special attention to Mengchia who was jogging along on firm steps.

"You see that old man behind us," said Joshui. "One wintry day, I was coming up. It was windy and hard going all the way. Halfway up the top, he felt he could not make it. He was coughing hard. I said I would get down and walk and send him and his companion home. Do you know what? I offered him the fare, and he would not accept it. 'Oh, no,' he said. 'I was to carry you up. Now that I can't, I won't take it.' I really had to force him to take it, and then he took it as a gift, rather than as his earnings. He is an ancient one. Where are we to find such people again?"

When they emerged from the grove, they were on the highland, which leveled off. Looking back, they saw the tiny village deep down below them. To their right, the slope fell steadily. Beyond this dark hillside, peak upon peak in diminishing blues and grays were piled up to the sky. Way out in the distance, a waterfall tumbled down, glistening in the sun, a thin, shining thread of silver. The mountain air was perceptibly cooler and had a pleasant bite in it. It was surprising that only a mile up, they had come upon a totally new world, where the flowers and trees were different and the air smelled like champagne.

"Isn't it heavenly?" said Peony to Mengchia.

"Is there game in these mountains?" asked the scholar of his host.

"There are hares—you can see them scampering around—and a kind of small-headed spotted deer. Plenty of groundhogs. I hear there are boars. I wouldn't really know. Do you hunt?"

"Rarely."

"I would leave them alone," said Joshui briefly.

"You live quite alone here."

"Up where I live, there is only a farmer's house besides ours. Once in a while, a shepherd comes up, and then we hear the mewing of lambs. Really we have nothing to offer you but the mountain air—plenty of it."

Mengchia liked him immediately. "You are a man after my own heart. But few people have your luck."

"Isn't that so?" said Peony, feeling very pleased. "It really takes some courage to come up and live so far out."

They were going steadily up toward the riverside where the house stood. Joshui said to the chair carriers, "I don't think we are going to ride again. Do you want to come up for a cup of tea, or do you want to go back?" The carriers said it might be getting dark soon, and they would rather go home early if they were not needed any more. Only one of the men came up with them. He carried the luggage and later would collect the pay for the others. Pointing to a gap on the bank side to the left, Joshui said, "A road leads through that gap to Yen Tseling's Fishing Terrace."

"It's wonderful. Tomorrow we must see it."

"The wind is terribly strong there as it sucks through the gap. It can blow your hat off."

"Wait a minute!" said Peony to Mengchia. "Tomorrow is the double-ninth. And your name is the same as that of your historical namesake. Isn't it a coincidence?" Back in the fourth century, during the height of the Romanticists, there was a Mengchia who had made the ninth day of the ninth moon famous. On this day, he had lost his cap without knowing it, and Mengchia's name has always been associated with it.

"I hadn't realized that," said Mengchia.

"Nor I. But Paiwei remembers it. We'll celebrate."

After a turn around the bend of a hilltop, Joshui's house came into view, hidden in a recessed crook of the crest. They soon saw a white feminine figure coming out.

"Paiwei!" shouted Peony, and quickened her steps.

Paiwei waved back a welcome, and then started walking down the hill to meet them. She seemed to glide rather than walk, with a swift, panther-like movement. She was extremely slender. Mengchia saw her fine features and very straight, pointed nose. Her hair had been brushed back smoothly and, like Peony, she was dressed casually, in a jacket and trousers. Her steady gaze was fixed upon the academician, whom she was meeting for the first time. They were introduced. She said, smiling graciously and revealing a beautiful set of white teeth, "I feel so honored by your visit."

Mengchia gave the usual courteous answer. He raised his head and read the name of the villa in inlaid glazed green.

"What a name for a villa!" Mengchia gave a small gasp of admiration. It would be hazardous to translate the name, "Puneng Wangching Villa." It would mean in essence the "little house still in the throes of passion," but has the connotation of being "not quite liberated from human passions."

"Wait till you see the view from the terrace," said Peony, joy and enthusiasm in her voice.

They went in. Paiwei hardly took her eyes off her distinguished guest, for she already knew her friend's secret and saw him more as Peony's lover than as a scholar. The interior was well lighted, airy, and spacious; the furniture was simple and had a take-me-as-I-am appearance. A pair of pink slippers lay prominently at a defiant angle in the middle of the wooden floor.

"Oh, Paiwei!" said her husband. "I thought you would tidy up the room a bit for our guests."

"Haven't I?" She smiled back sweetly. "I have done the best I could."

Peony's eyes narrowed in laughter. "What did I tell you?" she said to Mengchia.

"This is fabulous," said Mengchia, quite taken by surprise. "You have created a love nest here, a world of your own!" He made a mental note of the fact that the house would look less like a love nest if the pair of pink slippers did not lie in the middle of the floor.

There were unpainted shelves where volumes leaned and tumbled against each other. An opium couch stood on the right.

"Do you smoke?" asked Mengchia.

"No, it's just a decoration. Paiwei wants it there. It makes the room seem so warm, especially when the glass lamp is lighted at night."

"Come, let me show you my garden," said Joshui. He led them toward the terrace facing the river. Some two hundred feet below them was the quiet, deep green Fuchunkiang. A fishing boat was tied below a cliff, appearing like a dark leaf of bamboo. Across the river rose a mountain on the rocky edge of the river, now blazing in shivering red maples at the top, which still caught the sun, and paling into clouds of purple, brown, and golden yellow below. To their right, the river was partly hidden, but on the opposite bank they could see a stretch of country receding into the distance.

"Where is the garden?" asked Mengchia.

"This is my garden," answered Joshui with a quiet, incisive humor. "It changes four seasons a year, and what is still more marvelous, I don't have to spend a cent to look after it."

Mengchia understood. He repeated the words, Puneng Wang-ching. "True enough. Still in the throes of mortal passion."

They came back into the parlor. Paiwei took her friend and

showed her her room on the south, which Joshui used as a spare bedroom when he wanted to rest during the day. Joshui accompanied the *hanlin* to the library adjoining it. A jug of water stood ready on a side table.

"I trust you have everything you want. You will want to wash up and rest a little."

"It's perfect," said Mengchia happily, greatly pleased with the arrangement.

Joshui excused himself and went into the kitchen. Paiwei then took Peony to her own bedroom at the opposite end of the house for a chat. They did not come out till much later; they found Mengchia wandering around by himself, looking at a miniature landscape built outside the library window.

"Where is Joshui?" asked Mengchia.

"He is in the kitchen," explained Paiwei.

"Joshui is quite a cook," added Peony.

Joshui was a mystery to Mengchia. His name, meaning "like water," came from the great saying of Laotse: "The best of men is like water. . . . It dwells in lowly places that all disdain." Mengchia wanted to learn something of the character of the man.

"What does he do?" Mengchia asked.

Paiwei answered, "He does nothing and does everything. He is cooking a lamb's head in your honor now. He paints occasionally, when he wants to. He writes unfinished poems. But he is busy all day. He designs our furniture himself. He grows vegetables. He helps the farmer's boy water the garden . . . "

It still did not explain to Mengchia why he chose to live that way. A man must have a certain greatness to be happy and contented doing nothing. Probably a man of a grave humor and mordant wit, as the name of his villa indicated, who knew that human life being what it is, he should try to make the best of it, and at least try not to spoil it. In Paiwei's company, he seemed to have realized his dream of a contented life.

In the first place, for a man who did not believe in killing, to become an expert in cooking lamb's head was a contradiction and an example of his "still-in-the-throes-of-mortal-passion" thesis. He would not kill an animal, but he also would not be a vegetarian and give up meat. When he came out holding the earthen pot in his two hands, his face radiated a great joy and pride in this delicate concoction. There was no mistake about it; he was an expert. In texture like a *tête de veau*, it was served steaming hot. Mengchia could detect the flavor of wine and some herbs in it. The cartilages had been treated by heat until they reached just the right consistency of gluey softness; other ingredients had been added to give it an extra rich, subtle flavor.

"Up here in the mountains," he said to his guests, "I can't offer you much. But we have good lamb. With this and warm wine I hope you will be thoroughly relaxed and happy tonight. I think I have done it just right."

He stood up to select the best morsels and put them in the bowls for Mengchia and Peony, along with the scallions and mushrooms in the sauce.

A toast was drunk to the guests, and all expressed appreciation of Joshui's creation.

"Tell me," asked Mengchia, "why did you choose that name for your villa? A little sad, isn't it?"

" 'The best of men get out of the throes of passion,' and are, therefore, immortals," said Joshui, quoting Chuangtse. "We are not yet immortals, and can't be. Does it sound queer to you, *hanlin*?"

"Certainly it sounds like an appropriate name for a love nest."

"It has that flavor, perhaps. What I am trying to say is that we have this sentient life, the life of senses and feelings. I don't think we should decry it, but should try to make the best of it. Above all, we should not spoil it, the way men do in society and in politics. I have only three small rules for myself: Not to injure people, not to kill animals, and not to waste a grain of rice. On the positive side, only one rule: I should be grateful for the act of living, for all this growth and life around us. Even in the performance of the humblest chores, we should rejoice in this gift of life. Why did Tao Kan move his hundred bricks out every morning and move them in every night? I think he was enjoying the gift of life."

Mengchia understood; all the Romanticism of the fourth
century was coming out alive in his host. "I see you are trying
to accept this life, this life of desires and feelings, and make the
best of it. You certainly have made the best of this lamb's head."

Joshui always wrinkled his nose and the lines around his
mouth deepened when he was pleased or amused. He said in his
soft voice, "You've got my point. If there were no flowers, then
nothing need be said; since there are flowers, they must be
smelled. If there were no bird songs, then nothing need be said;
since there are bird songs, they must be listened to. Since there
are women, they must be loved and cherished. Since there is
such an exquisite, incomparable flavor in a lamb's head, it must
be brought out and tasted. Then the lamb will not have died
in vain. But I would not go out and kill a lamb. I wouldn't
mind if nobody ever killed a lamb. The same thing goes for all
life and for people's lives. Why can't we leave the people and the
beasts alone? That's why I will never enter government service.
Leave the people alone. They are good people. . . . I am sorry,
I am talking too much. I must have drunk a drop too much."

"On the contrary, I quite agree with you," said Mengchia.
"I see now why you and your wife are so happy. I heartily agree
that if the government governed less, the people would be
happier."

After dinner, the four of them went over to the library. Peony
begged Paiwei to show Mengchia her portraits. She selected some
two dozen of them. They were almost all sensitive studies of
human faces. Paiwei seemed to delight in portraits of peasants
and other poor people. Several portraits of a village idiot seemed
to give her a special pleasure. She explained that there was much
more character in the faces of common fishermen and trappers
and shepherds than in the well-fed and self-indulgent rich of
the city. These portraits were a remarkable tribute to her sensitivity to the life and feelings and character of the poor. There
was wonderful animation in her portraits of a crippled beggar,
a lunatic, and an old peasant woman all doubled up and supporting herself on a shepherd's crook. Joshui was helping to
show these portraits one by one in the manner of an adoring

husband. Sometimes she said frankly, "I like this," and sometimes she pursed her lips in modest deprecation when a compliment was paid to one of her sketches.

"What a life you two are leading!" said Mengchia in obvious
delight at discovering this young couple. "Frankly, I do not think
much of married life. Now I see you two living like a pair of
cooing pigeons, and I may change my mind."

Paiwei said thoughtfully, "What makes life beautiful, I think,
is love, the sentiment that goes out to life from us. There seems
so much in life that is ugly, painful—so much pain and suffering.
You see all those eyes of desire and mouths of hunger, all crying for satisfaction. There is so much killing and slaughter and
hatred of one another, in nature and in man. However, in man,
the imagination creates life afresh, and by giving a reflection of
life—not life in the raw—we are able to detach ourselves, and by
the love of all things in art, transform all the ugliness and the
suffering into something beautiful to look at."

"You see, she has quite a theory about it," said Joshui. Paiwei
looked really beautiful in the lamplight because she was radiant
with love.

That was Paiwei, all of it. Though Peony had felt the same
things, she was less articulate about it. Paiwei was often able to
help Peony give expression to the dark embryos of her thoughts
and emotions. In Paiwei's company, too, Peony could talk about
her innermost thoughts and feelings more freely than she ever
could with her parents or sister.

Paiwei now said like the tactful hostess she was, "You've had
a full day. I am sure you will want a good rest." She pointed to
a tea cozy with a full pot of hot tea and saw that they had
everything for the night. Mengchia's bed in the library was already laid out, while Peony's bed was made up in the extra bedroom next door.

There was a crisscross of fire in the eyes of Peony and Paiwei
when the latter said good night to them, and left.

"Do you like my friends?" Peony asked, when the door was
closed.

"Immensely. What a charming couple!"

"I wanted so much for you to meet them."

For the first time, they were really alone. Mengchia had a premonition of what was going to happen. He had longed so much to be alone and close to her. He had seen just a fleeting suggestion of a smile on Peony's lips when Paiwei left her. But he held himself back, feeling that he should not take advantage of Peony until she surrendered of her own accord.

Peony's cheeks were flushed and she avoided looking at him directly. He was sitting in Joshui's chair and was thumbing through a volume on the desk. She walked toward the desk and stood opposite him. Her beautiful oval face and dark lashes glowed in the soft light of the lamp, while her round belly pressed against the edge of the desk. Suddenly, she bent over and said, "What are you looking at?"

"Just a book of Joshui's."

Their faces were close, and he could see her quivering pupils in front of him, holding a charm and a mystery as old as Eve. And then her hand caught his, and she looked fondly at him. She seemed to be fighting a sense of shame within her. He kissed her hand lightly and tenderly and said, "Sanmei."

She broke away and said, "Do you want a cup of tea?"

She walked to the side table and poured a cup and brought it to him. He rose, too, and approached her. Their eyes met in a quick, embarrassed exchange of glances. She was looking at him and at the same time at the cup, holding it gingerly, so that she might appear occupied. He took the cup and put it on the table. Before he knew it, their arms were around each other, instinctively and simultaneously. Their lips sought each other and pressed eagerly, in an ardent fulfillment of longing and love. Her head was resting upon his neck. He heard her quick breath and felt the warm glow of her soft body. Suddenly she raised her face close to him and said, "Scratch my back. I feel itchy."

He did as he was told and put his hand under her inner jacket. It was the most unusual task he had ever been asked to perform.

"Up at the shoulder. Lighter please," she said as she inclined

her head upon his shoulder, softly giggling. "A little to the left.
. . . Ah! . . . That is good! . . . Lower . . . still lower."

Mengchia thought he had really never met a girl or woman
like her.

"Would you like to have some tea?" he asked and offered her
the cup she had brought, just to appear to be doing something.

She took the cup and sniffed the fragrant steam. "And you?"
She went and poured another cup for him.

"I don't feel sleepy at all," she said, sipping her cup of tea.
"If you are not going to bed yet, I will stay another little while."

"No, it is not even nine o'clock yet. I usually do some reading
till midnight."

"Then I will stay."

Mengchia was an older man. While he knew it would make
him infinitely happy to possess her entirely, he was still waiting
for her own surrender—and only if she wanted it. This was also
out of respect for her as his cousin. On her part, she had been
prepared to give herself to him completely this night, yet she
also checked herself, as she still admired this man from a distance. He took out a cigarette and pretended to be looking at
some notes on his Foochow journey.

She went and threw herself upon his bed, which lay against the
wall.

"If you don't mind, I will rest here, while you are working."

"Not at all." A man could be more embarrassed than a girl
at such moments. It took so much to strip themselves morally
and physically.

She snatched an old volume from behind the headboard and
tried to read. Some awkward five minutes of restless silence
passed.

"Tako," she said. "You don't mind my interrupting. Did you
never really fall in love before?"

"I believe I did once, when I was very young. I'd rather not
talk about it. Why do you want to know?"

"Because I want to know everything about you."

"Yes, I did love a girl once. She was beautiful. Heavens, she was beautiful! She threw me up for a rich man. That was the end of it."

"There is no love like first love," she said with a heavy sigh.

"Yes, you are right. At first, I was bitter. Then I quickly grew out of it. Love to her was just a game. I have fought shy of women ever since."

He had given a poor account because his mind was not on it and because the episode had been distasteful to him. He did not know what to do, and lit a cigarette. Pushing his chair back, he stood near the window, with his back to her.

"Will you hand me a cigarette?" he heard her say. He turned and saw her sitting up, covering herself with the quilt. He lit a cigarette and came and sat on the bed and gave it to her. Silently, without a word, she shaped her lips into an inviting circle and pulled him to her. They kissed for a long time, and she drank his kisses in as if she were quenching a long, tortuous thirst.

"Oh, Mengchia!" It was the first time she had called him Mengchia.

"Sanmei," he said as he smoothed her face lovingly. "You cannot imagine how I felt when I was separated from you—on the boat, on the road, on horseback, crossing the high mountains— I always imagined you to be at my side. I seemed so lost, as if I had lost a part of my soul. I longed for a word from you. I kept that short little note you left in the boat, with the two words: 'Write me.' It helped me so much, those few words from your own hand, to feel your presence with me."

"I did receive those two wonderful letters from you."

"I never want to leave you again. I am yours—forever, for life."

"I, too." She sealed it with another kiss, and said very naturally, "Put the light out. Come and be comfortable."

He went and put the light out. A clear moonlight came through the window, whiter and clearer than in the valley. He started to throw off his gown. As he looked up, he saw she was throwing her socks and things on the floor by the bed, one by one.

Then it was their bodies and souls melted together in an

ecstasy of pain and joy, as if all the pent-up longing of the flesh
was at last given expression in a flood of relief. They had become united as one. The *yin* and the *yang* joined, the firma-
ment shook and the stars fell, and nothing remained but a
giving and a touching of each other, and a feeling of being
carried back to an unknown region of primeval beginnings, of
the slime and the amoeba, the stinging jellyfish and the sucking
anemone. Only sensations of the flesh remained. It seemed that
they were perishing in a global darkness in an excruciating pain
and joy as if only in such death could they become gods and
creators of life. Then the whirling and swirling motion subsided
a little, while her hands roved over his body, searching, probing,
kneading, pressing, and stroking in sweet, endearing strokes.

"Are you comfortable?" she asked.

"Very comfortable."

"So am I." Little, quick, inchoate groans came from her
throat. "Please do not think evil of me. I love you—so madly."

"Don't you want to go back to your room?"

"No."

And so they sat and talked and loved again. It was a complete
surprise to him that there was so much love contained in her
small body. Now in the dusky half-light before the dawn, he
saw her face asleep, accented by her pouting lips and long, dark
lashes, the shutters of her mind closed, the quick flutter and
shift of muscles below her eyes subsiding into a calm like dawn
on a lagoon after a stormy night. Her white body had a perfection of form which was a happy surprise to him. How he
loved her then, the whole of her, her spirit and her soul, as well
as her body. He felt, instead of a certain *détente* after satisfaction, or a mere relief and escape from a burden of the flesh, a
new depth of soul in the intimate knowledge of her body, and a
new strength and purpose in life, because their union was not
just a carnal satisfaction, but a complete surrender of two spirits
made for each other. This night had given him a new dimen-
sion of love he had not known and not thought possible before,
and struck a new depth in his being because of the light and

power which she was able to give him and which entered into him.

He lighted a match and saw that the clock pointed to four. He tapped her lightly.

"Sanmei," he called. "You'd better go back to your room—for form's sake."

She barely answered, "Oh, no. It's warmer here," and fell asleep again.

It was not until the first signs of daybreak and a cock in the farmer's house was crying cock-a-doodle-do, that he was able to persuade her reluctantly to go over to her own bed.

It was a tribute to her youth that she woke up at eight without being tired. Everyone else was up, as Joshui was an early riser and Paiwei had made a special effort to be early today.

Peony did not need any make-up. As soon as she had washed, she came to the breakfast table, fresh as a daisy. Paiwei was alone at the table. She looked at her and asked with a quiet, discreet smile, "Has it happened?"

Peony gave a nodding smile.

"I could tell without being told," said her friend. "You have that honeymoon look."

Soon the men came in to join them. No one said anything improper. They were talking of a hike to Yen's Fishing Terrace half a mile from there.

Joshui said, "Either the land has risen or the sea has sunk a hundred feet in the last two thousand years; otherwise, Yen Tseling could not have caught any fish from that terrace."

Mengchia laughed a slow, quizzical laugh. "We have three tombs of Li Po, all claiming to be the genuine one. People believe what they want to believe."

"It's the sentiment that is important," said Paiwei. "Yen Tseling may not have fished exactly at that point. But people want to show their love and respect for such a glorious recluse."

At about ten, the party set out. At the gap, however, a stiff wind made walking difficult.

"I don't want to go," Peony said. She did not care much for

visiting historical sites. She lived so much in the present that she had little feeling for the past.

"If you are not going, let the men go. I have seen it many times," said Paiwei.

While Mengchia and Joshui went on ahead, the women friends turned back to the house.

A halo of last night's romance still hung around Peony's face.

"You told me you had broken with Chin Chu. How did he take it?"

"He had no choice. He asked me why, and I could not give a reason. I told him that I loved another man. He was still unconvinced. He never thought it was Liang *Hanlin*. Of course when a girl says 'I love another man,' or 'I do not love you,' what can the man do except resign himself to it?"

"You didn't say that you did not love him any more."

"Practically."

"But how could you, after all these years? It can't be true."

"It is true. . . . When I saw clearly that he could not divorce his wife, what was I to do? Live as his mistress? He suggested moving to Hangchow so that we could meet often. I had to make a break. What could I do except tell him that I did not love him?"

"Of course you can't mean it."

"I feel an infinite sadness for him. He was angry. He returned my lock of hair, and burned my letters. He took out my photograph from his wallet and gave it back to me."

"I expect he would. It must have hit him hard."

"It did . . . but we parted as friends in the end."

Paiwei remained silent for a moment. Then she said, "All that means nothing. He was just angry. I don't believe that he has stopped loving you, or can—or you, either."

They went on talking about her trip to Peking till the men returned.

In the afternoon, Paiwei proposed that they visit a favorite stream of hers where she often went to do her sketching. Near the stream was a small falls, only seven or eight feet high, which she called "my waterfall," and below the falls was a pool, scarcely twenty feet long, in which Joshui liked to go for a dip during the summer. The place was picturesque and secluded. Clean white boulders were tumbled about along the water course, and on both sides, pine and cypress had grown into a deep thicket.

Paiwei thought it a poetic idea to have a picnic of broiled fish by the stream, for she knew that her friend loved such things. Joshui had bought some trout in the village, and she now set about charmingly to build a crackling fire. When the fire was good and hot, she took out the fish and began to broil them, one by one, holding each fish with a pair of chopsticks over the fire. The trout were very small, barely four inches long; Mengchia was greatly amused to see the deep, childlike seriousness with which she broiled each tiny fish.

Joshui laughed. "It will only be a few mouthfuls, hardly worth the trouble. I've brought some sugar-treated smoked pike along."

"Oh, please!" said Paiwei, deeply wounded. There were tears in her eyes.

The four friends sat around the boulders by the side of the stream and started to eat. The fish were delicious, but each one was worth no more than two bites. Joshui was just about to unwrap the smoked fish, when Paiwei stopped him.

"Oh, please! I was going to make this a special occasion and you had to come and spoil it."

Joshui did not think it worth while finding out from a woman just how the introduction of smoked pike spoiled the idea of a picnic. He made amends by patting her shoulder silently, lovingly, and nuzzling her hair.

"Behave yourself," said Paiwei, feeling embarrassed. But it was obvious that she loved it.

"Come on," said Peony to Mengchia, "let's walk down the stream. We'll leave these two lovers alone."

"Which way shall we go?" asked Mengchia.

"There is a good spot below where we can get a view of the whole valley."

She led him by a path along the stream, walking in front in her youthful, swinging gait, and leading him with her hand.

Mengchia had never encountered a woman so magnificently warm and independent and whimsical.

"You know the place?"

"Yes, I've been there before."

They slowed down, their arms around each other's waists, body touching body.

"Are you happy?" she asked.

"I've never been happier before. This is a wonderful retreat. I suppose that when we are in Peking with your sister, we'll have to be more careful."

"I wouldn't worry. I am her elder sister, and I have my freedom. She will know all about our affair—she is bound to. But I have never seen a person more level-headed than Jasmine. She never speaks out of turn or lets an awkward word slip out of her mouth."

Halfway down the stream, they found a large flat boulder jutting out into the water.

"Let's climb up and sit there."

They sat shoulder to shoulder, and kissed and surveyed the sunset turning from bright gold to purple and dark mauve, while below them the village already lay in deep shadow.

In about a quarter of an hour, they heard Paiwei's voice calling. Peony stood up and saw them above. Paiwei said they were going home. Peony waved her hand back to them and shouted upstream, "You go home first."

She sat down again happily. "Now you can look all around, and there is not a soul in sight in this whole universe but us." She lay down on the rock, crooking up her pantalooned legs, looking immensely happy. He looked down at her and saw her light brown eyes reflecting the shadow-streaked sky and becoming a celestial green.

"You couldn't have chosen a better place than this."

Suddenly she sprang up and said, "Come on."

Mengchia was continually surprised by Peony.

"Where to?"

She gave him her hand, and together they leaped down from the boulder and walked toward the bank. She took him to a clearing which was completely shut out from view. There she stretched herself on the grass. At this moment she looked like a forest nymph, staring blankly at him or at the roseate clouds drifting high in the darkening sky.

"This is divine!" she murmured.

Vividly, Mengchia felt her beauty, her youthfulness. He sat down, contemplating her closely, his heart filled with a tight pressure.

"It is unsurpassable," he said.

"What is unsurpassable?"

"This moment—here with you. . . . "

She turned her eyes full upon him, silently gazing at him, her breasts heaving perceptibly.

"You excite me now," she said.

"You are a devil." He shifted and rested his head against her breasts, hearing her sweet whispers. Without looking at her, he said, "You knew this was going to happen when you took me down here."

She nodded. His defenses were down. Since last night, their relationship had changed; there was no longer any shyness and restraint. They had met as equals, he a complete man and she a complete woman. She stroked his head on her breast and said, "Be good to me. Make this a memorable day for me."

When they finally sat up, the short September day had turned into twilight.

"We must go home. They may be waiting for us for supper," she said.

She tried to rearrange her hair. He kissed her and thanked her.

"For what?"

"For giving me so much love, so much pleasure."

"You men have the wrong idea. You think of women as only giving pleasure, and forget that we enjoy it as much as you do."

As she was sitting up getting ready, he saw that her shoulders were stained with spots of green, and he picked a crushed firefly from the soft white flesh of her thigh.

"You!" she said, slapping his hand.

"Sanmei," he said, "since coming to know you, I love you

more and more every day. That was a beautiful whim of yours, taking me downstream here."

"That is because I love you, because you excited me."

Now she was fully dressed. As they walked away out of the clearing, he said, "With your nature, I don't see how you could have been a good, faithful wife to your husband for so long—or a very submissive daughter-in-law."

She shook her head and answered with her usual candor, "A good daughter-in-law, perhaps; a faithful wife, no."

"You mean . . . "

"It could not be. If I had loved my husband, I would have. But I did not love him. I detested him. . . . "

"How could you in such a secluded life?"

"Where there's a will, there's a way."

"You really dared?"

"I would dare anything for him."

"Him?"

"Don't ask me, please. It still hurts. Let this be my only secret from you." Mengchia, walking by her side, felt that her whole body seemed to tremble a little.

"I shan't ask again."

Her eyes were moist; she sighed deeply. "How I loved him! But it is something past and gone. That was before I met you. . . . "

Mengchia took the news in silence, and heard her say, "Tako, I love only you now, no one but you. . . . " She was almost pleading. "Please do not ask me. It still hurts terribly."

"Then I do not want to know. I mean only, how could you manage to do it?"

"As I told you, where there's a will there's a way."

He did not press her with any questions. Hand in hand, they retraced their steps upstream in the rapidly deepening gloom. When they reached the house, the sky was completely dark. Supper was waiting for them.

CHAPTER 9

A calm had settled upon Peony, a calm of quiet exultation. The knowledge of her secret love made her ignore everything and changed the colors of the world for her. She had her heart's desire. She thanked her parents for letting her go. She told everybody that she and her sister were going to Peking with the Liang *Hanlin,* and felt an infinite pity for all the "gossiping women and goose-stepping men" too busy with their old and established duties of the day to stop and ask what they were doing. This voyage to Peking was a door to a new life, her adventure of the spirit and her salvation, a quest of the unknown.

Really, it went off very well. At the clan celebration, everybody was told that the two sisters, the "Sanmei" and the "Szemei," were going up to see Peking. This was the great news. The sisters were presented to Prince Yi, the Military Governor, and were seated at the table with the guest of honor and the Prince.

At one point in the dinner, Prince Yi said to Peony's parents, "Any time you need help, come straight to me." It was a fine gesture, and was made to cement his relationship with the renowned scholar; but it also meant a good deal, in case of trouble. The people were at the mercy of the blind, slow-grinding bureaucracy, except for the lucky ones who could reach the Governor directly.

It was a great occasion for the clan when Uncle Sueipo confirmed the news that the Military Governor was coming to the dinner. In those days, when the Governor came out of his office on some official occasion, drums were beaten at the three successive courts as he emerged. Long horns were blown, and after the booms of three large firecrackers, the mandarin started off in his sedan chair of blue velvet, borne by four carriers, and preceded by footmen and cavalry. It was good to have such pageantry and respect for authority. Men and women got out of the way and stood on the sidelines, gaping and admiring as the Governor passed by. The whole town knew that Prince Yi was a friend of the Liangs.

The clan had borrowed a villa on the lake. Near the water was a lotus pond bordered by a long, winding red balcony where the guests could sit and watch the fish.

At the dinner, families sat with relatives they hadn't seen for years; everywhere there were children crying, mothers shouting, babies suckling at their mothers' breasts, men sitting down and hopping up—all in a noisy, happy confusion.

A few speeches preceded the dinner, as was the custom, to get the worst part over with, as it were. The clan elder read from a paper held high in his two hands, written by someone aiming at being literary, and not intended to be intelligible to the audience. His voice was inaudible, anyway, in the general hubbub. But he took it seriously, and it was an honest job, honestly done. He would halt in the middle of a sentence when he got caught, squint at the paper from different angles, and say, "What is this word? I can't make it out." Then he would gasp when he managed to interpret it and repeat the word several times until he was satisfied, feeling like a boatman who had somehow got his boat off a sandbar. From there on, it was easy sailing and his tempo suddenly picked up, and you could see that he was happy in safe waters.

Prince Yi's speech was brief, full of Mandarin talk and highly complimentary to the *hanlin*. When Mengchia spoke, a hush fell over the audience. Mothers hushed their babies and said, "It's the *hanlin* speaking." The word was pronounced as if it were magic, and even the babies felt a sense of fear. Eyes of admiration and of grateful recognition were directed to the scholar, the only one of their clan to receive the rank in the last century, to the envy of the other clans. A muscle danced in Mengchia's cheek, his brows puckered and smoothed out in quick alternation. He was touched. This reception by his clan meant more to him than any of the official dinners in Peking. "There is nothing like being at home," he started by saying. His bushy eyebrows twitched and his voice was softly vibrant.

His aunt, seated next to him, was proud and happy. As he got underway, he spoke with increasing conviction. Few understood him as he talked about Viceroy Chang Chih-tung's idea of "strength through learning." He said that a great country was always capable of changing and adjusting to meet a new situation, that China was now facing such a situation, that she had been safe on her ocean front and built her Great Wall to defend herself against menace from the north, but now the menace was coming from the open sea and she must quickly adjust herself and learn, and learn fast, or suffer a few more humiliations like the Opium War, the Sacking of the Old Summer Palace, and the recent loss of Indo-China to the French. "The Great Wall no longer serves a useful purpose," he said. "Foreign races, unknown to us in past history, have come from across the China Sea. Gunboats, gunboats, gunboats are making a mockery of the waves. China is facing a situation unprecedented in history."

Mengchia's speech was characteristic of the mood for reform on the part of a few thinking men, now led by Chang Chih-tung, who a few years later was to publish his ideas in his famous essay, "Strength Through Learning."

The Prince did not stay till the end of the dinner. When he excused himself, the guests stood up in his honor and the whole dinner was interrupted. As soon as he had left, the hubbub and the confusion resumed.

"How did you come to know the Manchu language?" Jasmine asked Mengchia at the end of the dinner. "I heard you talking Manchu with the Prince."

"I had learned a Mongolian dialect, which is different. But it has an alphabetic script rather similar to the Manchu script. So long as you have an alphabetic script to read, you can learn. But they all prefer to talk Chinese."

"Why?"

"Because it is the language of culture, of philosophy and poetry. The Manchus talk better Mandarin than we do. Nalan, the Manchu prince-poet, as you know, wrote Chinese. What poetry! What feeling! I will teach you Nalan's poetry. You cannot really appreciate his poems unless you know about his love life."

A light was playing in Jasmine's bright, round eyes. Everything Mengchia told them was new and exciting. What luck that she should be able to go to Peking with her sister and listen to him, day in, day out!

In spite of the sadness of departure and some general misgivings about Peony, the parents were very happy for their daughters. They thought it a wonderful opportunity for them, and hoped and believed that Mengchia would be able to find husbands for them. In a way, too, the problem of their widowed daughter was off their hands. The father said to Mengchia, "I see my daughters are really lucky to have such a teacher, and I hope they will profit from their stay in Peking under your guidance."

"I entrust my daughters to your care," said the mother, whose heart was breaking to see both her grown-up daughters leaving home this time.

"I shall take good care of Peony," replied Mengchia. "Jasmine, I am confident, can take care of herself."

"Whatever do you mean?" asked the elder sister with a rueful look.

"I mean I will take care of you and rely on your sister to take care of me."

"You mean the laundry and cooking? And you won't take care of me?" said Jasmine spiritedly.

"Don't be rude to your Tako," admonished the mother.

"No, I like it. I don't expect them to stick to formalities if they are to live in the same house with me."

That night before their departure, when the sisters were alone, Peony said, "Sister, we are going together. I'm glad that you can come with me. I'm sure you are all excited."

"Of course. To go to Peking!"

"Don't tell Mother, but I will tell you as your sister. I love him and he loves me. Is that clear?"

Jasmine replied in her level tone, "I thought I had sensed it. Mother, too."

Peony put a finger to her lips. "Hush, let her think what she likes, but don't say it. To you I am saying it. I love him—madly —what I mean is, I will live my own life and you will live yours."

"What you really mean is that I should not interfere."

"Exactly."

"If that is your worry, I tell you to forget it. I can take care of myself."

"Tako said you could."

A peaceful understanding was established between them. They lay in bed, each thinking her own thoughts. After a while, Jasmine said, "You wouldn't hurt him, would you? You must think of him, protect his reputation. . . . "

"Oh, you make me sick."

"Good night."

"Good night."

It was a real sacrifice on the part of the mother to let both daughters go. Jasmine was the father's favorite. She was the West Lake, her sister the more unruly Tsientang River; the famous bores of the Bay of Tsientang during the harvest moon could never ruffle the still waters of the lake—or could they? Younger than her sister by three years, she was completely womanly and mature, with a woman's set of intuitions about what to do and what not to do, what to say and what not to say. But the mother, with her more imaginative soul, living a life of quiet desperation, neither happy, nor unhappy, had a partiality for Peony, as if in Peony's adventures she was living her own youthful life again. It was shown in everything she did, in the pitiful garden she tried to make of the little free space behind the house, in the furtive snatches of song she sang with her daughters when the father was not at home.

They went by a Butterfield & Swire coastal steamer to Shanghai, and then by a Jardine Matheson boat to Tientsin. The sisters had wanted so much to go by the foreign steamers, which were a novelty—enough reason for Mengchia to overcome his prejudices against the sea. And, after all, they would reach

Peking much faster—by the end of September, before real winter set in.

Mengchia did not intend to make himself a naval expert. What could a mandarin scholar learn about the secrets of the modern navy? But he was on this mission, and beyond it lay Chang Chih-tung's idea that the menace facing China now came from the sea and not from the Mongolian deserts. With a keen, searching mind, he tried to understand what was new. On the voyage, he talked through an interpreter with the pilot, who was a tall Swede in a white cap, and learned many things about navigation. He was intensely interested in the barometer, the telescope, the quadrant. All in all, here was a race of men not to be despised by any means, especially when their gun turrets belched forth a thundering fire. Slowly he was forming his ideas for a report to Chang Chih-tung. Above all, as a student of historical geography, he was greatly impressed by the foreign systems of lighthouses and buoy markers and the accuracy of their maps. He had taken considerable pains in pasting up the woodblock pages of Yang Shouching's *Historical Atlas*. After getting hold of some postal maps made by foreigners in Shanghai, he decided that Yang Shouching's atlas could vastly benefit from a careful revision. He had compared and verified the distances between Peking and Kupeikou and Kalgan with his own notes. Both the cartography of the foreigners' maps and the printing, as printing, were superior to anything he had seen before. While stopping at Shanghai for three days, he was able to pick up a seaman's barometer from a chandler's on Kiangse Road; he was going to give it as a present to Viceroy Chang Chih-tung. Later, when he reached Tientsin, he visited the fort of Tangku and with great care tried to trace the route by which British and French soldiers had marched from Taku and Tangku to Peking in 1860, a march which ended in the sacking and burning of the Old Summer Palace. Against a lethargic, slow-functioning mandarinate and a petty, but very real, struggle for power inside the palace, there were a few men like Mengchia who felt the urgency for reform.

As their steamboat glided slowly up the Whampoo toward

Shanghai, a northwester blew the black smoke from the funnel across the smother and spray of frothy whiteness. Peony and Mengchia stood against the white railing, watching the smoke sweep over the waves. Peony's eyes narrowed and she cried softly, "How divine!" On both banks, a stretch of red brick warehouses, small factories, and tumble-down shacks made of corrugated tin flew swiftly by. The river was crowded with sampans, junks, and fishing boats; the steamer glided along slowly, tooting horns to give warning of her approach. Undaunted, the small sampans closed in to pick up, before the sea gulls could get at them, cans, bottles, vegetables, and bread being thrown overboard. A French and an English gunboat were lying at anchor, slim, with a sinister beauty, the invincible argument of diplomacy and the protector of expanding trade and commerce.

The Bund, with a sprinkling of tall buildings, including the Palace Hotel and the more impressive Hongkong and Shanghai Bank, made of cut stones and huge glass windows, extended a short quarter mile; it ended in the Hongkew Bridge at one end and the tarnished red-brick godowns, with huge tar-coated iron doors, at the other. Soon they were able to hear the trams clanging and see passing rickshaws and horse carriages. There were swarms of pedestrians in different shades of blue, the men in long gowns and queues, wearing black skullcaps, the women wobbling on their bound feet, often holding long-stemmed tobacco pipes. The younger girls wore brighter colors of rose and turquoise and lavender, the favorite colors of the period. There were Sikh policemen with black curly beards and towering turbans of khaki, white men in bowlers, with pinched and pirouette mustaches, stiff collars and fantastic long pants, and foreign women in still more fantastic hats, their ostrich feathers sticking out a foot high.

Even at that period, Shanghai was a hodgepodge of Eastern and Western mercantilism, the spearhead of a vast venture in cotton textiles and tobacco, a daring quest for pigs' bristles and soybean and tea, a crashing wave of an aggressive, thriving, touting civilization lapping the shores of the old continent. Mengchia was a little frightened.

They took two rooms on Foochow Road near the Kiangse Road section. Foochow Road was a continuous line of small shops where one could buy everything from umbrellas to musk and "magic oil" of Turkestan, from exquisite brocades of Nanking and "cut velvet" of Soochow to deer horns of Heilungkiang and ginseng of Shangtang. The sisters saw Mengchia spend three or four hundred dollars on ginseng alone as presents for friends. They found a Cantonese shop that specialized in carved ivory, tortoise-shell articles, amber from Persia, and incense from Cambodia. A Persian Jew by the name of Hartung owned whole blocks of real estate on Foochow Road, having faith in the future of this Oriental metropolis. Farther in, toward the Race Course, the limit of the city in those days, was the famed *tangtse* (singsong) district of women from Soochow; or if they were not really from Soochow, they at least affected to talk the soft, effeminate Soochow dialect, with rounded vowels, like the French *u, eu, eur*. These houses helped to give much business to the wine restaurants. The girls, on call to enliven restaurant parties, sat on the laps of their amahs in brightly burnished, private rickshaws, their powdered and rouged and invariably smiling faces garish in the white light of gas lamps at their feet. This gave the Foochow Road an impression of dazzling gaiety at night.

They were having supper at the Hong Far Low restaurant, in a private compartment. A poor girl in rags, twelve or thirteen, with a wan and underfed face, lifted the grayish-white door curtain. Holding a small pocket-sized folder in her hand, she begged them to let her sing for them, choosing from the song list in the smeared and smudged folder. Mengchia asked the sisters if they wanted to hear a song and they said they did not. The girl begged and begged. Out of pity, Mengchia asked her to sing a Kiangnan love ditty. It tore one's heart to hear the sentimental love song of *Tseyehko* from this famished little girl who was barely thirteen. A man whose gaunt shoulders showed beneath a shabby gown, too thin for these autumn days, was standing by. He was probably her father.

Kill the cock!
It is not dawn yet, koko.
The dew is wet on the road,
Do not go yet, koko. . . .
Come again, koko.
If you come,
We shall renew our love again.
But if you do not come,
Then I shall know—
And wait and pray
In an infinity of pain.

"Let me have a drink of water," the little girl said almost as soon as she had finished the last line. It was highly doubtful whether she had understood what she was singing. What she did know was that this was a song about a girl selling love, that this was the way the world was made, and that she could make six coppers from a song. On her face was written the sin and degradation of a big city.

"Poor girl," said Peony. "Give her something extra." Mengchia gave her six more coppers. The wan, pale face broke into a smile and disappeared behind the door curtain.

Repeated whistles and the louder clack of wheels echoing by the city wall told the sisters that they were near the end of their journey, the imperial city of Peking. On their right, separated by a moat some forty feet wide, was the centuries-old wall of the capital, divided into segments by outworks and turrets for gun emplacements.

This time it was Jasmine who was excited at the moment of their arrival, while it was her elder sister who smiled in a mood of sweet content.

"In another five minutes, we'll be there," said Mengchia.

Peony merely exclaimed, "It is so immense!"

"Of course it is."

The ancient city wall was there, a huge mass of gray bricks dappled with white lichen, standing forty or fifty feet high and extending for miles. As the ancient imperial capital, the name

Peking rang like magic in the sisters' ears. To Jasmine, no less than to Peony, it was a dream realized. You do not argue about Peking, you find it and accept it; some embrace it and some fall in love with it.

The train ran through a break in the wall and pulled up at the Chienmen station. Right in front of the station stood the Chienmen gate tower, some eighty or ninety feet high. There was a jostling of carriages and rickshaws. Liu An, Mengchia's houseboy, came up and notified his master that their carriage was waiting.

It was a glorious autumn day. While Liu An was taking care of the luggage, the sisters looked up at the gate tower, old and serene against the incredibly blue sky. Peony felt lost and happy in the busy traffic all around them.

"Why don't we take rickshaws?" she suggested.

"Why?"

"Because we can see better than in a closed carriage."

"It's not a bad idea. We can hire an open carriage."

"No, I say rickshaws." She knew her wish was law to Mengchia. He sent Liu An home with the carriage while the three of them engaged rickshaws.

It turned out to be a brilliant idea. One could see more. Here, directly outside Chienmen, were the busy streets where hats and lanterns were sold, and then the thickly settled area of restaurants and hotels. Passing the Chienmen, they came into the city proper. The rickshaws turned east, and on entering the Legation Quarters the rattle of wheels was immediately silenced by the smooth asphalt road. The French, British, Russian, and German legations stood in close proximity. Turning north down Hatamen Street, the view opened up and one breathed the air and sensed the immense space of Peking. Hatamen Street was seventy feet wide, the main road separated from the cart roads on both sides by open sewers. Although the official Chinese name was Tsungwenmen, the street was known to the inhabitants by the Mongol name, Hatamen. (The rickshaw pullers wouldn't know where Tsungwenmen was. "Why didn't you say Hatamen?") Soon the imperial yellow of the palace roofs became visible to their left, sweeping broad and low, one behind the other, now glittering in the October sun, the heart of the Forbidden City itself.

Near the Tungtan Pailou (decorative gate) on the main street, a few turns to the east from Tsungpu Hutung brought them to Mengchia's house. Like all Chinese homes, the house had an unpretentious gate in black with a red circle. Liu An and the carriage driver were there to greet them, along with the cook. An old man with watery eyes and a thin white beard filled the position of the *menfang* (concierge), who in official residences controlled the admitting and rejecting of visitors. Mengchia had kept him for years because he considered himself as "out of the running" for an office, and therefore wasn't interested in impressing anybody. There was also a mangy dog, coughing in competition with the old gatekeeper. The dog began to jump and sniff and wag its tail at the returning master, and then tried to sniff at the newcomers, to Jasmine's great disgust.

Mengchia's living rooms were at the rear court. Like all houses with an inner courtyard, it had a cloistered effect, homelike and secluded. It was unbelievable how quiet a house could be in the *hutungs* (alleys) of Peking. The parlor in the center was hung with scrolls and furnished with severe hardwood chairs. Portraits of the *hanlin*'s father and mother hung on the wall, over a long, high table of teak, inlaid with rubbed walnut and curling downward on both ends. Mengchia's bedroom was on the west and his library on the east. All in all, it was not a disgraceful residence for a bachelor *hanlin*, nor was it pretentious. The library was the room that was used the most, being the working den of the scholar. A large table, covered with papers and books, stood close to the window opening out on the yard. The room was lined with book shelves, orderly but crammed with books. On the north stood a couch beneath a small, high window, and next to it, two low easy chairs grouped around a small tea table. A brazier had already been lit to keep the room warm.

The sisters were shown to their rooms in a separate court to the east of the library. When Mengchia was living alone, he had not made much use of this court. Apparently this was the inner court where the family of the former owner lived, with a charming yard paved with fine, peppered green stones, the inevitable goldfish jar, and a small garden, now untended and gone to seed. All the houses of Peking were one-storied, so that no one should be able to raise his head, as it were, above the palaces.

The rooms had been made ready for the cousins, although additional furniture would be required. Liu An said that he had thought he ought to wait until the young ladies were here and could pick things for themselves.

"How do you like it?" asked Mengchia.

The sisters declared that they were charmed with the court. Peking and this court held for them all the excitement and delight of novelty. It spelled ease and comfort and a standard of living higher than their own at Hangchow, with servants, a cook, and a private carriage.

In the days that followed, many additions were bought, and Chouma, a woman of forty from the Tsingho district, was asked to come in every day and do the washing and the cleaning. Outside of his former housekeeper, Tingma, Mengchia had never cared much for women servants; he felt that most of the time they spoke only gibberish, and gossiped without any regard at all for the facts.

With the cousins at home, a change came over Mengchia's life. The affair at Tunglu had given him a new sense of life, like a draft of spring wine. He felt as if his spirit were crossing to a new frontier. He talked with a new-found ease over the dining table, as he had never been able to when Tingma was there. He found that he was ready to talk because the sisters were ready to listen, Peony usually quietly and Jasmine interrupting with avid questions. Over the dinner table, he talked ramblingly, without restraint, and felt that he was understood and respected and loved. He had a feeling of being *home*, or of having found the meaning of it. Not infrequently, he was overtaken with a sense of intrigue and guilt. The arrangement might be considered unfair to Peony. But she had wanted it. Whatever the cost, he knew that his whole being required the presence of her spirit, the company of her love, the sound of her voice. It was a necessity and a need of his soul. Here was Peony, ready to defy social conventions to live with him a life of illicit but exquisite love. He did not see how he could find a husband for her and live without her. This was the flaw in their emerald of love. One did not think about the flaw, but admired the incomparable brilliance of the love itself, shining with a fire of unique intensity. How tragic a small accident should make their marriage impossible; if she were a cousin with a different family name, they would have a marriage of undreamed-of happiness and harmony of spirit. But in a way, too, the secrecy of their affair added a spice and bite to their passionate clinging to each other.

Some regard for form was kept before the servants. Nothing overt was done. Whether in the study, or in the dining room, a pressure of her arm, a glance of sweet, silent understanding from her beautiful eyes, or the purposeful contact of body and hand while examining a book or reading a letter thrilled him like the sudden leap of a flame in the wind. He felt proud, with a royal sense of intrigue and adventure.

All this Jasmine saw and understood, feeling it neither right nor proper for her to say anything. She had seen the period of her sister's affair with Chin Chu and her attempt at suicide when Chin Chu had married another woman.

There was one thing about Peony; she changed her mind too much. Once she said to Mengchia, "This is terrible. No matter how I wear my hair, I always want it the other way." Like Paiwei, she often changed her hair-dos.

CHAPTER 10

During the first few days, Mengchia was busy making and receiving calls and delivering his official reports. He was practically never at home for lunch or supper, official life being what it was. He had never pursued the routine round of dinners, which seemed to be the most effective way of cementing friendships and securing promotions; he had managed to escape from the social round as an "eccentric genius." But after half a year of absence, dinners and renewals of friendship were unavoidable. He would come home when he could, at about three or five in the afternoon. At night he'd have to go out again for supper and wouldn't return until ten or eleven. Once or twice he remained with his friends after a wine feast and made the *tachawei* ("tea rounds") in the houses of their girl friends in the Pata Hutung singsong district. But his friends saw that he was bored and impatient to go home early.

He would come home and find Peony waiting for him in the library, curled up on the couch and playing at reading. Rarely would he find her sitting up properly.

Without getting up, she would say "Come!" and draw him to her, and rub her lips against his, never saying a word, but always kept her glimmering pupils fixed on him, enjoying him, running her soft, warm fingers through his hair and tickling him around the nape of his neck with the playfulness of a kitten. And he would tell her whom he had seen and what he had done, and she would listen so quietly that he did not know whether she were really listening or not. Only her grayish-brown eyes dilated and wandered, to rest again amorously on his face. Mengchia used to work over his papers or read far into the night, content with her presence in the room. The servant usually left a pot of tea in the old, shiny, woven bamboo tea cozy. On cold evenings, the heavy blue curtains would be drawn across the windows, papered with *maochih*, which rolled up and down and was better than glass for keeping out the cold air. With the opaque *maochih* paper, she preferred to have the lights out and the curtains drawn to the sides, permitting a hazy half light. Then Mengchia would say he was getting up to do some work and he would light the lamp again. She would retire if it were late and slip into her room through a small side door next to the book shelves.

One night, she said to him, "I have something to show you." She handed him a foot-high envelope in thick white *maochih*, as was used for official dossiers. It was framed in heavy blue lines and on the lower left, a vertical line in deep orange printed in woodcut bore the stationery mark of the Kaoyu Salt Tax Bureau.

"I want to show you what my husband did. You will then understand, when you see the names of women and the money he spent on them." She explained that she had found this at her home after she came back from Tunglu; it had been delivered by a boatman from Kashing. There was a notation on a slip of paper pasted over the upper left-hand corner of the envelope with the words: *For Mrs. Fei Tingyen, Personal,* with two round loops beside the word *personal.* The Kashing family had sent it on to her, thinking that it contained some papers of her own. It turned out to be private letters of her husband and a thick diary and a small book of accounts. The Bureau at Kaoyu had sent some trunks and pieces of furniture, together with this special envelope for the widow of the deceased. They did not know that she had already left the Fei family.

"It is nothing new to me. But you won't blame me, will you, when you see the little folder? It was Precious Pearl, Silver Apricot, and Little Cassia who got the most from him."

Mengchia went over the folder with casual interest. There were items of a night's dinner and entertainment running to eighty or ninety dollars. This was all part and parcel of the life of an official. There were, however, some items of income which caught his attention, with names, dates, and figures, usually with three zeros at the end. Tingyen wrote a fine hand in neat figures. Of course the dead man had been living beyond his means.

The diary was more explicit. On a number of pages Tingyen had pasted love letters from his sweethearts. There was a jumble of stray entries, such as "unsuccessful encounters," "the woman is unbelievably stupid, after all my offers." His notes on his colleagues and his chief were none too complimentary. And finally he had made notes on cases of smuggling and bribery, negotiations and threats like this: "I know Yang will pay up. He cannot get away with less than fifteen thousand, and that is on top of two thousand five hundred for myself alone. Will speak to Shueh about him tomorrow."

It was hard to understand how Shueh, the Chief, could let this pass into other hands. Probably he had not known about it, or had not bothered to look at the contents. The clerk had found this in one of Fei's locked drawers at the office; they had forced it open.

"Do you know what this means?" Mengchia asked gravely. "In the hands of a prosecutor, it means a ghastly misdemeanor in which the entire staff of the Bureau is involved."

"Why don't you report it, then?"

"You hated your husband, didn't you? But he is dead now."

"I don't understand you Peking officials. If this is a violation of the laws of the empire, don't you think it needs cleaning up? What is he to me?"

It seemed to him that something deep was burning inside her. That unfortunate match had for a time destroyed all her longings and passions. She still remembered the hollow laughter of her husband, the exposed, naked soul and heart of a man, unscrupulous and hellbent for success, and the time when the slightest noise would make her start and she was afraid of light. All the embers of resentment and hatred of a frustrated young wife, so happily buried and forgotten in the last half year, were still smoldering and rankling in her, as only one who had gone through it could know.

Mengchia lighted a *shuiyen* and blew short, blue puffs into the silent study. The water pipe, made of beautiful white copper, was his favorite form of smoking when he was at home and relaxed. Each bowl was good for only a few puffs, and there was too much lighting and refilling. For his busy hours, he smoked cigarettes.

At last he said, "You do not want to come into the limelight of the court. Nor do I want to see you involved. Certainly when the case is up, they will ask you to testify, since the direct evidence involves your husband. It's true, Prince Yi can do a great deal to protect you. It depends on how the case is built up. If I turn this over to the prosecutor's office, he may jump at it either for his own career or for another big squeeze on the millionaire salt merchants of Yangchow. This diary contains all the leads for a thorough investigation, with names and dates and sums that exchanged hands. It will be a notorious scandal unless the salt merchants hush it up in time. . . . "

Her answer was curiously feminine as she drawled with a weak chuckle, "It will break my mother-in-law's heart. She has been so correct, so anxious to keep up appearances. . . . I don't mind so long as my name is kept out of it."

"Of course the investigation will be kept secret by agents sent out by the Censorate. I'll tell them to keep you out. You just knew nothing about it, which is true, isn't it?"

"I knew nothing except the philandering. I didn't even know the names of the girls. He never told me, of course. But how will they be able to get the evidence without this diary?"

"Leave it to them. They have their methods. Someone will go there, befriend the hotel waiters, pick up names, or even try to mingle with members of the Bureau. It may take months. Town gossip. Barber shops. When there is a case like the one mentioned in the diary, everybody in town knows about it except the higher officials. Precious Pear, Silver Apricot, Little Cassia. These girls know a lot. It is too easy."

"You mean these girls will talk?"

"They can be made to. Don't be afraid. These documents will be returned to you. A copy will be made." After a while he said, "I will keep this, then, and think about it. There is no hurry."

It took some time for the sisters to fall into the pattern of life in Peking and get used to its strange new colors and sounds. Peking meant an incredibly clear blue sky, the crisp and dry days of early autumn, the magnificence of the palaces, the quiet and tranquillity of the homes in the *hutungs*, and the chirp of sparrows and magpies and woodpeckers. Coming from the south, they thought the city typically northern, with its openness, its bright, solid, sunlit colors, and the humor and gaiety of the populace.

The sisters used to go in their carriage to Tungan Bazaar, which was only a short way from their house. They would get out and walk through the rabbit warren of canopied streets, where one could buy anything from fruit and Shanghai sweet-meats to textiles and clothing materials, or have a snack at one of the small restaurants, or attend a famous theater for Peking operas where Tan Shingpei, the king of the actors, and later, Mei Lanfang, used to play. It was an open-air theater, shabby and crowded—but the singing was magnificent. Or they would go to the fair at the Lungfo Temple, where one could pick up paintings, genuine and forged—mostly forged—ink rubbings of ancient calligraphy, scrap iron, and old scissors, and brand-new leather shoes, and all sorts of art objects like small jade buckles and snuff bottles of unusual delicacy. Or when Mengchia was with them, they sometimes drove out to Tienanmen Square, in front of the Forbidden City, where the Imperial Palaces were.

It was utterly right that Peking should be the seat of the Dragon Throne of the Son of Heaven. Nature, the imagination of man, the hearty, human life of rich and poor, the babbling, laughing populace had made the city what it was. Generosity is the word—generosity in time and space and the spirit of man. You could see this peculiar atmosphere anywhere you stood on the Hatamen, which was two or three miles long and broad and straight as an arrow, where the gate tower on the north or south rose into the clouds as in a painting. Tienanmen Square permitted the gathering of a hundred thousand people. The effect was probably created by its immense proportions and its low, wide, and sweeping lines, the product of the mind of men used to the open spaces of the desert. Peking would rather spread and straggle than be hemmed in or soar up in space. Genghis Khan had conquered the old Chin capital, his grandson Kublai Khan had built it, a Chinese Ming emperor had rebuilt and completed and expanded it in the fifteenth century in the present form as we know it, and the great Manchu emperors Kangshi and Chien-lung had beautified it. The force of history supported it and carried it along, immense and generous and vigorous always.

The Liang sisters were dazzled by the strange, white glitter of the city. The strength of the north, open, clear, unaffected, blazingly pure like the white sun and the blue sky itself, so different from the soft haziness of the south, greatly impressed them. Here were glamour and simplicity combined, the imperial glamour and opulence of the court coupled with the bland and satisfying rustic tranquillity of the private residences. From a short distance near the Tungtan Pailou, one could see pavilions with glazed roofs of blue and turquoise and deep lavender, bordered in glittering gold, and below, the long, crenelated walls of the Forbidden City at the back of the palaces, rising over a twenty-five-foot-wide moat, ending on the northeast in a decorative tower with manifold, overlapping gables in yellow and emerald green.

Nature was generous with its blue sky and sunny winter and its glorious suburb of Western Hills, dotted with exquisite temples. Human art had created a sense of grandeur and serenity and peace. But nature is often taken for granted by its inhabitants, and so is the creative architecture of man. It is the life of the people which makes one love the city. For its inhabitants, Peking was like an immensely knowing and tolerant mother, or like a big banyan tree providing a home for a great variety of ants, flies, and other insects. It was the millions of gay, poor, rickshaw pullers and polite restaurant waiters and milling crowds around temple bazaars and tradesmen and their wives and children that carried it along and stamped it with their patience and good cheer and instinctive good manners.

Sometimes the three of them would have an exciting supper of barbecued mutton, Mongolian style, at the famous Chengyanglou. The barbecue was made at an open court, where the guests stood with one foot on the ledge around the grill, holding a slice of mutton with their chopsticks over the flames and eating it straight from the fire, so that none of the flavor would be lost. They would come home after dinner and sit in the library and make small talk, or discuss books and painters and poets with no end of anecdotes about the eccentricities of famous scholars. Or Mengchia and Peony would play a game of chess while Jasmine wrote letters home.

The evenings were quiet. The *hutungs* had a music of their own at night. Against the stillness in the outer gloom, the long-drawn-out cries of peddlers selling noodles or dumplings and the wonderful iced persimmons of winter, penetrated the night, sweet to the ear. A hot bowl of dumplings served in syrup was wonderful as a midnight snack.

One night, they were amusing themselves by composing verse. Mengchia showed them samples of a special form of verse. He would give the first line of a verse and the sisters were to complete it, always using the word *ipanerh . . . ipanerh* (half and half) to describe a state of mind or condition of things. The subject was "An Autumn Scene."

When there is a bite in the air,
    JASMINE: and the leaves half brown, half gold,
    PEONY: and the quilt half warm, half cold,
The cranes cry high in the sky,
    JASMINE: and the rushes half bend, half dance in the wind.
    PEONY: and the maiden half regrets, half pines for her beau.
A light knock comes at the midnight door,
    JASMINE: half like a fallen leaf, half like a broken bough.
    PEONY: her heart half frightened, half pleased with surprise.
But it is neither twig, nor leaf,
    JASMINE: half like a flower, half like a foggy form.
    PEONY: half an acquaintance, half some forgotten friend.

"Now comes the real test of your skill," said Mengchia.
The late visitor stands at the door,
    JASMINE: his legs half in, half out.
    PEONY: she half covers her face, half steals a glance.

Jasmine pouted her lips and said, "I refuse to go on. It is getting impossible."

Mengchia said, "Of course, this is sentimental poetry. I just wanted to test your skill. Unless you want to be excused . . . "

"All right. Go on."

He gave the next line:

His voice like the spring breeze,
    JASMINE (after thinking a long while): his eyes half open, half dreamy closed.
    PEONY: she half gasps a welcome, half swallows the rest.

Jasmine said, "This is terrible, getting naughtier and naughtier. At this rate, they will soon be in bed. I'd better get out."

"We will stop then," said Mengchia and added to Peony, "You seem to have read the *Moutangting* play well."

"I read it when I was thirteen."

Mengchia said to Jasmine, "I think your view is more objective. You look at love from the outside, your sister from the inside."

Jasmine was not shy. She said in a quite open tone, "There was love before there was poetry. And the *Book of Songs* is full of love, beginning with the celebration of the love of a prince and his wife. There is love wherever there is life. It all depends on how it ends up."

And so, amidst play and laughter, the sisters learned a great deal about the secrets of verse and prose, and gradually became familiar with the intricate forms of Sung love lyrics.

Mengchia noticed that he could never make Peony read through a book. She was talented and wrote easily in a beautiful hand, but she had no patience for details. Her thoughts were her own and he was happy to notice this; he believed that when she had accumulated enough thoughts and experience, she would break through and become a good writer.

One day she said to him, "I will never read a whole book when I can read half of it, never half a book when I can enjoy a page or a paragraph, and never a whole paragraph when I can enjoy a line or a phrase. It is enough."

"As you never walk when you can stand, never stand when you can sit down, and never sit down when you can throw yourself on a couch."

"I am lazy, I know, happy with my solitude."

"But that is your personality. I don't ever want you to be different from what you are. Since I first saw you, all the other women I pass in the streets seem completely superfluous. They just aren't you. There is only one Peony; there cannot be two. Some may have your looks, but not your voice, and if they have your voice, they have not your spirit, your way of life."

"What is my way of life?" she asked contentedly.

"The whole of your personality. The way you sit, the way you stand, as Tingma once said—the way you move, hanging your hands by your sides and throwing your head up when you walk—the way you look at life, your searching and longing for a beautiful life. . . . And you are passionate, uninhibited, mature. . . . I don't know how to express it. . . . "

Peony beamed at him. "I don't know what has come over me," she said. "Since meeting you, I cannot write. I remember waiting for your letters. That was when I was at my mother's home before you arrived. I would be taking a pencil in hand to write, then I would slowly lower it and drop it; when talking, I became silent; when silent, I fell to thinking; when thinking, my thoughts flew far, far away, wondering what you were doing at that moment."

"Write exactly as you are talking now. You will one day become a very good writer, I am sure."

"I do so want to write."

CHAPTER 11

When spring came around, Peony was seized with a restlessness. It was a kind of malaise she could not understand herself.

More and more she wanted to be alone, and tended to withdraw to her own room. The tendrils of her longing reached out for something unknown—she did not know what. She was still very fond of Mengchia, but her love was not the spontaneous, effortless, perfect thing it had been at Tunglu, or better still, at their meeting on the boat to Ishing. More and more, she would go out alone and lose herself in the company of men at teashops, wineshops, and places of public amusement. An inner urge drove her on as if she were looking for something lost or forgotten in this world.

Her sister had asked her why she wanted to go out alone and not drive out with Mengchia, and she had replied, "I don't know. Sometimes I want just to be left alone, completely alone by myself." She had planned to live with Mengchia and now she had her wish. She wasn't unhappy, but she was not completely happy. Mengchia felt it, felt vaguely that he was in the way. Or perhaps it was satiety. The world of moonbeams must give place to the sunlight of common existence and companionship. But that was not it either; she seemed haunted by a shadow, a feeling of vague restlessness which she could not describe even to herself. Peony knew that she adored Mengchia as she had never adored another man, but there was something lacking in him—perhaps it was the youthful image and fire of Chin Chu.

Or perhaps it was simply the primeval instinct of woman to find her destiny in marriage and home. There was something inherently unsatisfactory in such an illicit relationship. Or perhaps it was Peony herself, dreamy, sensitive, and eternally yearning for the unknown.

So she followed both an old habit and a new prompting, irresistible and imperious. She found escape and relaxation in roaming the city and seeking places of amusement where the crowd was thickest. After all, it was her youth, too.

As in her gamin days, she chose to wear a common, nondescript blue cotton jacket and a pair of dark blue pants, much too tight for her and the worse for wear. In the rest of that blue-clad humanity, she could lose herself. It made her feel happy and secure. Her attire surprised the servants when she came out. The idiosyncrasy certainly did not surprise Jasmine.

She took a rickshaw and went out to Tienchiao, an area of popular entertainments outside Chienmen, in the outer city. She had a surprising gift for learning very fast where the crowds of the city were (for she talked easily with strangers in the streets), where she could find that common friendliness and open hospitality and absence of convention which hampers the social intercourse of the upper classes, where strangers could meet and talk without being introduced and could call each other by their first names after five minutes.

At Tienchiao she found what she wanted; she lost herself happily in that pleasure-seeking populace. Young couples jostling, bent old men with white beards munching sesame cakes and leading grandchildren by the hands, other children peeing in public, their pants cut away in the center for convenience, maids with baskets in hand chasing each other with ringing laughter. And over and above everything, the boom of gongs, the rattle of small hand-drums. Nearby a swish, a whack, of muscle striking muscle, the boxers exhibiting themselves with well-timed *ow's*, *ah's* and *yow's* which aided in the rhythmic expelling of breath.

Peony watched as one of them clapped his hands before giving a high kick aimed at his opponent. The latter caught his shoe and with an easy lunge threw him off balance. He fell backward on the ground, knowingly, rhythmically, and in the next second sent his opponent reeling backward with a powerful kick in his belly. The ring of spectators clapped and cried, "*Yow!*" which was also the way of applauding an opera singer at the end of a favorite aria—an elephantine "*yow*" which came not from the throat but from below the diaphragm. The ring of spectators pressed in and the circle became smaller and smaller. One of them took a rattling iron chain with a heavy, wrought-iron drill the size of a coal scuttle handle, and began to lance at the spectators, each time pulling back that sharp metal point precisely before it struck a spectator's nose. The ring of onlookers receded.

Now the two boxers, each naked to the waist, clasped their hands together, shaking them up and down as they wheeled on their heels, and said, like the gentlest of persons, "Beg your pardon, uncles and brothers. We guests of the rivers and lakes are selling medicines. We dare not boast of our skills. Any among you elder brothers and uncles with better skill and greater prowess will pardon us for our poor show. We crave your indulgence." The voices were throaty, ringing with a vigorous resonance. It was part of the boxers' routine at the beginning and end of a show; it kept them out of trouble when traveling in strange cities.

Peony liked one of the young boxers. He had an attractive shock of hair and a clean smile, revealing a set of white teeth. Using an upturned gong as a tray, he came around the circle collecting cash. "Plasters for killing pain! Ten cents a package! Plasters!" he shouted and from the way he was shouting, he seemed to be enjoying it, too. When he saw there was not sufficient cash thrown in and that few people had bought any plasters, he looked at the tray, shook his head and started joking for sympathy. Bending his arm to make his biceps leap at will, he said, "Look! . . . Hey! Don't walk away, you son of a bitch!" Pointing to his wide-open mouth and slapping his stomach with energetic whacks, he shouted, raising his head, in an appeal first to heaven, then to men: "Oh, heavens! *Tsamen* sell our strength for a bowl of rice"—now lowering his head—"Can *tsamen* go without eating? *Tsamen* selling our breath, our perspiration for a bowl of rice. Come on!" The bystanders, moved by this elemental appeal to hunger, began to throw in copper cash. "That's better, son. That's better, good uncle."

Peony threw in a dozen coppers, her eyes staring at his heaving, muscular chest dripping with perspiration. The young boxer glanced up in surprise at her generosity, and then took a second look at her lovely figure. She started to push her way out. But the boxer kept his eye on her. With the freedom of the uneducated, he shouted after her, "Hey, *kuniang*, don't run away! Hey, *kuniang*!"

She loved his calling after her that way, and looked around at him. The boxer turned the words into a folk song for the public's amusement:

> *Kuniang*, don't run away!
> You are taking my heart with you.
> *Lang-ah-lang-ti-tang!*
> *Kuniang*, where are you going?
> If you come, bring my heart with you.
> *Lang-ah-lang-ti-tang!*
> If you don't, I shall come to you.

> *Lang-ah-lang-ti-tang!*
> *Kuniang,* where do you live?
>   (in falsetto)
>   Sanchiachun,
>   Behind the willows,
>   On top floor.
> Oh, *kuniang!* Yow!

Peony looked at him very hard; he was very appealing. But he was no longer singing to her alone. She walked away smiling. From nearby came the sound of a rattling trident. Another boxer was rolling it around his shoulders and back and arm. Some bystanders were starting to form a ring around it. Farther on, a magician was producing out of thin air a bowl of steaming hot soup noodles from a square piece of gray cloth held in his hands, his arms bare, his body naked to the waist, with the onlookers on all sides of him.

From the distance came the sounds of hand drums and a piercing Turkestan flute. She ran toward it. A woman was lying on her back, on a table, her upturned legs supporting a hand ladder ten feet high. A girl of ten was ducking and weaving her way up and down through the rungs. A man, apparently the father of the child, was tapping the hand drum and asking for contributions. Cash was thrown upon the ground by the admiring onlookers. Now the girl climbed down, and the mother sat up.

The hand drum hastened its beat. The girl picked up a short flute and blew a shrill melody. The mother, grotesquely covered in pancake white and circles of rouge, started to sing and dance. Everyone joined in. The public knew this song of *Fengyang Flower Drum* well. Fengyang was the name of a tribe which wandered from the north to the south, making a living by acrobatics and song and juggling. Peony joined in with the rest. Everyone clapped and tapped his feet to the rhythm, kicking up clouds of thick gray dust. The woman jiggled her hips in a wild, shimmering motion, while the catchy, lilting rhythm of the song was accented by the fast plop and boom of the

hand drum. The audience loved it and asked for more. It was
rowdy and noisy, and produced a great deal of laughter.

Peony was enjoying the trip enormously. In that milling
crowd of people, she found her natural element. Then the girl's
sharp flute sounded again, exquisite, like something which came
from the Mongolian wilds.

> Wotishin [sweetheart], I love you,
> Wotishin, I adore you. . . .

The short phrase was repeated in every verse. Peony's body
automatically swung with it. The melody, soft and sensuous,
was faintly but recognizably Arabic in origin. The incessant
drumbeat carried it along and the shrill flute took up the intervals. It gathered speed toward the end, exciting and tugging at
the heart, stirring up unsatisfied longings. She waked up with
a start when it ended with an abrupt plop of the drum.

Incognito, merging with the raw, smelling populace, she saw
an open teahouse beneath a matted awning and went and sat
there to rest her feet, lost in thought, on the verge of tears.
What was it she was looking for? She did not know. She felt
only a nameless ache in her heart and an overwhelming sense
of lacking something, wanting something. She was young and
very attractive with her bare arms, tight jacket, and pants. Men
filed past her, handsome and ugly, flabby of flesh, and muscular.
She always found that whenever she went out alone and sat in
a teahouse, pensive but thinking of nothing at all, someone
would start to talk to her. Waiters, young and old, would speak
to such a pretty girl with that warm, indefinable smile. She was
frank and easy with all—it did not matter who they were. Oh,
she knew men. She did not need them sexually, but she loved
the free and easy and exciting atmosphere around them. Was
she searching for a lost love, or for an ideal she could not find?

That spring, Mengchia heard news from his friend in the
Yushihyuan (Censorate) that a big case of salt smuggling was
about to break. It involved a well-known salt merchant of

Yangchow who had collaborated with the Salt Tax Bureau of Kaoyu using official boats to transport smuggled salt, thereby evading the heavy salt tax. The Chief, Shueh, and a number of *likin* (internal customs) officers were involved. It meant that, if the prosecution were successfully concluded, there would be heavy fines and exile for the salt merchant, and disgrace and a long sentence of exile, or possibly capital punishment, for Shueh. A mass of data had been collected on the spot. Shueh and the merchant were charged with willfully depriving the government of its revenue with full knowledge of the laws of the empire. It depended on how the case worked out. If persistent misconduct were proven, Shueh would be beheaded in autumn in Peking.

Naturally, the case had many ramifications. The merchant, Yang Shunli ("Obedience to Heavenly Reason") was desperate, running about like an ant on a hot pan. He had enormous influence and hoped that his money could talk for him. He had sent a private representative to come up to Peking and study avenues for a soft approach. But the *yuchih* (imperial censor in charge of maintaining law and public morals), by the name of Liu Tseng, was a man who took his job seriously and was known for his integrity. It was not known whether Liu had adopted the personal name "Tseng" before or after he became censor; at any rate it means "clang of iron." There was no way of softening the blow, and the merchant's representative, who had come up in deep winter, went back in less than a month.

Meanwhile, in the middle of February, Bureau Chief Shueh and Yang Shunli had been arrested, and a warrant had been sent out for a number of key people and witnesses involved, who were subjected to individual questioning. Their dispositions were recorded. Those who co-operated with the government, such as the singsong girls, Precious Pearl and Little Cassia, were released, but remained under observation.

It came pretty close to Peony. The crucial testimony was, of course, the diary and the little book of accounts in her husband's own handwriting. While the evidence was overwhelming, Shueh and the others continued to deny all knowledge of the affair, and shifted the responsibility to some underlings, whose families the rich salt merchant promised to take care of.

This primary evidence was now in Mengchia's safekeeping. Copies had been made for the Censorate's office. (The Censorate had the duties of an attorney-general, as far as the nation was concerned, but also had the additional odious duty of admonishing the Emperor on his personal conduct.) The case was now in the local courts of Kiangsu, passing rapidly from the *fu* to *tao* (magistrates) and eventually to the civil governor of Nanking, and subject in the last instance to review by the Taliyuan, the equivalent of the Supreme Court. Mengchia repeated his request to the censor in charge to build the case around the confessions, leaving out the diary as a personal favor to his cousin-sister. The latter had performed a service to the government by submitting the evidence against her deceased husband. Although Fei's name was clearly implicated, nothing would be gained by disgracing the dead, and since Mrs. Fei herself had known nothing about the smuggling, the censor promised to keep her name out of it.

Also, at this time, there was talk of Peony's going back to Hangchow to see her parents. She wanted to. Mengchia could not understand why. If she were still worried about getting involved in the salt scandal, he would send a letter to Prince Yi, as far as the case was concerned, asking him to put in a word with the civil governor of Nanking. Theoretically, the civil and military governors (*tsungtu* and *shünwu*) were equal in rank, and although they had separate areas of authority, the words of the military governor, who was a member of the Manchu Imperial House, usually carried weight with the Chinese civil governor. It would be the easiest of all things to arrange: a word spoken over the dinner table would be enough. Accordingly, Mengchia wrote a personal letter to his friend, Prince Yi. That settled it to their satisfaction, and Mengchia put the smuggling affair out of his mind.

At the beginning of April, soon after the spring festival of *tsingming*, Peony received a letter from Paiwei. Their letters were as intimate and frank as their conversations. There was nothing Paiwei might say which Peony could take offense at. Among other things Paiwei wrote:

Peony:

I always admire your spirit of independence and your daring. And I am sure you are seeing things in Peking which I hope I shall see one day with Joshui. You must be living a dream, you lucky devil. People tell me about seeing the Temple of Heaven in moonlight and I am reserving that pleasure to see it with you—perhaps later when you are more settled. It will be a good excuse to visit you. . . . You don't know what you have done to Chin Chu. It breaks my heart, I am telling you. I was horrified when I saw him during the spring holidays when he came down to pay respects to his ancestral graves. His hair was unkempt and his face was gaunt and he had a hard look. One might say that his features have changed. It is a hard face, but underneath he is broken. He told me that he is living with a harlot in Shanghai. From Soochow to Shanghai is only an hour by train. I must tell you something which I did not tell you before. He came up in November after you left and went to that place down the stream and passed a night there. In the morning when he came up to the house, his eyes were bloodshot and haggard. But he tried to keep up a brave appearance. Now he is changed. There is nothing you can do to change him back, I am afraid. He never mentioned your name once when I talked to him. If he is bitter, you cannot blame him. Because I have known him so long, it hurts me to see him. . . . In time, he will be able to adjust himself, I am sure, for as you know he has got a lot of strength in his character. . . .

Peony could not finish reading it. She felt alternately hot and cold and had a feeling of terrible congestion in her chest. The letter did not say that he had abandoned his wife; apparently he had not. How many things a harlot could do openly that a society girl could not! She was sure that the harlot did not deserve him or that he really wanted her. She felt a faint,

sick tug in her guts and a hot flush on her face which were almost painful.

The news filled her with remorse. Since he could not divorce
his wife, it really wasn't her fault that she could not consent to
live as his mistress, as the harlot did. And there was no point
in writing to him; it would only cause more entanglements and
make it harder for him to forget her. That was that. Let the
cheap prostitute, whoever she was, have him and help him to
regain himself.

That night she woke up at midnight and couldn't get back to
sleep. She got up and, unable to find her slippers in the dark,
limped barefooted to her desk, lit the lamp, and sat thinking.
The soft glow of the lamp and the silence of the stars were so
like the midnight hours she had spent at Tunglu with him
that her heart seemed to leap up in her throat. She set her
lips together tightly, took a brush in hand, and started to write
to Paiwei. As she looked out the window, the midnight sky
was peppered with a thousand stars, while across the heavens,
the Milky Way hung slantwise—the "Silver River" which separated lovers in the sky, according to a popular myth. She could
hear the soft voice of Chin Chu whispering in her ears about
the unquenchable longing of the Cowherd and the Spinning
Maid in the sky, "permitted to meet once a year like ourselves."
She imagined she could even hear his quick breaths.

> Dearest Paiwei:
>
> I was shocked to read your letter and learn what has hap-
> pened to Chin Chu. I kept on asking myself, Was it my
> fault? I am not writing him. I suppose he will never forgive
> me. But I am more afraid to write him lest it should reopen
> an old wound. I can say this only to you. My heart and soul
> have long been given in ransom to him, and as hard as I
> try to forget, I have no will of my own. I do not know what
> has come over me. I can no longer find my bearings. I feel
> like a ship tossed at sea. What can I do?
>
> Since coming up to Peking, Paiwei, I have not been able
> to find the happiness I hoped for. The situation is rapidly
> becoming ridiculous. It is all my fault, I know. My cousin is

as perfect as I could expect in a man of his age. No, not even the difference of twenty years could stand between us, if I could forget Chin Chu. That I cannot, you know. His love is in my blood and hair, in my bones and marrow, in the most intimate depths of my being.

What am I to do? Tell me, what shall I do? My heart is torn to pieces. I had to give him up because I could not forever meet him once or twice a year. What was I to do with myself the rest of the time? You will understand. But how can I forget? From the very beginning, our meeting was both painful and exciting, the joy of holding each other always accompanied with the heart-sinking dread of having to tear ourselves apart again. While he kept his head, I had a perishing fear of going back to my unloved husband. I abandoned myself more fully in the knowledge that I alone could give him complete union of soul and body, and tortured myself to give him pleasure. My sensibility was so keen those rare times that we could meet, that I blinded myself to reality, and lived in the ecstasy of being his wife.

The effect of such secret meetings was that my senses were sharpened almost unbearably. I became a woman fully awakened, sensitive to the stars at night which looked down upon me, and the moon which kissed me and the breeze which came through the window and caressed my arms and back as I lay half naked in my room—an awakened sensibility without the possibility of being satisfied. My malaise, my headaches, and my fear of light wrecked my mind and transformed my body into a thousand tender, shredded fibers of wounded sensibility. I had a feeling of insubstantiality of all that surrounded me, and barely retained enough sense to go back to my brute of a husband and go through the duties of wife and daughter-in-law like an automaton. . . . What's the use of reviewing the past? All I am telling you is that I am confused and do not know what to do.

I am frightened of myself and doubts and fears begin to rise. Is it because of my love for Chin Chu that I cannot give Mengchia the undivided love which he craves and which I once used to feel? It must be hard for Mengchia, I know, for he is so good to me. It is strange, but I have come to think of him as "*our hanlin*," and not as a lover. My heart is in ransom. What my body does, I do not care any more. Can you understand me? . . . This letter is as disjointed as my feelings.

Yours,
Peony

CHAPTER 12

The April air throbbed with love songs of birds and the Western Hills were inviting. All over the countryside, life had returned to the dry sod of winter's earth. The Jade Fountain Hill and the Patachu ("Eight Great Places"), besides Emperor Chienlung's deer park at Shiangshan and the Temple of the Sleeping Buddha, afforded an endless variety of places for trips in the spring.

One evening after supper, Mengchia and Peony were sitting in the library. Jasmine had gone into the kitchen to give orders to the cook for the next day, and was going back to her room to freshen up. She preferred to keep out of the way when she knew they were together. It was much cozier in the library, she knew. As she was passing to the other court, Mengchia called to her:

"Szemei, come and have a talk."

"What about?"

"Just have a talk. It's nicer in here."

"All right. I'll be right back."

In a few minutes she came in, her face wearing the natural bloom of youth, her hair done over again into a queue of shining smoothness. She had changed into a simple blue cotton jacket and trousers, similar to Peony's, such as she used to wear at home. The jacket had shorter and narrower sleeves than a party dress, for the latter had very ample sleeves usually with broad, bold trimmings in the fashion of those times. But the effect was no less stunning. She threw a quick glance at her sister who, in spite of herself, was feeling uncomfortable, and quickly seated herself on a hardwood chair, a picture of youth. Her eyes caught sight of Peony's slippered feet resting on the rim of the cold brazier, her body snugly ensconced in the fur-lined easy chair.

"Why are you looking at me?" asked Peony.

"I am not looking at you," Jasmine said, her eyes open with surprise. She turned an innocent glance at Mengchia and said in a low, serene voice, as if nothing had happened, "What were you talking about?"

"About you."

"About me?"

"Yes, I was saying how lucky you came along . . ."

"I know, you two live on air. I don't underestimate myself. A house is a house. Someone has got to look after it. Don't you feel good sleeping in clean sheets? I really mean it."

"I really appreciate what you've done."

"It seems to me we are short of sheets. I am thinking of buying some more. May I?"

"You do not have to ask. Just go ahead and buy whatever you need."

"Seriously, what were you talking about?"

"I'll be going away for a half month or so. You've seen the Peking–Tientsin Railway. The Emperor has authorized building an extension to Shanhaikuan. Work has been going on for two years and is now about finished. It will parallel the Great Wall, more or less, but will enable us to move troops in a day, whereas it would take about a week of forced march to cover the same distance. With the foreign troops permanently stationed at Tangku, we cannot afford to be encircled. We must be able to move troops fast from Manchuria. I am going to examine the work on the new railway with a group of British and Chinese engineers. His Majesty is so pleased that he is thinking of starting a new line connecting Peking with Jehol. The two British engineers have been begging me to accompany them to see the Ming Tombs, the mausoleums of the Ming emperors. I was thinking that if you sisters would like to come along, this is a splendid opportunity."

"Oh, the Ming Tombs!" There was keen enthusiasm in Jasmine's voice.

"The journey to the Ming Tombs will take only two or three days, and the weather is just right for a spring outing."

"Wouldn't you like to see it?" she asked Peony.

"No. Why should I see the tombs of the dead emperors? I would rather stay at home."

Mengchia interrupted. "That was why I thought we ought to have a talk. Perhaps you can persuade your sister. If you do not go now, you won't have another chance until much later, and it may be hot. And then who knows? . . . I may be called to another place."

Jasmine said, "I would love to come. And we can see the Chuyungkuan Pass near the Great Wall that I've been dreaming about."

"Sister, if you are really interested, you go with him."

"No. If you won't go, I won't go either." Jasmine's voice was firm and determined.

"You go with him," said Peony, "if you wish so much to see it."

"No, I won't if you don't come along."

"Well, that's that," said Mengchia, his voice heavy with disappointment.

Mengchia was to leave on the seventeenth. On the night of the sixteenth he said to Peony, "This is the first time we are to part since you came up. I hope you will take good care of yourself. Go out and relax and be happy. I shall write you as often as I can. But it's only for a fortnight or so."

Surprisingly enough, in their embraces, Mengchia found her eyes slightly moist.

"Why are you crying?"

"I don't know."

"Aren't you happy?"

"Of course I am."

"Why don't you come along? Don't you want to see the Ming Tombs and the Great Wall? You can see both in one trip."

"It's only that I—I want sometimes to be alone."

"Why?"

"I don't know."

"You are not worried about your sister?"

"No. I trust her completely."

"And you are right."

Something had come between them; he did not know what.

"It's your moods. Have a good sleep and tomorrow you will feel better. Just tell me when you want to be alone and I shall respect your wishes."

So Mengchia left the next day for Nankow in the company of the British engineers. Every two or three days the sisters received a letter from him, addressed to Peony, consisting of two or three pages written in his bold, angular hand. He was careful in those letters not to go beyond the usual expressions of "longing" and "remembering" at the beginning, and of hoping that they were well and in good health at the end. Peony would scan the letter first and then show it to her sister. He had the knack of evoking an image by a short phrase, subtly suggestive of intense emotions, such as "clouds over the pass suddenly opened," or "flying teals coursing the sky," or "I hear the Mongolian flutes' sad notes at night," which went so well with "thinking of you."

One of his letters contained a poem:

> I arise from dreams of thee.
> We were holding hands together and free,
> And would never let them go.
> The day is richer for me.

> I arise from dreams of thee.
> Freed from this separation and pain.
> Oh, if this be bliss, then let me sleep
> And never wake up again.

During the master's absence, the servants were more relaxed, food was simpler, and there was not much to do. The sisters had the carriage to themselves; spring was inviting and there were so many places to go. Once they went out as far as the

Bluecloud Temples (*Piyunsze*) at the foot of the Western Hills, a place with a dagoba of Hindu origin, which commanded a view of the entire city of Peking with the yellow roofs of the Forbidden City in the center. Both enjoyed it but felt they missed Mengchia. It was a beautiful, clear day, completely cloudless, but it was not much fun for two women to go on an outing alone. Jasmine, being a conservative girl, never thought it her business to be looking for a young man. She would not even talk about it; it was her parents' business and her cousin's to find a good match for her. It was just not discussed, so clear were her elders' duties.

One afternoon Peony went back to Tienchiao alone. The day when the boxer had looked at her and sung a courtship song to her had left a pleasurable memory in her mind. It is good for a woman to be admired and looked at and flirted with by a young man with such a clean smile and white teeth, even though she may be engaged or married. That man had all the appeal of manly youth and handsome shoulders and strong limbs.

She went on the chance of meeting him again—not that she felt there could be anything serious between them. She loved the swift grace of his movements and his powerful, heaving chest. She would like to hear him sing that song to her again and see his white teeth gleaming in zestful laughter as he sang, "*Lang-ah-lang-ti-tang!*"

She stood around watching the boxing exhibit. To her chagrin, the young man was not there. Two other boxers were giving a show, one on the defensive and the other chasing him around; but the smaller man, running away and on the constant defensive, stole the show because he always managed to give a dastardly, unsuspected kick or blow which felled the other, before he started running away again. It was like a cat-and-mouse act with the mouse as the hero. The spectators loved it. There was the same "*hee-ho-hah!*" with which the smaller man challenged and baited his chaser. Of course it had all been rehearsed as an act, but the public loved it, especially when the smaller fellow showed such agility and merciless skill.

Peony laughed with the rest and was holding a handkerchief

to her mouth on account of the dust kicked up by the two men, when someone tapped her lightly on the shoulder from behind. She turned around and recognized the sparkling eyes and broad grin of the boxer. They exchanged an easy, carefree smile.

"It was you, *kuniang*, wasn't it, at the show half a month ago?"

Peony nodded a smile. "Why aren't you in the show today?" Then she added in a softer voice, quite innocently, "I came to see you."

"Really? What's your name, *kuniang*? You didn't mind my singing to you that day, did you?"

"Not at all. I loved it. I knew you had to have your fun." She found it easy to be talking to a young man of her age.

"What's your name?"

"I have no name."

"Well, Miss Anonymous, then. Not at

> *Sanchiachun,*
>> *Behind the willows,*
>>> *On top floor*

I hope?"

He was being facetious, but he hummed those lines with a lilting, catchy rhythm. She was fascinated.

"Come on!" he said, and without caring whether she wanted to or not, pulled her away. She followed gladly, amused at his forthright simplicity.

They went into a teahouse in an enclosed patio beneath some pear trees, and ordered tea. There was the distant sound of drum and cymbal and some high-pitched singing coming from an open theater somewhere. She studied him carefully. He was not husky or big, but he had beautiful cheekbones and a firm chin; his face was smooth, lean, and muscular. In that corner under the shade of the greenery, the light struck his sharp, lean profile. A moving, rippling white reflection from somewhere danced playfully on it and illuminated his tousled hair.

"Why aren't you in the show today?"

"I am an amateur. I was a guest performer that day."

"Amateur?"

"That is, it is not my profession. They are my friends. You don't know the brotherhood of boxers. We are all brothers. They thought me good enough and offered me a chance to give an exhibit. Wasn't bad, was it?"

"It was very good. You must tell me your name."

"Fu Nanto. I live right here in the city."

His simple, artless smile made her feel secure. He gave her an admiring look and said, "My, you *are* beautiful!"

No one had ever said it in quite such a direct, open fashion.

"Nanto," she said, calling him by his first name, "what do you do?"

"I have a small shop and a bit of land in the country. Boxing is my sport."

"What else do you do?"

"For sports? Shuttlecocks. There is a wonderful Shuttlecock Club around here. I will take you there one day. And *taichichuan*, eurhythmic dance. I am a slow man. I am no good for books." He spoke slowly, methodically, but clearly. "Tell me," he said, "who you are and where you live."

"No," Peony smiled, shaking her head, knowing that if he learned she belonged to a *hanlin's* family he would be scared away.

"Don't be so mysterious," pleaded Nanto. "Are you from some rich family? One would think so, to look at your face." He glanced up and down her body in such a way that she felt he was looking right through her.

"I am of a common family, Nanto," she said.

"Not married? Tell me if you are. I want to be warned."

"No." Then she added, "I lost my husband."

"Then who are you?"

"Miss Anonymous, as you say. You are a man and I am a woman. Isn't that enough?"

As soon as she said this, she quickly realized that she had made a slip of the tongue, but it was too late to take it back. He might misunderstand.

She rose to go.

"Where can I see you again?" He did not ask if he could see

her again. She looked at his clean smile and straight look and shock of black hair and replied, "I don't know."

"When can I see you again?"

"I don't know . . . it is so far out here. I live in the East City."

"I live in the West City. If you will be good enough to tell me where I can find you."

"You want to very much?"

"Very much. Come on, I will walk a short distance with you. Then you can go home if you don't want to tell me where you live."

She found it pleasant to walk with him. As they approached Chienmen Boulevard, their steps fell into an easy, jogging, jaunty pace, the rhythm of youth. His arm was gripping hers and it was powerful and strong. Both knew and both pretended not to know that the hand on her arm had come into contact with her breast and was brushing against it.

"I suggest the wineshop at the Tungtan Pailou, directly west of it, where we can meet. When can you come?"

"Any time, any day. Say, tomorrow, five o'clock?"

They agreed. He found her a rickshaw and reminded her, "Tomorrow, five o'clock."

The encounter with Fu Nanto took her mind off her brooding; it was an innocent, pleasant flirtation. She found him diverting and relaxing and easy; it was not like talking with a scholar. Nanto had no abstract ideas and no pet theories of any kind on human life. He was probably innocent of books, but gave her the sensation of a young bloodhound, healthy and strong and ready to meet life in the raw. Also, she was sure there would be no emotional entanglements. Mengchia was one thing, Fu Nanto was another. The two categories were quite separate and she did not have to be afraid of herself.

This impression was confirmed and increased during the following meetings. She would go out about five o'clock, take a seat at the open-air wineshop, and look out at the passing scene in the street. It was already the end of April; the days were lengthening, and it was still quite bright at six.

Hatamen Street presented a scene of constant activity. Black-faced boys, their white teeth standing out in sharp contrast, might be passing by, driving mule carts heaped with sacks of coal. A train of camels might be jogging along, slowly, having just arrived from the coal mines of Mentoukow, the drivers invariably wearing black turbans wound about their dusty heads. Tibetan lama priests trailed their bright orange cassocks; they belonged to the magnificent Yunghokung monastery in the north city, endowed by Emperor Chienlung. Or there might be one of those beautiful, long, colorful funeral processions that Peking loved so much. The procession would extend for two hundred yards, with professional men in grotesque uniforms, shabbily florid with green and lavender, carrying parasols, drums, gongs, big red wooden signs engraved with gold characters, and Tibetan horns seven or eight feet long. These professional men purposely marched at long intervals so as to spread out the procession and give a false sense of glamour. . . . Then there might be fights, accidents, a woman falling in the mud to the amusement and hearty laughter of everybody—so ready for laughter was the Peking populace—and beggars, priests, nuns, Manchu women with their tall black folded headdresses and thick-soled shoes, dogs snarling or fighting for a piece of bone, and the eternally babbling and laughing rickshaw pullers. . . .

The wine- and teashop life was the real life of the city, where the rich and poor mixed and had the right to enjoy themselves as they watched the world go by. The wineshop smelled of *pehkan*, freshly baked wheat cakes, and fried mutton. Close by the *pailou*, there was always a group of parked rickshaws, waiting for fares. The pullers, too, would come into the shop, grating their cloth shoes caked with mud, and leaving large clumps of mud on the wineshop floor. They would ask for a drink of *pehkan* (70 per cent alcohol) and start to babble, the perspiration dripping off their cheeks. Some would take off their long shabby gowns, park them on the back of a chair, and start to retie their trouser belts, airing their groins in the presence of the public. Some of them were husky young men. Peony watched with fascination as she heard the raw obscenities sprouting from their lips; some of it she did not understand, such as *chipa*, which she thought meant literally a chicken drumstick.

She would order four ounces of *shaoshing* and take up her position at a small, unpainted, but well-scrubbed table. If Fu Nanto was not there, someone, perhaps a soldier in uniform, would strike up a conversation with her. She was young, so pretty, and so uninhibited. Courtship belongs naturally to the young. She was well dressed, but it was quite possible that the way she came out alone, some people might mistake her for a "semi-open door," or private courtesan in business.

Fu Nanto would come and sit there, sharing with her the joy of the street. In a way, he dominated the scene. He was the life of the street personified; he allowed nothing to happen which was not as it should be, which was not fair play and fair game, according to Peking custom. He kept an eye on what was going on. Once there was an argument in front of the wine-shop about a rickshaw fare. The man was from Shanghai and insisted that he had paid enough, and the rickshaw man was clutching his chest, saying that he had not. Fu Nanto walked up and asked the stranger, "Where did you take the rickshaw from? How much did you pay him?" The stranger told him. Without a word, he gave the rickshaw man a whack and told him to be gone. The rickshaw man was gone like a whirlwind. Fu Nanto came back and told Peony that the man was taking advantage of a stranger in the city. "No *wangfa!*" he shouted; *wangfa*, whatever it means literally, was all that was right and proper and ancient. He appeared really angry, as if it was an insult to Peking itself.

Once he took her out to the Shuttlecock Club, which had both men and women members. It fascinated her to see the way he could kick a shuttlecock to let it land on his upturned fore-head, and knock it off again with a toss of the head to catch it with a hind kick. He disdained buttoning up his jacket which flopped about while he leaped and swirled. He was as agile as a monkey. Once they spent a whole day climbing the old Mongol City walls, north of the city. She practically fell on top of him when they descended, and he had to carry her in his strong arms.

She found him invariably entertaining and without a single theory in his mind. She suspected that he was half illiterate but made up for it by his clean smile. His heroes were the red-faced Kuankung and the black-faced Chang Fei of the Three Kingdoms, as he came to know them on the popular stage. He was good company always, but there was no question of involving herself or falling in love with this man.

However, it was certain that she felt attracted to him. She was fascinated by his sparkling eyes and youthful laughter, so different from the mature, pensive look of Mengchia; also, his skin was firmer and smoother than Mengchia's, and he had nice hair. As men often find a purely physical appeal in a young girl's body, so Peony found excitement in the company of a young, muscular man closer to her own age. It was natural. If somebody played a trick with Peony's heart and emotions, it was nature herself.

Fu Nanto came regularly to the wineshop. Some days she successfully resisted the impulse to go, and would spend the time with her sister. Jasmine was sure that there was something on her mind. She was just a little too anxious to finish a letter she was writing in order to be able to go out at four. Or she would yawn and protest that she did not really want to go out but there was nothing else to do. Also, she plucked her eyebrows with extra care and spent a few more minutes in front of the mirror before she set out for the wineshop.

Peony was aware that if she let the matter drift, she would certainly not be able to stop this affair, which had begun so innocently. She kept away for a week, and resisted the impulse to go all the more, because of that slip of tongue, which had seemed to invite further intimacy: "*You are a man and I am a woman. Isn't that enough?*" Fu Nanto had misunderstood her motives, she was sure. He came every day and waited for her, but found that Miss Anonymous had stopped showing up. He came and sat at a table, scanning the street for a pretty girlish figure that might turn out to be Miss Anonymous; finally he went away, doubting but still hopeful, inventing excuses for her failure to appear.

One morning, about eleven, she ran into him where the Tsungpu Hutung ran into Hatamen Street. (Hatamen Street should have been called a boulevard.) He had seen her from the back and dashed up, calling to her, "Don't run away, *kuniang*, don't run away!" She turned around and saw him. It was Nanto, unmistakably, a pleading look in his eyes behind their bright gleam. She uttered an impulsive "You!" which seemed to mean a thousand things in his ears.

"Where have you been? I have been to the wineshop every day. Why didn't you come? Have I offended you? I have roamed the streets in the hope of meeting you." The sentences broke like little snaps.

"I am going home."

"You cannot get away from me."

"I am going home. I beg you."

"Then I will follow you."

But she did not move, her feet glued to the ground. Her heart palpitated like a pair of buckets going up and down a well on a pulley. She felt her legs yield below her as he took hold of her hand and forced her to turn and go in the same direction. They fell in step and, in spite of herself, she felt wonderful as his hand gripped her right arm and pressed it.

"Where are you going?" she asked.

"Anywhere you say."

She wanted to get away. She had met him in public places, but she knew nothing about him. Fu Nanto begged, "Will you come with me to a hotel where we can talk at leisure and get better acquainted? I promise you I shall not bother you."

"How can I be sure?"

"I swear by my mother. And because I love you. Tell me anything you wish, and I shall do it."

"Jump into that ditch."

Fu Nanto really jumped. The open sewer was some two feet deep, running between the center pavement and the cart roads on the sides. The muddy shallow water splashed up. When he climbed out again, his face was splattered with clots of mud.

Peony laughed. Taking out a handkerchief, she wiped his

face for him and said smilingly, "You are crazy. I was only joking."

"But I am crazy—for you."

She studied him carefully. He was a very young man, perhaps immature, but he loved her as only youth could love, she was sure.

"If you promise to behave, I will be friends with you. Just friends, you understand?"

"Anything you say. Why are you so mysterious?"

Fu Nanto was convinced that she was not in that "semi-open door" business, and this increased her mystery and charm for him.

"May I ask, are you married?" she asked him.

"What if I am? Does that make any difference?"

"No, not if we remain strictly friends."

He began to tell her about his marital troubles, what a spiteful woman his wife was, and how he must not look at another woman in the street or at the theater.

"Come on. Let's take rickshaws. I know a good hotel where we can talk quietly."

The hotel was small, just back of the "street of lanterns" outside Chienmen, where traveling tradesmen stayed, decent but inexpensive. Hand in hand, they climbed the dim staircase. Peony felt her legs soft as rubber, her heart beating violently. The very act of secretly going up with him excited her and gave her the thrill of doing the forbidden.

They closed the door behind them. He called for a pot of tea. While waiting for the tea, he took her by surprise and imprinted a kiss on her neck and then begged her pardon. But she knew it was coming, of course, from the way he had squeezed her behind on the staircase.

The boy brought the tea and the door was closed. A key was turned. Peony, feeling terribly guilty and embarrassed, seated herself on the bed with her hands in her lap. He wanted to come close, but she said, "No. You sit there. We want to talk, don't we?"

He obeyed her and took a chair by the window, never taking

his eyes off her. He poured a cup of tea for her and a cup for himself. The tea seemed to calm him down. He was able to collect himself a little, and began seriously to tell her about his wife. He said he had not married a wife, but a jailer. Then he told her how he had not been himself the last few days, thinking of her. That very morning, he had had words with his wife because of his continued absence from home these past days, and he showed her the place on his forehead where she had clutched his hair and torn off a few locks from his scalp.

"It is still red, I am sure."

Peony looked. There were purple clots on his hair.

He drew nearer for her to see, and then seated himself on the bed beside her, his hand pressing hard on her thighs.

"Please don't. Look at your shoes!" She pointed at them and broke out into a ringing laugh. He laughed, too, and rose and stamped on the floor.

"Take them off. You can't dry them that way."

The thought amused them both.

"You don't know how funny you looked when you climbed out of the ditch."

She started to laugh hysterically, and he joined in, enjoying the joke on herself.

Just then, there was a series of loud bangs on the door. Fu Nanto turned pale. Their laughter ceased and they spoke in whispers. "It cannot be the police. It must be my wife. She has followed us here, I am sure."

"What am I to do?"

A woman's voice screamed through the door: "Open up. I know you are there. Open up!" More bangs.

"Now you will see some action," whispered Nanto, quietly, calmly. "I am going to open that door very suddenly. You hide behind the door. Slip out at the first moment, before she has a chance to see you."

"Coming," he called loudly. He tiptoed to close the window and darken the room. Almost noiselessly, he turned the key in the door, while holding Peony by his left hand. All of a sudden, he threw it wide open and in the same breath dragged the woman in so forcefully that she toppled over. At the same moment, he pulled at Peony for her to go out. She ducked under his arm and dashed out into the hall.

She ran pell-mell down the stairs without waiting to hear what was happening inside the room. The hotel clerk was looking at her, but she got out safely into the street, ran a few paces, and found a rickshaw. By the time she reached home, she had sufficiently collected herself.

"Why, you're back early today," said her sister.

"I was so bored," she replied.

CHAPTER 13

Mengchia had been held up longer than usual and returned on the tenth of May. He was tanned from the journey, but looked a little tired, perhaps because he had arrived in a heavy downpour, most unusual in Peking for this time of the year. He said the trip had done him good. He had gone on horseback as far as Tanchihshih and Miaofengshan, deep in the Western Hills, on a four-day trip to work off his fat.

Upon his return, he had to attend a conference on the new railway project connecting Peking with Jehol, as a man whose sound knowledge of the whole region was depended upon.

After three or four days, he was able to stay home, and proposed that they take a drive to the Altar of Agriculture. It was far out at the south end of the Chienmen Boulevard, near the front gate of the Outer City, and contained a beautiful stretch of mulberry trees. It used to be the custom for the Emperor to go on winter solstice to offer sacrifice at the Temple of Heaven, across the Chienmen Boulevard, and for the Empress to make a ceremonial picking of mulberry leaves for feeding silkworms in spring, thus symbolizing the importance of the farmer and his wife in the life of the nation. Actually, the Altar was called "Farmers First."

Jasmine had not come with them, for she had the tact to leave them alone, since it was so soon after Mengchia's return. Forgetting all about her widow's mourning, especially here in Peking, where nobody knew her, Peony had put on a white dress printed with large blue flowers, which made her look quite breathtaking in the spring sun. Her hair was swept up at the back, with a few carefully arranged locks hanging over her forehead.

He talked about his long journey, and then about the romance of *The Western Chamber*. It was Peony who had brought it up.

"Do you know why *The Western Chamber* is the most popular of all love stories?" he said. "Because it is *stolen* love. No one dares. But Inging dared. There is a reckless, compelling quality about it. And after all, what is so wrong about a fully grown girl having a stolen romance? The story couldn't hold the reader's interest if she were properly engaged and legitimately married and then made love to her husband. Love always tries to break frontiers. The insufferable part about the story is that Changsheng, really the poet Yuan Chen himself, turned heel and deserted her and married a rich man's daughter. That is the part called his 'repentance' for his 'youthful folly.' The worst thing is to copulate with a girl and then moralize about it. It was written in remorse, but I wish he didn't moralize about it to justify himself."

"But you do approve of Inging?"

"I don't approve and I don't disapprove. That is to say, I do not judge her. She was young, mature, ready for romance. The way she and her widowed mother stayed up in the mountains, she had never met a tolerable young man. Changsheng came and her young girl's heart responded. She gave herself to him entirely. Granted that it was passion, pure physical passion. She was young, very young—I believe she was nineteen. Who are we to judge?"

On an impulse, she started to tell him about her encounter with Fu Nanto. She was unbelievably candid. He listened attentively. But as she proceeded, she suddenly decided to change it and embellish it, just to test his reactions. There was no wife in the story she was telling him. She had lost control of herself. "I didn't want it, honestly, but I did it. And he was wonderful, tender. I felt awful afterward, but at the moment I did not know what I was doing."

His face did not betray the slightest expression and he merely said, "I was young once. I, too, did a number of foolish things."

"You will pardon me?"

"There is nothing to pardon. That you are passionate, I know." He bent to kiss her. "You are the tenderest, the most marvelous thing in my life, unique, unique, unique. If you take away this love from me, I—I do not think I can take it."

"You have not changed your opinion of me after what I told you?"

"No, I haven't. I can't. Whatever you do. . . . You see I need you so much I must be strong, too. I have to guard myself. Frankly, there is a difference of age between us. I will guard myself against anything."

"Against what? Against me?"

"Against your youth, your impulsive, whimsical nature. Youth must have its romance. You know now why I was not surprised when you told me about the boxer."

She half felt an impulse to tell him the truth, that she had not really slept with Fu Nanto, but decided to leave it as it was. "I do not understand you," she said. "You are too good to me." She rested her weight on his arm.

"So you don't. Nor do I. It's a love that wants to give and give, to see only that you are happy. It makes me happy to know that you are happy. . . . Can you understand that?"

"I can," she replied sweetly.

Upon their return in the afternoon, Jasmine told them with a tired face that there was a letter from his friend, Prince Yi of Hangchow. No, she had not read the letter, which was lying upon his desk. It was sent by a messenger from Prince Tuan's Palace. Naturally, she had given the messenger a handsome tip of twenty dollars. Mengchia was agreeably surprised that she had already picked up the style and customs of Peking. She added that there was a man from Yangchow who wanted to see him, a man well dressed, mustached, and talking like one of those professional unemployed scholars, *shiangshen*, that is, scholars in the country living on their wits. He appeared greatly disappointed, but in a nervous way, when he was told that the *hanlin* was out for the day and said he would return the next day. He seemed to have important business.

Mengchia looked at the visiting card. It was from Yang Shunli, the arrested Yangchow millionaire. He understood and was sure that the man had been sent by Yang as his representative to "make arrangements." How would Yang and the others know about the evidence in Peony's possession? Maybe Shueh's secretary had peeped into the diary before sending it on. This secretary could have told his uncle Shueh about it when the case broke.

Mengchia at once gave orders to the doorman to turn the visitor away with a firm "Master not at home" when he showed up.

"If he is willing to wait?" asked the old gatekeeper.

"Just say not at home. I am not in the city—say anything. He will understand."

Mengchia was angry. Turning to the sisters, he said, "I bet you that man is coming up with a big bribe. I know the type. Those dangerous, floating scholars without visible means of support, fattening on lawsuits and connections and selling of influence. Invariably talking the language of the Sages, with an air of affected diffidence and culture and knowing all the simulated laughs and chuckles, the correct clearing of throats, the tremendous affection and respect for their interlocutors. They waste your time. A high-class prostitute might make a hundred dollars a night with the same efforts. A polished scholar might make a thousand. Both are prostitutes—what's the difference?"

Jasmine was plucking nervously at her gown. Peony suddenly noticed how wan her sister looked.

"Are you ill?" asked Peony of her sister. "You seem tired."

Jasmine replied that she was fine, but her eyes were clouded and lacked the usual stable luster. She was an expert at concealing her feelings.

There was a note of forced gaiety in the small talk that followed. Conversation was irrelevant, trivial, and filled with awkward intervals of silence. During the tea in the library, a little more conviviality was restored.

Mengchia opened the letter from Prince Yi. It said nothing important—that the matter had not yet come up to the civil governor, but he would certainly take it up when it did, and of course he or his cousin-sister did not have to worry. Then he read the court bulletin, a four-page affair. It said that the Chief of the Salt Tax Bureau and two merchants of Yangchow had been arrested. The case had come up to the *taotai*, and the Governor, having heard about the impudence of the culprits, had instructed the *taotai* to make a complete and thorough report. Mengchia knew as much. Most probably the bulletin report had come from the Governor's office itself. The significance of the published report was that the Censorate was committed to vigorous action and no settlement out of court was possible. Having a personal interest in the case, Mengchia said he would call on Censor Liu and find out more about it.

"Are you sure that I shall not be involved?" asked Peony.

"I am quite sure. Leave that to me. And even if the prosecution should want information from you, you can say honestly that your husband never discussed these things with you—that you did not know."

Fu Nanto had completely disappeared. He failed to show up again at the tavern. She went to Tienchiao several times and he was nowhere to be found. She was once bold enough to inquire of the boxers, but the latter pretended not to know anything. She wondered what had happened to him. Was his wife so bad as to shut him up or force him to stay away?

Like a criminal returning to the scene of the crime, she went to the hotel where she had last seen him and loitered there, half expecting and half imagining that Fu Nanto would appear and walk into the shadow of the hotel entrance. If he should appear with another girl, she would go right into the fruit shop opposite and hide from his sight. Her eyes were glued to that dim rectangle of light defined by the door posts, over which hung a glass sign covered with cheap red characters: "Lien Sheng Chan" (the Inn of Continual Advancement), the most vulgar name conceivable. Commercial inns could not keep away from two basic themes for travelers: one, the search for a gushing fountain of gold, and two, the continual hope of ever-lucky official promotion.

The sensation returned to her of walking arm in arm with him on Hatamen Street, matching her steps to his jaunty, youthful stride. This sweet reverie held her mind suspended for minutes. Then her eyes came into focus as she saw a strange face, probably that of the hotel clerk, emerging in that gloomy rectangle under the glass sign. She panicked and turned on her heels and ran.

The days were getting hot. "Oh, well," she thought. She was not that much interested in him. But the question of what had happened to him kept coming up in her mind. Very soon she discovered there was another area of public amusement at Shishahai, just back of the Forbidden City. Partly out of ennui and partly out of a desire to find him, she went there.

The Shishahai was a region of cornfields and large lotus ponds under old, shady *yang* willows. The name indicated that there had once been "Ten Monasteries" on the "lake," but there was only one small temple left, unpretentious, in terra cotta, with two white circles for windows. The bodies of water here were connected with the North Lake inside the Forbidden City through a floodgate. It was pure imagination to say that the perfume in the air came from the powder and perfume of the imperial concubines in the Palace; but one was willing to concede the point when a cool breeze wafted in the sweet scent of lotus blossoms. Here were willow-covered walks and paths and squares where young boys and girls gathered to while away a summer afternoon. The wide, shady areas and the stretch of blue water made it popular in summer. The place hummed with the clanging of brass saucers of the sellers of cold drinks. Some entertainers had shifted to this area from Tienchiao, which, at this time of year, was scorchingly hot. At night, the place was bright with candlelight, bamboo lanterns, and large oil lamps throwing up black coils of smoke, their reflections caught in the water. One did not have to go home for supper, since the place was jammed with peddlers selling noodles, cold cuts, dumplings, and a dozen unusual delicacies, all afternoon long and all night, until midnight.

But Fu Nanto was nowhere to be found.

Jasmine saw how her sister's life had changed. In the past month or so, Peony sometimes went out at eleven in the morning. She often came back late for lunch. She went out again at five, spending half an hour plucking her eyebrows and looking into her mirror, and combing her hair. She was in a flurry when she went out and in a flurry when she came back. If Mengchia was there, she threw her jacket on the back of a chair and felt it her duty to devote an hour or so to him every day. But certainly her heart wasn't in it. Mengchia missed the warmth in her eyes, but said nothing.

"Do you know what you are doing to Tako?" Jasmine said to her one night.

Peony merely pouted her lips and did not reply.

You know without being told when a lover's ardor has cooled. It is in the coldnes of the eyes and the tone of the voice, in the absence of warmth or the desire to be close. When Mengchia came home now, there was no longer that bright, spontaneous light in her eyes. One day, as he sat at the dinner table waiting for her to turn up, he asked Jasmine, "Where is your sister?"

"Out somewhere. I wouldn't know."

"Was she like that at home?"

"Yes, sometimes."

Jasmine was silent, implying that she would rather not talk about it. She looked anxiously at his impassive face. Not the slightest trace of shock or annoyance was evident. "Well," she thought, "it is her story. She can tell it to him directly if she wants to." But she could not fathom what was going on in his mind.

The younger sister saw everything. Her sister's whirlwind romance with Mengchia did not surprise her, nor did her more recent moodiness. Calmly appraising all she saw, she kept silent. Once, Madame Chang Chih-tung had suggested a match for her, but she had refused. She also knew that there was no hope of marrying her cousin. These things were safely buried inside her, giving a firm sense of direction to her life, like a rudder to a boat, making navigation easy. Besides, Mengchia was irreproachable as far as she was concerned. Mengchia actually said things to her that he would not say to Peony. Even in the discussion of Nalan's love poems, they had reached a level of communication that was free from intrusion of personal feelings. And if she thought everything about him was perfect, including the gray in his temples, and knew that her heart palpitated a little whenever he came home, it was easy to believe that she adored him as a scholar, for his vast scholarship, his brilliant ideas, and his classic elegance of style. She was happy indeed to fit into the very comfortable position of a devoted and admiring girl disciple who happened to be his cousin, picking up stray bits of knowledge at the breakfast table, where they often met before Peony got up.

One day Peony went back to the wineshop at Tungtan Pai-lou. The woman cashier saw her, got down from her desk, and said, "Why, *kuniang*, you haven't been to see us for so many days. We thought you had left the city."

"No, why would I leave?" she replied. She thought the woman's question was strange. A sad smile hung upon her lips. She opened and shut her mouth again, but the woman had read her mind.

"Come here," she said, and whispered something in her ear.

Peony gasped as if time had suddenly been suspended. She put her hand to her mouth, horrified. With a feeling akin to shock and remorse, the full impact of what had happened dawned on her—the fearful consequences of a casual act. Fu Nanto had been arrested for killing his wife, and her maiden family had had him prosecuted. What really happened that day in that dark room nobody knew. It could well be that his wife, hurled with such force into the darkness by the powerful hand of a boxer, had crashed her head against something hard, perhaps one of the sharp iron bedposts. Now he was awaiting trial for manslaughter.

The woman cashier had given Peony the news, making it clear that she had nothing more to say, that she wanted no part of what had been going on between them. Out of the corner of her eyes, she saw Peony sinking down into a seat, still with open, wondering eyes. Just as silently, Peony rose again, pushed her chair back, and shuffled with her usual lazy steps out into the street.

Of course she could not help him; she had to stay out of the picture.

In the days following, she steeled her heart into thinking that, in the first place, it was an accident; in the second place, Fu Nanto had told her about the fights going on between himself and his wife before he met her; and in the third place, she had not even slept with him once, although she might have. But try as she would, she couldn't stop feeling guilty. She would wake up in the middle of the night with an uneasy, tremulous feeling, as if she had made a bodily contribution to the ruin of a family. Then her head cleared, and she was able to reassure herself that she was not to blame.

Mengchia was busy these days with preparations for celebrating the completion of the Peking-Shanhaikuan railway. As he felt Peony's remoteness, and her conscious efforts to disguise it, he had the uneasy feeling of walking upon slowly sinking ground, upon ice which still held, but with already detectable cracks and flaws. His eyes still brightened with joy when he saw her come home, but her response was strained and affected. Over her hung a veiled look, the look of sympathetic friendship, but it was like a heavy, still backwater, lacking the quick bubble of a spring.

As he came to know her in her most unguarded moments, his intense feeling for this devastatingly beautiful cousin was increased, instead of being diminished; but it had also turned outward and his first keen shock of delight in her person became a kind of protective love. To him she was as lovely as ever, but she began to worry him. He could see that she was walking upon clouds, fed by her own sensibility and imagination, searching for some ideal young hero, questing for some impossible golden fleece. He was reminded of how, just a year ago, she had yearned for him with such intensity. Now he saw clearly that she was feeling this same almost life-crushing yearning for someone else. He was fascinated; it was like watching a somnambulist walking toward the brink of a precipice. All he could do was to stand by and lend a quick, helping hand if she should ever need him. It was a good thing that she did not try to deceive him.

Jasmine could not understand this. Her stubborn loyalty to her sister made her tend to conceal what she knew from him. She knew a lot—little words escaping from Peony in unguarded moments, veiled looks at dinner, covert yawns in his company, her going out alone so often, her candid confidences, including things which would make an ordinary girl blush. These things which make up the stuff of gossip lay in a tabooed ground between her and Mengchia, partly because she wanted to protect her sister, who, after all, was responsible for her stay in Peking, a stay which she wanted very much to continue uninterrupted, and partly because they were things which an unmarried girl did not speak of with a man. On Mengchia's part, his intimate feelings for Peony were too personal for him to discuss with another person, even her own sister, and he was too proud to pry about the woman he loved. So a pall hung over the most important changes in the relationships of this family.

It was like watching a play in silence, during which the members of the audience were forbidden to express any feelings or compare their reactions until the curtain was down on the last act.

Then, too, in trying to understand this clan sister of his, Mengchia thought of her principally as youth burgeoning in love, tinged by love, as the first blush of the morning sun tinges every delicate petal of a blossoming rose. She was fully awakened at twenty-two when many women at thirty were not. But her love had also the mark of immaturity, of the sheer violence of youth; little did she know of the refinements of a more experienced, more esthetic enjoyment of sex. She could have love without love-play. It was like drinking a glass of wine and draining it at one gulp, instead of taking it in slow sips. It amused him that she had not responded to several suggestions of his to see the great court in the Audience Hall of the Palace when she first arrived; only later did she accede, upon his urging, with a startled afterthought, "Oh, yes, I must see the Palace." She would much rather have fun at Tienchiao. These were the limitations of youth, distorted by a personal frustration. She was, however, so dear to him now that whatever she did, he tried to see it from her point of view; he did not want her to be different.

One night, she slipped into the inner court about ten. She was about to enter the hexagonal door leading to her own room when she saw the light in his study. She went in, as she always did, to have a little chat. No doubt she still cared for him in a friendly way. Their eyes met for a moment in silence. Then he smiled and said, "Did you have a good time?"

"Very."

She went and sat on the edge of the couch and said, "Why do you work so hard? Why don't you relax?"

"Oh, I always have things to occupy myself with when I am alone."

"I am sorry," she said with a half sense of guilt for leaving him alone.

An awkward silence intervened. He made a gesture to kiss her, but she shook her head. She stood up, threw off her jacket, and curled up on the couch, as was her habit. He stopped for a second, then looked at her longingly and said, "You don't want to kiss me now?"

"No. You don't mind?"

"I don't," he said unconvincingly. "Now go to bed."

"Wish me good night."

"I wish you good night."

She went out by the rear door of the library, characteristically forgetting her jacket. Then she remembered it, turned back with a smile, and planted a fugitive kiss on his forehead.

He saw her disappear behind the door, her hair falling over her shoulders, like a dream phantom of tragic beauty. She exasperated him and infatuated him at the same time. His heart sank with a terrible gloom of loneliness.

What pained Mengchia most was the thought that he had thought of a way by which they could have got married now if she still loved him. By a simple change of family name, they could have done it. It was not unusual for one branch of the family to adopt the son of another branch, if it was without an heir. This was important in ancestral sacrifice, "to continue the altar fire." This *kuochi*, or "crossing the branch" among cousins could give Peony another family name if, for instance, she were formally adopted by Uncle Su Sueipo. Aunt Su was his mother's sister, and Peony would become a Su. No one had done this "crossing" except for ancestral worship and for inheritance of property; it had never been done just to satisfy convention in a marriage between cousins of the same family name.

He had thought about it while away on the trip, and had meant to tell her. It could be done, although it would have been unusual. Several times he was about to discuss it with her, but she had so cooled toward him that he had hesitated to say it. He buried the thought and never mentioned it again.

CHAPTER 14

September was approaching. The air palpitated with shuddering, browning leaves, warning them of the cold winter ahead, reminding them of the seasons pulsating in the trees' delicate veins, telling all creation to conserve, to forestall, to save, until spring should come again. The Western Hills and the parks of the city responded with a blaze of glory in red and purple and gold and burnt brown. The bones of the grass and trees grew brittle and the winds acquired a dry hiss instead of the muffled, orchestrated murmuring of summer. The crickets' song intoned from wall corners and stony cracks and beneath one's bed. On the hills, lambs grew heavy wool and Peony entered the saddest period of her life.

Mengchia was called daily for consultation with the Viceroy. A great ceremony was set for the fifteenth, when the diplomatic corps of the foreign nations would be invited to participate in the inauguration of the Peking–Shanhaikuan Railway.

Mengchia was going out at six o'clock to a dinner arranged by a British engineer. The latter was very anxious to introduce him to a few men friends of his. Mengchia had grown fond of the Englishman on their visit to the Ming Tombs last spring. Their conversation was halting when the Englishman's interpreter was not around, but while both men failed to communicate precise ideas, their despairing gestures and smiles and tremendous good will only strengthened the bond between them. At least, Mengchia had learned the phrase "got it," and the Englishman, on his part, had learned to say its equivalent in Chinese, *dungde*. So there was a great deal of *godit* and *dungde* when they talked. Their admiration for each other was mutual. The engineer's name, Peter Cholmeley, had curiously been transformed into "Mr. Dream Pear Cha" (Cha Meng-li), as his name card indicated. Cholmeley admired the intelligence of the mandarin—although he hadn't the ghost of an idea what a *hanlin* was—and particularly liked his wide-awake curiosity, his desire to learn, and the quickness of his understanding. The Chinese interpreter, who was from Shanghai, did not have a large enough vocabulary to explain what a member of the Imperial Academy meant, but told the Englishman that a *hanlin* was "big name, big name, Number One Topside." On his part, Mengchia both admired and studied this foreign man from across the ocean, fascinated by the fluffy, golden hair on his arms, most inconceivable for a Chinese, as well as by the freckles on his long, thin, sad face. He had never come so close to an Englishman before. Every gesture of his hands, every expression on his lips was something new and revelatory. His Jesuit friend, at least, had black hair, which was one thing less to understand.

Their close association developed when the engineer, hobbling about in his khaki shorts and boots, chatted with him as they walked on top of the Great Wall. All this—the Englishman's swift, sharp movements, his bodily strength for a scholar, the way he rolled his cigarette and kept it between his lips while talking, his quick, sharp commands to the foreman, and the fact that a scholar did not wear a long gown, made him cry out to high heaven to learn all about the foreign devils who built locomotives and telescopes and cameras and made such excellent maps.

Before going out to the Englishman's dinner, Mengchia said to Peony, "You were so good to come to Peking with me. I felt I had no right to do this, but we were madly in love and we couldn't help ourselves. Lately, I am afraid you have changed. . . ."

"No, we are just fond of each other as before, are we not?"

"I am. I realize that these things cannot be forced. They do not fit into patterns we set for ourselves. . . . Why did you never speak to me about your first love? . . . "

To his surprise, a deathly pale expression came over her face. Then her body shook and on her face was written an agony of despair. As he sat on the arm rest and bent down to touch her hair and face with infinite tenderness, she all of a sudden flung her arms around his neck and clung to him and broke down pitifully, sniffling and sobbing and boo-hooing like a small child.

"We belonged to each other. . . . They took him away from me." Her soul's anguish seemed to pour out in these brief words. Then she raised her pale face and said, "Pardon me. Be good to me. Help me."

It hurt him deeply to hear these words. She spoke almost like a child. In that moment, he understood. He understood why she could never truly love another person, himself included. When she disengaged herself, the front of his gown was wet. He had been brought immeasurably closer to her.

That evening, Mengchia brought his English friends to his home about ten o'clock, having sent word to the cousins that they were coming and that, moreover, it was all right for them to come out and meet them, according to foreign customs.

These foreigners were always immensely interesting to the sisters, who had seen a few missionaries in Hangchow. They always referred to them as *yangkueitse*, or "foreign devils," with a feeling of amusement, in the same way that little children were often referred to as *shiaokuei*, "little devils"—lively, mischievous, endearing, and devilishly clever.

The guests were received in the parlor, and after a short time, the sisters emerged, splendidly dressed in their "at home" black silks, without jewels. One of the guests had been in China for over a dozen years and was considered an expert at the Embassy. He was not averse to showing off his spoken Chinese to his compatriot and engaged the sisters in a lively conversation. He had an accent, but was really quite fluent. After tea, they were taken to see the library, and the Sinologist treated Mengchia and his woodblock editions with great respect. They were shown his collection of writing brushes, an antique inkstone, and one enormous volume, one of the few surviving books of the great Yunglo Library, which had been destroyed by fire. It was a beauty. The volume was eighteen inches high by nine and a half inches wide, handwritten with the best shining ink on heavy *shuan* paper, and bound in yellow brocade.

Jasmine's fair, round face and her serene poise made a strong impression on the guests. Dream Pear Cha, while unable to talk with her, glanced at her repeatedly as she sat discreetly, listening with demure eyes and not saying a word. She had that wholesome freshness of a girl of twenty. The Sinologist engaged the elder sister in conversation. Her eyes danced and she was frank and warm and completely at ease. All in all, Mr. Dream Pear Cha was taken with the two sisters and suggested to them that they should come along to the preceremonial run to Shanhaikuan.

Peony refused to go; but on the sixth of September Jasmine went with Mengchia to Shanhaikuan, where the Great Wall joined the China Sea. They had two wonderful days there, hiking over the nearby mountains to the beach. The Englishman had not thought the water too cold, and had taken an afternoon swim. Jasmine was neither shy nor demonstratively excited; and the Englishman kept remarking on her wonderful poise and dignity. It was a thoroughly enjoyable trip for her. She stood before the old, fortified gate and listened to Mengchia expounding the historical significance of the pass. The inscription of the tower said, "The Number One Pass of the World."

They came back after four days to find Peony in a state of nervous expectancy, anxiously awaiting their return.

On the eighth of September, two days after they had departed, Peony had received a telegram from Paiwei, in exactly six words:

T'A PING LA: NI SHU LAI
(He is ill: you come quickly)
(signed) PAIWEI

Not a word more. These words sunk into her with a metallic weight by their very brevity. She never had doubts that the "he" in the message referred to Chin Chu. It could be, of course, Joshui, Paiwei's husband, but there would be no need for the deliberate ambiguity in the text. Evidently, Paiwei thought it important enough to send a telegram, a mode of communication new in those days, and not yet in general use by the public. She had learned from Peony's letter how much she still loved Chin Chu, and thought it unpardonable if she did not let her know.

A thousand questions surged up and choked her; she could not think. Was it Chin Chu? Yes, it must be. Just how seriously was he ill, and what kind of illness? Was the message sent by Paiwei, or by her at his request? He must have desired her presence at the moment, or Paiwei would not have sent it. Then she remembered a phrase which Chin Chu had said in passing: "I am dying slowly, bit by bit." It couldn't be true. Things didn't happen that way, except in novels. These hypothetical possibilities went round and round her mind until she felt giddy.

A decision was easy to make when the heart dictated no other alternative. She sent a letter at once and went out to mail it herself, telling Paiwei that she was leaving at the first available opportunity, and enclosing a letter to Chin Chu, as follows:

Dearest,

I am coming to your side wherever you are, well or ill. Be comforted, my heart, I am coming and shall never leave you again. I am passing my days here like one half-asleep and all the foolishness I have committed on account of you. I have realized my mistake.

This is a hurried letter, as I shall be coming to you at the earliest possible date that I can get away. I want to say only three things here: First, please try to get well for my sake. I will do anything, give anything, if I can help you get well. Second, I am coming to your side. I am leaving Peking for good. The city where you stay shall be my city. I shall stay in the humblest shack and shall be the happiest person on earth if I know that you still love me as much as I love you. Let me be your friend, wife, mistress, whore—it does not matter.

And third, do not ever doubt my love for you, I beg you.

Yours for ever,
Peony

The days of waiting for her sister's return passed in a dream for Peony. She wanted only to tell Mengchia of her decision to go home and ask his help.

Mengchia and Jasmine returned to find her usually animated face grave and unsmiling. She showed Jasmine the message of six words from her friend.

"I am going home. I must, by the first available boat from Tientsin."

"What is all this?" asked Mengchia, sensing that something of great importance had happened.

It was going to hurt, she knew it.

"I cannot lie to you," she said. "I have been living an illusion. He is ill. I must go and I am going by the first boat. Will you help me?"

Mengchia knew without being told where this woman's heart belonged. Suddenly he had a feeling akin to hate. Why had she started the romance at all? Why did she want to come to Peking? Had all her words of endearment been lies? He remembered that once she had said to him that the trip to Peking was her "salvation."

"We will talk about it later," he said briefly and left for his room.

Jasmine forgot all the excitement of the trip and all the things she had wanted to tell her sister. It was Chin Chu, of course, she knew. How was this going to affect their lives, her own included? She knew her sister's impetuous nature; she had always had her way, even with their parents, and she knew Mengchia well enough to know that he would let Peony go if she really wanted to leave. She sensed almost everything that was going to happen—her sister's definite break with Mengchia and no possibility of her ever coming back. That much was certain. She felt angry, outraged, as Mengchia must have felt, at the betrayal of his love and devotion. All the time she was unpacking her own things and Mengchia's she felt a sense of disaster; her headstrong sister was going to do something which was just not right. When she ordered the bath for him, she was informed that the master was going out.

"He is going out?" Peony asked, puzzled.

"He is very upset," Jasmine answered. "Sister, you are acting crazy."

"I was never more sober. I know my own mind now."

"What are you going to do?"

"I am going to Chin Chu. He is ill. He is asking for me. Is that not enough?"

"But do you realize what you are doing to Tako?"

"I am sorry for him."

"What about me?"

"Why should it affect you?"

After the brief exchange of staccato sentences, each fraught with meaning, the sisters felt as if a great gulf had opened between them. Each was occupied with her own thoughts. At last, Jasmine said, "Why don't you have a bath?"

Peony looked up at her younger sister sharply and said, "Leave me alone."

"Really, after a bath, you will feel better and your mind will be clearer."

"Can't you leave me alone?" Then she checked herself. She

saw Jasmine getting out fresh clothes, and her heart softened. "Jasmine, you are wonderful. I admire your presence of mind. You'll make a wonderful wife for somebody."

"I know," she answered curtly, in a tone suggesting that she had heard it a hundred times before. "There!" She shoved a handful of underwear to her sister, with an injured expression.

Left alone, Jasmine realized the gravity of the situation. She alone seemed to see all the implications. One way or another, her sister was involving herself tragically—falling in love with her cousin-brother, then changing her mind to go back to Chin Chu again. What was to come of it? What could come of it? She was surprised at her own tears when she felt how deeply her sister was hurting Mengchia. She had come to know him so well, and greatly admired in him certain mature qualities of intellect and character which her sister did not see. By feminine intuition she knew that the cause of her sister's falling out of love with her cousin was the difference in age. Peony was altogether too flamboyant, flitting around too much on the surface of emotions, but he was too great a man to be played with by a girl seeking passion, not love. Peony had confused the two. It was these mature qualities that Jasmine admired in the man almost twenty years her senior. She did not blame her sister. No girl could be expected to remain satisfied with such an illicit relationship.

The full measure of Mengchia's maturity, the stature of the man, was evident when he returned for supper after an entire day with the Viceroy, looking as if nothing had happened.

They left him alone in his study, busying himself with some official documents. When the sisters saw his heavy concentration they felt relieved. At this moment, he was pursing his lips, meditating, his writing brush lying upon the inkstone. The habitual, happy smile and light of playful thought in his eyes were unmistakable. Peony had been the first to come into the study and had taken up her position in an armchair. Seeing him occupied, she took a volume and said not a word. When the younger sister came in, Peony looked up with a finger across her mouth. He picked up his brush, and rapidly wrote some remarks on a document. With a sense of happy accomplishment, he pushed back his chair.

"Let's go for supper," he said. The amazing self-control of the man! Peony's eyes caught the familiar, bright look whenever he glanced at her. She felt a vast sense of relief.

He set the tone of the conversation by telling Peony about their trip. The younger sister joined in with her own remarks about the Englishman.

"The most unbelievable thing about these foreign devils," she said, "is the hair, the HAIR, about their chests and arms"— The word *hair* was forcibly expelled with due emphasis.— "Their complexion, nose, color of eyes are all bizarre. There is always something too much on their faces, up and down, up and down. The unbelievable thing, however, is that when they speak or laugh, they are just like we are. Isn't it interesting? One engineer rolled up his sleeves to show me the curly black hair all over his arms—you should have seen!—and then he laughed exactly like a schoolboy. And the way they look at a young girl or woman is what you see at Tungan Bazaar, except that we say *yow!* and they whistle. When I had to jump down over a high step, near the Great Wall, two of them competed in lending me a hand. . . . "

"One fellow," added Mengchia, "slapped her bottom after she got down, and the other spoke to him in a sharp voice. We didn't understand what he said, but I am sure he was giving the other man a sharp rebuke."

When they were back in the study, he opened by remarking casually to Peony, "It is most unfortunate that you will be missing the execution of Shueh, your ex-husband's chief. It will take place at Tienchiao on the seventeenth. I just learned about it at the office. Two Yangchow salt merchants—I don't recall their names—have been sentenced to exile. I am sure they are some poor devils bought off to take all the blame and serve as scapegoats. The real culprits have escaped scot-free with their millions.

Of course, their firms have to pay a heavy fine, which does not hurt them too much."

"Nothing is said about my ex-husband?" Peony asked.

"Not so far as I can see from the court bulletin."

Just as casually, he fixed an intent eye on his cousin-sister and said, "I have booked a ticket for you, leaving Tientsin in a few days. It is your wish to leave as soon as possible, is it not?"

Peony tried to discern in him some trace of sarcasm, but she knew there wasn't any. His tenderness, his love for her, was unshaken.

"Yes," she managed to utter, and looked at him with silent gratitude.

He rose, fumbled about with his papers, fished out an envelope, and said, "Here's a banker's check drawn upon a local bank in Shanghai. You will need it. Tomorrow I shall buy some deer horn and ginseng. Whatever your friend's illness is, they will be useful. The best are always from the north. They can't get such quality in the south."

He saw his cousin-sister's head fall upon the arm of her chair and he touched her gently. She looked up with almost a frightened expression, an expression of surprise.

"Peony, your friend is my friend," he said briefly.

It had been easier than she had thought possible. If he had been another man, she would have said that he was wonderful. But she was used to that ever-tender look of his and was not displeased to note that the spell she had cast upon him was not broken. She managed to say, "I do not know how to thank you. With you I have no pride any more. Perhaps in some future time, I shall be able to repay you for all that you have done for me. . . ."

Then he sat down beside her, talking of irrelevant things. She had a feeling that a chain was being forged to hold her forever to him, a chain that nothing in time or space could break. It was too strong.

Jasmine observed all this silently. She forgot about her disapproval of her sister's affair with Mengchia, and wished that she would change her mind and remain, instead of embarking upon another fatuous, impossible adventure. She was at her best in concealing her feelings, so she said nothing.

The next day was spent in shopping. Peony was occupied with the thought of getting to Hangchow as quickly as possible. All her friends and relatives would be expecting gifts from her from Peking. She had in mind, particularly, presents for her father and mother and her little nephew Ren-Ren, whom she loved very much. She had already bought a beautiful, imported jewel box of a very intricate design for Paiwei.

After the siesta, Mengchia told her that he would be able to accompany her on a shopping trip, since he knew the best places to shop.

"I thought you had to go back to the office."

"No. I got everything in the morning. I want to spend the last afternoon with you. It is our last day together. And I may not see you again for a long time."

She smiled contentedly. She knew that their friendship would last as long as they lived. When the fires of passion had burned out, his love, which amounted to an adoring fascination for her, would always remain. Her heart warmed toward this man with such a self-denying love, and she regretted she could not reciprocate.

They came home, their carriage loaded with parcels. They had been able to secure eight ounces of the best ginseng from Shangtang and four ounces of deer horn from Heilungkiang. Back in the library, Mengchia again examined these items critically by their color and smell, and declared himself satisfied. At the last moment, he sent Liu An to obtain dried snake gall bladder for reducing fever and restoring the digestive system.

All this meant a great deal of packing, which, with Jasmine's help, lasted till half-past eleven that night. In spite of her anxiety, Peony was very happy.

Peony knew, and Mengchia half suspected, that this was to be their last night together. Jasmine had tactfully left them alone.

He talked very much like a retired lover who had withdrawn

in favor of another man whom he had never seen. Ever since the day when she told him about the affair with Fu Nanto, they had not slept together. His *amour-propre* prevented him from imposing on her, and he knew that even passion was a physical quantity which, like water, dries up in one direction when it is directed to another. He had even refrained from kissing her on the lips because she had twice rejected him.

That night, while she was lying on the library couch, he took the opportunity to say to her in a tender, but dispassionate tone: "Sometimes I understand you, and sometimes I don't. Not entirely."

"What do you mean?"

"Because you have not told me everything."

"Do you think I was lying to you when I fell madly in love with you?"

"I have thought about it a great deal. You have acted throughout like a coquette."

Peony made a hot denial.

"I will be very frank with you. I said you have acted like one, changing your love once every so often. It cured me of my madness. I began to think a great deal, as we think about something we do not understand. Frankly, I thought you were a bad girl in the usual sense of the word, enormously attractive to men, but without character."

"You still have that opinion of me?"

"Let me finish. Remember, you never spoke of Chin Chu to me. When you broke down the other day, crying pitifully at the mention of your first love, I saw the light. It must be a wonderful thing, a marvelous thing, the love you still feel for your lost lover. I do not think of you as a coquette. I admire the beauty of your passion for him. That is the first thing I want to say to you. The second thing is that, although you have changed, I haven't. No matter what you do and where you are, you shall remain the most beautiful thing in my soul, the purest and most shining fiber in my being. I do not know how to say this. But you will understand. You may leave me in body, but you are still in me, in my heart. You will never leave me. I shan't even try to forget you. It can't be done. My spirit shall be with you always. You walked into my life and gave it a light and a power I had not known before. You asked me several times why I did not go out and amuse myself. The fact is, whenever I thought of doing so, I thought of you. You shall remain in my heart, the one and only one. I said to myself, there is no substitute for Peony. . . ."

All of a sudden, there was a catch in his voice. He was silent a moment as he tried to control himself. When he spoke again, his voice trembled. She heard the words wrung out of his tormented soul, words which she was to remember a long, long time, lingering in her memory whenever she was alone:

"*Sweetheart, you took me to heaven, then you threw me out. I accept my luck. I have nothing to say.*"

It sounded like a cry from the depths of his heart, a song of eternal remorse.

An irresistible impulse rose in him, as he looked at her face, her adorable face, and he pleaded with his lips for a kiss. She looked at him seriously now, the grayish-brown light in her pupils shifting and flickering, and she drew her face close to his and pressed on him one of those reckless, abandoned kisses which he used to know so well. Something joined them together in heart and mind at that instant, and as he held her tightly, breathlessly, he heard her faltering breathing and felt the hot tears trickling down her face. At that supreme moment, their souls were united, and in it, too, were united their past and their future, all that had gone before and all that was to come. Time was deprived of its meaning. She leaned back on the couch, and he leaned over her. Her head was thrown sideways, while their hands and mouths sought each other and remained locked for a few precious minutes.

"We shall be friends forever," he said.

"Yes. A little bit more than friends, don't you think?"

With this they parted. The love which was sealed at that moment needed nothing else. It was a love which rose above young passions. For Peony, it was something new.

Unfortunately, Peony's train the next day was the one which was being used to celebrate its first official run. All the important ministers were present, including two Manchu princes and the entire diplomatic corps. While Mengchia had no official duty to perform at the ceremony, he felt it his duty to stand by Grand Councilor Chang Chih-tung, as he received the felicitations of the envoys. He ran between the grand councilor and the sisters, who had seated themselves in a compartment on the train.

A number of mandarin hats with peacock feathers were fluttering around the station platform. The mandarins, swathed in deep lavender brocade jackets and black silk boots on white soles, lent an air of great dignity to the occasion. They wore flat-top black official hats, broadening upward, with a tuft of peacock feathers at the back; and their various ranks were easily distinguishable by the small button at the top, made of either crystal, coral, or precious gems. A rope had been looped around the platform, with imperial guards in green and red standing by importantly, so that for the moment it looked like a regular court scene. The foreign envoys were conspicuous in their long, narrow striped pants, a most ungainly costume to Chinese eyes. They were joking and laughing among themselves, but on the whole, they managed to convey a sense of gravity and dignity which matched that of the mandarins.

Prince Chun read the formal speech. Long horns were blown and drums were beaten. The band, with flutes and mouth organs predominating, played the popular tunes of the day; to foreign ears the high, thin melodies sounded more like bridal music than military.

At a whistle from the shining new locomotive, the crowd started to applaud wildly. The band struck up a strange new melody that had been composed especially for the occasion. Today, everything was new, including the railway guards' and conductors' uniforms and the red flag of the signal man. Mengchia had deserted the ceremony during Prince Chun's speech and stolen up to the car where the sisters were.

"You'd better go down now," said Peony to her sister and

cousin. They were interrupted by a Manchu princess in a tall, black headdress squeezing past them through the corridor. Mengchia said a few hasty words to Liu An, who was accompanying Peony on the train, and would see her safely to the boat. After much pushing and jostling he and Jasmine were able to make their way to the platform. They looked back and saw Peony's smiling face in the window, happy and excited. The engine started with a blast and quickened its puffing, like a man gathering breath for a long run. The shining blue express chugged slowly out of the station. Peony waved a hand and was soon lost amidst a row of fluttering hands and handkerchiefs.

Three days later, Liu An came back to report that the young mistress had been safely put aboard the S.S. *Sinkiang*. "We had to stay overnight at the hotel, and didn't get on board until this morning, when the boat was ready to sail. . . . What is it?" the servant asked. "Isn't she coming back—not at all? I thought she was just going for a visit."

Mengchia's eyes closed just a second, as if he had been hit in the face. Then he asked in a level tone, "Did she tell you that?"

"Yes, sir. She said I was to take good care of the master and Mistress Jasmine."

"Did she have a good cabin and was everything all right?"

"Yes. And furthermore, there was a very nice young man going on the same boat who promised to look after her during the voyage. He seemed a very decent young man, a college student, I understand."

He fumbled in his coat pocket and produced a name card.

Mengchia read the name, and sighed deeply. "Oh, Peony!" he muttered under his breath.

BOOK TWO

CHAPTER 15

When they returned from the station, Mengchia and Jasmine entered the court, and were suddenly overwhelmed with a feeling of desolation. A lonely magpie, cawing on the black lichen-coated roof, accented the silence in the house. As they went inside, Chouma was passing through the hall with an armful of laundry.

"I have picked up the sheets," she said to Jasmine. "If Mistress approves, I shall take down the curtains, too. You won't be moving to Mistress Peony's room, will you?"

"No, why should I? I shall keep mine."

As she walked into the library she caught sight of two letters and a bulky package lying on the desk. At once she recognized her sister's hand. Of the two letters, one was addressed to herself, the other to Tako.

What was it that Peony wanted to say which she could not have said in person? She handed the letter and the package to Mengchia. His features were tight, his eyebrows twitched once or twice, always the sign of intense concentration in him.

A deathly silence descended upon the room, as each took his letter and sat in one of the easy chairs below the north window.

Dear Sister:

I am not coming back. Our paths lead us apart. What I am doing may appear strange to you, and I am aware that Tako may be hurt. He still loves me, and I feel an infinite pain in leaving him. You may help him to get over his passion for me, but I do not think that he will completely erase me from his memory. Why must it be so? I have learned a great many things about myself in the past year, but the only thing that can never change is my love for Chin Chu. I have no control over myself. Tako has been wonderful in his understanding. The only thing I can say is that if I hurt him, I did not, and do not, mean to.

Your sister has been unfortunate. Was it my fault that I could not marry Chin Chu, and married that lout, and was it my fault that I loved our cousin who cannot marry me? I do not know why I must say these things to you now. Perhaps I want to justify myself in your eyes.

Believe me, I feel an infinite pain for Tako. When I am gone, take good care of him. I am happy, yes, immensely happy, to go back to Chin Chu. Whatever fate has in store for me, I do not care. Love and pain, love and sadness are always inseparable. You are younger, and perhaps when love catches up with you, you will know.

Your elder sister,
Peony

She let the letter fall upon her lap. She looked at Mengchia, the open letter in his hand, and was overcome with a feeling of pity for him and sadness for herself. She never saw a face so crushed and yet so angry at the same time. He seemed to be aware of her watching him, and averted his glance quickly, squinting downward. Something was fighting for control in his mind as his lips compressed into a quivering silence. Veins were throbbing in his temples. In the next instant, he looked up as the tight lines softened around his lips.

"Well?" he asked.

Jasmine looked at him intently for a second, before she said, almost too coolly, "I apologize for my sister. She is sorry for what she has done. . . . Here, do you want to read it?"

She had stood up. She shoved the letter into his hand before he could answer, and walked through the library door to her own room.

He felt relieved to be alone, and admired Jasmine's wonderful tact. He had read Peony's letter to him, a brutal note, contrasting with the most graceful expressions, like the backward glint of a leopard slithering away. Why was it necessary for her to be so hard and unsparing since she was going away? Her words had the icy hardness of a kiss of death.

Dear Tako:

With infinite sadness of heart, I am writing you this note because I do not have the courage to say these things to you in person.

I know you are the only person capable of a great and unique understanding, and I pray that you will understand me, your unlucky cousin-sister Peony.

I cannot lie to you. I do not want to deceive you. I cannot tell you why or at what moment the brutal fact surged into my consciousness and my soul.

I do not love you, and shall never want to see you again.

I loved you once, madly, blindly, with all the passions in my heart, but I suppose it was the novelty and the fascination of the unknown. Now that I know you, I have awakened and realize that what I regarded as love was merely admiration for the man who changed my life and taught me to laugh.

I still admire and adore you as a man and thinker who breaks the bounds of Neo-Confucian Puritanism and teaches every man and woman to live and fulfill his instincts, according to the natural goodness of his heart. This I owed and still owe to you.

I understand your sorrow, for I feel it, too. But I do not love you as you love me, and I cannot force myself to show what I do not feel.

Forget your cousin-sister Peony. Do not come to me, for I shall disappear definitely from your life.

In sadness,
Younger-sister Peony

There was a wanton quality in the letter which he could not quite account for. It was like listening to a beautiful symphony orchestra that was suddenly disrupted by a monkey, leaping across the stage with a raucous screech. A bitterness surged up in Mengchia and his throat felt tight. The crash of his dream left him stunned and defenseless.

What puzzled Mengchia was the sharp cutting stab in her last sentence. He knew well the cooling of her ardor in the past months. What was the necessity of saying all this after their parting? He had, indeed, made every allowance for her behavior; he thought he had understood her. Here was candor without warmth, betrayal without apology, parting without tears. It suddenly brought to his mind his first experience of love; his desertion by the girl who had changed her mind to marry a rich husband, with the same animal hardness of feeling. It only established more firmly his conviction that the first law of womanhood is the complete possession of a man—to marry him, and then to direct, guide, and dispose of him as she sees fit. In destroying his love, Peony had destroyed more than his love. She had revived in him the misogynist reflections that woman will claw and tear to obtain possession of a secure home in which to raise her young—that hers is the same instinct essentially as the nest-making instinct in birds—and that in so doing, woman is not necessarily heartless, but is only obeying the first laws of an ageless instinct. The wise confirmed bachelor is the cunning fish which takes what bites it can and escapes the wide-spreading net of sucking mouths and hypnotizing eyes.

His eyes caught a postscript, written in haste, contrasting with the neat and graceful lines of the letter itself. It was evident that she had added this, perhaps late last night after the crushing, burning, revealing kiss which had surprised them both.

> P.S. Forgive me. Forgive me for everything. What I have written, I have written. Here I am giving you my diary, a part of my innermost self. Perhaps it will help you to understand me better.

Mengchia left the large package unopened, as he considered it of no real importance. If it contained an explanation, he wanted to read it coolly and objectively, as if it were a historical document or someone's diary of a century ago, without the personal involvement he felt so keenly at the moment. Why did she have to say, "I shall disappear *definitely* from your life?" Decisive, cold, and ruthless. He felt as if he were reading the letter of an accomplished and experienced courtesan, that Peony must have written such letters before, in breaking off a relationship she no longer wanted. The tools of the trade. The fact was, she was clearly leaving him to seek another love, to start another romance. He would read the diary in three or four days, perhaps a week afterward. He needed to take complete stock of himself and regain his old equilibrium.

"Why are you looking at me like that?" asked Jasmine at dinner the following day.

"Am I? I am sorry," said Mengchia. "I did not mean to."

Mengchia's eyes had a look of deep concentration, so searching and penetrating that a less level-headed and self-assured girl would have winced. Jasmine saw the torture in his soul, his absorption in himself, and the terrible loneliness behind his steady gaze.

"Aren't you thinking of my sister?"

"Hardly. Of womanhood. Of the nature of woman. I am sorry I was looking at you to find . . ."

"Find what?"

"To find traces of deceptive womanhood in you."

"Did you find any?" Her glance, wan and tired and bitter, switched away from him. "You might look harder. . . . "

"I am terribly sorry."

"Then do not judge me by my sister." She bent her head and blew her nose in a handkerchief which she had pulled out from the jacket button under her armpit. Then she turned a serene face toward him, as if nothing had happened.

"Do you want me to go away?" she asked. "I can always go back, you know."

"Do you want to?"

"No," she said and added more softly, "unless you want me to. You have read my sister's letter to me. She hopes I will stay.

I like Peking so much. I like this house and you and my own room and the benefit of learning so much from you. No one could ask for more. If you want me to stay, I will. I want to. My sister . . . have you read her diary? . . . No? . . . I know she keeps one. I do not pry. . . . " She said the last words proudly.

Mengchia felt on the defensive. "Then I beg you to stay . . . Please do not misunderstand me. I have a definite feeling . . . it will be different." He cocked his ears.

"What is it?"

"I thought I heard her voice, your sister's. I must be crazy."

"It's natural, after she has been in the house so long. Sometimes I hear her voice, too. Last night, I woke up in the middle of the night, and was going to call to her, then suddenly remembered that she was gone. . . . But why haven't you read her diary?"

"I don't want to. Not for the present. I want to feel sufficiently remote from her when I read it."

She continued to eat her dinner, and then burst out angrily, "The cook is getting impossible!" She pressed a bell and said to the boy, "Take this soup away. Tell the cook not to serve this dishwater. Isn't there better stock?"

The cook appeared a moment later, hardly daring to look straight at the young mistress. She gave him no chance to explain. "Don't think you can get away with spoiled fish while I am here, however you cover it up with ginger and vinegar. Just look at this. . . . "

"I bought it at the market this morning. . . . " explained the cook weakly.

Jasmine scarcely heard him. "The master will be eating in for the next three or four days, lunch and supper. I see the eggplant terrine is all gone. Have some more made, or buy some at Tungan Bazaar. Remember, the master loves it."

Turning to Mengchia after the cook had gone, she said, "He is crazy. Because we were away and the house was upset last week, all the servants are getting slack. . . . Only Chouma is going about as usual. She picks up all the soiled things without being told. I like her very much. Have you seen the curtains she washed and ironed and hung up in Peony's room?"

Without his knowing it, Mengchia's face had relaxed. It was good to hear her feminine gibberish.

"Let's have tea in the study," he said.

It was their first evening alone together. The atmosphere was so new and yet so old. He felt he had never really *looked* at her carefully, and he surveyed her anew, even though he had seen a thousand times before her direct, open, clear eyes and the dimple appearing and disappearing at the corner of her mouth.

"How do you know I love eggplant terrine?"

Jasmine smiled contentedly. "A woman sees things. I can't imagine your living alone. You wouldn't know what you were eating, would you?"

Mengchia basked in all this womanish concern. He could not resist the feeling of pure contentment and peace that the younger sister's presence was giving him. It seemed so right for her to be sitting there with him, erect in her chair with her legs close together, coy and demure, so different from her sprawling, languorous sister. Her voice was delicate and low, without the bell-like jingle of Peony's. Between her sips of tea, she would raise a hand and with slender fingers carefully adjust a brooch on her hair. The general contour of her face and the proportions of her features bore a close family resemblance to Peony's, but the dreamy remoteness of her sister's eyes was not there; Jasmine seemed like a purified version of Peony.

"Something has changed in this room. What is it?" he asked.

Jasmine smiled. "Haven't you noticed? This morning when you were out of the house, Chouma and I switched the curtains. I found the blue satin bedpiece there." She pointed to the neatly folded bedding in blue and white on the couch. "Don't you think the blue is nicer? I always love blue. The old violet one is being washed. Do you want it back?"

Mengchia remembered how fond Peony had been of violet, especially for her pajamas.

"No. It's pretty there. I thought the room had changed—it looks sunnier."

After they had had their tea, Jasmine asked, "Do you want to work now? If you would like to be alone, I'll go back to my room."

"No, unless you want to. I am so used to having you sisters around. It can be very lonely at times."

"Then I will have some charcoal added and just sit here and read. This afternoon I felt lonely in my room, too, since my sister is gone."

For the first time he enjoyed a calm and peace which he had not felt in a whole year, almost as if he were a ship entering a harbor after buffeting a night of storm.

The sense of personal humiliation which Peony had inflicted still smarted in Mengchia. He discovered, to his surprise, that he had not stopped thinking of her and was calculating the days when she would be in Shanghai or back in Hangchow. He would never trust another woman again, and found relief in the cynical idea that all women were alike, that what had happened to him was merely what he should have expected. Still his heart palpitated when in his mind's eye he saw Peony's smiles and heard her voice, and he had an overpowering sense of her absence, of hollowness on returning home.

"The bitch has left me. I have lost all."

Jasmine saw this restlessness in him, and inwardly pitied him, but she said nothing. On the third night, he said to her after supper, "I am going out."

"Work?"

"No, just to call on a friend."

He wanted to convince himself of the hollowness of woman's love, and savagely set off for the Pata Hutung, to find solace in a woman's embrace, and at the same time wreak the vengeance of his spirit on all womanhood. It would be interesting to bring love to its lowest animal level and dissociate it from all sentimentality. But it was not convincing. He went again the following night, for in spite of himself, he always found a human response; the prostitute he slept with was also a person, with warmth in her affection, capable of intense attachments. Some of them were, in fact, weak and silly and begged him to visit them again. Try as he might, love, even base, bought love, could not be a purely physical thing for him. He could not stop thinking of Peony as he had first seen her on the boat—sincere, frank, sensitive to all the fine things in nature, filled with a joyousness for living, a unique spirit different from all the other women he had ever known.

He stopped going to the Pata Hutung. Busy or idle, his mind had only one thought: Peony. He tried to go out and meet more people, interest himself in official matters, but it was no use. Every minute of the day, she was with him. He tried to think evil of her—that she was cold, and ruthless, and cruel—but it was of no help. His head tried hard to find reasons for forgetting her, but his heart felt differently. Physically, he felt that his heart was bleeding, that this love was like a throbbing pain which he felt all the time. Then he tried to convince himself both that she loved him and that she did not love him. Each view was convincing and then, completely unconvincing. He felt that in our deepest emotions, we do not know our own mind—perhaps until a crisis comes. Yes, she liked to run after young men. What did that prove? Passion and real love are two different things. . . . In this state of suspension, he simply couldn't get her out of his mind. He developed the ability to deal with important matters and be thinking of her at the same time. At night, when Jasmine had retired, he lay awake. She was definitely gone. The song of eternal remorse recurred to his mind: *"You took me to heaven, then you threw me out."* He stretched out his arms in the dark and knew that she was not there. He silently called her name and knew that there would be no answer. He was seized with a terrible loneliness in his soul. This happened the first night and every night. There was no reprieve. Then he knew that he was doomed to feel like this for the rest of his life; from the well of loneliness there would be no escape. And he knew that there was no use writing her. What good would it do?

He knew then that he would never be able to reach the point at which he could read her diary dispassionately as he had hoped to. It was Jasmine's feminine curiosity that urged him to do it. She saw the package unopened and tucked away on a shelf behind his desk, with the white twine around it still intact.

"Why, are you afraid to read it?"

Mengchia was defensive. "No, I just thought I would let it cool off a little. I hate to be upset. I should not be able to be objective."

"Why don't you let me read it? I am her sister and am dying to read it. And I can be more objective than you because I know her better."

"You read it for me, then."

Jasmine threw a square, direct glance at him. "She wanted you to read it. And I would rather that you did. Face it, and you will feel better."

"Why do you say that?"

"You don't get rid of a mystery by leaving the mystery unsolved. I am sure my sister wasn't bad. She was just born differently from me."

She took the package from the shelf and placed it in front of him and said, "There! I shall leave you alone. And if there are things in it that you do not understand, things about my family or her past, you can ask me."

Mengchia thought it most unusual for a young girl like Jasmine to take such an attitude, and as he saw her disappearing behind the library door, he felt compelled to admire her consummate tact and intelligence.

The entries were, with rare exceptions, undated, but it was fairly easy to establish the approximate dates by the events referred to. Some of the entries recalled their first meetings, but all of it was apparently written in the last year in Peking. These were desultory jottings-down of her thoughts as she struggled with her own mind. Some of them occupied three or four pages; and again, there seemed to be months when the diary was untouched. The phrase "my love" and "he" were often confusing, referring as often to Chin Chu or Fu Nanto as to himself. Thus, an entry of one sentence was totally useless: "Oh, he is wonder-

ful!" or "I know I shall never love another person in this life."
Whom was she speaking of? Reading the diary was like living on
a planet with four or five moons, so that he did not know, and
probably Peony herself did not, which moon was "kissing" her
with its silvery light through her window. Some of it was shock-
ingly frank, some of it showed her capacity to analyze herself
ruthlessly.

"As I grew up, and learned many things about adults, I decided to live every moment intensely until I should be tired out
or have no more feeling. Yes, I am a rebel. I always was a rebellious and capricious child and nobody could make me do what
I did not want to do." . . . "The one thing I crave is total and
entire liberty. Is it because my father is so severe and authorita-
tive that I long so for it?" . . . "The stars look down upon me
and I have no rest. I can feel them—like his wonderful sparkling
eyes looking at me, and then they seem very close." . . . "I do
not know why I am so weary this spring. The breeze coming
through the window touches me like a lover's caress."

Of her relations with Mengchia, she was astonishingly explicit and often contradictory, showing the searching torments
and conflicts in the depths of her mind. One passage is typical:

"Today I went out with him to Tienchiao. I imagine he went
on account of me. He is a disappointment. All right, I am low-
brow (*shialiu*) as he says, but I love it. There was the riffraff, the
jugglers, bear shows, and children running around with running
noses, and all the dust and noise. There was a father half naked,
standing on the belly of a young girl twelve or thirteen, her legs
crooked backward and her whole body bent like a bow on the
ground, her face and neck stretched tense in pain, and her
mother going around collecting cash from the bystanders. I
could cry. But he seemed quite composed. Is he getting old?
All right, these are the things that touch me. I love the swirl and
bubble of all this *life*, of everybody so full of life. I love the
tragedy and the vitality of the crowds. Didn't he see it? Then
we went over and sat at a teahouse in the open. I started talking
with one of the young waiters. I suppose the waiter took me for
his mistress because I was asking about the most popular 'drum-

singers' and I got to talking with him about a lot of things. Men are always friendly talking to a young girl. I ran off with the young waiter when a magnificent blind minstrel singer passed by, singing to a guitar in a throaty voice and the crowd gathered around him. The man stood up, resting one of his legs on a stump. 'Brothers, uncles, and aunts, listen to your *laotse*, your daddy, sing.' The crowd laughed and roared. He was tall like a Manchurian and wore a wisp of a beard like a pair of brackets, his face shining like a sheet of bronze and powerful and strong. With his open, sightless eyes, he seemed heroic. You could see his stomach heaving as he opened his powerful throat. He was singing 'Chaochun Leaving the Fort.' That face, that voice, combined with his total blindness, made him look tragic and very impressive. But he didn't care. You could see that he didn't care! What a man! They say the blind make better musicians; perhaps it is true. You feel you could follow such a man to the ends of the earth. What caused his blindness? Perhaps some romantic adventure? Who knows? I was so enthralled. I must have stood there listening to the singer for twenty minutes, and forgot all about Mengchia. I came back chattering with the young waiter. I thought he might be jealous. But he was not a bit. Oh, he is magnificent!—I mean Tako, not the Manchurian singer." . . .

"I want to be all to Mengchia, and I want Mengchia to be all to me. Perhaps he may wonder why ours has not been a platonic friendship, a communion of two spirits on a high intellectual level. Since coming to live with him, I have, unlike Jasmine, purposely kept away from discussions of ideas and books with him. I am so afraid that I may become one of his girl disciples, that a teacher-student relationship might replace that of lovers. I want to meet him on a level of equality: he a complete man and I a complete woman. In the field of ideas and learning, I can never be his equal." . . . Then, further on, a very curious note: "Is he capable of physical passion, as I feel when I am with him, of a total surrender of the body and obliteration of the spirit? I must have shocked him during our first night at Tunglu. I could see it on his face. I wanted to be a whore to him, giving myself in total surrender. I wanted him to abuse me, penetrate me, destroy me. And what was he doing? He is too refined for me. Lots of fireworks and no action. It's all love-play, but not love—all cerebral. I don't need love-play. Now what woman wants a cerebral lover? His greatest pleasure seems to be esthetic. He says love is not just a piston-and-cylinder affair. Maybe, but— " . . . "I do not understand love, the greatest mystery on earth, a mixture of the sublime and the ridiculous, the animal and the spiritual. Is such a thing possible? Is there love without physical passion? What woman does not want to be destroyed by the man she loves, to be entered into and torn inside out, to be ravaged? Am I a bitch? But I am." . . . "Our two levels can never meet. I have discovered my mistake. I do not mean that he is not passionate. He is. But how do you like to see your lover smoking and chatting naked in bed while you burn?" . . . About Fu Nanto: "Love is physical. That day when I saw him climb out of the ditch, his face and clothing splattered with mud, he conveyed a wonderful feeling of youth and physical power for me. I laughed at his folly, jumping into the open sewer because I told him to. The thing that I cannot forget is his jogging, jaunty steps as we turned toward the Tung-tan Pailou. His quick, alert steps, his immense shoulders, his muscular arm gripping me until it hurt. I was so aroused that if his wife had not intervened, I knew I would certainly surrender. Against my wish, and my verbal denials, I was leading him on. I discussed this with Mengchia, and he agrees with me to a point. He said that the sex appeal of a woman to a man is *entirely* physical, and the reverse is true for woman. Where does this get us?" . . . "I maintain that the splendor of love, its beauty, and even the ardor of its longings are possible only when the lovers are separated or thwarted and our mind and imagination play the devil with our senses and work up a kind of hypnotizing vision of love. Is there love without sadness, without longing? The longing is the love, as I know from my love for Chin Chu. Would I love him so much if he were living daily with me as my husband? Confess it, Peony, be honest with yourself." . . . "Love is the mother of tragedy, of the tragic spirit.

Or else it becomes a shallow farce or a three-meals-a-day affair. As to why it is so, I do not know. I must ask Mengchia about this point one day. Perhaps I shall be able to love him again when I am separated from him, when I shall have lost him." . . . Again: "Who in the world wants to read about legitimate love? All the great love stories of history have an illicit element in them. The moment the bride enters the sedan chair toward the bridegroom's home, the novel abruptly ends, and it is just as well, because the reader is not interested any more. True fishermen are more concerned about the big fish that got away than over those they have caught."

A more philosophic note bore the underlined heading: "*The Lopsided Universe*. It is true that the universe comes from the balance and interplay of *yin* and *yang*, the negative and the positive. But it is equally true that the universe is constantly in a lopsided state. Either the *yin* dominates the *yang*, or vice versa. All activity comes from imbalance, from pull in one direction. Hence love means sorrow, for love is a pull of one being toward another of the opposite sex. I know Mengchia loves me with all the force of passion and emotion with which I love Chin Chu. Hence the tragedy. Rarely in a family or a state is a perfect balance established. Hence the quarrels, disloyalties, hatreds, wars, and rebellions. In nature, the changes of season, the clouds and rains and storms and snows are due to this lopsided state of one force overcoming another. Something is always upsetting something else. Therefore, nothing lasts. Even so is human love. What a pity!" . . . One of the last entries takes up this note again: "I am completely upset by what has happened to Fu Nanto. The cruelty of it, for which I must take the sole blame. Well, I must say that I upset Fu Nanto. I really had no desire to cause him to kill his wife. He is sitting in prison. What's the use? But he also upset me. The touch of his skin and his gripping arm killed my love for Mengchia. These reverberations go on. And now, to my profound sorrow, I am upsetting Mengchia's life, just as I upset Chin Chu's. Mengchia who has done so much for me. Why must it be so complicated? Everything lopsided."

"Oh, if our longings could float and join together;
If our dreams should one day become real;
If all the creation were spread before you and me alone;
If at the coming of the night and the breaking of the
dawn, my hands were joined in yours;
If we should fall in the rain and roll together drenched to
the skin;
If the moon giving light to the earth should shine upon
us united in one place;
If our eyes were not looking at a blank, but yours into
mine and mine into yours—
Is there a greater happiness than this, two beings who so
love one another?"

Such outbursts were not infrequent. Addressed to whom?
To Chin Chu? To Fu Nanto? To Mengchia himself? Certainly
not the last, since they were living together. But the following
note, at the very beginning of the diary seems to indicate how
happy she was in finding Mengchia:

"In meeting you, you taught me to admire all the beautiful
things created or to be;
To perceive the softest, sweetest sounds, the slightest caress
of the breeze.
In my hours of sorrow, you taught me to laugh; in my
solitude, you bring comfort and take away my loneliness.
Oh, the tenderness of you, your comfort and your love flood
my soul like a drenching downpour. . . .
I believe that our souls have already been united across all
time and space, and that every single one of our feelings and
impulses was inspired by a force which transmits that love
and binds it together, although it does not know us, nor is
aware of our existence.
I know, as each minute passes, that there is no power which
can separate our souls, and that this love which unites us shall
last through our life and death.
Now nothing can separate us any more. We belong to each
other. Through all changes of matter, the soul is the strongest."

Another note was about her friend and in it there was a reference to Jasmine which took Mengchia completely by surprise.

It was a revelation! He had never suspected Jasmine's secret love for him, so carefully had she guarded herself against any betrayal of her feelings.

"Of all the beings in this life, the one I love most is Paiwei. Because we are both women, we reach a complete understanding impossible between men and women. How I admire her subtle intelligence, her sensibility, her view of life which is so in accord with mine. Thus there is nothing to intervene; it is like a moon in a cloudless sky. She will do anything for me, as I know I shall do anything for her. When she and Joshui fell in love, I did not tell her that I loved him myself. I could not cause her the infinite pain if she knew, and I am glad that I did not. Oh, Paiwei! She is more than my own sister. I remember one rainy day we were sitting together watching the raindrops racing down the windowpane. Our joy was complete, and she said, 'This one is me, and that one is you. See which one wins the race.' Then they merged before they reached the bottom, and we broke out in uncontrollable laughter. No one would understand us if they saw us then. Yes, we are like two drops of water. As for Jasmine, I love her and hate her. Our temperaments are completely different. What I cannot stand is her silent rebuke. If she would only say what she thinks. She just does not. But in spite of all our differences, I love her and admire her immensely. One day I said to her, 'Don't deny it. I know you love Tako.' 'What if I do? He is yours.' Is this like my refusing to tell Paiwei my love for Joshui? Or is it different?

"Only once did we discuss my love affair with Mengchia. 'Sister,' Jasmine said to me, 'don't misunderstand what I am about to say to you. I am not *lishueh* (Puritan). At least I don't think I am. But for a girl, the first and last thing is to have a husband and family. You are fooling yourself. I mean you are wasting your time. Don't you see that you will not want to get married, so long as you are carrying on with him?' I cannot agree with her more."

Peony was imaginative, sensitive, and passionate, but beneath her dreaminess, her recklessness, perhaps she was searching for what all women search for, what they have searched for since the beginning of time—an ideal husband. Like all women, she was anxious to build her nest. She tired of a passion without the prospect of marriage. All her loves were like

> "A bird in rain and storm,
> Which frantically builds her nest,
> Lest my neighbors laugh and scorn,
> And say I have no house or home."

"It is my ambition to be a mother of many children," she wrote. "I cannot have children with him without disgracing him and myself. Yet my deepest need is to have one little Mengchia that I shall raise and suckle at my breast."

All the seeds of her being were crying out to be fertilized. Like a burgeoning flower, she was sending out waves of intoxicating scent to attract the bees, lest they die of their own sterile pollen. The gorgeousness of the peony bloom is a cry of self-pity:

> "She envies the heavy-laden bough of pears,
> And tries to smile more beautifully and smiles in vain."

Perhaps Peony was not ready to nest, or perhaps she would never be ready. She loved being free; perhaps this is what drove her to knock so frantically on one locked door after another—doors that were locked from within. Chin Chu, Mengchia, Fu Nanto: they were all men she could never marry. Yet in her diary came this note of torment:

> "Oh, for ten such Fu Nantos,
> Let me have one child of my own,
> And I shall live and die content."

"It is too complicated to be a woman," she once told Jasmine.

CHAPTER 16

As the perfume of flowers intoxicates the bee, so did the beauty and intensity of Peony's feelings intoxicate Mengchia after reading these notes. No matter what cynics may say of love, all

his values had changed: the colors of the world had changed for
him because he had for once known the love of a woman. We
can no more explain than judge what he did so soon after Peony
left him; we can only explore. The music of Peony's passion
for him had stopped, but its echo remained. It was as if his
whole being were an open wound, sensitive to the slightest
touch, seeking something, anything, to stifle its throbbing pain.
Heartless as Peony had been in spurning him, and cured as he
was of his consuming passion, his tenderness for her remained,
coloring all his thoughts and feelings. He had expected that in
their last night together, she would turn to him once more,
maddened by passion as they had been at Tunglu. But her love
was dead; there was no doubt about it. At their parting there
were no tears, but only the smiles of a good friend. The flame
of passion had completely burned itself out. Still, he was sure
that if she had turned back that moment and decided to stay
with him, all the chords in his heart would have responded with
an undreamed-of resonance, like a temporarily suspended and
resumed symphony. All the pores of his being would have
opened, tuned to every vibration of her voice and the sight of
her face and limbs, uniting them once more electrically and
inexplicably.

The reading of the diary confirmed only one fact, the sincerity of her sorrow in discovering the death of their love. And
even then, she seemed terribly remote, not at all like a living,
passionate woman, but like a flower with a poisonous scent that
could destroy him, or any other man, if she wanted it to.

A week later, as he was breakfasting with Jasmine, he told her
he was going out. Then he changed his mind, and decided to
lie down again. Jasmine did not discover this until Chouma came
and informed her, "Master is in his room, door shut." Jasmine
went to his room immediately and found that indeed he had
closed the door. She tapped lightly and hearing a faint answer,
opened it gently. All was dark within; he had closed the south
window and only a faint light from the back came through. It
took her some seconds to adjust her eyes and discover him lying
in bed with his clothes on.

"Are you ill?" she asked in a voice of deep concern.

"No. I just thought I would like to lie down a little. I'll be all right after a little rest."

She came and gently felt his forehead with her hand. It was burning. She took his hand and felt its pulse; it was strong, firm, but jumpy.

"We must send for a doctor."

"There is no need."

"You are very ill with a high fever."

"Nonsense, I have never been ill in my life. I will lie down. Another couple of hours, and I'll be well again."

"If you want to," she said hoarsely, "at least take off your gown and shoes and socks and cover yourself well. I shall make you a pot of *kanho* tea."

"All right, I guess I will."

He sat up briskly but with a nervous motion. In the dusky half light, she could hear his quick, heavy breathing. He started to get undressed and, finally, unable to extricate himself, permitted her to undo the last button of the gown which had kept him trapped. Then she pulled off his shoes and socks for him. She tucked him in and left, not without a last touch on his forehead. When she came out, she wiped the beads of perspiration on her forehead and could hear her own heart pounding violently.

She paused for a minute to recover her composure before she went to the kitchen on the west and sought out Chouma.

"The master is not well. It's Indian summer, the tiger-after-onset-of-autumn. I want you to go home and bring your bedding. You will have to spend a few nights here looking after him."

The doctor came in less than an hour. He had come by their carriage, for the driver had been instructed to say that it was urgent and he was to wait. On the way, Dr. Cheng, a scholar-physician of great dignity of mien, had learned from the driver something about the household, and vaguely gathered that the patient had been greatly upset by the departure of a cousin-sister.

When he came in, Jasmine concealed herself at the back of the room, behind the bed curtain, according to good form. She saw that the first thing the doctor did was to open the patient's eyelids and study his eyes for an instant. Then he asked for his right arm and, placing his wrist on a pillow, felt the pulse for a long time. Mengchia was able to answer a few questions in a hoarse, tired voice. Then with the same urbane dignity of manner, the doctor rose, and assured the *hanlin* that he would soon be able to get well, but that he was to relax and not occupy his mind with anything.

He excused himself and asked for brush and paper, and was shown into the study.

Jasmine hurried out after Chouma, and followed the physician into the study.

"I am his cousin," she said simply. "In a matter of this kind, I cannot leave it to the servants. Tell me, doctor, what is wrong with him?"

The doctor looked steadily and decorously at the desk while he listened to the low, concerned voice of the young girl. Then, with a quick glance at Jasmine, he replied in his best professional tone: "*Shiaochieh*, you need not be alarmed, but I must inform you that the illness comes from a disturbance of the spirits of the body. It is a case of distraction of the mind; the *hun*, or soul, has dispersed and the *p'o*, baser spirits, take over. He must have undergone some emotional distress. His eyes tell the story. His pulse is strong, but jumpy and irregular, a result of too much *yang* fire and insufficiency of *yin*. But his vitality is good, very good. You are giving him *kanho* tea, I saw. Keep on giving him that. I will prescribe a mild purgative to flush out the liver fire which clots up the whole system, and causes the wild, runaway pulse. What he needs is to nourish the *yin* water and sustain the *yang* fire. In addition, he needs something which will allay his spirit, calm his nerves, and strengthen his vital force."

He began to write a prescription of twelve or thirteen ingredients, most of which were familiar to Jasmine, and gave the instructions. He looked searchingly at the young girl, and felt reassured by her steady, intelligent eyes. The patient was going to need care.

"Is there anything he must avoid?" she asked.

"Oh, yes, no fried food. It would only clutter up his system. I am trying to flush out his system first. When he sweats, as he will after the medicine, rub him well with a towel and cover him up. I will stop by tomorrow. What he needs is plenty of sleep. He may get worse before he gets better, but do not be alarmed."

The doctor detected a faint blush on the girl's face as he was giving the instructions. Finally, he said, "Remember, care and rest of his mind are better than any medicine." With a confident, professional tone, he said good-by. Jasmine saw him to the landing of the inner court.

Jasmine set up a rigorous routine. A portable clay stove was installed on the landing of the court, and the driver was given strict orders to remain on call. Chouma came with her bedding, and a light couch was set up in the central parlor against the wall of the bedroom. She was told to forget the housework completely, for her time would be fully occupied. Jasmine attended to the brewing of the medicinal stew herself. She had an easy chair installed just outside the bedroom door, which was kept half open. There she would be able to hear any call from her cousin and at the same time keep a sharp watch over all that was going on in the house.

The next day the doctor found that the pulse was steadier, and was satisfied with his diagnosis. He went over to the study, his head bent, his features tightly drawn. He rapidly wrote a prescription and looking at Jasmine, said: "*Shiaochieh*, I need your co-operation. Have this prescription made up. Do not be alarmed. I am giving him something drastic. Do not give him any food except some light soup if he asks for it." Handing her the prescription, he said, "Give this to him after supper. He will rave and toss about and yell with pain and may even become violent, but leave him alone. After half an hour or so, the pain will subside and he will pass into a peaceful sleep. All you need is to watch over him. When he comes out of his sleep, give him the other stew, and he will be all right."

Jasmine set her jaw tightly and said, "You can depend upon me, doctor."

She followed the instructions, and when supper time came, she told Chouma to keep out and closed the door. With the bowl of medicinal stew in hand, she tapped him lightly and awakened him. He opened his eyes and saw her holding a bowl in her hands, close to his mouth. There was a challenging smile on her girlish face.

"Tako, take this. The doctor says that it may throw you into paroxysms of pain, but it won't be long, and it will put you into a good sleep."

Mengchia saw her glancing steadily at the bowl, which she was still holding close to his lips. He tasted it and his face contorted violently. He tried to push it back, but Jasmine was unyielding.

"Are you afraid?"

"No. It has a frightful taste."

Obediently, he took the bowl in his hand, but Jasmine did not let go until he had finished it in one gulp.

Mengchia's eyes were closed in a gesture of horrible distaste. Some of the stew spilled out of his mouth, and Jasmine wiped it off. Suddenly he broke out in a terrible cry of anguish. "It will kill me! It will kill me!" he shrieked and his eyeballs rolled in fright and agony, and he clutched at his bedclothes, wild with a sharp, scorching pain. Silently, Jasmine watched his convulsions of pain, as he doubled up and tossed from side to side and threw his arms about. His hands clutched at a bedpost and with a tremendous swing he rolled over, shouting, "It is killing me!" The force was so great that Jasmine, who was standing close by, was knocked down and fell over, her hand pressing on a chip from the porcelain bowl which had crashed onto the floor. Chouma, hearing the noise, banged hard and drummed at the door, but Jasmine sat on the floor and watched him as he writhed in pain, never taking her eyes off him. The yelling and shrieking were horrible to hear; it was as if his whole body were burning up.

She got up and stood at a safe distance. After ten minutes or so, his arms were thrashing about with less force. The screams were lower and the convulsions less frequent. His wild eyes began to droop out of exhaustion. Gradually the screams of pain subsided and gave place to low, weak moans, while his chest heaved up and down.

Jasmine advanced and asked, "Tako, how are you? Is it better now?" But he did not hear her. She saw the agony gradually subside, slowly giving place to calmer and more regular breathing. She approached and felt his forehead. His eyes were closed and a deathly pallor had come over his face. The face, a moment ago hot to the touch, was now cold. All blood and life seemed to have ebbed out of him.

She opened the door.

"He is asleep now," she whispered to Chouma.

"But your hand is bleeding, and look at your face and hair. What has happened?"

Chouma pointed to the daubs of blood on her neck and chin. Jasmine then discovered her palm was bleeding where it had been cut by the broken chip of porcelain.

"This is nothing," said Jasmine. "I will go and clean up. You watch here and don't make any noise."

Jasmine returned after a few minutes and had a light supper, saying she had no appetite. Lights were kept on in the hall and in the bedroom, and the big charcoal brazier in the study was moved in to keep the bedroom warm. She told Chouma to watch him during the early part of the night, while she moved over a lamp and settled down in the easy chair in the hall, with a volume in hand. The patient was sleeping peacefully; but she wanted Chouma to be on the alert in case he called out for a drink of water or something.

Then at midnight, she told Chouma to go to bed while she took over. The light was flickering in the autumn wind, so she moved the easy chair over to the bedroom and continued her reading there. Now and then, she dozed off, to wake up and find him still asleep and breathing regularly. She had a chance to study his beautiful profile, so immensely impressive in sleep. His face seemed narrower in sleep than in daytime.

Mengchia remained in a deep coma the following morning. The doctor came at ten o'clock, verified what had happened, and said that it was all as it should be. The *hanlin* might sleep another twenty-four hours, until the effect of the medicine wore off. Then he was to be given the second stew, which would strengthen his heart and his greatly weakened system.

The same thing was repeated the following night—either Chouma or the young mistress was in attendance, never leaving him for a minute. She had the stove going and the stew ready to be served to him as soon as he woke out of his coma. Only once or twice, he choked or coughed or mumbled something unintelligible in his sleep.

Early at dawn on the third day, Chouma came in to find the room completely silent, the master still sleeping peacefully, and Jasmine dozing with a half-opened volume in her hand.

"*Shiaochieh*, you can retire now," she said.

"No, I must be here when he awakes. I have to give him the medicine."

"I will give it to him. You have not taken off your clothes for two nights. You must get some proper sleep or you will break down yourself."

"How can I sleep when he is ill? No, I will stay. You go and have your breakfast and clean up the place."

A cough was heard from the bed, and then silence. The two women stopped talking.

Chouma tiptoed out of the room. After a few minutes, Jasmine heard a movement in the bed and another cough. She rose from her chair and approached silently. He turned and his hand moved. He opened his eyes and saw Jasmine looking down at him with eyes of infinite tenderness.

"What time is it?" he asked.

"Day is breaking."

"I must have slept the whole night."

"No," answered Jasmine happily. "You have been asleep for one day and two nights."

His face showed surprise. He opened his eyes wide and looked about the room. The oil lamp was still burning. It was still dark outside.

Jasmine gave a relaxed smile. "Was the medicine terrible? You were writhing in pain when you took it."

"Was I? I don't seem to remember."

Jasmine came out and called out to Chouma to fetch a basin of hot water, while she went to heat up the stew. When Chouma arrived with the basin and towel, Jasmine went in. She would attend to the washing herself. She wrung out the hot towel and wiped his face for him. He saw the tender, happy look on her face. When he said he wanted to change his underwear, she abruptly left and said to the woman servant, "You help him change."

"Ay-ah," she heard Chouma say, while she was fanning the clay stove. "*Laoyeh*, your cousin-sister hasn't slept a wink for two nights. I told her to go off to bed but she wouldn't. And you didn't see the cut in her palm. You pushed her to the floor. You were yelling so it could have brought the roof down."

When Jasmine came in with the stew, Mengchia gazed at her so intently that she had to look away. His eyes rested on her bandaged hand, and he said weakly, "What happened? I didn't know."

"Oh, it's nothing," she said. "The important thing is that you are getting well. The doctor will come around ten. We are sending the carriage for him, as usual."

His eyes rested on her again for a fraction of a second, but it was long enough to make her blush with embarrassment.

The doctor came, heard the report, and complimented the *hanlin* on having such a capable cousin-sister.

"When can I get up?" Mengchia asked.

"Not for a few days yet. That medicine took a lot out of you. Stay in bed and let your mind be at ease. I will let the Grand Councilor know that you are incapacitated for a few days."

"I have done so already," said Jasmine at the side. Both men looked with approval at the young girl.

"It is true," said Mengchia. "When I tried to get up a

moment ago, I found my legs shaking, and I had to grab a bed-post for support."

The doctor felt his pulse and nodded his head. "There is still some irregularity," he said, "but if the *hanlin* will follow my instructions and stay in bed, you will be up and about in a week."

The days which followed passed quickly. Jasmine kept him company, or was not very far out of sight whenever he called for her. Neither of them mentioned Peony's name, he feeling as if he had gone through something he wanted to forget, and she for fear of disturbing his heart again. Jasmine seemed to have lost some weight, and her face looked sad. On the other hand, a new awareness had sprung up between them, so that they frequently avoided looking at each other directly. Once he took her hand to examine the cut. She quickly withdrew it and left the room.

Mengchia thought of the words in Peony's diary. "Don't deny it. You love Tako," and her reply: "What if I do? He is yours." He also remembered hearing her say as he was coming out of his sleep, "How can I sleep when he is ill?" He had never suspected it, and now he knew, and it showed in his frequent glances at her.

Mengchia decided to get up on the sixth day. Jasmine proposed that a change of scene would be good for him, and that he should move to the inner court, facing the small garden on the east. The inner court was more intimate and quiet, with a small rockery, a few potted dwarf *poyang*, and the big earthen jar containing goldfish.

"Where will you sleep?" Mengchia asked Jasmine.

"I can sleep anywhere, in sister's room, or here in this bed-room, after it has been cleaned up. I have arranged for Chouma to sleep inside."

It was decided that the master was to sleep in Jasmine's room, facing the garden, while she would move out and sleep in the western room which had been occupied by Peony; Chouma would have a couch in the central room, for convenience "in case he wanted anything during the night." This girlish fore-thought and defensive arrangement amused Mengchia.

The inner court was so much brighter that Mengchia thought he would use it for his living quarters until winter came, at which time he would move back into the main court. Previously he had spent very little time in the garden, but now he liked it. This also seemed to reflect a change in his state of mind. The central room was now converted into a dining room, where he and Jasmine had their meals.

One late afternoon, Jasmine, after a shopping trip, walked into the garden to find her cousin sitting on a stone bench. He was so deep in thought that he did not seem to notice her. She knew so well his look of concentrated thinking. Afraid to disturb him, she was about to leave when he said, without raising his head, "Don't go. I want to discuss something with you."

She turned back and stood in the shadow of a date tree. Minutes passed, and he said not a word. From time to time, she looked at him, afraid that he would ask her about her sister again.

At last, he fixed a strange, incomprehensible look on her and said in a hoarse voice, "Jasmine, come here." He rose slightly and tapped on the stone bench where she could sit down. She approached, slightly flushed, and took a seat beside him.

"Jasmine," he said, looking at the ground, "will you marry me?"

The girl's heart leaped to her throat. "What are you saying? How can we?"

"We can," he said, still with an absorbed, grave expression.

"But we are cousins of the same surname!"

"We can arrange to have that changed."

"But how can we?"

"A brilliant idea came into my head as I was thinking. A *tangmei*, that is, a cousin of the same name cannot, but a *piaomei*, maternal cousin of a different surname, can. Aunt Su Sueipo is very fond of you. Why don't we ask her to adopt you legally? It is a mere technicality, that is, if you are willing."

Jasmine felt overwhelmed. The name change had never occurred to her; the idea ricocheted inside her head like a bullet. She stared at the date tree in silence, trying to absorb the shock.

Seconds passed and she felt her insides turning and blood rushing into her heart like a warm, comfortable bath flooding her entire body.

"Do you want to, seriously?" she asked, afraid of her own voice.

"I need you. I have realized that. I need you very much. I have thought this thing over carefully for several days now. Your sister and I were fighting a futile battle, against ourselves."

Her shock of surprise gave place to an unexpected happiness.

"How are we going to do it?"

"It is a technicality, as I say. It came like a flash. Just a *kuochi*, a legal adoption and changing to another branch among cousins within the family. I know my aunt has been very fond of you. You are her adopted daughter, aren't you? All you have to do is to formalize it, so that you will be Unce Sueipo's daughter and your surname will be Su, and not Liang. Of course you will have to have your parents' consent, but I think they will be glad to give it. Besides, it will be only a formality—a piece of paper."

Jasmine was still trying to let the idea penetrate and see all its implications.

"You have not answered my question. I am asking you."

She placed her hand in his and pressed it. "Tako, is this true? You will make me the happiest and proudest wife in the world. At first, it was Peony. And I never thought it possible. Now you could not drive me away from you if you wanted to."

Her finger brushed away a tear, she was so overcome by her sudden, unexpected happiness. She let her head rest against his shoulder.

"I should have known," he whispered sweetly. "I did not know that you cared for me. I mean, in that way—until I read Peony's diary. All along I should have seen that it was you I loved. But I was blinded. And now I need you more than ever."

He kissed her lightly—a fugitive kiss on the soft hair curling at her temple, and felt the pressure of her arm tighten around his back. He turned his face and looked tenderly into her eyes, and she surveyed his face closely, up and down, and seemed to take in and love every part of his forehead, his cheeks, his mouth, his chin.

"Won't you kiss me?" he asked.

"I am ashamed." She hesitated for a moment, then printed a quick kiss on his lips and ran inside.

No news had been received from Peony, and none was expected, as it was not her habit to write. During her marriage, sometimes half a year passed without her mother or Paiwei receiving a letter from her. It was all a matter of mood with her.

The October sky was lined with a white fleece of clouds, and the north wind from the Mongolian plains blew a new chill into the city of Peking, making the leaves of silver poplars on the Western Hills vibrate and shiver like lanky white ghosts. White cranes in perfect arrowhead formation rode high in the sky upon these winds, carrying them on their annual voyage to the south. Teals and wild ducks, which had fattened in the summer, abounded among the reeds and marshes in the Mongol City and in the northwest section of the Outer City. The Shishahai now presented a desolate appearance; the sellers of cold drinks were gone and the yellowing stems and curling, pitted leaves of lotus in the ponds marked the end of another round of summer romance. But the autumn air was crisp and invigorating in Mengchia's garden. On the hedgerows, small-eyed asters peeped from the ground and chrysanthemums were making ready for their perennial debut. A woman's touch was evident in the beautifully arranged rows of the chrysanthemum plants which Jasmine had bought from the Lungfo Temple Fair; they had been planted all around the hedge at measured intervals, each propped up by a piece of split bamboo. The air was perfumed with wafts of fragrance from a giant magnolia tree at a neighboring house, and now and then the tangy smell of burning stacks of dry leaves, acrid but pleasant, reached this secluded corner. The garden had been transformed. New gravel had been spread along the mud walks. Where there had once been rotting weeds and fallen twigs, a whole moss landscape in varied shades of dark greens and frosty blues had been created. Already a *lamei* (dark plum) was planted against the window in anticipation of snow in deep winter. One could almost imagine the delicate scent of these yellow forsythia-like blossoms stealing across the cold air, as Mengchia sat gazing at the branches through the window before his redwood desk.

Mengchia was delighted to see this transformation. In the window of his room stood two chrysanthemums in pots of glazed white; in fact, pots of chrysanthemums had been distributed in all the courts.

The old mangy dog had been put out of the way. Mengchia did not know about it, until one day, upon returning in his carriage, he noticed that the dog, which usually yelped and pawed on his arrival, was not there.

"Where is the dog?"

"The young mistress had it poisoned. She said it coughed too much, and should be put out of its misery."

Mengchia's convalescence took longer than they had anticipated. The disease of *chengchung* (heart palpitation and jumpy pulse) did not disappear like a cold; the doctor had told them not to expect it to.

"Whatever worries you have, you must put at the back of your mind. What you had was a case of dispersion of the *hun*, the soul in control of the body. When it departed, the six humors did not know what to do. If I had not prescribed that drastic treatment, it might have lasted for years. Now I am glad it is over." Turning to the cousin-sister, he said with a look of approval and admiration, "I am glad you have made such a change in the house and garden. Nothing will hasten his recovery faster than to make him happy and feel contented and relaxed. It will take some time, but I am sure in a couple of months he will be completely well."

"Make him happy?" She did not know why she blushed.

"Yes. This is called *attack the heart by the heart*. A happy man recovers quickly, especially in a case of this sort." He supplemented this with a significant look, to make sure that Jasmine had caught his meaning. Her girlish heart felt a tick, but she said, "How about work?"

"A little of it is good. The mind wanders when the heart is not there. It is good to give the mind a definite direction. Once the *shinhun*, the heart-soul, takes control, the mind functions again."

Jasmine was familiar with the principle of homeopathy—to "attack poison by poison," "to attack the heart by the heart." For some old channel which has been blocked up, a new channel must be opened.

The golden autumn afternoons usually found them together sitting in the eastern garden. There was always something to watch or to do in the garden. Sometimes Jasmine would collect the dead leaves and make a small bonfire. Still weak, Mengchia lounged in a wicker chair, basking in the mild October sun. He watched her lithe young figure moving about, gathering leaves and poking the fire, so wholesome in her good cheer and so occupied with her work. Hers was always a soothing presence, radiant in her virginity. How successfully she had guarded her secret love for him! He might never have known.

Then when the evening chill set in, he would move in, and lie on the couch and ask her to sit by him. She would come and now and then feel his pulse. The soft touch of her white fingers and the jade bracelet circling her wrist moved him strangely. With a serene smile on her lips, she would always say, "It's wonderful. Your pulse is getting stronger each day."

He covered her hand with his and said, "It's never accurate, because my heart palpitates faster every time your hand touches mine."

"Don't talk nonsense," she chided sweetly.

"But it is true. You are my best doctor."

How he desired her at this moment! He pulled her down to him and gave her a warm and passionate kiss. She sensed danger and said, "Please don't," and stood up to pour *lungching* tea for him.

It was some two weeks before they received replies from Uncle Sueipo and from Jasmine's parents. Mengchia and Jasmine had not wanted to be explicit. Without giving reasons, they had asked simply for the official "adoption" of Jasmine as Sueipo's daughter, making her "Miss Su" instead of Miss Liang. It was a rare day when the *hanlin* wrote his mother's sister, and when he did this, they would naturally suspect there was a serious purpose behind it. Jasmine had been corresponding regularly with the aunt, and she added a letter in her own name and another to her parents. The replies could not be expected until the end of November.

Usually before the supper hour, when they had come in from the garden, Mengchia would be having a sip of *wuchiapi*, a liqueur recommended by the doctor as a heart tonic, and Jasmine would be having a cup of tea. Chouma would be busy in the kitchen. Lying on the couch, Mengchia would draw Jasmine near to him; and with her hand clasped in his they would talk of various things—everything, except the subject of Peony, which they consciously avoided. There were times when he snuggled close to her breast and buried his head in it and asked her to hold him tight.

"Does this make you happy?" she asked, remembering what the doctor had said.

Then he buried his head still deeper without reply, and she stroked his hair and held him at her breast, caressing him gently as she would a child. "Relax and sleep if you can, if it makes you happy this way." Her mind wandered far away, to her parents, her sister, and the people she knew in Hangchow.

"I wonder when Uncle will reply to our letters."

"It will come."

"I know that my parents will gladly give consent if they guess, as they certainly will, what we have in mind—"

"Of course," he said and turned over, looking up at her closely and very tenderly. "Then I shall write and ask for your hand—and you will be my dear little wife."

Her heart was full, as she bent over him and said, "Is that true? Can it really be true?" He pulled her head down toward him and she bent over and their lips joined in ecstasy. Deliberately, she slid her body down and stroked his cheeks and warmed him with the warmth of her body, saying, "Now I want you to get well quickly—for my sake and for nobody else's."

Then his eyes looked up and down and about her as if she were something new and wondrous to behold, and she moved a little, and gave a happy sigh.

"I am a lucky girl. I never dreamed that I would be so lucky —to be loved by you and needed by you."

They heard Chouma's rather too obvious cough. She always did this as a sign that she did not wish to intrude when she came to set the dining table in the hall. Jasmine had told her in confidence that they would soon be engaged to be married, and Chouma, who admired as well as respected the younger sister more than the elder one, was happy for her. So she would always cough and Jasmine would sit up and rearrange her hair, all as a matter of good form. Everything was fine except that the simple, honest servant had to make it clumsily obvious with her cough, as if to say, "I know you are doing wrong, young Mistress, but it is only me."

So it happened that Jasmine gave herself to Mengchia three days before Uncle Sueipo's formal letter arrived. They had been so close, and every day they could feel the new love welling forth between them. That afternoon, when a roseate eastern sky sent soft, diffused light into the room, Mengchia begged Jasmine to do it. She heard his quick breathing as he buried his head in her breast.

"Do what?"

"Do it. I need you now, the whole of you."

She was silent, feeling that one day this was bound to happen. Then she drew his face toward her and kissed him gently, lovingly.

"Will it make you happier?"

"Yes."

She permitted him to make love to her, while she flushed all over with her own warmth and his, until she was no longer conscious of what was happening but, closing her eyes, knew only that in giving herself totally to him, she was fulfilling herself, that a key was opening into the most intimate secrets of her being, that this was the ecstasy of pain and bliss, of true union and belonging. And she was vaguely very happy and proud to become this man's wife, to hold him in her arms and to own him and be owned by him.

"Did I hurt you?" he asked.

"No. You make me very happy by making me yours. It had to be painful to have something to remember. I felt it was like the birth of a new being in me, this awakening of love. I am a woman now. It had to be painful."

Later, on another occasion, she said with an arch smile, "Some experienced women think that they alone are capable of passion, and that a virtuous girl is always cold. It isn't true. The most virtuous women can be the most passionate. They only want to wait for the right man, as I have found you. Of course not every girl can find one like you."

It was after this that Mengchia permitted Jasmine to read her sister's diary. Pointing to the passage where she had confessed her love for him to Peony, he said, "Read this. It is a turning point for me. I never thought that you would care for me—in that way. I never knew, because you were so impeccably correct. You never allowed yourself to show it."

Jasmine's eyes scanned the passage quickly, biting her lower lip. Then she looked up at him, meeting his glance with a curling smile.

"Is it true that your sister was a little jealous of you and forced you to confess your love for me?"

"Not jealous. That was the time when she was mixed up with Fu Nanto. She behaved abominably and went out nights leaving you alone. I said a word or two, and then she turned on me and said, 'I know you love Tako. Don't deny it.' So I answered, 'What if I do? He is yours.' But I was no threat to her. She had no reason to be jealous then."

This was the first time Mengchia had permitted himself to mention Peony or the diary. His heart palpitations and his desire for Peony were gone; but it also seemed to him that he loved Jasmine because she appeared to him like a purified version of Peony, the true Peony herself, the Peony he loved and not the distorted version he had happened to know.

"You read the diary; then tell me what you think," he asked Jasmine.

Nothing could have delighted Jasmine more. "I think I know more about her and understand her better than you do," she replied. She hugged the manuscript to her breast and went and curled up on the bed to read it. It made delicious reading. Sometimes she blushed, sometimes she looked up and paused to recall things to her mind; and sometimes she bent close and squinted to make out a word, searching for clues to things she had not known before. Peony had told her about Fu Nanto; certainly she had not told her about the incident at the hotel. And she had only heard about the Shuttlecock Club.

"And here, at the very end, I see why she did not want to go to Shanhaikuan with us. She was brooding about Chin Chu. That was why she did not want to go with us. Now I see."

Late that night when she had finished reading, he said, "Tell me what you think. You can be more objective. I am too involved myself."

"I don't know that I can be objective. We grew up together. I don't know that I can judge her at all. When you know a person as well as I know my sister, you can't say that a person is good or bad. She is a bundle of things. All I can say is, as all our relatives say, she was a little rebel at home. I was a quieter girl and she was three years my senior. She is unique, totally unlike other girls that I know. Always vivacious, extremely clever, full of spirit and high caprice. She was so pretty and lovely that my parents spoiled her. She used to storm into the house, throw things about, and when Mother scolded her, she just opened her big eyes and rolled her tongue and smacked her lips. She was very obstinate and impatient, and always had to have her own way. She would argue and argue until she won. Father and Mother could do nothing with her. Of course, when *you* came home and praised her before all the clan uncles, people regarded her as very extraordinary; she had been blessed personally by the *hanlin*. She was unusual, and much prettier than I. I knew that."

"I would say that each of you is beautiful in your own way."

"No," said Jasmine. "She is much prettier. I know that. Such a perfectly straight nose and such well-formed lips. My mouth is too wide."

Mengchia was amused by this bit of self-criticism. Unquestionably Peony's mouth and her peculiar smile, her luscious lips, were exquisite; and Jasmine's face lacked that absolute perfection and fineness of features—her face being rounder, with a firmer jaw. But all the same, he liked her for her utter frankness with herself and her generous view of her sister.

"Later, when she was sixteen or seventeen—that was when she first fell in love with Chin Chu—Father used to forbid her to go out, but the more Father tried, the more she rebelled. She went out all the same to meet her lover, and Mother, being sympathetic, connived at her absences and helped to conceal them from Father. She managed to meet him two or three times a year—even after both of them were married. People would say that she was bad. Other girls in such a situation would learn to forget. She couldn't. You don't know how she cried in bed —how she suffered. Once she came home after seeing Chin Chu. How she cried! She actually bawled out loud in bed and the next morning her eyes were swollen shut. If she had married Chin Chu, what a wife she would have made! After that, she just didn't care. Would you say she was a nymphomaniac because she was looking for a lost love which she could not find again? All the rest followed because she could not be the wife of the man she truly loved. Chin Chu married someone else. It wasn't his fault—his parents arranged it. Mind you, she is much more intelligent than most girls. I remember her reading *Moutanting, Peony Pavilion*, at the age of thirteen. The reading did her some harm, one might say, by opening her heart for love. But she was just made for it. . . . She was always honorable, straightforward, believed in everybody, and was highly sensitive to the beauties of nature; but otherwise she was not really different from anyone else. I think she was just *more* of these things than anyone else."

"You have read her farewell letter to me?"

"I have."

"What do you think? Tell me frankly. It has puzzled me greatly. Why did she have to be—so harsh? As if she wanted to hurt me purposely."

Jasmine's lips were drawn downward. She hesitated, choosing her words carefully. "It seems—so ungrateful. I may be too subjective—she is so different from me. She is more brilliant, and therefore more reckless—more—impetuous, more—aggressive. Of course it was totally unnecessary to make such a complete break with you. She need not have said 'I shall *definitely* disappear from your life.' After all, you are still her cousin. . . ."

"But as a girl, you might see a girl's point of view better. She was very much in love with me, as you know. How could such a passionate love die so casually and easily, without, so far as I can see from that farewell letter, a modicum of sentiment left?"

Jasmine pouted her lips. After a minute's pause, she said, "It has puzzled me, too. I knew her mind changed when she went about with that boxer—whatever his name. . . . But there is a passage in the diary which struck me when I read it."

She thumbed through the pages and, stopping on a page, pointed it out to him:

"I am restless these days. Our love has become a burden to me, and perhaps to him. I do not see how I can go on living with him as a lover for life. We discussed this. Of course I loved him with all the love a woman can give. But always there was the hope that somehow we could be married. How proud I would be! I suggested that we go to Hong Kong together, where we could assume other names. Why not? Is not love more powerful than everything else? But now I see I was demanding an impossible sacrifice from him, a sacrifice of his whole career, his position as a scholar, loved and respected at court and everywhere."

"You see," said Jasmine, tucking a stray lock of hair behind her ear, "the diary was written for herself. I understand what it means, although the connection may not be clear. As a husband, you would be splendid; as a lover, you are useless to her, to put it crudely. The young boxer rates higher as a man to sleep with. I do not say that she meant consciously to exploit your love for her. But it is easy to see that, as she says, she could not see herself hanging around you in an ambiguous relationship for the rest of her life. You were a burden to her, as she says. Her love for you must have stopped at that moment. She must have wanted to be free from you to look for some other man. It is all instinctive, of course. . . . Now I am afraid for her. . . . She may do something rash. . . ."

After a pause, she added, "I don't know what she will think when she learns that we are going to be married."

"She won't feel jealous of you; you can be sure of that. I was led to believe that she loved me very much. Her love for me is dead, dead as a stone."

"I mean what will she think when she learns that you have thought of changing my surname, which you never thought of when she was with you."

"Oh, that!" He gave a loud laugh, perhaps just a bit louder than was necessary; he still felt a twinge of guilt that the device he had thought of in connection with Peony was now being applied with such ease to Jasmine. Yet he loved Jasmine, and could not bear to tell her the truth. "The idea just came," he said, "in a flash, like an inspiration. It's like what I do when I have to cudgel my brains trying to think out something novel and simple and fresh in my work with the Grand Councilor. The most difficult thing is freshness of thought; most bureaucrats get all tangled up in habit and routine."

"Are you sure that the adoption will solve our difficulty—will be all right?"

"It is all right. I have not studied the *Liki Commentaries* without knowing all about the six relationships—first cousin, second cousin, and rites at ancestor worship, et cetera. This matter of surname is pure foolishness. I would not be able to marry a girl from Kweichow if she had the same surname, even though she were related to me only by going back five hundred years. Actually, as Uncle Sueipo's daughter, you will be much closer to me, my first cousin, but it will be all right because your surname will be Su. What society wants is that the wedding notice shall go out with Su Sueipo's name as your father's. Everything will be legal, and I shall ask the Grand Councilor to officiate for us."

All formalities were completed as expected. Their intention to get married was communicated to Jasmine's parents and to Su Sueipo, and their consent obtained. It was a great surprise to Jasmine's parents, coupled with the unexpected and more complicated return of their elder daughter. Jasmine's wedding was set for January of the following year, and would take place in Peking.

CHAPTER 17

In the beginning of October, Peony walked into her Hangchow home, accompanied by a carrier-load of elegant brown varnished trunks of split bamboo. She was stylishly dressed in a black, satinlined jacket, broad-sleeved, as was the fashion in those days. The broad white lace trimmings around the neck were exaggerated to form a scalloped shoulder piece, so that the black jacket itself appeared to start low over her chest. She wore a fine skirt of black toile over white, which she had picked up on Nanking Road in Shanghai. Her hair-do was elaborately puffed up and curled around her temples. Dressed in the latest fashion, she might quite easily pass for a lady from Shanghai.

She knocked at the small black gate of the brick house she knew so well. She had come back unannounced and anticipated many questions. What was she to tell them? That she had broken off with her cousin? Or that she had come back to see Chin Chu and continue a hopeless romance with a married man?

Her mother opened the door and narrowed her eyes just a second before she recognized the fine lady who was her daughter. She seemed to have aged considerably since the departure of her children.

"Mother, I have come home," Peony said, walking straight into the house, dragging the weight of her body on her tired feet. Then she plumped down on an upright chair and stretched her legs out, letting her arms flop down by the sides. The mother was struck by her heavy, wearied expression no less than by her sudden return.

"What has happened?" she asked anxiously. Peony was still her favorite, because she gave her so much worry, and needed her so much. Never in the last four or five years had Peony given her a moment's peace of mind; and now, it seemed, she needed her mother's love more than ever. "What has happened?" she repeated, as Peony continued to stare blankly ahead. "Where is your sister?"

"She is in Peking. She is all right, Mother. Nothing has happened. I left Peking ten days ago by boat to Shanghai. Mother, I have decided to come home."

The last words were spoken with a methodical, weighted tone, implying that a great decision had been made. The mother was used to her caprices. Then a tear trickled slowly down Peony's cheek.

"Mother, please don't blame me. Chin Chu is sick. I have come back to see him. And I am not going back any more."

The mother said nothing, as her eyes darkened with horror. But she merely replied, "You'd better not let your father know this." Tender as ever, she pulled her daughter to her feet, as if she were still a child, and then went to the kitchen to prepare some tea, while Peony showed the carrier where to leave the luggage. Coming back with a tray of tea, the mother sat with Peony on the stools around the square dining table, and they told each other all the news of the family in the past year.

"You are the one who has never failed me," Peony said as she squeezed her mother's wrinkled hands on the table.

"Your father and mother are getting old. I feel it in my bones. Since you went away, it has been very lonely in this house."

"Now I have come to stay with you. Aren't you happy?"

The mother's face melted with the warmth which had come back to this deserted home, and her fine eyes glowed.

When her father came home in the afternoon, Peony and her mother had already agreed not to mention the reason for her return. The father's welcome was tinged with irritation at his daughter's unpredictable behavior. Peony gave an irritated and not too satisfactory account of why she did not want to stay in Peking. Her father lectured her a little on her inability to stick to anything she had started, and Peony nervously stood up and went to her room.

Peony was extremely anxious and impatient to see Paiwei and learn from her how ill Chin Chu was and where he was now. She bought a seat in a boat going up the Fuchunkiang the next day. There were fifteen or sixteen passengers, and the boat was crowded. She sat alone, hugging her knees in silence, oblivious to everyone around her. She wondered if there were any chance that she might find Chin Chu in Paiwei's home—it was not a likely possibility, but the very thought set her heart to pounding fast. And if she were to meet him, what was she to say? She was so lost in reverie that before she knew it, the boat had stopped at Tunglu.

Nothing seemed right on this journey. Her eyelids twitched from nervousness. The sky was overcast, and when she went ashore, a heavy fog lay like a white shroud over the waterfront. It had been raining and the air was saturated with a clammy, oppressive dampness. The benches and tables in teahouses were coated with a fine spray. Dogs slunk around with their tails between their legs and now and then shook the water off their backs on the mud floor.

A twilight dusk had descended, although it was only five o'clock. Peony had some difficulty finding sedan chair carriers willing to go up the mountain some two miles away; they claimed that it would be dark when they came down and the tracks would be treacherous. On top of that, she found that she had dropped one of her earrings on the boat. She felt afraid, too, to go up that deserted mountainside alone, for she was much too well dressed and did not trust the strangers who were to carry her. But so sharp was her impatience that she decided she would risk it, since night had not really set in. She paid what she considered an exorbitant price and engaged a sedan chair. Leaving everything to providence, she closed her eyes, as the sedan chair carriers stumbled up the tracks of red clay, sticky and slippery in the rain. Successive gusts of whistling wind and singing rain whipped around them. After about three quarters of an hour, the sky started to clear, although the fog still swirled around the foot of the mountain. The wind stiffened and flapped the oilcloth covers of the sedan chair noisily, and Peony found herself shivering, partly from the cold and partly from her anxiety to hear about Chin Chu. In another ten minutes, she saw lights in her friend's house.

Her heart quickened as she descended from the chair. Joshui came to the door, quickly joined by Paiwei.

"Peony! What a surprise!" Paiwei cried.

"Didn't you send for me?"

"Yes, but I didn't think you could come so quickly."

"Where is he?"

"In a hospital. Come in first."

The two friends embraced warmly. They were overjoyed to see each other after the year-long separation.

In Paiwei's company, Peony felt somewhat better. It relieved her to talk about Chin Chu and Liang Mengchia. With Paiwei, she had to make no explanation or apology for what she did. Paiwei was as incurably romantic as she was.

"He is in a missionary hospital at Liuhota Pagoda. Some intestinal infection, I was told. He's been sick for six or seven weeks and looks much emaciated. The doctor wasn't sure whether to operate or not. I am glad you could come so quickly. How could you leave the *hanlin?*"

"I came as soon as I could. No one could stop me. How serious is his illness?"

"It looked pretty bad half a month ago. I thought you would never forgive me if I didn't let you know. He doesn't know you are coming. I did it on my initiative, and I couldn't tell him and raise false hopes because I was not at all sure that you would come."

"Paiwei, thank you so much. Only you can understand my feelings. I am through with my cousin. I am not going back." She talked on while she divested herself of her heavy jacket. The servant brought in a basin of hot water and towels. They talked, as she walked about washing her face and depositing her jewels on a table. "I would leave my cousin even if I had not heard from you," Peony said, pulling off an earring. "See? I lost one of the pair in the boat."

Paiwei's eyes opened and fixed on her for a second. "Tell me why." She ignored the earring.

"It takes time to explain. It did not work out."

"Lover's quarrels?"

"No."

"He loves somebody else?"

"No."

"Then why?"

"I don't know. I just found that I did not love him, not really."

They were now seated around the marble table on which Paiwei had set a pot of hot tea.

"You mean, you found he was not the god you thought he was, and now you are disillusioned? No one is perfect. I thought you were madly in love with him."

Paiwei had thought them a wonderfully romantic pair of lovers. Now she felt very sad, as if it had happened to herself. She never believed he could marry Peony—that was out of the question—but he would never marry anybody else. Did it really matter if they were never married? They would be lovers for life. What a romance between a scholar and her friend!

"Shall I tell you something?" she said to Peony. "When you and the *hanlin* were up here and passed a night down near the stream, Joshui and I were discussing you two. We thought you were beginning a romance like Cho Wenchun and Szema Shiangju, because Wenchun was a young widow who had just lost her husband, like you, and Shiangju was a poet, like Liang *Hanlin*. You had to go and kill that dream for us."

Peony's face looked solemn. She tried to put her feelings into words, but could not. "Some things I will tell you later. Not now." Then her face softened into a smile. "One good thing about him is that he isn't jealous. I met a young man called Fu Nanto. Mengchia knew all about it. I told him. He said he wanted to see me happily married if I could find a good man. If he had got mad and raped me, I believe I could have loved him again. Can you understand me? After I told him about the affair, he said he understood and never imposed himself on me. Maybe I was disappointed. I shouldn't have been, but I guess I was. He was all patience and all understanding. That killed my love for him. This does not make sense, does it?"

Joshui smiled. He put his cup down on the table and said, rather sardonically, "I think I understand. What you women love is a little brutality. The more a man beats his wife, the more she becomes a slave to him."

"Don't talk nonsense," said Paiwei. "Women don't want to be slaves."

"But they do. They love a little spanking on the bottom once in a while. It makes them feel they can infuriate someone, that someone cares."

"Don't take him seriously. Joshui is joking," said Paiwei. "There should be a perfect intellectual understanding between a man and a woman who are lovers."

Joshui answered, "That would be companionship, not love. What woman wants a good mind while making love? She wants a handsome torso."

"Will you stop monkeying around when we are talking?" said Paiwei in an affectionate rebuke.

"Joshui has something there," Peony said. "But perhaps it doesn't have to be quite so brutal as he describes it."

There was a moment of silence. Joshui, properly chastened, kept quiet. Paiwei was piqued; she had always had a highly romantic ideal of love—unearthly, poetic, almost celestial—a love such as she and Joshui shared. Peony was thinking of the boxer's "handsome torso" and wanted to say something, but she hesitated in front of Joshui. Joshui had just explained for her something she could not understand herself; namely, why she would rather sleep with a common boxer than with an academician. At last, she said, throwing a glance at Joshui, "I think Joshui is right. What a woman really wants is a handsome, young lackey, not a poet."

"You two are impossible," said Paiwei. "Aren't you a little mixed up, Peony?"

"Who wants intellect in love? You want passion and muscles—a suspension of the mind. . . ."

"Peony!" protested Paiwei.

"Anyway, I left my cousin a note, telling him that I do not love him, and am not going back. I said I would disappear definitely from his life."

"How could you?" Paiwei asked, her eyes round with pained surprise. "Does he not still love you? Why did you have to do that?"

"I don't know." She paused and added, "I think we are still good friends. The last night we were together he looked very sad. I kissed him, which I had not done for months. He still loves me. I could tell from his kiss. But he didn't touch me. I wish he had. I mean he was always a gentleman. That does not make him a good lover. I told him so. I said I still admired him as a poet and a man, but would not have him as a lover. . . . I was quite frank."

"You said that?"

"Don't look so horrified."

"What did he say?"

"He said that if it was so, it was so. If he felt something, he did not show it. What could he say? He said he did not want an admirer, he wanted me, my love. Since I did not love him, there was nothing more to be said."

"You really did!" said Paiwei. "I remember you said you would die if you had to live without him! Why, of all persons . . ." She broke off. In her mind, she had an image of someone drawing a knife and slashing a famous Yuan land-

scape or laying a rude hand on a delicate porcelain bowl and
sending it crashing to the floor. "It could have been beautiful
if you and he had worked it out!" she said. She gave a half-
meditative, half-reproving look. "I suppose you were disillusioned from all the illusion you had built around him. Still,
I do not think you did right to turn your back on him so abruptly."

"Why, Paiwei!"

It was the first time that Peony felt irritated with her friend,
perhaps because she herself was so unhappy and nervous that
day.

"I am sorry," said Paiwei, seeing that her best friend looked
really displeased.

They smiled, looking into each other's eyes. "Don't be my
conscience," Peony said weakly.

The talk had upset her. Peony went on to tell them many
things about Peking, even the new Peking–Shanhaikuan Railway and the tall Manchu princess she had seen in the train and
her dress.

"You saw the Great Wall, of course."

"No, I didn't. Jasmine did. She and Mengchia went on a trip
to Shanhaikuan. I didn't."

"You must have seen some famous collections of paintings."

"None at all."

"What were you doing all this time in Peking?" Paiwei
chided her as only one's best friend could. "No museums,
nothing?"

Peony shook her head.

Everything was wrong tonight. Like the loss of her earring
on the way. Like the twitching of her eyelids as she started
out that morning—a foreboding of bad luck. No one was closer
to her than Paiwei, but even she disagreed with her tonight,
and had different ideas about love. It was just enough to disturb the perfect harmony of spirit that had always existed between her and her friend.

That night, thinking that the two women friends had much

to say to each other, Joshui vacated their bedroom in favor of the guest.

"I will sleep outside. You two want to talk all night, I am sure."

"It is so thoughtful of you," said Paiwei, looking gratefully at her husband.

The two women talked till the gray hours of the dawn, as they used to talk years ago. Peony really loved her as she loved no one else, and as she wept in her embrace, their friendship and confidence in each other was restored.

"Are you happy?" she asked Paiwei.

"Of course."

"I mean living so far out from the city, completely alone with one man."

"Our love is perfect. I am happy and contented, loved by one man whom I adore."

"Don't you sometimes want to go down and sit in a wine-shop, see people, and be seen by them? In a way I was happy in Peking. I had complete liberty. I had no obligations to anyone for the first time in my life, I had *total* liberty. It sort of satisfied me. I didn't tell you about Fu Nanto, a boxer. I didn't want to in front of your husband. I don't know what has happened to him now. He was sent to jail for killing his wife. . . ." She told Paiwei the whole story of her meeting with the boxer.

"I didn't tell you about the man I met on the boat to Shanghai. He was a college student who happened to be on board, and he was extremely nice—he did everything special to make me comfortable. He was not yet engaged or married, and had a refined face, and I liked him. I was so bored, so bored with everything that I did not care. The first night he wanted to make love to me, and I refused. The second night, I gave myself to him. I tell you I did not care. My heart belongs to Chin Chu, but in my body I didn't care. There was a stiff tail wind, sending the ship tossing and rolling. But it wasn't the ship that was tossing and rolling, it was he. It wasn't making love, it was a savage dance. . . . What do you think of me now?"

"You are promis——"

"Promiscuous. Say it. I tell you I am not. I have always wanted to find an ideal, something which means something to me."

"I know you have been chasing your own shadow since you lost Chin Chu."

CHAPTER 18

Peony's heart pounded and her steps quickened when she saw the three-storied Liuhota Hospital, a red brick building with a curving roof by the side of the broad and deep Tsientang River in the suburb of Hangchow. She had to stop for breath; she wanted to be calm and happy when she returned to her love. There was a chill wind coming down the river which made it difficult for her to fix her hair. She did not know what to say. She had missed him so much in the past year. She felt off balance; Chin Chu was her center of gravity—she fully realized it now. It was true that she had told him last year that their affair was finished. But she had come back to make amends. She would tell him that she was through with her cousin and was coming back to him. She buried her pride because she knew she needed him. He couldn't still be angry, and if he was, she would take away his anger. She had asked Paiwei if they had discussed her. They couldn't very well have done so as the nurse was in the room. Paiwei had taken the trouble to bring Peony's letter to Chin Chu personally, because she could not trust anybody else with it. She had found him not at home and then was told that he had been taken sick and was in a hospital. It was there that Paiwei had seen him last. Chin Chu did not think there was any chance that Peony would come. He had given her up. Paiwei had been shocked to see him so emaciated. She had the impression that he was out of his mind and was suffering terribly. She had seen his whole body shivering in rage when he came up to Tunglu and learned that she had been there with her cousin and was throwing him overboard and had gone to Peking because she was in love with the *hanlin*.

She was all mixed up and her head whirled as she approached the red building, enclosed by a high white wall. At the entrance was a clump of bamboo trees swaying in the wind, a mass of deep green with sharp-pointed graceful leaves, drawing moving silhouettes against the winter sky. She knew only one thing she would say to him: "I have come back and will never leave you again."

A smell of iodine and other medicine peculiar to a Western hospital assailed her nose as she entered the hall. It was full of outpatients. Some were sitting on the benches around the wall, with babies in their arms, but many were standing in a queue. Across a counter, some nurses in white and a foreign doctor were busy with bottles, scissors, and bandages. Peony felt suffocated.

She told them she was a friend from Peking who wanted to see Mr. Chin Chu.

The nurse on duty said there was no Chin Chu, but a Chin Chutang of Soochow.

"That's the one."

"But you said you wanted to see Chin Chu."

"Chutang is his poetic name." She was annoyed at the self-important woman, who thought herself modern and enlightened because she was working in a foreign hospital; to her all Chinese people were ignorant and superstitious. Actually, she probably couldn't read the classics or any other Chinese literature because she was brought up in a missionary school.

"Can you write his name?" the Chinese woman asked.

Peony controlled herself. She wrote down "Chin Chu, poetic name Chutang." The woman saw her handsome writing, looked up, and smiled.

"He is in Number Eleven. I will take you to him."

The room was on the second floor at the end of the hall, facing west. Peony's heart pounded violently. The assistant in white knocked and opened the door.

"A friend has come to see you," she announced, and hurried out with an air of abrupt efficiency.

A solitary iron bed stood against the wall. Chin Chu was asleep; his hair was long, his face unshaven and haggard and green with pallor. A hand lay motionless over the sheets, the knuckles standing out sharply.

Peony's throat tightened. Tears came to her eyes. Her hand gently touched the mass of black hair she knew so well. She studied the smooth forehead and the sunken, but still handsome, chiseled features of the man she loved. How he must have suffered, she thought, and her heart was bitter with remorse for having deserted him.

She bent down to sniff that smooth forehead and hair. "I have come to you," she whispered gently. "I have come back. Your Peony has come back."

She heard only a gentle, steady breathing. She kissed his eyelids. His eyes opened, at first fitfully; and then, suddenly, he was staring at her with a tired, haunted gaze. His face betrayed no emotion. Focusing a hard look on her, he said slowly but clearly, "Why have you come?"

"But Chutang, it is I. Are you very ill?" Her hand touched his cheek in a stroking gesture. He did not smile, did not take her hand.

"Why have you come?" he repeated hoarsely, with a tinge of bitterness in his voice.

"Why, Chutang, what's the matter? I left Peking as soon as I heard you were ill."

"Yes?"

"Chutang, it is Peony, your Peony. I am not going back. I am coming to stay with you, to see that you are well."

"Yes?"

Then, choked with surprise and anger, she stopped talking. It was clear then that he was still angry. She had known Chin Chu's anger before—sharp, incisive, impatient, with an unending flow of curse words in Soochow dialect, for he reverted to Soochow when he lost his temper. Just how furious was he when he discovered that she had gone off with her cousin?

However angry he had been then, his voice was tired and weak now.

She drew up a chair and laid her head down on the sheets where his hand lay. She kissed his fingers, but his hand did not move. An ineffable feeling of hurt pride surged up in her, yet in spite of herself, her tears trickled down on the outstretched hand, which was cold as ice. The tears poured down her cheeks.

"I love you, I love you, Chutang. You do not know how much I love you." She was sobbing now, uncontrollably. "I shall love no one but you, my Chutang."

Slowly he withdrew his hand. His eyes were still staring blankly at the ceiling.

"How can I believe you?" he said in a hollow voice, drained of all strength.

She raised her head and looked at him. "How can you say that, when I have come all the way from Peking to see you? I love no one but you. I need you. You are my heart, my life, my all. Believe me. Now I know."

"You have said that before, and I guess you have said it to him." Without moving his head, his eyes looked downward at her clinging figure.

"To whom?"

"To your cousin." His dead calm was frightening.

Peony was exasperated. "I found out my mistake. Now I know it is you I love, nobody but you."

"I have no confidence in you."

She was enraged, and was hurt deeply inside.

"But I have proven it to you. I have left him—definitely."

"Why shouldn't you decide to leave me definitely again, as you did before?" He made a motion to sit up higher. She helped him and patted the pillow, imprinting a stolen kiss on him. In former meetings he would already have caught her in a hot embrace. She retreated and sat back.

"All right, tell me," she said, looking at him intently.

"Why do you come to disturb me again? I have got over my folly. I had peace—peace of heart such as I had not known for a long time. Yes, I was furious when I learned of your crazy

romance. You had to have your new romance. Then I understood you—understood you completely. Granted, I loved you
once. We loved each other. But now, frankly, I do not know
what to think. . . ." His breath was short.

"But I sent you a letter from Peking. I told you of my decision to come back, any time you wanted me. I just wanted to
be near you, to be your wife, mistress, concubine, whore. I
don't care. Didn't you receive it?"

"Yes, but I never opened it. I threw it into the basket. If you
want to know, I burned all your remaining letters to me last
spring when I came back from Tunglu."

"But look at me. Look into my eyes. I am here. Don't you
believe me?"

"What can come of it? Nothing—nothing except pining and
longing and meeting you perhaps once a year. Don't you see?"
Suddenly there was a dangerous fire in his eyes. "Don't you see
that it is better that we give up each other and thinking of each
other?"

The degree of his hatred now was the measure of the anguish
he had suffered when she had coolly cast him aside, like a pair
of old shoes. He had never been the same man again. He
hardly knew that he existed; it was as if a piece of his flesh had
been torn away.

Peony stared at him, fascinated. Color had returned to his
cheeks. Chin Chu was always handsome and impressive to her
when he was displeased with something, when he hurled slippers and cushions against the wall and dashed cups on the
floor. She liked that fire in his eyes, anger on his lips, obscenity
on his tongue. There was brutality in him. He was so handsome now.

On an impulse, she leaned her whole body against his, captured his face between her two hands, and covered it with her
ravishing kisses, crying, "Chutang, my Chutang." He wrenched
his head sideways to free himself and suddenly he lunged forward and pushed her away.

"Go away! And don't come and disturb my peace again."

Peony staggered backward. Her face burned, as if he had

struck her across the mouth. She crumpled up in a chair, crying into her hands.

"Don't cry, but wipe your tears and go away. My wife will be coming in a few days. Don't try to come and see me."

Without turning her head, she rose slowly from her seat and dragged her feet across the floor. She walked out without even closing the door behind her.

Outside, the Tsientang shimmered in the bright noon sunshine. There were people in the teahouses and small eating places in the stalls along the river bank. She walked away, scarcely knowing where she was. Her head reeled with the thought that Chin Chu had misunderstood her, would not believe her. She had seen Chin Chu's fits of temper before, but she could not believe that he could be so harsh and bitter. Some fifty feet up the bank was a small ferry landing, where two or three small rowboats were tied. There was no one there. She sat down on the planks and looked at the broad river glistening in the sun, flowing endlessly into the sea.

She had only one thought, how Chin Chu had misunderstood her true love for him. She was not bitter, but only felt remorse for the suffering she had caused him; she was immensely distressed to see him so ill and so emaciated. It hardly mattered to her whether he wanted to see her or believe her; the important thing was how she could help him now.

She was exhausted when she got home. A thousand-mile journey to see her one and only love, and at the end, nothing. She felt oppressed with a sense of terrible loneliness. The idea of helping Chin Chu became an obsession with her. The next morning, when her father had gone to his office, she took out the medicines she had brought from Peking, and prepared the ginseng stew. She did not know what to do with the deer horn and the sun-dried snake gall bladder. Taking the things to a medicine shop, she asked the employees for directions. The root of the young deer's horn had to be shaved into very thin slices and heated over a very slow flame. It was difficult to prepare, and she begged them to have it ready by the next day.

It was already long past noon when she brought the tonic drink, in a bamboo basket, to the hospital. She knew it would be difficult to bring it in. She waited at the gate to meet the nurses as they came out. After a while, she saw two nurses off duty passing through the gate.

Putting on her best smile, she asked, "Which one of you is in charge of Room Eleven?"

The tall one answered. "I am. What do you want?" Her name was Miss Mao. She was about twenty-five, and rather thin, with high cheekbones. Already there were lines around her eyes, which was unusual for one so young.

"I have brought some ginseng soup for Mr. Chin in Room Eleven."

"It is against the rules," said Miss Mao.

"Please, I have come all the way from Peking to see him. Please, this may help save his life."

Miss Mao eyed her curiously and guessed from Peony's embarrassed look and tone that the girl visitor was perhaps Mr. Chin's sweetheart. She said sympathetically, "You can send food, yes. But the matron must know about it. Why don't you come in and ask the matron?"

She followed the nurse toward the building.

"Are you his wife?" the nurse asked her.

Peony blushed and spoke a hardly audible "No." Then she added, "We are very old friends."

The matron saw her and smiled.

"Oh, you were here yesterday." She was not as schoolmarmly correct as she appeared to be the day before.

Peony tried very hard to persuade her.

"It's ginseng, you know. I got the best quality from Peking. If you had seen the root, rich and darkly transparent! The best of Shangtang. It costs fifty dollars an ounce—would you believe it? And I shall bring deer horn tomorrow—and snake gall bladder."

She seemed desperate. When she had finished talking, she felt foolish. The matron gave her a significant look, and said,

"Ginseng, yes. But I would not know about deer horn and snake bile. I cannot permit it."

"But you know it may save his life. Won't you please?"

"Who are you? I mean what relation to the patient?"

"We are friends, very old friends. Please!"

"I can see that. His temperature went up yesterday after your visit. I shouldn't advise you to see him. It is not good for him. As for this, of course, I believe in our old medicine, deer horn and all that. But I have to get permission from the doctor." She opened the lid of the pot and sniffed at the darkish-brown fluid. Then she looked up with a smile. "I will speak for you. Doctor Fey is always curious about Chinese medicine. He may be interested. Wait a minute, it may be a good idea for you to bring samples of the medicines for him to look at. Will you do that?"

Peony thanked her and prepared to leave.

"Why isn't his wife with him?" she asked Miss Mao on the way out.

"We hear that his wife has just given birth to a baby. She may be able to come in a few days, I am told."

Peony's face betrayed an uneasiness; Miss Mao's curiosity was aroused.

"Of course you know his wife."

"Yes, I know her." Peony gave a direct look at her. "I must be honest with you. I am not his wife and would rather not meet her."

"I see."

They had come out through the corridor. Miss Mao had guessed it all—it was undoubtedly a secret love affair.

"Can I trouble you for a minute?" asked Peony.

"Certainly." Partly out of curiosity and partly because of something in Miss Mao's own life, she felt sympathetic. She guided Peony to a glass-encased porch furnished with some benches and a few cane chairs. It was a room where the convalescents could sit in the sun and watch the small goldfish pond in the garden. The porch was now deserted. Selecting a comfortable chair, she said, "Sit down. I'm not on duty now. Where are you from?"

"My home is here in the city. But this time I came all the way from Peking. Tell me, what is his illness?"

Miss Mao began to tell her that the patient had been brought to the hospital six weeks ago with a fever and dull, intermittent pains in the belly. "It is intestinal fever. The doctor suspects some kind of Oriental disease caused by intestinal infection, but is not sure whether to operate or not. In any case . . ." She saw the pain in Peony's face and the tears rolling slowly down her cheeks. She touched her on the shoulder and said, "I am sorry."

Peony blew her nose and said without raising her head, "If he dies, I shall die, too. He wanted to marry me. They took him away from me." She sniffed into her handkerchief again.

"I understand," said Miss Mao. "Come on, cheer up. If there is anything I can do, I will do it for you. You bring those Chinese medicines tomorrow and we will see what the doctor says."

"If you will help him to pull through, I shall never forget you."

Miss Mao was quite touched by her young, appealing voice. Had she herself suffered from a broken romance?

"Is there anything you want me to tell him?"

"No. Just tell him that I have brought the Chinese medicine. Say it is from Peony."

The nurse accompanied her to the gate, and Peony barely remembered to murmur a weak good-by.

In the weeks that followed, Peony was seen daily on the street facing the river, where a number of shops had sprung up. Young locust trees lined it on the hospital side and a few persimmon trees cast shadows on the side near the river. Some hundred yards off was the ancient Liuhota Pagoda, with more shops and stalls. This was a comparatively quiet region outside the city, where tourists and holiday-makers would come to spend a pleasant afternoon.

Doctor Fey, the American physician, a spry, lanky figure with a brown mustache, had asked to see the deer horn. It had been explained to him that it was taken from a young deer in its first year. It had to be chopped off after a hot chase, immediately after the young deer was caught, at the moment when the deer's young blood had rushed into it. It was cut carefully at the base, and included the cartilaginous substance where the horn was soft and still being formed. Presumably, at the moment, the blood carried some special chemical substance which nourished the growing horn. The American doctor was willing to experiment with the old remedy and note its effect, especially when he was confronted with a baffling case for which other remedies had failed. As for the dried snake gall bladder, he knew it contained concentrates of liver bile, but he had never had the chance to investigate the efficacy of snake bile. It would not kill his patient, but might help his digestive system. It was great news when the bile concentrate brought the patient's fever down.

Dr. Fey had, as a matter of fact, given up hope, and had confided his feelings to the nurse. He suspected intestinal cancer. Miss Mao could not bring herself to tell Peony; she had seen the flush on Peony's face and the quivering smile when she reported the reduction in temperature.

After hearing the good news, Peony went out, her head erect, a smile of personal triumph on her lips. She wanted to be alone. She walked to the ferry and sat on the deserted jetty of wooden planks. With her arms hugging her knees, she listened to the autumn song of the winds on the Tsientang River.

Chin Chu's wife arrived a few days later, and started to visit Chin Chu every morning. Peony could always tell when the wife was there by her carriage, parked outside the hospital wall. She used to come early, and when she saw the carriage she would go off to sit on the ferry landing.

It had now become a daily habit with her. There she sat day after day, listening to the muted gurgle of the broad, deep river and the whistle of the winds in the hillsides, now turned brown and purple in the autumn. Often a group of sailing boats, setting out to sea, was visible in the distance, their sails glimmering in the afternoon sun. Chin Chu was getting well, she was sure, thanks to the deer horn and the snake gall extract.

More often, she went to the hospital about two o'clock, when she was sure the wife would be at home, on account of the newborn baby. She waited for Miss Mao to signal her from the window. Chin Chu had a corner room on the second floor and she used to take up her position, sitting on a rock near the white wall, in the shadow of a clump of bamboo trees.

The nurse, in a sweet conspiracy, would signal her when the patient had been given an injection to put him to sleep. This was the nurse's idea, and Peony, afraid of upsetting Chin Chu, agreed. She could wait until he was out of danger before she talked to him again.

It would be the siesta hour, when the hospital was quiet. The matron would be sitting in her office in the main hall. Peony would enter by a side door, pass through a room full of bottles, climb the creaking side staircase, and slip into Room Eleven, where Miss Mao would be waiting for her. She would be allowed ten or fifteen minutes in the sickroom; there she would sit, mutely watching Chin Chu as he slept, the veins perceptibly throbbing in his temples, his emaciated face calm and composed in sleep, his bony profile and straight nose standing out against his stubby mustache and tossed black hair. In low whispers she would inquire from the nurse how he had slept and if there had been any sign of improvement. Sometimes he would toss in his sleep, stretching out a thin white arm on the white sheets, and she would touch his sharp white knuckles ever so gently, and perhaps impress them with a stolen, silent kiss. Then she would leave, happy and content.

She could not stay away from the hospital. A force compelled her to stay close to the place where Chin Chu lay wasting away. She asked nothing of Chin Chu, but wanted only to be near him and enjoy the luxury of being alone with her infinite sadness. She would go up and sit near the ferry, or enter one of the teahouses, and take a table overlooking the river.

Toward five o'clock some of the medical students and nurses would come out and the teahouse would come to life again. To the nurses, she was known as "the friend of Room Eleven."

Luckily, there had been no mishap. The wife always arrived in her carriage, which could be seen from the window overlooking the river. Once the wife had come when Peony was in Chin Chu's room. Miss Mao stomped noisily down the corridor to give warning, and Peony was able to leave by the back staircase. And once she caught sight of Chin Chu's figure moving across the window; he seemed to be looking in her direction. She was sitting on the rock in the shadow of the bamboo grove, and was not sure whether he had seen her or not; most probably he had not, as he disappeared from sight the next instant and was not seen again.

One day, she noticed that the shadows of the maple trees on the hospital wall were barer somehow. She had grown familiar with the sight of those intricate shadows fluttering on the white wall as the sun went down. But now the flickering shadows were no longer the same, and she suddenly realized that all the leaves had fallen; only the bare branches remained.

She had not counted the days, those days of a strange peace and quiet, the quiet of the autumnal evensong, as she called it, and of voluptuous sadness and beauty. Miss Mao's reports had always been encouraging—at least never alarming—until suddenly she grew suspicious. The deer horn and the snake liver extract were not accomplishing the miracle she had prayed for. Her spirit of buoyant hopes and confidence gave place to doubts and fears. And then one afternoon Miss Mao informed her that her friend was in a coma, and had been for over a week. These visits had always been a strain on the nurse. Miss Mao could not bear to tell her the truth.

CHAPTER 19

Peony could never tell either Paiwei or her parents how it happened. One late afternoon, she saw that the shutters of Chin

Chu's window had been closed. She waited in fear and her heart sank within her. It seemed like ages before the nurse came out and informed her of Chin Chu's passing away. Peony's lips seemed to dry up suddenly, and the blood left her face and ears. She had no tears. Miss Mao saw the pale figure walking away like an automaton along the river toward the city.

The next morning she was found by a monk behind a temple three miles away from the hospital, on the way to Hupao. The monk found her sleeping by a thicket near some giant boulders, and thought that she must have been a girl abducted here by someone and abandoned; yet her hair was not in tousled disorder, her quilted black silk jacket was well buttoned; there was no evidence of a struggle. The strange thing was that she must have waded across two shallow streams in the night, for there was no direct path from Liuhota Pagoda to Hupao. Or if she had taken the path by the lake, she must have trudged some six miles in the moonless night in a state of somnolence.

Peony did not know whether she was awake or dreaming when she felt someone shaking her. She opened her eyes. The ravine in that early morning lay in the shadow of the peaks of Tienchu. The shafts of light which came over the peaks revealed a virgin forest of giant pines, silent except for the eerie songs of birds, invisible and far away.

"Who are you? Why are you here in this deserted place?" asked the monk anxiously as she sat up with wondering eyes. In a stupor, she saw the lanky young monk in an ash-gray cassock towering over her. In the center of his shaven head were nine burn scars, in three neat rows.

Embarrassed at the monk's look, she tried to get up, and then gave a sudden shriek, as sharp pains shot through her foot. The monk helped her up, and she leaned the weight of her body against his shoulder. To the monk's astonishment, she gave a weak smile of immense satisfaction.

The monk was doubly surprised to hear her say: "It's wonderful. He has forgiven me. We've made up. It's such a wonderful, blissful feeling." She was speaking half to herself, slightly shaking her head. Then she looked up at him. "Do you know love? It is a wonderful thing."

Dew was glistening upon the sycamores and persimmons, as the morning sun stole over the peaks and sent pools of light into this isolated, deserted valley. Deep pockets of the ravine were still hidden by a blurred vapory canopy of morning fog. The place was strange, the man she was walking with was a stranger. It was as if they had reverted to a primitive existence and were the only two human beings on earth.

Anxious to relieve himself of this fleshy burden, the monk helped her over to a large flat rock where she could sit down. "And now," he said, "will you tell me who you are and what brought you here?"

"I don't know."

"Try to remember—how did you get here?"

"Never mind who I am. I am so happy. He is mine, completely, and he cannot get away from me now. It is forever."

The monk was sure now that she was out of her mind, that something terrible had happened to her.

"Who is 'he'?"

"Chin Chu, of course. Of course I know *you* are not Chin Chu. I can see that. You are taller, and you haven't got his sparkling eyes and his lovely, soft small hands. We made up, you know. We decided to forgive each other. And now we cannot quarrel any more, because he is inside me, completely."

Her eyes were focused on the distance. Almost immediately they closed and she fell asleep again. Her body was rocking and the young monk held his arm around her. As her body gave a sudden lurch sideways, he caught her in his arms before her head hit the rock.

He laid her gently down and in great trepidation ran back into the temple some twenty yards away, stumbling and looking back in disbelief, as if fleeing from a *yaksha*, a female evil spirit.

A few minutes later, the monk appeared again with an old priest and led him to the place where the prostrated woman lay. The old priest took her hand and shook it, but she was fast asleep.

"What shall we do?" said the priest. "I have never seen anything so strange in my life. We cannot leave her here, and we must not take her into the temple. We should be liable to a charge of concealing a woman for immoral purposes."

"At least let us take her in. She was talking with me, quite excitedly, only a short while ago. She must have walked in her sleep to this place. She was talking about her lover. He will most probably come and find her."

Between the two of them, they managed to raise her limp, sleeping body. The young monk carried the lovely burden into the temple where they laid her on a mat on the temple floor.

"There," said the old priest. "She will probably sleep for some time. We will watch her till she awakens, and can give an account of herself."

The old priest tested her forehead with his outstretched palm and declared that she had no fever. He pushed up her sleeves and saw a bautiful jade bracelet. "She must be from a rich family," he said. He searched her for any papers or clues to her identity, but found in her pocket only a handkerchief and some dollars and coins. Her hands bore several superficial cuts, and her shoes were coated with mud. It was a complete mystery. He called to the kitchen help for a cushion, and then loosened the button at her neck, and slid the pillow under her head.

The temple servant and another acolyte were now standing around watching the sleeping woman. The old priest gave orders to have someone sit by and keep watch, and have strong ginger tea ready in case she were to wake up.

Peony finally awoke around dusk, and was astounded to find herself in a temple. She stared at the monk in disbelief when he told her how he had found her lying on the grass that morning, and repeated some of the things she had said. She still looked dazed.

In a few seconds she had her bearings, and then she remembered Miss Mao. The awful realization of the fact of Chin Chu's death, definite and irremediable, flooded her with a sense of loss and utter defeat. Her dream was finished. She was alone. Her head hung to one side, and she shivered with an irrepressible spasm, and started to weep, her whole body shaking, her stifled sobs swelling uncontrollably, wetting the cushion where her head lay. The young monk offered her ginger tea, but ignoring him, she crumpled up in a bundle of anguish and misery, pounding the cushion helplessly with her hand. The monk attempted to ask her what had happened, and she answered, "Chin Chu died. My Chin Chu died," and then she started to cry again with choking, heart-rending sobs.

The monk pulled her up, and forced her to take the bowl of ginger tea. This steadied her and restored her mind to full consciousness.

"What time is it and where am I?"

The monk told her.

"How far from the city?"

"Three or four miles."

"How did I get here?"

"We don't know if you don't."

She was quiet now. She looked helplessly into the distance. In that instant she fully realized what had happened, but still felt a little confused. Distortions of dream and reality crowded her mind like alternate pictures of the most absolute happiness and utter despair. Suddenly she remembered that she had not been home and her parents must be worrying about her.

It was long after the supper hour when Peony arrived home by sedan chair. Her parents had been terrified when she failed to return that night. Her father had taken the morning off to go to the hospital and find out where she was. Miss Mao was greatly distressed to find that Peony had not returned home. Chin Chu had died, her father was informed, and the wife was there now, weeping in the room. Miss Mao cautioned him into silence, lest the wife should hear about Peony. According to the nurse, Peony had received the news in silence, and then walked off in the direction of the city.

The father's patience was near the breaking point. When Peony returned home that night, he was ready with an accounting of all the things she had done in the past years. The father saw her swollen eyes, her listless face as she descended from her sedan chair. So this silly fool of a daughter had come home. He choked with anger, and would have shouted at her had not his wife tugged at his elbow and said, "She has come home," implying that nothing further should be said.

Now that she was safely home, the mother's suspense was over. Peony's safety was the only important thing. In spite of all urging to eat something, Peony said she had no appetite. She was offered some porridge, hardly touched it, and went to bed.

The next morning, Peony woke up, still dazed, confused, and unable to disentangle her fantasies of a final reunion with her lover and the cold, naked fact of his death. The father had breakfasted and gone out. Before he left, he had said to his wife, "I can never understand this child of mine. It's lucky she's got a home to come back to. First, the break with her husband's family. Then, she has to go to Peking with her cousin. Then she changes her mind and comes back. And now . . ."

"She is young. Everybody's young once," the mother cried defensively.

"That does not mean she has to be man-crazy. What next?"

He had come, bit by bit, to learn about her infatuation with Chin Chu, a married man—her former lover, he understood. He had strongly disapproved of her daily visits to the hospital in the past several weeks. What a scandal if the wife should find out! But every time he tried to remonstrate with her, Peony flew into an argument, maintaining that she was of age and a widow, that she knew perfectly well what she was doing. Peony lacked neither the ability nor the spirit to defend herself. He consoled himself with the thought that at least, now, her paramour was dead.

The mother found Peony lying in bed, her eyes staring blankly at the ceiling. She brought her some mince meat and the rice porridge she had left untouched from last night.

"Now, eat," she said, seating herself upon the edge of the bed.

Peony took the tray. She reached out and gently touched her mother's hand.

"Mama," she said, "you are the most wonderful person on earth."

"My child, you gave us such a scare yesterday. Now eat and you will feel better."

But she clung to her mother, and then started to weep, her mother patting her as she would a child.

She stayed in bed that day, and the next, overcome by an extreme lassitude, like one returning from a long journey. Once in a while, she trailed around the house in her slippers, and then went back to bed again, shutting the door behind her. She craved the solitude and preferred to be all by herself, thinking, reading here and there in a desultory fashion, and doing nothing at all. She could thus lie in bed for hours, living with her own thoughts, her own memories, and her own dreams. And she yielded to the fathomless and wordless fantasy, so real to her, which to her replaced the bodily presence of Chin Chu. At times it seemed that Chin Chu was nearer to her, now that he was dead. She could not recall the scenes in her delirium which she tried so hard to remember, but she felt still vividly the distinct music and tone of them. It seemed that Chin Chu and she were floating in a world of clouds and vapor, alone, happy and united, free, weightless in a world of moonbeams, saying to themselves, "Now our troubles are over." That vague, sweet, intoxicating feeling of immense and limitless freedom to love each other remained like a haunting echo in her mind.

Chin Chu's death was the most important turning point in her life. It was final and irreparable. She felt liberated. She had to reorient her feelings and start a new life. The many wounds in her soul waited to be healed. She was almost excruciatingly sensitive to the slightest noise, to the touch of objects soft and warm. She was undergoing a great convalescence, as real as if she were recovering from a long disease.

She lay in bed for hours, just thinking. Chin Chu, had

he lived, would be alternately petulant and tender, short-tempered and endearing, heartbreaking and heartwarming by turns, and he would grow old and change. But Chin Chu, by his death, had assumed the image and the cloak of an immortal love. He was enshrined like a young martyr, beyond the touch of time, beyond change and beyond death itself. She labored, when she felt better, at pasting up his letters, notes, and poems, including the envelopes which she had saved, and binding them with a silk thread in a handsome volume covered with brocade in an intricate design of black and gold. She made up another volume of her own notes, poems in manuscript, and random lines, in wild disorder like her thoughts—unfashioned, unfinished, and unending. She added to these notes when wandering thoughts and strange images came to her mind; they were always exaggerated and colored with emotional power—phrases like "that magnificent, dark sweet slumber in his breast" and "the sweet, white light of his fingers against the starry night." These thoughts were her life, her most intimate feelings.

She spoke these thoughts aloud to herself, as she spoke to his letters in the brocade volume, and it was as if he were in the room. Sometimes her mother smelled burning paper from her room. She had written many of these sacrificial prayers to his spirit and said them and then lit them by the flame of the candle to send them to his spirit. It was strangely satisfying. These cherished memories were her life, and she began to love the solitude of her room, feeling his presence surrounding her. Her soul was at peace.

Peony's father was greatly pleased that she was no longer running around the city like a bitch in heat. One day at supper, he asked her: "Now what are you going to do with yourself?"

"I don't know."

It was about this time that Peony's parents had received the letter from Jasmine asking for her legal adoption by Uncle Sueipo, an astonishing request, inexplicable, except for one reason only. Mengchia himself had written to the uncle.

Coupled with the elder daughter's return, this made it pretty clear. The parents resisted the impulse to ask her about it during the first days of her shock, for fear it would upset her. But one day, she was well enough to ask about her sister, who had always kept up a regular correspondence with her parents.

Her mother told her and concluded, "Now what can it be if Jasmine is not going to get married to your Tako? It isn't for Uncle Sueipo's property. And if your uncle wanted to adopt an heir, the request should have come from him."

Peony was aghast, completely stunned.

"What do you think? You never told us what happened between you sisters and your cousin."

Peony's face blushed as she stuttered, "Oh, Jasmine! . . . Yes, she loved him secretly, I know. It must have happened after I left."

She spoke no more and went back to her room. To her, as to the family, it was such an unexpected turn. She herself might have married him, certainly would have, if they had been able to think of a way to do it. She did not know what to think. She felt an uncomfortable wave of jealousy and yet she could find no reason to blame Jasmine for it. Whose idea was it, hers or his? If Jasmine had thought of it, why had she not suggested it when she, Peony, was so much in love with Mengchia? Tako was now to become her brother-in-law; yet he could have been her husband.

Then it became clear to her—she did not know when the certainty arose in her mind—that Mengchia loved her still. She knew it from her own experience. Even as her love of Chin Chu could not die, so Mengchia must still love her now. Love was an eternal self-giving liquid, flowing from inside, craving return —but returned or not, it was there. Chin Chu had rejected her as brutally as she had left Mengchia. Now she had found out that it made no difference; she was sure that Mengchia would forgive her if he truly loved her, as she had forgiven Chin Chu's remorseless cruelty. She remembered Mengchia's final words on that night: "No matter what you do, you shall be the most pure and subtle fiber in my being." It was so true, she was sure of it.

It would be poetic, so marvelous if she didn't marry, or if he never heard from her again and could preserve that sanctified image of her in his mind, as she did of Chin Chu.

She already had an idea that she wanted to disappear—she must disappear from his life as, indeed, she said she would in her farewell letter—not only for Jasmine's sake, but for her own.

On the twenty-sixth of November of that year, the Chin house at Hangchow held a memorial service for Chin Chu. The notice had gone out in an obituary folder, beautifully printed in Sung-style script, outlining the distinguished career of the young man, who was survived by his wife and a son and two daughters, the last only a few weeks old. Much was made of his being a good son at home, of his brilliance and his marital felicity. On the doorjambs of the gate hung festoons of white chrysanthemums set against evergreen leaves. Inside, the spacious hall was filled with square, redwood tables. The guests, who had overflowed into the court, filled the house with a noisy hubbub, punctuated by the periodic ceremonial wailing of the family and the blare of horns and short trumpets.

The Chins were an old family in Hangchow. The deceased young man, being a *churen*, belonged to a class by itself, the class of officials and scholars in the government service, who had secured their degrees by passing the imperial examinations; they were bound by their own set of loyalties and connections in official circles. There were also many old friends of the family, of the grandparents and parents—bankers, well-to-do merchants, owners of large firms—whose carriages stretched far around the block and overflowed to a main street. A small band of short brass trumpets and drums played at intervals, alternating with the wailing of the men and, especially, of the women. The male relatives walked about with a white band around their foreheads, chatting with the guests. There was a clinking of jade and gold at one end, where the women were crowded, whispering loudly to each other. The lady guests kept a sharp watch on those who came in to pay their respects to the casket in the center of the hall, and commented on them, straightening out the family relationships for each other's benefit—who was who and related by what aunt or cousin or in-law to somebody else. It would seem that in a city like Hangchow, hardly a person of the same upper class was unknown, who could not be easily identified by some lady now chatting inside the hall.

Peony had seen a notice of the memorial service in the local newspaper, and also a copy of the long biographical sketch at the home of a friend. The Chin family was making a social occasion of it, and for two days the newspapers carried a paid announcement of the service. Usually the arrangements for a formal funeral took several months; but the Chin family had its cemetery plots already on the Phoenix Hill. The memorial service was to take place on November the twenty-sixth and twenty-seventh, so that all friends and acquaintances might pay their respects to the dead, and on the twenty-eighth there was to be the funeral procession.

Peony had looked forward to that date for a week. She had to attend. It was inconceivable that she should absent herself at the last rites of her lover. She could easily slip in unnoticed.

She went in and found the place filled with guests. She saw the casket and behind it a portrait of the deceased. Her heart was pounding. She walked up and stood for a minute after making her three bows, looking like one in a stupor. Suddenly she whipped out a handkerchief and tried to smother a sob. But the more she tried to control herself, the louder became her sniffs. Her knees wobbled and she fell by the side of the coffin, embracing it with one arm and crumbling up like a doll in tears. She could no longer control herself and in her great misery she did not care. Before anyone could quite realize what was happening, her frenzied sobs and uncontrolled weeping rent the hall.

Dramatically, silence fell upon the guests. This was no ceremonial weeping; she was crying her heart out, in great gulps, unrestrained and oblivious to all who surrounded her. She knocked her head repeatedly against the casket, uttering disjointed words and syllables that were cut short by her tears and impossible to make out.

Everybody asked, "Who is that woman?" Nobody knew.

The wife stood rigid, like a frozen statue. First mystified and confused, then clearly suspicious, her eyes were riveted on this young and beautiful woman whom she had never seen or heard her husband speak of. She guessed it must be the harlot from Shanghai he had been living with. She inquired from the others. No one could say, as her face was covered. This sweetheart now had the effrontery to appear in public and weep at the coffin— her husband's coffin! She was in a rage.

Her eyes blazing, she came up close to the weeping woman still squatting on the ground, hugging the side of the coffin.

"Who are you?" she demanded.

Peony looked up. She didn't know what to say. Through dimmed eyes, she saw the white, powdered face of the shouting, ranting woman looking down upon her. Before she could answer, a hard whack across her cheek made her smart. Peony raised her hand to avert another blow.

"How dare you! Get her out!" the wife was shrieking. Men and women closed in, astonished at what was happening. Peony picked herself up and tried to run away, but the wife had caught her by the collar, her primitive anger mocking the refined appearance of the gentle fair sex. A male relative tried to pull them apart and forced the wife to let go her grip. Still ranting and panting in quick gasps of breath, she tossed out a stream of abuse in local Soochow dialect: "Bastard! You mongrel whore! Heart-stealing wench damned to the eighteenth hell! See that the devil slit your jelly-roll in half. . . ." The profanity was part of the local Soochow. She certainly would have torn her hair out if a man had not hastily escorted the unknown visitor off the scene and outside into the court. The wife stamped her feet and spat at the floor where Peony had knelt, and then at her husband's coffin where her hand had touched it. Peony, covering her head between her arms, hastily made her way out into the street.

The memorial service was suspended for some twenty minutes. The wife could not be persuaded to go on with the ceremony, and someone else took her place at the end of the coffin.

It was verified that the wife had stopped crying for her husband from that minute on, and did not appear again that afternoon.

CHAPTER 20

Peony had created a scandal that day that was the talk of the town. What she did was unprecedented in the annals of Hangchow history. The men loved it, made ribald jokes about it, and in general wished that they could have such a pretty woman to weep over their coffins. The society matrons were outraged and infuriated by it; wives began to look twice at their husbands; a few younger women and unmarried girls envied Peony for her courage. If Peony had controlled herself, she could have come into that public gathering, made her bows, and disappeared, unrecognized. As it was, she had created a scandal for herself, her lover, and his family.

Such an event provided material for delicious gossip. Those who left early regretted that they had not stayed longer to see the scene of the two women caterwauling before the man's coffin. Those who came late and heard about it afterward regretted that they had not come half an hour earlier. The visitors of the day were made up of a fair cross-section of the highest society of Hangchow. The story, carried by word of mouth, went from family to family, from teahouse to teahouse, with the usual distortions and added conjectures passing for facts. It came out that she had made daily secret visits to the hospital, that she was his secret sweetheart all those years when Chin Chu was known to be a model husband. It further came out that she was the famous Sanmei of the Liangs, and that as a widow, she couldn't "keep the lone bed" and left her husband's family only three months after his death. (Her episode with Mengchia happily escaped public notice. There was nothing reprehensible in the sisters' going up to Peking.)

The wife was so mortified that she hurriedly left for her Soochow home after the funeral, having thoroughly lost face in public. She would not mind so much if her husband had kept a harlot and been discreet about it—just so long as nobody talked.

As for Peony, she regretted what she had done, but also felt a sense of selfish exultation. She did not see how, knowing of the memorial service, she could have stayed away or how, having gone, she could have avoided breaking down the way she did.

"Now look what you have done!" the father fulminated the next morning. "The story will be all over town in three days. To go and weep at the *wrong coffin*, the coffin of *another woman's husband!* What a scandal! And you had to go and do it! . . . Do you know what you were doing to that family, to yourself, and to me?"

Peony was silent and only stared blankly.

"Did you ever stop to think of your father? As a child, you were always capricious, willful, had to have your own way. Why did you have to pick a married man?"

"He loved me, and I loved him. He married against his will. He told me he loved me, not his wife."

"So you still met him after he was married! I am ashamed for you. . . . You didn't have to flirt. . . ."

Peony felt suffocated. Her father would never understand her. She slammed the door and walked out of the house to be by herself. Once outside, she drew a breath of relief. Oblivious to everything, she passed the crowded market in the next street, and after a few turns in the narrow alleys, emerged at the lake shore. This was the poor area of town; a fishing jetty, with broken, creaky planks, led to the water, littered with garbage of vegetables and fruit peels. A prowling dog was sniffing at the water in vain. She went up along the bank, passed a third-class hotel where she knew some prostitutes had taken rooms by the month. The thin coating of white plaster on its walls had peeled off into irregular plots, like islands on a map. A faded sign hung at the gate, bearing the name "Wangshanlou" (Hillview Hotel), taking its name from the Hillview Gate in Hangchow. Further on were some cheap restaurants and teashops. She went into one of them; there was no one around at this hour, except a few waiters cleaning up the tables.

She felt so depressed that she came out again and turned back south, following the bank until she came to the *Tsienwangmiao* (temple dedicated to King Tsien of the tenth century). The hard court of red clay in front was planted with cypresses, a sanctuary for birds where shooting was forbidden. Passing it, she went and sat on one of the stone benches near the bank.

It was the first time in a month that she had seen the West Lake, which now lay before her—a picture of stillness under a sky of heavy, somber, grayish clouds which hid the highest mountain peaks from view. There were only one or two boats on the water. Looking across the lake at the Paiti Embankment, she saw the place deserted, a cluster of small pleasure boats anchored on the shore line.

She was seized with an immense sense of loneliness, after a month of emotional stress ending in disillusioned hope and a broken dream. She felt all played out, her heart as bare and dry as that wintry landscape before her. Life seemed to have passed her by. Nobody understood her, nobody except Paiwei. Everything seemed dry, unimportant, and devoid of meaning.

Days passed. She remained in that state of vacuum, hugging her own memories, and nursing the throbbing heartaches whenever she thought of her lost love. As she no longer cared to answer back, her father kept needling her with taunts of her past follies, mentioning the fact that he had been made the target of many sly jokes among his colleagues.

At this time, there was further excitement in the family. Besides Peony's escapade, Jasmine and Mengchia had written to ask for the father's permission for marriage. The wedding was to take place in Peking, and they expressed the hope that it might be possible for them to come down and see the parents after the wedding, as was proper—perhaps in spring or summer. This cheered the parents' hearts a great deal, but at the same time they were glad that the wedding was to be in Peking. Coming on top of the gossip and the furor about their elder daughter, Jasmine's marriage with her cousin would cause more wagging of tongues. Legally, Jasmine would have a different surname, but socially, who would not know that she was a Liang marrying a Liang?

Peony, too, was glad that they were not coming down south immediately. It would be awkward and embarrassing after all that had happened between Mengchia and herself. She thought of him as a kindly old man, with whom she had once been infatuated. Once the name of Mengchia was like a magic word standing for all that was good and beautiful and wonderful; now in its place remained only a faint echo and a mockery of her own youthful passion. The affair was over, and she would rather be left alone. She had forgotten Mengchia. Instead, the letters from Peking called up those marvelous days at Tienchiao and Shishahai, their plebeian gaiety and popular entertainments. There was nothing in Hangchow to compare with them. Hangchow was poetically and quietly beautiful, but it was too quiet for her young soul. Neither Jasmine nor Mengchia mentioned her name in their last letters. This was deliberate policy on Mengchia's part, thinking it pointless to stir up the ashes of a dead fire.

The local papers had, of course, carried the story, much toned down, of the broken-up memorial service. She had no idea that she had become a celebrity in the town gossip. Her solitary walks inevitably carried her to some teahouse or other, where she felt relaxed in the company of men from all walks of life, as she had in her Peking days.

One afternoon, in one of the teahouses, a respectably dressed man came in, wearing a black silk skullcap topped by a red button and carrying a long-stemmed pipe. A habitual customer, he ordered a pot of tea and sent for a barber from a neighboring shop, as he preferred to have a shave here rather than in the cramped and stuffy shop. The loud-voiced bespectacled barber came in. He was a man of fifty and a bachelor whose face oozed unctuousness and smiles in equal proportion. He had won many customers by his entertaining talks. He could easily fill a daily column, entitled, "The Things That Men Do." For a crop of his hair, his customer could always get in exchange a crop of news and stories and the latest jokes, told with salty comments from the barber's own secure, detached point of view. He had a way of standing above the troubles that beset his fellow men. From the moment a customer was seated till he had finished with a few plops on his neck and shoulders, his customer was regaled with a miscellaneous flow of gossip—wild, improbable, but salacious and highly entertaining.

Peony sat in one corner and heard the voluble barber say: "Would you believe it? Recently there was a woman who cried at the wrong coffin, the coffin of another woman's husband! This was at the Chin house at Chenchiashiang. The wife's tears dried up completely, at once, when she saw her husband's sweetheart fall over the coffin, crying her head off, and discovered her husband had such a sweetheart, and he was supposed to be a model husband, too! They tore each other's hair out in front of all the guests. Imagine the uproar! And this happened in one of the best and oldest families of Hangchow. You know what I would do if I were that dead man?"

"What?"

"I would knock at the coffin from the inside and say, 'Shut up.' "

The people at the teahouse roared.

Peony blushed to the roots of her hair. She threw down a few coppers and left hastily, hoping that no one had seen her.

Another day, she hired a small boat, so that she could be quite alone. It was the day before winter solstice and a number of young people had come out to celebrate. She told the boatman to row to the Inner Lake, and stretched herself out on a low chair, letting her thoughts wander at will as the boat scudded gently along. At Tuanchiao, she heard young voices from another boat. As she came near, she could hear the young people engaged in an energetic discussion of the now famous memorial service incident, punctuated with boisterous laughter. One man was defending the strange young woman, saying that it was what a true lover would do, and should do, and more-over, could not *help* doing upon seeing the casket. She threw a quick glance at the boat, and shut her eyes, pretending to be asleep. The others in the boat thought otherwise, and disparaged the lover for bringing disgrace upon the family.

The love story of Peony and Chin Chu had the elements of sex, bravado, and adventure which make a good ballad. In less than two weeks, a teahouse professional storyteller had woven it, with many embellishments, into a connected story, a living romance. From this, it was but a short step to becoming a modern ballad, sung by blind minstrel singers to the accompani-ment of a three-stringed *sanshuan*. Like the popular ballad of "Ingtai and Sanpo," it both amused and excited the admiration of the listeners for what a pair of passionate lovers had dared to do.

Peony now changed her habits, and preferred to stay at home. Wherever she went, she had a feeling that people were looking at her. She used to love going to a teahouse on the Hupin Square where she could watch people over a cup of tea, and listen to a storyteller at sunset, telling about the romance of the *Three Kingdoms* or the cycle of the *Heroes of the Lake*. Now, whenever she saw people talking in whispers, she imagined they were discussing her and she would blush nervously and steal away as quickly as possible. She chose the less frequented places along the sea wall, or the canal district, where busy traffic was going on and people had no time or inclination to look at her.

Yet the *Ballad of the Red Peony* had become popular:

> There was once a lady, two-and-twenty was she,
> Can't tell where she's from, or what they name her.
> It was God made her so, to be loved and to love,
> And in truth, to be fair, you can't quite blame her.
>
> Her neck was like a swan's, her voice the nightingale's,
> She was all the wondrous things spun together,
> Her eyes were like a lake, and her smile like a breeze,
> And her heart fickle as the April weather.
>
> Be she sprite or woman, be she Fairy Caprice,
> As far as her looks go, they don't come any better.

The toast of the town, and the curse of the wives,
Fatal was her charm to all who had met her.

Her husband died when she was twenty-two,
There was ne'er a better or merrier loser.
The mien of a goddess, the heart of a woman,
And they christened her "The Outgoing Cruiser." . . .

The ballad, composed anonymously, as usual, by some hack
writer, made maximum use of the fact that the unknown woman
was a widow who had left her husband's home after three
months, and aimed for effect by painting her as a *femme fatale*.
It appealed to the popular, middle-class prejudices and en-
trenched morals. However, there were many on that day of the
memorial service who were profoundly moved by what they saw,
and whose sympathy was drawn toward that tragic sweetheart,
in purely human terms. Many were sympathetic to the lover
rather than the wife; the tragedy of a girl caught in love always
elicits a human response, especially among the poets. Nothing
excites the imagination so much as a thwarted love affair, or an
illicit love, or a *crime passionnel*.

There were many incurably sentimental poets at the Shiling
Club. Many of the scholars knew Chin Chu and it was now a
matter of common knowledge that the lovers had enjoyed a
mad romance before marriage. Often a theme was chosen after
lunch at the Club, so that the members could show their skill
at versifying. Nine out of ten poems romanticized about the
lover's sorrow, her weeping and remorse, as it was practically
impossible to romanticize about the maddened, jealous wife.
These poems circulated from mouth to mouth among the
literati as rapidly as gossip among women. Peony's name was
rocketed to literary fame, which embarrassed her still further.

It was rapidly becoming impossible for her to remain in her
home town. Hiding in her home and harassed by her uncompre-
hending father, she felt suffocated, and longed for a chance to
escape to a place where she could be unknown and search out
her destiny.

Paiwei and her husband came down to the city to spend the New Year holidays with Joshui's relatives. She found her friend quite changed. Peony looked quiet and tired; her sweet melancholy and her softer voice and slower speech gave her sedate dignity that Paiwei had not seen in her before. Paiwei and Joshui lived such an isolated life that they had not heard about Chin Chu's death, and learned about it from Peony's own lips. The two friends were so close that Paiwei lived through the agony herself as she heard the story. When Peony showed her the brocade-bound volume of Chin Chu's letters and her friend's eyes lit up with an almost unearthly frenzy, Paiwei knew that there in that little volume lay buried a dream of passionate love which had absorbed and changed her whole being. Yet Peony could not go on like this, hugging her young grief.

"Why, you cannot hide yourself all day in your room. You must pull yourself together. . . . What are you going to do with yourself?"

"I don't know. I am happy as I am."

Paiwei was pained to see the sad, sweet smile on her friend's face, as Peony said, "Nothing is important any more. You know the day of the funeral, I felt a tremendous urge inside to go and follow the casket. My mother stopped me for fear I might not be able to control myself and might disgrace myself again. She actually locked me in. She was right. I could not trust myself. And all the time I felt I was not living, I was not here, I was dead and somewhere else, being buried with him."

After they had talked for about an hour, Peony seemed more composed, more her usual self. Paiwei sought out the mother to have a talk with her alone. The mother had never liked Paiwei, thinking her a bad influence upon her daughter. Surprised to see Paiwei come into her room, she gave a stiff, perfunctory welcome. Paiwei saw the look of preoccupation on her face.

"Mrs. Liang, may I have a word with you? I am worried."

The mother lifted an expectant face.

"Sit down. I am glad you came. How do you find her?"

"She is all right. Naturally she has not got over it. Mother Liang, you were young once. If you only knew how much Chin

Chu meant to her. I do not know what you think. She is not really frivolous...."

"I understand my daughter," said the mother defensively.

"I know. You know as well as I do that everything a young girl does, she does to find the right man. She really loved Chin Chu, and never anybody else. Remember when she tried to commit suicide when he was engaged? She may seem frivolous, but she is not. I am her best friend, I know. And now she is afraid to go out and meet people. I understand there is a great deal of gossip about her, as if she had done something immoral, shocking, horrible. She told me about the ballad. They are calling her the 'Red Peony.' I know the name will stick."

Mrs. Liang listened with her narrowed eyes creased in absorbed attention.

"I believe you do understand her," she said, and sighed deeply, staring earnestly at Paiwei. "I cannot talk to her father about her. But, Paiwei, I believe you do understand. Did she tell you that she has gone up to weep at his grave on Phoenix Hill?"

"She had not told me."

"I am worried. She will go crazy. Her father mustn't know. Imagine a young woman going out alone at night to that hill. Anything may happen. It's not far from here. You must dissuade her. Her father was furious when he discovered she had gone out after supper. Tell me what I should do."

"She must get away from here. I will invite her to stay with me after the holidays. She needs somebody to talk to. Time will do the rest. Mother Liang, you must not worry too much. She is young. She will get over it. I know."

The mother looked at her anxiously. "I want to believe you. This child has given me so much worry. Did you hear about Jasmine?"

"Yes, isn't it fantastic?"

"What did Peony say about it?"

"She laughed. You wouldn't mind my telling you a secret. She believes that her cousin is still in love with her and that Jasmine is getting it on the rebound."

The mother's eyes visibly darkened. "She can't be in love with her Tako still," she said, as if she were begging Paiwei to confirm the fact.

"No, she assured me she is not."

"Well, this child of mine has given me so much worry. You remember how gay she was. She was unhappy in her marriage and I don't blame her for coming back. Then she wanted to go to Peking. Then she changed her mind. And now . . ."

"That is because she is different. She feels things that others don't. She is unique. She says that she was born like that. She ought to find a man."

"But she won't talk about it. She says she is happy and resents people discussing her problem. Paiwei, you said a moment ago that everything a girl does is explained by her looking for the right man. Of course. How can she find a man that she will marry? I have been thinking of nothing else. But she must get over this crazy mooning about her dead lover. You can help her. Take her out. Life must still go on."

"I will. But she is of such a passionate nature. Sometimes I feel she must be protected against herself."

The short talk changed the mother's opinion of Paiwei, as if a barrier had dissolved, letting a new warmth flow between them, based on the sharing of a common secret and their genuine, deep concern for Peony.

"Don't say anything about it to her," said the mother. "She will be angry if she knows we have discussed her."

CHAPTER 21

The New Year passed. After the New Year party, Aunt Su told the mother that she noticed that Peony had suddenly grown up and a thoughtful look had come into her eyes. She was not sulky and aloof, but was most of the time silent, listening to all the talk with a resigned and detached expression. In the following fortnight, Peony was in Paiwei's company every day and this helped a great deal to restore her spirits. They saw their mutual friends, or went out boating; visited the Jade Spring Temple to see the giant carp two or three feet long kept by the monks in a pond of spring water; took long walks along the Nine Streams and Eighteen Rapids. One day they went out to drink tea at Hupao, famous for its spring water. Another day, they went to see the Tomb of Yofei, the great patriot general who resisted the Kin invaders at the end of the Northern Sung Dynasty.

By the time of the *Shangyuan* lantern festival, Peony appeared quite recovered. In the evening she was going with Paiwei and Joshui to look at the exhibition of lanterns which each family had made in a contest for novelty of design. Along the Hupin Square, booths had been set up by the great families—an old tradition handed down from the Sung days when Hangchow was the national capital. Young ladies, married and unmarried, did not mind being seen that night, where they sat in their booths or walked about, commenting on the exhibits. The young women and girls wore fiber flowers in their hair and were looking their best in the reddish glow of the lanterns. All restrictions were suspended and the city gates were not closed that night. The square was jammed with young men and girls. In the empty spaces along the shore line, children were setting off firecrackers and rockets which soared into the sky and came down in showers of sparks, burning out before they reached the water.

It was their last night before they were to go up to Tunglu. After making the rounds, Peony strolled with Paiwei and Joshui to the shore of the lake, where they sat on the stone landing, preferring the quiet there, and watched the lighted boats threading their way among lotus-lanterns in their nests of green leaves, floating on the lake surface.

"I think I want to go away," said Peony thoughtfully.

"Where to?" asked Joshui. "To Peking?"

"No."

"Where would you go?"

"I don't know. I can't stay here. I feel stifled. Some place where I am unknown, where I can be myself again—Shanghai—Hong Kong."

"But how? How will you support yourself?"

"Why worry?" Peony answered with spirit. "All I know is that I must leave this place behind me. I can do any work, as servant, kitchen maid—any kind."

"Yes, and get us all worried about you," said Joshui.

"I'm not afraid. What do I care? Oh, look!"

On the embankment, five or six small rockets soared into the sky, trailing tails of light, and exploding into showers of yellow and purple. The lake was illuminated for a second. Paiwei saw Peony's white profile against the dark face of the lake, her head erect, a curling smile on her lips. Paiwei felt that Peony was her old self again, as spirited and restless and full of mischief as she'd ever been.

Joshui liked to bully Peony; he knew that she liked it. "Oh, no," he said vehemently, "you'd hate it after a week."

"A week of what?"

"You were talking about doing any kind of work, being kitchen maid and all that."

"You don't believe me?" Peony answered with spirit.

"I don't. What you need is to find a man to love. Isn't that right?" he asked teasingly.

"All right, find me a man, a man who adores me as you adore Paiwei."

"But you had such a man. The *hanlin* adores you. You didn't want him."

Peony paused in silence. Joshui had touched a very tender spot. She was aware of an uncompleted passion, like a rocket which has shot up into midair and failed to fan out in luminous glory. One might call her affair with Mengchia a failure, but whatever the label, it was now accented by Jasmine's success. She had her moments of gnawing doubt as to whether Mengchia had, or had not, thought of the obvious and simple solution of changing surnames while she was still with him in Peking. She drew a heavy breath and said, "You know the saddest thing in life? Not the death of a lover, but the death of love. How sad it is that even love must change."

Paiwei's gilt slippers gleamed like two streaks of light as she swung her trousered legs against the landing, her hand resting in Joshui's lap. Peony's memory shot back across the years to the time when she and Paiwei, then sixteen or seventeen, had first met Joshui, as their boat lay tied to the willow-covered bank at Tuanchiao. And the marriage had made no difference to their friendship. The half-moon of Paiwei's face hung over the water's edge, her legs spread wide apart as no decent women would in public, even in that semidarkness. She could do this and continue to be her real self because Joshui not only approved, but adored her for it; it was proof of a harmony that was rare and enviable.

"How long have you been married?"

"Four years and seven months," replied Paiwei, half guessing what was on her mind.

"And still a bride."

"Yes, and still a bride," Paiwei crooned gently as she cast a swift glance at Joshui. She tapped lightly on Peony's thigh and said, "Come on, let's go back. We want to catch the boat early tomorrow."

"But why?" protested Peony in pained surprise.

"We have to get up early to catch the boat at seven."

"But tonight is *Shangyuan*, which comes only once a year! I won't go home yet. Not at this hour!"

The excitement on Peony's face told Paiwei that she really meant to stay. She remembered the days long ago when they had come out of the theater with Chin Chu at midnight, and she had to accompany Peony home, over her protests. She recalled the nights they had spent together, talking, during a trip to Yutsien. The instinct of the night owl was upon her. She needed this excitement, this abandon of *Shangyuan* when no explanation was needed if she returned home late, especially since her parents knew that she had come out with Paiwei.

"You go home first," Peony said to them. Joshui gave his wife a nudge, and they walked away arm in arm, after being assured that Peony didn't want them to accompany her home. Peony thought that she, too, would not mind going home now if she were like Paiwei, with a Joshui walking by her side. If she were away from this city, living all alone, would not every night be *Shangyuan*? It was this total liberty that she craved—this was one of the reasons she had decided to leave Mengchia. She wanted a widow's liberty, an independence complete and without obligation to anybody.

"Her restlessness—isn't it strange?" Joshui said, as they passed the fringe of the illuminated square into the opaque darkness of a small street. Paiwei was thinking the same thought, but she listened in silence. "You've got a job, or we've got a job," Joshui continued. "We'd be doing her parents a great favor if we could find a poet or painter for her husband. She needs love."

"Do you think it is all due to her reading?"

"No, it is in herself, the way she is made. What she did at the hospital is really touching—secretly visiting her lover behind the wife's back and watching him while he was asleep after he had rejected her so brutally. Chin Chu never got over her betrayal of him, of course. You've broken her spell now—taking her out of her daydreaming. I was worried that she would never get out of it. Now she has, but the change is too sudden. I bet you she is ready for love tonight—and it will be whoever comes along first. I saw that liquid luster in her eyes. The mood of the lantern festival, of course. But it is so sudden."

"Yes, I wonder," replied Paiwei.

Joshui's soft chuckle ended in a weary sigh. Paiwei clung to his arm. They listened in silence to their own footsteps on the pebbled road.

"What are you sighing about?" asked Paiwei.

"About Peony. I saw her eyes glistening in the dark when we were sitting upon the shore. I can't make her out. How, according to what she said to you, she could stop loving a man like Mengchia so abruptly. Did she stop loving him after she knew the boxer, or did she fall for the boxer after she found she could not love him? And according to what she told you, there were quite a few others—"

Paiwei tried to defend her. "Men fall for her. It's not her fault. She is so pretty."

"Yes, pretty and naughty. Prettier than many, and naughtier than most who have not the courage to do what she did."

The lantern exhibit had passed its peak. Most of the booths were deserted and dark now. Idling men and groups of young girls still kept the square alive with their frolic and occasional bursts of laughter, but more and more people were disappearing into the outer darkness. A huge lantern on the boat jetty, the size and shape of a seven-foot pagoda, was now only half lighted; most of the candles had gone out, and it looked like a distorted and grotesque lady appearing in the street without all her make-up. On the water, specks of light sparkled here and there, the lotus lanterns having drifted far out and dispersed in different directions. At the opposite shore, bands of liquid silver reflected the lights in the villas. Tonight the moon was hidden behind broken patches of clouds, revealing indistinctly the low banks of mauvish-gray mists hanging across the midriffs of the mountains.

Up on the terraced towers of the Paiti some three hundred yards away, the bright lights of the Louwailou appeared deceptively near across the darkened water, and above it, colored lanterns splattered light on vague, moving forms on the terrace of the Shiling Club. Peony thought of the afternoon when Mengchia took her to that Club and his hand enclosed hers in that first exciting gesture of love. All that had passed between them since seemed like a capricious and unresolved dream, unanswerable to reason. The faintest echo of music and song pierced the night. There was activity at the Club, she was sure. On an impulse, she decided to walk in that direction.

As she emerged into the area of white light in front of the restaurant, the strains of music and laughter floated over the treetops. She looked up. Two lighted dragons, their heads meeting from opposite directions, over a large lighted ball representing a pearl, stretched across the base of the balcony. Notes of a woman's singing voice mingled with screeching, scraping strings. On the stone steps leading up to the Club was a series of artificial moons, partly hidden by foliage.

There was nobody at the gate. With the courage of *Shang-yuan*, she went in. A couple coming down the steps met her at the entrance. "Can I go up?" she asked. The man, surveying her young figure and taking her for one of the singsong girls, answered, "Of course."

Men and women were spread in pairs in the shadowy arbor-houses and terrace of the garden. Peony felt choked with a tremendous feeling of loneliness. She sat on one of the stone benches just below the balconied terrace. An unaccountable lassitude seized her as she heard the gay voices of men and women above and saw the distant lights of *Santan Inyueh* (Thrice-Mirrored Moon) in midlake, now appearing like an indistinct enchanted isle.

Peony sat quite alone for a long while. She knew full well that a young girl sitting alone on a night like this was bound to attract some attention. After a while, a couple strolled by, then turned back to take a second look. Leaving his partner, the man approached her and asked diffidently: "Pardon me. Aren't you Red Peony? I may be mistaken, but, pardon me, I was at the memorial service and I was the man who got you out from that crowd."

Peony flushed a little, as she looked up at the stranger. She was neither offended, nor encouraging, but gave an inconsequential nod to his question and hung her head again. The stranger moved away.

In a few minutes, three or four men came down, hovering around her like hummingbirds. They implored her to go up and join them. They were jovial and friendly and made her feel that her presence would be an exceptional honor to them.

The clubrooms tonight were filled with well-dressed men in silk gowns, and young ladies with glistening pearls on their shining hair-dos. Men and women gathered around card tables inside, or spread out in the open terrace in groups, submerged in the soft, intoxicating glow of the colored lanterns. Green and red wines stood on the table and there was much chattering and laughter. No wives, of course, were present.

The three or four friends made her sit at their table. Peony liked their friendliness and informality, and enjoyed being surrounded by admiring men. Soon others came to join them. Word had passed around that "Red Peony" was among them. The courtesans, especially, gave her the intent, curious look due a celebrity. Wine was passed around and Peony made a pretense of drinking just to oblige and respond to their cordiality. There was much teasing and joking going on. Some of the courtesans sat sedately behind their friends; others leaned over the men's shoulders with their arms around their necks. Some of them were imported beauties from Soochow or Yangchow, and even out here spoke only the soft, feminine Soochow language of love.

Peony's attention was drawn to a striking young man, in his early thirties, seated at the far end of the table. He had a truly extraordinary face. There was a gay, bubbling smile constantly playing about his lips, and his skin was extremely white and smooth; in fact, he was utterly beardless—his upper lip and chin were so smooth that he looked as if he'd never need to shave. Although he wore thick glasses, the sparkle in his eyes lent a jolly vivacity to his face.

He sat silently by himself, staring at Peony. The man sitting next to her whispered that this was the well-known poet, An Tonien. Peony gazed dreamily at An Tonien for a bare second, and then turned her attention to the man beside her. But she was watching An Tonien out of the corner of her eye. So this was the famous poet. Mengchia had spoken very highly of this man, that day he took her to the Club. Peony remembered the five-foot-high scroll with An Tonien's extraordinary couplet about the Tsientang and the Phoenix.

One of the men across the table leaned over and loudly addressed her as "Red Peony." At that, An Tonien blinked his eyes and then suddenly leaped out of his chair, uttering a "Haw!" Everybody in the room turned around and started to smile broadly. His friends were used to his uninhibited ways.

Before she knew it, An Tonien was standing over her. He pulled up a chair, wedged it between Peony and the man sitting next to her, and seated himself.

"Haw! So you're Red Peony!" he shouted with enthusiasm. His smile was completely childlike. Peony flushed. You don't cry "Haw!" into a pretty lady's face, as if she were a prize horse. But for some reason Peony wasn't offended. She started to smile—this man was amusing. The next thing she knew, he was drinking out of her glass. Then he banged the glass down on the table so hard that the wine splashed out.

"Tonien, it's her glass!" somebody shouted, but he ignored it. Peony noticed his extremely white, tapering fingers, which might almost pass for a woman's.

"So you are Red Peony!" he repeated.

Still smiling, Peony glanced at him quickly. "I'm sorry to intrude," she said, not knowing quite how to respond to this extraordinary man.

"Why, this is *Shangyuan* night. And we are deeply honored."

"What a place here! And what a night!" she crowed.

"I am glad you like it. As a matter of fact, I was quite bored until you came."

"Oh?"

His eyes rested on her with a serious look and his voice was low as he talked with her protectively, like one handling a fragile blossom. Peony was excruciatingly beautiful when she looked this way—with her pensive, half-awake, veiled expression, seeing one thing, her mind thinking of another thing, in a world of her own, detached from all that was going on. An Tonien saw her chin supported in her hand, and was fascinated by her inviting, mysterious smile that seemed to conceal so much. His mind formed an image of the half-open peony as the lines came to him:

> The flower, half unfolding, half withholding,
> Pauses in quivering hesitation,
> Hanging a smile upon her dreamy lips
> That none may know her love-essence within.

Then, remembering the story of her crying at the coffin, his mind dwelled on those fathomless light-brown eyes which held such a deep mystery, and were now and then illumined by a rippling laughter.

"Come on!" he said. "I will show you around." He stood up and pushed back her chair for her. She rose and followed him.

"Tonien, you can't do this. Don't take her away from us."

"You people are not fit to talk with her."

"Tonien! Tonien!" cried the others. Evidently he was very popular. He was regarded as the best of the local poets of Hangchow, but his prose was equally poetic. He was born into this world to marvel at its beauty, and he seemed to see the world as a child sees it. He had never been known to speak a bad word about anybody; consequently, he was popular with everyone. Yet, in spite of his fame, he had no personal vanity of any sort.

Peony followed him through the various rooms as he pointed out certain scrolls written by contemporaries, including his own, and a part of a copper tile that came from the Copper-Sparrow Terrace of the time of the Three Kingdoms (third century). In one room, people were standing around a table watching a game of chess. Passing into a small terrace on the east, they came out into the open again, and stopped for a moment to see the surface of the lake buried in the fitful luminescence of the moonlight. Peony remembered that she had stood here two summers ago with Mengchia, viewing the distant Tsientang like a white band one late afternoon.

"Do you write poems?" he asked.

"Not really, Tonien," she replied. She liked to address men by their first names, even when they had just met. "I write only when I am very excited, or very melancholy."

They followed the winding footpath down the garden. It tilted upon a slope covered with many fruit and flower trees, and was provided with stone benches and white and blue porcelain drums which were used as garden stools. Gentle drifts of wind made the trees shiver noisily, but it was not cold in this city that never knew snow.

"Are you alone?" he asked.

"Yes."

"Do you have to be back home early?"

"It's only my parents. But this is *Shangyuan* night. . . . Why do you ask?"

"I was going to suggest that you might enjoy a drive along the lake. My carriage is below."

"I would love it."

Peony was pleased to receive such an invitation and have company tonight. It was just what she was looking for. Time and again, she had found that she could easily make friends with men, but she was particularly pleased now, because she knew that An Tonien was a painter-poet of established local reputation. She liked the way she was treated with respect. And he was quite handsome, slightly taller than Mengchia. A man's company gave her comfort as Paiwei's company could not. With a sense of adventure, she entered the carriage.

They went up the embankment, passed the tomb of Su Shiaoshiao, the beauty of centuries ago, and following the turn of the road, took the drive toward the western shore.

"I understand your husband died some years ago."

"Yes."

"And you have no one—I mean no one looking after you."

"Only my parents."

The closed carriage made a sharp swing to the left after passing Yowangmiao as it turned into the shore line of the Inner Lake. The sudden turn threw them together violently. "I am so sorry," he apologized.

An Tonien's behavior took her by surprise. Scholars were one thing; poets another race of beings—sentimental, unconventional, and incurably romantic. When she entered the carriage at the Club, she was prepared for an unusual, memorable experience, for something crazy and overpowering, a temporary illusion on this night of nights, to sweep her off her feet and make her forget. He had been, on the contrary, as correct as a schoolmaster.

The Inner Lake lay now like a polished mirror on their left, fringed with the frosted white branches of the willows on the Suti. The silence of the night was broken by the rumble of the wheels and the steady, easy clop-clop of the horse. Neither spoke for a moment, but she could almost feel a palpable uneasiness on his part. Was it the magic of the night which caused his voice to tremble and falter when he timidly asked her whether she was completely free and alone. She felt her own inward excitement, a conflict of feelings that she could not quite put into words. She suddenly wished that he would break the ice of self-restraint, that she might touch and hold his body close to hers and with a wild abandon bury the sorrows of all that had gone before. At the same time, a feeling of quickening uncertainty loomed up before her, and made her feel as if she were sitting on the cliff edge of an unknown vista, dark as the night. Could it be possible that here at last was the love she had been seeking for? Why this shyness and timidity on his part? Or, as Chin Chu had done in their first meeting, had this poet put her on a pedestal with a halo over her head and forgotten that she was a woman? His quietness now contrasted sharply with his gushing enthusiasm at the Club.

His voice was tremulous when he said, "I am glad I took you away. That was no place for you with all those painted women."

"Why?"

"Because when I saw your face beneath the lanterns, I knew —I was certain—that you did not belong there. And those men there, they had no right to talk to you as if you were just one of those women."

"What do you think I am?"

"You are unique. You are wonderful, wonderful!" He was exuberant and enthusiastic again, but his voice had a dreamlike quality, as if he were talking to himself.

"Why?"

"I don't know. I heard the story of what you did at the funeral service. I was sorry that I had left before the incident. It was something glorious, magnificent, what you did."

"And you don't think I did something wrong?"

"No. You were big, bigger than all of them. They could not understand you. You are a kind of Tu Liniang. You must be."

Peony gave a bemused chuckle. It was pleasant to be compared to the heroine of *Moutanting*. The romance of *Moutanting*, of love overcoming death, was her favorite story. She said, "Many people think Tu Liniang a foolish, sentimental girl."

"Don't you believe it. The romance is popular with men and women, with old and young alike."

When they had come back to the Suti Embankment, An Tonien offered to drive her to the Yungchinmen. That was where she said she wanted to get off.

"Oh, dear," she said, standing beside the carriage, "I didn't realize it was half-past one!"

"Would you mind sending me some of your verse and prose compositions so that I can have a look?"

"I should be delighted."

"Send them to the Club, not to my home. Just address them to An Tonien. I do hope to have the pleasure of seeing you again."

"Maybe. I shall go up to Tunglu tomorrow. I shall let you know when I am back."

An Tonien stood by the carriage until her young figure faded into the darkness.

CHAPTER 22

During the two weeks she was up in Tunglu, Peony could not stop thinking about An Tonien. What impressed her most about him was that, like a sentimental poet, he had called "magnificent" what others had called scandalous. It made her feel very friendly toward him. He seemed to fit into her picture of a man who would approve of her way of living and understand her. She was impatient to return to Hangchow. She had not willed it, she had not sought it. The romance had come to her, and was no less enchanting for being just "poetic" rather than carnal.

Joshui was quite impressed. As a resident of Hangchow, he had heard stories about An Tonien—who had not? For An Tonien was a "personality" as well as a poet, combining the sensibilities of a child with the gifts of a mature pen.

Friends told a story which took place one gray day while An Tonien was studying in Tokyo. Some friends had come to visit him, and were informed by the Japanese maid that the master had gone out for a walk. He had taken an umbrella with him, because it looked as if a storm might be brewing. The rain had already started to pelt down outside, and the friends decided to wait for his return. A short while later An Tonien came back; his gown was drenched through. His face was radiant as he described to them how glorious the rain had been—the thunder, the lightning, the changing dramas of the clouds, followed by the appearance of a magnificent rainbow. "But how did you get so thoroughly soaked?" his friends asked. "You had your umbrella with you." An Tonien replied, "Oh, did I?" The umbrella was still under his arm.

An Tonien was a great admirer of beautiful women, Joshui reported, and had made a few singsong girls famous by a few quotable lines he had written about them. It was his habit to rave about beauty in nature and in women. And because of his singular personality, he was able to make friends with scholars older than himself, like Lin Chinnan and Yen Yuling. Although his mannerisms were extravagant, he was, at the same time, completely unaffected, completely uninhibited, completely authentic.

Joshui informed Peony that An Tonien was living with a woman, by whom he had a son. Joshui thought that this romance between Peony and An Tonien was a mere romantic fantasy on An Tonien's part; and that on her part, Peony was merely transferring her love for Chin Chu to another man. This was Joshui's opinion, as she learned from Paiwei. Joshui did not believe her when she told them it had been purely

Platonic that night when they had driven around the lake. Paiwei, herself married and contented, suffered for her, but did not know how to advise her. "Take care, Peony," she said on parting. "I do not want to see you wounded again." She had her misgivings. But she also knew the flamboyant quality of her friend, who was capable of throwing everything and everybody aside in her search for love.

Peony met An Tonien one afternoon at the Club. She had sent him a note on her return and they had met by appointment. The thrill of uncertainty accompanied this second meeting, as each was to verify and see in the light of day what had perhaps been an illusion of the lantern festival night. It was most assuredly a difficult test.

He rose to greet her with the same boyish excitement. His face and manner, however, showed a hesitating bashfulness. Their first questions and answers were like furtive leaps of the mind, darting in different directions, brief, and ending in irrelevant smiles, the words themselves meaning nothing, the tones of communication everything.

"I am sorry I am a little late," said Peony.

"No, not at all. It is a fine day."

"It was quite windy when I came."

"Oh, yes, quite windy, as a matter of fact."

"It is a fine day, nevertheless."

They looked at each other and both felt enormously amused at their determination to agree about the weather.

"You said you would bring some of your verse with you."

"I don't know if it will meet your approval." She suddenly felt at home and her words came naturally. "What I want to ask is that you write something for me to frame up on my wall. My uncle Su Sueipo has one in his parlor. Will you?"

"That is a small request."

"Oh, you are magnanimous."

They settled themselves around a low tea table in one of the small side rooms. An Tonien sat back in a low easy chair, blowing out puffs of blue smoke. She sat opposite, erect, alert, a smile on her pretty lips, but nervous and dying for a smoke.

"May I have one?" she finally summoned up enough courage to ask, pointing to a package lying on the table.

"Oh, I beg your pardon. I had not thought of it."

He hastily grabbed a package and offered her one. Lighting it for her, he said, "I didn't know that you smoked."

"Do you mind?"

He gave a relaxed chuckle. "Why should I?" He watched her take a slow, luxurious puff. "I hope you didn't think it rude of me to invite you to ride with me the other night."

"Oh, no!" She smiled. This approach was unexpected. Did he think of her as a goddess? "Come down to earth, Tonien," she thought in her mind.

The servant brought in tea and a dish of sesame candies and was told to bring in a package of cigarettes.

The servant came back a few minutes later and laid the package of cigarettes on the table. An Tonien saw a tinge of a suggestive smile on the servant's lips, and shot a stern look of reproach at his retreating figure. So, then, she was his goddess.

"Oh, no," she thought to herself. "This cannot be. An Tonien, the poet who writes with such power, such sensitivity. What is he so shy about?" She discovered with a pleasant surprise the seriousness with which he took poetry, and his modest estimate of his own work. Here was unmistakably an idealist; it was clear that he idolized her as the girl who had cried at the wrong coffin. It was possible that he admired the love more than the lover.

"I am dying to see your verse compositions, Miss Liang," he said, as he offered her a second cigarette.

"Call me Peony."

"Peony then. Have you brought some with you?"

She fished an envelope out of her pocket, and blushing with excitement, held it out tremblingly. He took it and glanced down the page approvingly at her clear, graceful hand.

> Evening clouds hide the hilltops; the winds
>   rustle my heart;
> I sit alone in the dusk and watch unknown to him.

Fluttering shadows of maple leaves danced on his
    window when I came;
Now the leaves are gone, the shadows bare,
    and he is still not well.

He went on to the next verse which was in the intricate meter
of Sung *tse* lyrics:

His face so wan
    Once full and round;
His mien so calm,
    Once torn with love's rage
        —Rejecting me.
I came a thousand miles
    To hear his voice.
    To hear his voice.
I'd come again a thousand miles
    And see
    His face torn by love's rage
        —Rejecting me.

"Quite a feat," An Tonien exclaimed with enthusiasm. "This
repetition is difficult. You have achieved it quite naturally."

"Oh, Tonien! To have your approval! You must teach me."

"I intend to. Your cousin Liang *Hanlin* taught you, I am
sure."

"A little." She did not know why she blushed. "I want you
to teach me."

"He is a master of prose, both the elegant and the familiar,
perhaps more than of poetry. You were lucky to live with him.
Unconsciously you must have learned a lot. Poetry is a difficult
art. It cannot be made to order. It comes only at moments.
I suppose one must listen for those moments when a line hits
you, floating out of nowhere, as a composer hears a phrase of
melody in the night. It is not easy. These moments do not come
by themselves. One must think in beauty, feel in beauty, live in
beauty. It is the training of your whole personality in response
to the elevated, the significant, and the subtle things of the
spirit. It's all hard work and discipline. And after all your pains,
you look at your work and feel that it is second-rate, or medi-

ocre, as I find mine to be. I don't think I have written four or
five poems that can stand comparison with the ancients. Perfect spontaneity is such a difficult thing. The rest is all rubbish,
a rehashing of what others have said a thousand times before,
and better."

"You are modest."

"No, I am speaking the truth."

"But you are regarded as the best poet of Hangchow!"

An Tonien looked up at her, pouting his lips deprecatingly.
"I would like to think so, but I do not. What people here
think does not matter. Who understands? A lot of what passes
for poetry is sheer verbiage—not the genuine article. Perhaps
that is why your cousin has published so few of his verses. They
are always genuine and elevated in tone, and the people don't
understand them or appreciate them."

"Mengchia told me that poetry is the voice of the heart, and
the basis of it is passion, true passion."

"Oh! I agree." His eyes were glowing. "Passion, or love, or
whatever you call it. We are dealing with an invisible thing no
one has been able to define. Love has as many shades and colors and tones as there are lovers. Sometimes it is not more than
an illicit affair with a butcher's wife. True passion is as rare as
the appearance of saints—the romance of Wenchun, the remorse of Tang Minghuang, and the quintessence of love expressed in the story of Chien-niang. And of course Tu Liniang.
Love is like that rare, disembodied song of a bird you can
never see. When it does land on earth, it dies. It cannot survive
in captivity. The song fades and changes in color and tone
when the lovers are united. The only way to preserve its color
and its beauty is through death and separation. That is why
love is always tragic."

Peony essayed a diffident disagreement. "But true love, I am
sure, exists everywhere," Peony said, "and not only once in five
hundred years. Except it is not celebrated in poetry. What
about the butcher's wife? She can have true love, too."

"You may be right. Even the rainbow is not so uncommon
as we think it is. But I was speaking of the quintessence of

love, that ephemeral devotion of spirit which can exist only in the imagination, the love essence distilled and caught in poetry. Wenchun, fanning a clay stove as a restaurant waitress after she had eloped with her lover—she had that divine essence of love. But then Wenchun, gaily dressed as a court lady, soon found her lover-husband running after other girls, as you well know. The first divine frenzy was swallowed up by the realities of the situation, as is too often the case." He smiled at Peony. "I do not deprecate the love of a butcher's wife. It is of a different order. True love is an enormous thing, a powerful thing, an obliterating thing, which transforms a person. I believe very few persons are capable of it. . . . And I think you are one of them."

Then he looked at her with a searching, adoring, burning look which frightened her a little. What a confounded idealist, she thought. No wonder he had to take her away from the crowd of singsong girls that night. What did he think he saw in her? She placed her hand on his arm and said softly, "You will make me very happy if we can be friends, if you will let me see you again."

"You know I want to." He sat up, and in an effort to conceal his feelings, emptied the cold tea in her cup into a spittoon, and poured her a fresh cup. "Have I bored you?"

"On the contrary. I never enjoyed anything more."

"I would rather talk with you than with anybody else. Here in Hangchow, how many people can understand what I say?"

"And I?" she asked coquettishly.

"I thought you would understand. You stand out in my mind as something unique."

"I am afraid I shall disappoint you."

"No, you won't. I feel it. That is why I am so anxious to have your friendship."

"What do you do?"

"Oh, I go to the office. In the Governor's Secretariat. One has to make a living. I have a wife and a charming son. I have a happy home, if that is what you mean—like anybody else."

"Why do you say 'like anybody else'?"

"I mean I am a good husband and a good provider and pay taxes and all that."

"And all that," she repeated after him.

"Don't misunderstand me. I admire my wife. She is a wonderful woman. She is as much as a man can expect in a wife, and as I told you I have a lovely boy of ten."

"I shall be pleased to meet them one day."

"You will."

Peony felt relieved that An Tonien had told her about his wife and had not tried to deceive her.

Peony came away from the meeting with an inward excitement, qualified by doubt. An Tonien excited her in a different manner; he had a slimmer build than Mengchia, was younger, and talked with marvelous youthful zest in a beautiful flow of words. From his attitude and everything he said he had let her think that he adored her and thought of her in ideal terms; the memorial service incident was to him a moment of glory of a great love, worthy of celebration in song. On the other hand, he had never laid a hand on her; he was making it a literary love affair; he would teach her about writing prose and verse, not as man to woman, but as a writer to a girl admirer. And he certainly had made it clear that he had a happy home with a wife and a child.

It was, therefore, all the more astounding when she received a letter from him, enclosing a folded scroll of his calligraphy, a letter of two pages, partly discussing literature, with suggestions about some authors she might want to read, and partly telling her about his own life, all in a cordial, impersonal, correct tone, betrayed by a highly personal reference to herself: "Your voice is soft and melodious and your hair-do goes so well with your face." A great question rose in her mind. The very disorder, the rather foolish, inconsequential jumble of words in that one line indicated that he was concealing a profound personal feeling for her behind all the verbiage. Why did he not ask her to see him? She wrote him a short reply, thanking him for the scroll, which she said she was going to frame and hang by the side of her bed. She added cryptically in a post-script, "I miss you very much since I saw you and am a little bit lonely. I feel exactly as you feel. What name shall we give to this sentiment, which is so unlike anything I have felt before?"

A second letter came a week later, still without asking for an appointment to see her. Was he deliberately restraining himself from plunging deeper into a budding romance? Was he afraid of himself, or of his wife? The tone was still impersonal, touching on nothing important, a jumble of irrelevant talk, avoiding the one thing he wanted to say. On the other hand, he did say how anxiously he had waited for her reply and he sent along two portraits of her "as I remember you in our first meeting," which spoke much more clearly than words. She was sure, then, that he loved her intensely, but was afraid. Was this all? Was it to be a romance carried out in correspondence? She wrote back:

> My dear friend:
> Thank you, Tonien, it is true, then. Your letter has put me in a dream from which I do not wish to wake up. If it is so, I shall enjoy intensely every moment that you offer me of your presence.
> I am so happy to learn that you were anxious to hear from me, just as I anxiously waited every day for your letters. Our anxieties are the same; our longings the same.
> My hands trembled when I held your portraits of me, as I traced every loving line of your sketch. My hands tremble always when I receive a note from you.
> You must tell me everything, everything that you think, or feel, everything that you love. Why should we restrain ourselves when time passes by and we are so anxious to see each other?

She went into a very extensive account of herself, her child-hood, her marriage, her search for an ideal, for "something that meant something" to her. "If you have anything to tell me, or confess to me, do not hesitate, and I shall do the same."

His reply asked her to come and meet him the following eve-ning at a certain hotel on the canal. They would go somewhere and have supper together and talk things out. But the letter—this time a long one—was also frank and full confession of his dissatisfaction with himself, as a man and as a writer, and of his yearning for a new life vouchsafed by this new, inexorable, compelling love which sent him to "heights of beauty and depths of despair." He said something had "happened" to him, something "inexplicable and unprecedented," and that it had changed his world for him. It lacked all his previous self-imposed restraint.

The letter was a shock to her, although she had more or less sensed his feelings; it suggested the full and final closing of an artificial gap between them, no less important for its being withheld so long and carefully.

She went to her appointment with her heart aflutter. She had found in him, at last, a man who felt as she did about love, and gave promise of an ideal life, such as Paiwei had found in Joshui, a couple who shared the same point of view. She was sure that she could love him and that she wanted him. Yet she knew also that she was going to meet a married man with a family. It seemed to give their love the necessary bitter-sweet flavor which she relished. She had learned from her experience with Fu Nanto that a young man was less mature; and of course more mature men were generally married. How could a young boy of twenty-two, like Fu Nanto, understand the full, rich content of love and torment in a full-grown woman? An Tonien offered her everything she wanted—he was a handsome, youthful-looking, yet mature man, who worshiped her because she had done the unusual.

An Tonien had chosen a hotel on the canal where it was most unlikely that they would be recognized. Its secrecy appealed to her. The dark passage only added to the excitement as she was being led to his room.

She tapped lightly and An Tonien came to the door, greeting her with that youthful, keen delight which sent a thrill through her heart. Their eyes met for a brief, pregnant second. He looked a little embarrassed as he whispered softly, "Peony!" and then suddenly pulled her close to him in a long, lingering kiss and tightened his arms around her. She let her head rest on his shoulder, enjoying the warmth of his body and this surrender of the deepest part of herself. Her whole body shivered with excitement. Then she raised her head and, still holding him close, covered his face with light, fugitive, endearing kisses.

"Tonien, you cannot imagine how happy you make me." She could feel the tightness of his arms around her and the hunger of his warm mouth as his lips imprisoned hers. This flooding of passion had transformed him completely—he was no longer the self-contained poet.

"Forgive me," he said, stroking her hair gently. He looked inspired.

"For what?"

"I don't know. You know how I feel about you." There was an almost childlike naïveté about him. He pulled her toward a chair. Peony seated herself on his lap, still clinging to him, feeling that she was melting inside. When she was like this, she was half inarticulate.

"Tonien, will you do something for me if I ask you? Is it too much to ask you to love me very much, and never forget me?"

"I never felt so deeply about any other woman before. Why do you have to say that?"

"Because I am so afraid."

She slipped her hand out of his grasp and went over to the window.

Tonien followed her and putting his arms around her turned her to him and kissed her passionately. Tears were shining in her eyes.

"Afraid of what?" he asked.

"Afraid of losing you. I need you. I've come to the end of the road. When you kissed me a while ago, I knew that I loved you, that in your love I was able to free myself of my love for him." She threw her arms around him and kissed him passionately, and then suddenly interrupted her kisses to beg him for reassurance: "Tell me that you will love me very much? . . . Say it again . . . very much? . . . You will never, never forget

me?" Tonien replied with a kiss which was tender, and passionate, soft, lingering, incomparable, unforgettable.

Holding her supple body in his arms, he felt a thrill. He was
in raptures and his eyes showed it. He knew how profoundly
he had been struck with her since their first meeting, how no
matter how he had tried, he had never been able to put her out
of his mind. He had come to seek an assurance that she loved
him as much as he loved her, and now found this overflowing,
complete, and unquestioned love on her part.

He pulled her away from the window and seated her ador-
ingly on the bed, while he drew up a chair opposite. She tucked
up her legs beneath her on the bed and made herself comfortable, slipping a pillow behind her back. She was ravishingly
beautiful, with her delicious white skin and her lovely lips
parted slightly, as she gazed at him in silence. "God made her
so, to be loved and to love"—the line from the ballad came
to his mind with the full impact of its truth, as she lay back,
still looking at him with those dreaming, light-brown eyes
flecked with the moonlight shining through the window. Her
silence at such moments added the charm of mystery to her
beauty; by saying nothing she was saying everything. He drew
near to her and, taking her hand in his, whispered: "Peony,
listen to me. I adore you. How can I put my feelings for you
into words? I dared not hope. It took me two or three days to
write that letter. I dared not believe that you would love me.
But I had to say it, hoping that you would not be offended.
You do not know what you did that night in the carriage,
when we were thrown against each other—remember? You
know all my life I have been searching for an ideal. Yes, they
say that I am a fairly successful man, have nothing to complain
about. I have many friends, a good home, and a fair job. But
sometimes I feel a craving for love, for a great uplifting, consuming love. I felt empty, can you understand what I mean?
You know you are a very unusual girl, don't deny it. Do you
know that one look from you and one whisper of your voice
can change the color and tone of this whole city for me? That
room where you sat that afternoon was never the same for me

again. You cannot know that. You transformed it. Every time I went to the Club I felt an impulse to go into that room and just look at that chair where you sat."

Peony gave a low, sweet chuckle, as he continued. "You left, but you have transformed that room. Your presence was there. I ordered tea for two. The servant laughed. But I sat there alone. A curious thing: I remember that we had those white-and-blue cups, and that you drank out of one of them. I remembered because I poured the tea for you and it had a tiny chip. No, do not laugh. It is so difficult to tell you. It is a miracle. There is a feeling, an excitement about that cup touched by your lips. I would put it there and I would not touch it, would not drink from it. Because your lips have blessed it. And I remember where your feet rested under the tea table as you filled that chair with your lovely self. You see how awkward I am in trying to tell you the impossible. I am silly, am I not?"

He paused a little. Peony's countenance had become serious. He went on, inspired: "I dared not love you. I dared not hope. Yet I find myself now transported into a region I had not known before. I have committed follies before—I have been foolish. Now I am silly. To be silly is better than to be foolish."

Her arms slowly closed around him and she uttered a groan, "Oh, my An Tonien!" They lay like that quietly, living in another world.

"Do you want to?" she asked. "Take of me what you will. I am yours." She was passive and let him possess her completely.

It was one of the most perfect loves she had known.

Then she felt a new release and influx of happiness, a flood which overwhelmed and obliterated her past and emancipated her from the obsession with Chin Chu.

CHAPTER 23

These secret meetings in the same hotel continued, causing a great upset in her family. As she came to know him better, she became more relaxed and was fascinated by his enchanting simplicity of spirit and the joy he took in everything. Her father did not know about the affair; he was out of the house during the day when An Tonien's letters came, although he had seen the scroll given to her by the painter-poet. But now her frequent absences from supper began to annoy and alarm him. He could not speak to her without needling her. Almost before the words were out of his mouth she would start defending herself sharply and with considerable spirit, saying that she was a grown-up and married daughter and knew what she wanted. She lied eloquently and coolly and was quick with her words. "Does that child of ours ever fail to do what she wants?" the father said to his wife.

Now her behavior at home worried even her mother. Peony either shut herself up in her room for hours, or went out, walking on clouds. She was touchy and fidgety and looked as if she were possessed. It was so like the time when she was in love with Chin Chu before his marriage.

"You are in love with that man, I know. You cannot fool your mother. And tonight you are going to meet him again. But he is a married man. What can come of it? You must control yourself and stop this folly. It will only ruin you."

Peony's eyes blazed. "But, Mother, I love him as much as he loves me, madly. There is no power on earth that can separate us. He is mine, do you hear?" She shouted the words "I love him" and her voice was so shrill that her neighbors could have heard it. Her father was not in the house at the time. "Try to stop me! I am going to leave this house if you do."

Her mother sighed deeply. Her face was a knot of deep and helpless sorrow. Tears came to her eyes. Her mother had always loved this child deeply, had always yielded to her. It was her great weakness, and in the episode of Chin Chu, she had aided by covering up for her. She would sacrifice everything for the happiness of her child. She pulled up a corner of her jacket and wiped her eyes. Her head hung pathetically, knowing that there was no longer peace in this family. She had lived in constant tension since the sisters went to Peking. Now tears gushed forth from the well of her loneliness. Her despair was intensified by her desire to cover up this misguided adventure from her husband.

Peony put her arms around her mother and tried to soothe her. "Please, Mother, don't grieve for me. Don't you see that I love him as I love you? Mother, don't let anything come between us. I couldn't stand it."

Then her mother raised her head. She gave a feeble sigh and said, "What are you going to do? You told me he has a wife and child."

"I don't know."

"You don't know! I don't want to see you hurt. That is all your mother is thinking of for you."

"I haven't thought about it. All I know is that in his presence I am completely happy. It is a strange thing. I have stopped grieving about Chin Chu since I met him. You should be happy for me."

"I would be if it really made you happy. But how can he marry you? I was young once like you, and made my mistakes. But I was cured of them." She paused for want of strength.

"I will discuss it with him, and will let you know, Mother. But you will keep it a secret from Father, won't you?"

"I will. But your father would be a fool if he couldn't read it in your eyes."

Peony went to the kitchen, poured hot water from a kettle over a face towel, wrung it out, and came back to her mother. With the towel she rubbed the old woman's eyes and face lovingly, talking all the while. "You are the best mother in the world," she said.

"You really are in love with that man, aren't you?"

"Yes, he is crazy about me. He is the man for me, I know. How can I explain his love for me? He puts me in a dream world. He makes me feel so important. He needs me as much as I need him." Then she chuckled. "He thinks of me as Cho Wenchun."

"Yes, but Szema Shiangju was not married and did not have a son. One of you is going to get hurt. I fear for you, and I hope it will not be you."

"Don't worry, Mother. I know what I want. But do not tell Father yet."

The hotel people knew these lovers now. They were used to seeing couples come in, rent a room for an hour or so, and leave. They greeted them like old customers and did not ask questions. An Tonien had tipped them generously.

At the next meeting, Peony said to him, "What are we going to do? We cannot go on like this. I hate all this secrecy."

"I have been thinking the same thing."

His face turned very serious, and he took her hand in his. "Will you marry me?"

She was taken completely by surprise.

"But how? Are you serious?"

"I am. I have come to a conclusion. It is painful, but it is the only thing I want. I may say I love my wife and my boy. But it is not the same thing. I am prepared to cut loose. She can have my boy. I will provide well for her. But I must have you. You are the most wonderful thing in my life. It is the only time I have ever felt truly *one* with a woman. They call this love, I suppose. I will abandon all, sacrifice all. We can go and live in Shanghai. Tell me that you will."

"Oh, Tonien!" She covered him with kisses. "I will be your wife. You will make me the happiest woman in the world."

"And I know you will be the most beloved, most adored wife in the world."

"But when?" she asked.

"Oh, it will take a little time. I have considered it. The Secretariat is very busy in spring with all the reports and accounts that will have to be prepared before the *Tuanwu*, the fifth day of the fifth month. I cannot just throw it up and quit. Then I may have to liquidate the house and garden. I shall need three months. It is very sad, of course. I do not think she will want to live in the same house."

"You have not told her?"

"Of course not. All this I am planning in my mind. What makes it so difficult is that she has been such a devoted wife to me. But I have made up my mind."

Peony was lost in silence. After a while she said, "Are you sure you want to sacrifice all this for me? . . . It makes me feel responsible. Of course this is what I want, to marry you, but only if you are doing it out of your own free will entirely. What about your boy?"

"It is a difficult question. I feel that I ought to let her have the boy, because it will be a double blow and she has done nothing wrong. But I know that he will still be my son. She is not the kind to go after another man and remarry. If she does, I will fight for my son. But that is a remote possibility."

Peony was staggered with the news. He had really thought out all the details. So she said: "That means we will elope and settle in Shanghai. Is that what you are planning? Are you sure you won't regret it—that our love will not be a burden to you?"

An Tonien reassured her. She trembled a little. "I am so afraid," she said. "Afraid of losing you. Do we have to wait that long?"

"Don't be childish. It's only for two or three months."

"Something may happen to change your mind. All my life I have been impatient. Imagine now, when I need your presence every day and every minute until the next meeting."

"Be patient. We'll see. Maybe I can arrange for us to leave earlier. But you realize I am pulling up all roots. I have to think of all the details."

"Details!" Peony answered, with a light, contemptuous chuckle.

*   *

"Peony! I have wonderful news for you!" She was now used to that keen, excited voice of his. According to him, something wonderful was always turning up.

"What is it?"

An Tonien crouched with one leg on the bed and pulled her to him. "I have spoken to my wife, and we've agreed to have a girl come in and be governess for my little Lulu. We'll be able to see each other every day. . . . "

"You don't mean . . . you don't mean for me to come and live with you under false pretenses and carry on this way?" The proposal sounded childish to her.

"Now listen. It is not like that. You can go back to your home in the afternoon. I just want to be able to see you at lunch. It's a wonderful idea. We do not keep an amah for Lulu—that is my boy's name. I spoke to my wife about it. You come and take care of him. He is only ten, a lovely boy. We call him *paopei*, treasure, at home. That will relieve her. You come in the morning and leave at four or five. My wife likes the idea. I'll be out of the house except when I come home for lunch."

"I'd rather not."

"Now, Peony. All I ask is that I can see you at lunch. We can see each other every day. Isn't this what you want?"

"I do want to, very much. Except I feel it is not right."

"It is better than this meeting in these filthy surroundings. I promise you that I shall be entirely proper. It will help me if I can see you every day in the open. I don't mean we shall carry on. Can you do that? Until the day I shall have to make the difficult announcement to her?"

An Tonien had impractical ideas, but had the ability to make them sound convincing by his enthusiasm. Against her better judgment, she yielded, on the clear understanding that she should be a real governess and they both would behave decently and properly while in the house. The idea of seeing him every day was very appealing. But she had a feeling that they were like two innocent children playing a game of adventure and mischief.

The day before she was to take on her job, she said to Tonien,

"I don't know what to think. I know that we need each other. It will be better than this. But it makes me feel queasy. Are you very sure we can go through with this arrangement?"

"I am sure. My wife trusts me completely."

"That makes it more difficult, doesn't it? I don't like to hurt people. I have nothing against your wife."

"If that is on your conscience, let me tell you once and for all that I am doing this because I want to. I didn't reach the decision on an impulse. But this I know. I cannot give you up. It is what I desire, what I want. It is my decision, not yours."

When he came to take her in his carriage, he was amused to see her dressed in a simple blue cotton print jacket and trousers. With her hair done in a pigtail and without make-up, she really looked like a young maid. He was intrigued at her daring.

"You will be Miss Yao," he whispered to her. "Lulu is already dying to meet his young governess. Do you like children?"

"I adore them. When I was in the Fei home, my only joy was in talking and playing with the children of my sister-in-law. I love everything about them—their laughter, their tears, their mischief and sorrows and anxieties, their voices, their innocent eyes. One moment they are crying, and the next moment they are laughing. It is my greatest ambition to be the mother of many children."

"Then you will adore my Lulu. Promise to behave."

"I promise."

The carriage went up a broad path in the direction of the Paosuta Pagoda. They descended at a house with a white wall and a small black gate. Charming peach trees blooming with pinkish buds were visible over the wall. As they descended, Peony stopped for a moment to admire the view of the Inner Lake a hundred yards below.

"Come on, Miss Yao," he said to her.

Peony caught sight of a boy standing in the doorway, a finger on his lip, looking shyly at the stranger with large, solemn eyes.

"Lulu. Come and meet Miss Yao."

The boy came slowly forward, biting away a smile on his lip, his face slightly pale. Peony felt she had to restrain an enormous impulse to hug him to her breast. "I shall be so happy playing with him all day." She winked at An Tonien. She extended her hand to Lulu and said, "Come, come with me." Lulu allowed his hand to be captured by the young girl who was to be his teacher and companion.

They had to climb a dozen stone steps to the house, which stood on the sloping garden. Mrs. An was in the kitchen.

"Lisa," her husband called. "The child's teacher is here."

Lisa came out and looked intently at the young girl, who was introduced as Miss Yao. Lisa was in her early thirties, dressed in black, her hair brushed smoothly toward a bun at the nape of her neck.

"Pardon me," she said to Peony. "I was out in back and didn't see you coming." She gave a quick glance at the girlish figure and said, "You are so pretty. I am sure you will find the work pleasant. Lulu, you like Miss Yao?"

The boy nodded, his hand still in Peony's hand.

"We'll be great friends," Peony replied.

An Tonien excused himself, saying that he had to go to the office. Peony's heart warmed toward the slight woman as she showed her the house, talking nervously, but very graciously. In the kitchen, she saw the cook, a fat old woman with a cataract in one eye. Coming out of the kitchen, Mrs. An said, "I am so glad I have someone to talk to. My husband is away all day. How he picked you! He likes pretty girls, I know. He is so poetic. You will find him a very kind and considerate man. You'll have nothing to worry about. He will be home for lunch, then take a short nap and go out again. I am sure you'll like Lulu. He is a darling."

"I do," Peony said quickly.

"He is very quiet. Perhaps he is lonely. He doesn't go out and play with the other children much. Perhaps I am selfish. He is my life, my everything. I do not know what is wrong with him. The air is beautiful here. Yet he is so pale. You will take him out and let him play in the open more."

Peony found her heart palpitating as she listened. Mrs. An

was young, of medium height, and dressed very neatly, but her cheeks were a little sallow. She could see that she was a lonely woman, modest, and very anxious to please. Her incessant chatter seemed to hide an emptiness somewhere.

"You see," she went on, "we have such a quiet, happy little home. My husband, as you probably know, is quite a poet, well known for his calligraphy. I don't go out much, and am content to stay at home. It is not like my mother's family, with three uncles and aunts and all the children living together. My aunts all envy me for having such a small family, living by ourselves all alone."

Everything went off smoothly. When An Tonien came home for lunch, she found that he had meant what he said. At lunch he was vivacious, chatting gaily with his wife and Peony, and teasing his boy with wild, improbable adventure stories. Peony left for her home after playing with Lulu on the hillside and giving him his bath. Some days, her work kept her late, and An Tonien came home to find that she was still there. He played his part superbly, never allowing his love for her to come to the surface.

Her work was pleasant. She used to take the boy out to play in the grassy park nearby, while she sat thinking of the strange things that had happened to her. Peony's heart yearned toward that boy who had such a beautiful smile. Even the pallor on his face made her love him more. She would sing to him and tell him stories, and Lulu was so fond of her that it broke her heart when she had to leave to go home each day. They had become inseparable. Early morning, she would come back and find Lulu waiting for her at the path, standing on a rock where he could see her coming from below. Then she would hug him, and their day would begin.

On some days An Tonien came home early and took them all out for a drive. She had a curious sinking feeling about this picture of family happiness, which, as she well knew, was going to be shattered in a couple of more months. She belonged in this family, and yet she did not belong, like a Siamese fish thrown into a goldfish bowl. Sometimes she would be so preoccupied with her own thoughts that she was completely silent during the drive.

"Aren't you happy with us?" An Tonien asked.

"No, I was just thinking. I am sorry." She admired his mask of complete deception.

"She is such a companion to me," said the wife. "And Lulu likes her so much."

It was so tragic. She swallowed hard. Mrs. An saw it and laid a gentle hand on her. Peony began to sniff aloud. Mrs. An's hand tightened on her.

"Don't cry," she said with real warmth of feeling. "If there is anything that displeases you, tell me."

"Nothing," Peony said. "You are so kind, Mrs. An."

"I mean you are young. I don't blame you. Any girl of your age wants a home of her own. I am surprised that you are not already married. A pretty girl like you is often too choosy." She turned to her husband and told him the string of lies which Peony had told the wife—how many young men had wanted to marry her, but how she wanted to wait until she found the right man. "Take a tolerable man, marry him, and raise some children and have a home of your own. Do not live in a fantasy of love and romance. Once you have a home and children of your own, it does not matter too much whether the husband is handsome or ugly. What do you expect?"—turning to her husband—"I think she is too romantic."

"Yes, I think she is," said the husband. "After all, she is young. Don't blame her."

In one of the prearranged meetings at the hotel, An Tonien asked her, "Well, how do you find my family?"

"I've learned something," she said. "Is all marriage like yours?"

"What do you mean?"

"I've tried very hard to see your life with your wife. I want to justify myself, to see if I am doing wrong. She spends so much time making an attractive lunch for you. Yet it was heartbreaking the other day to hear her talk about marriage. One would say you have a happy home and are happily married. Yet she talked of marriage as if it were just a good, dependable business arrangement."

"I am sure ours will not be like that. Don't be too disillusioned. As a matter of fact, I am tired of this kind of life."

At the hotel that night, Peony lay in bed silent for a long time. Her head reeled in confusion. Life was such a mix-up. Why did she have to fall in love with a married man? They had not kissed and embraced each other for so long that the pains and longings of the past came back to her in a flood. She thought of the men she had loved—Chin Chu, Mengchia, Fu Nanto, and now An Tonien. "Oh, Tonien, kiss me," she groaned, and in their kiss she seemed able to forget, to be once more fulfilled with a passionate love which inundated her whole being.

"Do not leave me," she said. "I shall not be able to stand it. I am so tired. Hold me tight, Tonien."

Later she said to him, "You men are stronger. I have no more will of my own."

He knew that the tension was too much for her, and she was going to pieces under the life of deception. "I am sure you will be all right when we are together. We may be able to get away in a month. I shall not have the courage to tell her. But I will tell her that I have to go to Shanghai, and later write her a letter. What hurts me most will be to lose my boy."

In spite of these reassurances, it was a strange, painful meeting, ending up by Peony crying herself to sleep.

CHAPTER 24

Some two weeks later, Lulu fell ill with a high fever. At first the mother thought he had caught a cold, as the boy always did with the change of weather. His forehead was burning to the touch. Peony was as frantic as the mother. The first day she stayed very late and went home after supper. The second day, when the boy's fever still had not gone down, she offered to stay overnight. Mrs. An scarcely left the boy's bedside. The doctor was called in and prescribed the usual medicines for bringing out perspiration. But the boy's fever remained, and all the light had gone out of his eyes. The windows were shut, and the boy lay quietly, hour after hour, with his eyes closed. He did not complain and took the medicine quietly, knowing that it was good for him. But his coughing increased and he complained of pains in his breathing.

When the condition became critical, An Tonien asked for leave and stayed at home to help. The house smelled of medicinal herbs. The mother sat dazed by the bedside, refusing to leave it to take a rest. At night, she refused to go to bed, but took catnaps lying on the couch which had been brought in. Sometimes the three of them sat and watched the child's difficult breathing. The doctor was making visits twice a day and seemed as worried as they were. It was pneumonia which was fast eating away the life of the child; the boy scarcely opened his eyes for more than five minutes before he was asleep again and was awakened only by his own painful coughs.

Peony returned home after staying up three nights with them. Mrs. An and her husband urged her to go home for a night's rest and thanked her for her help. The next morning she woke up late and arrived at the house to find the door of the sick room closed. She lightly tapped and opened it; the mother was kneeling by her boy's dead body, weeping in heart-rending sobs, and her husband standing helplessly by. He nodded to her and said briefly and simply that the boy had passed away about half an hour ago. Mrs. An had almost collapsed. She huddled over the bed, her legs crooked beneath her, her arms still clinging to her only son.

Peony, too, fell by the boy's bedside. Her tears bathed the boy's face and his limp hands. Then she remembered the mother. A great bond of sorrow had united them. The boy's death seemed to be killing her. Finally, between the husband and herself, they raised the limp body of the mother and assisted her to the couch.

Peony's eyes slowly sought those of An Tonien. Covering her face with her hands, she ran out of the room. She sat on the landing of the front steps, trying to breathe freely, resting her head against a pillar, thinking. Suddenly she felt she wanted to flee the place, but her legs were numb. The idea, clear and definite, came to her that she could not marry An Tonien, could not let him abandon his wife now, no matter what the cost.

An Tonien came out and found her sitting by herself. She turned and looked up.

"How is she?" she asked.

His face was grim as he said, "She is asleep. This is very hard on us. It will take her a long time to get over it."

Suddenly strength came back to her, and she got up.

"Come with me," she said as she descended the steps.

Stopping at the gate, she said to him, "My mind is made up, Tonien. You must let me go. Stay with her and be good to her. She needs you now, more than ever."

"But, Peony!"

"Let's not argue. I can't do it. Let me go. This is the end."

She cast a lingering look at him, and walked with firm steps down the path. An Tonien stared after her until she had disappeared around the bend.

Peony kept herself out of sight. She dared not even go to the boy's funeral, knowing how easily she might change her mind. The loss of Lulu was more than the loss of the boy; it meant the giving up of a happiness she could see within her grasp, the snapping of a life line she had been clinging to. Yet very clearly she felt she could not go through with their plan, involving abandoning of the poor mother at such a moment of sorrow. She could not kill the woman. "Probably this is the only good thing I ever did in my life," she thought to herself.

An Tonien must have felt the terrible truth in her decision and admired her for it. He doubted that he could have gone through with their original plan. The hour of sorrow for their son had made him realize how good his wife had been to him all the last dozen years of their marriage. He said to himself that he loved her truly, and seemed to be able to regard his infatuation with Peony as an unrelated affair. Now with his son gone, he saw that he had been foolish, that events had forced him to see the inexorable consequences of his action. He understood and did not try to communicate with Peony, but his love for her changed into deep respect. He had not been mistaken in her, for everything she did appeared to have a heroic quality. He behaved exactly as a grieved father and dutiful husband should in this hour of trial, but was constantly oppressed with the thought that in trying to be a good husband, he was obeying the imperious will of Peony who had wanted it to be so.

Peony was now the flower which was traditionally (although erroneously) described as bearing no seeds, based on the popular idea that a glamour girl made a bad mother. Her mother detected a new note of sad resignation. She had been forced to accept, but had never approved, her daughter's plan to elope with a married man and wreck a home, and was glad that she had changed her mind. "Mother, if I had never seen his wife, I would have done it. Now I can't. I just can't kill her."

It made good sense, but what next?

"All I care about," said the father, discussing Peony with his wife, "is that she settle down. I've had enough of it. How would you like to hear your daughter discussed by your colleagues? 'She couldn't keep a lone pillow or bed. God bless her!' If she does not get a man and settle down, she may end up as a tramp."

Some similar thought must have been going through Peony's mind. As she lay in bed, she felt as if she were falling down through black space, completely torn from her familiar moorings, distracted and without direction. Her mind flitted between grief for the boy, who had been so close to her, and the loss of An Tonien, and a thousand little futilities of her past and present. The reality of what she might have done to Mrs. An was forced upon her. She could not go back on her decision.

She could vividly see the wife receiving a letter from Shanghai, her shock at learning of her husband's desertion following so close upon the death of her son—how it would be impossible for them to feel happy together under those circumstances, how An Tonien might be bitter with remorse, might even hate her for it. Yet to give him up was like cutting her heart out; it was a denial of her deepest yearnings, so much did she need him now, yet so unattainable was her wish. When would she again find such a man and such harmony of spirit? She stared blankly at the scroll which he had written for her and which now hung upon the wall facing her bed.

Though she had passed sleepless nights in the last ten days, tortured by the pangs of trying to give up An Tonien, her youthful appearance did not suffer from it. On the other hand, she developed a deep, dark look of pain that only enhanced her beauty. Most men, she found, would come crawling to her at the crooking of her little finger. But all she wanted was to marry one—an ideal man she had created for herself. Nor did she care much now if she went out alone and sat around in wineshops and knew that men were talking about her. She was aware that the more notorious she was, the more the men loved her. And she would look cynically friendly and didn't mind talking with those who wanted to exchange a friendly word with her in the atmosphere of a wineshop. To her, all men seemed to have codfish eyes, and this amused her. All codfish were alike. All were weak and disappointing in one way or another. Few men were able to excite her, but she liked men and enjoyed the comfortable superiority of knowing that whenever she wanted to, she could make one of them a slave to her feminine charms just by throwing him a smile or a glance.

The news disturbed her that Jasmine might be coming to visit her parents this summer as a returning bride with her husband. The very thought suffocated her, made her immensely ill at ease. Whenever Jasmine wrote to her parents, she enclosed a word of love for her sister. She had not written Jasmine, and she did not know what her parents or Aunt Sueipo might have reported about her. They might have told her about the new romance with An Tonien. She would indeed have been proud if she had married the poet, but now they would hear only about the crash of the romance. She also remembered that she had been unnecessarily cutting in her farewell letter to Mengchia, saying that she never wanted to see him again, and that she would "disappear definitely from his life." She had not counted on his becoming her brother-in-law. What would he feel about her now? She was sure that a love so deep and powerful as Mengchia's could not die. Both Jasmine and Mengchia would feel better if she were out of the way—above all, Jasmine, who knew all about her and Mengchia. She had no wish to becloud in any way her sister's happiness. "It will be the second good thing I ever do if, for my sister's sake, I am out of the city when they arrive," she thought to herself.

She had an intense desire to escape from Hangchow and all that surrounded her, to break through the mesh of memories and associations of Chin Chu, An Tonien, and her family, and feel clean and whole again. Vaguely, too, she felt she wanted to punish herself even though she did not say it to herself. She would abandon all that was dear to her and escape and be entirely alone and free, picturing herself living in a far-off island, or deep in some remote mountain, where she might even live contentedly as a farmer's wife. There would be nothing wrong with that. She knew she had youth and good health, and would enjoy a simple life of tranquillity and peace.

Once more with Peony, to dream was to desire, and desire brought with it an impetuous decision to do something, to start immediately. Where would she go? Shanghai, the big city, frightened her. She had a feeling that she would be dragged deeper and deeper into more adventures. Shanghai, that great conglomeration of races, the hunting ground of the rich pleasure seekers, whirlpool of retired officials, merchants, warlords driven out of their provinces, underground gangsters, "white pigeons" and "salted pork" (slang for confidence girls and call girls), mistresses, gamblers, prostitutes. She longed for a sweet love, tranquillity, and quiet. In spite of herself, she was incurably romantic, and the last thing she thought of was to marry for money. No, Shanghai was not for her. Nor would she go to Peking, although under other circumstances she might have. She had such pleasant, enchanting memories of her Peking days. Whenever she thought of Peking, she thought of space and sunlight and a blue sky, and of the exuberant, laughing, leisurely populace of the streets. The whole city had that clean, elemental, northern strength, so unspoiled in spite of its age-old culture.

But, of course, she would avoid Peking. The idea came to her, as ideas come to all of us when we are in a receptive mood, that she might go to live in the home of the school-teacher, Mr. Wang, and his wife, in Kaoyu. She had such pleasant memories of Mrs. Wang, the schoolteacher's wife, cheerful, strong, big-hearted, motherly, and utterly dependable, who had been so unexpectedly helpful during her husband's funeral. She remembered her sweet, well-behaved children. She would be able to help in teaching in Mr. Wang's school, or at the worst, could help in any capacity in Mrs. Wang's house. The more she thought of it, the more the idea attracted her. Oh, no doubt, her parents would oppose the whole idea of her going to some remote place to live by herself. They would not understand what caused her to make such a decision. It would be painful for her parents. Was she going to disappear from home and family and friends entirely? That was basically what she wanted. But she would insist that she knew her own mind. She had to go if only to escape from the whole environment which was suffocating her.

She wrote Paiwei a long letter, telling her of her decision.

I have come to a crisis in my life. The affair with An Tonien has clarified things for me. You know all my life I have been searching for an ideal, for something of meaning. I have changed, and yet I have not. I am still searching. Jasmine is coming and I feel uneasy about meeting them in the present stage of my life. If they seem happy—and I am sure they are —I shall not be able to stand it. And if they are not, I certainly wish to be out the way for fear of myself or of what— you understand what I mean. . . . As for love, I am a little tired.

I do not think I can take much more, after Chin Chu, and after the events of last month. I have not given up. The kind of love you and Joshui have found in each other still seems to me ideal. I long for it. But since Chin Chu's death, I seem to have grown up. You say that I am floating in air—am I? I do not ever want to fall in love with a married man again. Somewhere, isn't there a simple love in simple surroundings, a clean, clear joy of living, without pitfalls and tragedy?

I am still searching, dear Paiwei. Mr. and Mrs. Wang are such nice, dependable people and they have lovely children. That is love, too. Paiwei, I am coming down to earth. My mother says that I have changed. Maybe I have.

Yours with love,
Peony

CHAPTER 25

When Peony made known her decision to leave Hangchow, her father took it stoically; his unimaginative mind had been so upset by so many things she had done in the course of the past year that in his more tranquil moments he wondered how he could have produced such a child. His mind staggered under the weight of the scandals she had created, one of which, the latest, she had barely escaped from. He knew by past experience that her words flew faster than his, and that to dissuade her from a course of action was a pure waste of breath. And now at last, it seemed that she might finally have come to her senses.

"I am turning over a new leaf," was the way she had put it. He felt a chill as she said it, not being sure whether this was just a fleeting mood of repentance, a momentary flash of good sense; but he was willing enough to take it at its face value. From her description, Mr. and Mrs. Wang seemed the nicest sort of people for his daughter to live with.

Paiwei and Joshui came down especially to see her off. They found Peony the same vivacious, pretty girl she had always been; she was not brooding over her recent sad break with An

Tonien. In Paiwei's presence she was always quite gay and talked more than her friend. One of the last things she said to her was, "Paiwei, you may not see me for some time. And the next time you see me, you may find me dressed in a cotton peasant dress, with a sun-tanned face and gnarled hands, chaff in my hair, and a baby at my breast. Why shouldn't I marry a man, just a man, simple and honest, and have my own children?"

She wrote regularly to Paiwei and to her parents from Kaoyu. Then one day her father was shocked to receive a letter from Mr. Wang, the schoolteacher, saying that Peony had suddenly disappeared without a trace, and that he greatly feared that she had been kidnaped by a gang on her way back from the school. There was no indication that she had expected to go away, since her room was as she had left it every morning. For that matter, her own letters home did not indicate anything except that she was happy with the change of place and work. Mr. Wang suggested that she could have enemies. The parents had heard her mention once the case of smuggling and bribery involving her husband, and the execution of the Chief of the Salt Tax Bureau. This had taken place shortly after her departure from Peking in September of last year. Peony had not seen the execution, but had been told about it by Mengchia. She had said that a good many people were involved. But she had given no details and no names, and had mentioned the incident casually, as if it were something over and done with, of no importance to herself.

Both parents were frantic with despair. Speculation at such distance was futile. The father said he had felt all along that something was bound to come up, that Peony was not going to settle down as a schoolteacher as she had claimed. It would have been nothing short of a miracle if his daughter had led henceforth a normal, uneventful life, like any other girl. What might *not* have happened with Peony living completely alone in a strange city, and she so young and attractive, with a temperament as fluid as quicksilver. She had simply too much glamour, like a gorgeous butterfly whose bright colors led to its own undoing. A drab-colored butterfly would stand a better chance of escape from enemies. And this was literally true of Peony: no matter what she wore, an old dress, a new dress, black or mauve or violet, whether she put her hair up or let it down, she radiated an instinctive, compelling, extraordinary charm. And she walked with that lazy shuffle, her shapely arms swinging easily at her sides, her head thrown up as if in communication with a dream in heaven. She could easily have been spotted by the underworld of traffickers in women. What a prize she would be! After a period of compulsory seclusion, she could be put up to be sold as a concubine, and not at any ordinary price. In the hands of the underworld her captor could ask, and obtain, a couple of thousand dollars without any difficulty, for she would be regarded as an "accident of nature," a woman a man would risk his life and fortune for.

Mr. Wang had said in his letter that the police had been searching for some clue, any clue, and were dredging the lake and the canals for her body, in case of an accident. But, according to the police, it was more probable that such a young and pretty woman had been kidnaped. Mr. Wang would let them know if there were any news.

Mr. Wang's second letter was even more discouraging. Peony had totally disappeared; she had left aboslutely no trace. Mr. Wang was inclined to believe that she had been kidnaped, since such a thing was certainly not unknown. The parents' worst fears were confirmed. The fear that their beloved daughter might have been sold for immoral purposes was a specter which overshadowed their minds and paralyzed their thinking. It would be a fate worse than death. Fear fed on itself and they could not dismiss it from their minds. They were hoping hourly for further news. If at moments the thought came to the father that his daughter had invited such trouble to herself, he kept his own counsel; it was his bad luck that at the evening of his life he should be struck with such sorrow. He saw his wife pass the days in silence, waiting every day for further news. They consulted with Uncle Sueipo, who immediately thought of writing to Mengchia, informing him of the situation and suggesting that he start at once and visit Kaoyu on his way home, to try to get some news on the spot.

The father was terribly anxious that the news should be kept within the family and that no further scandal should provide the Hangchow public with food for gossip.

Curiously, the mother was more optimistic. "I know Peony will return," she told her husband. In her heart of hearts, she believed that this was just another escapade of Peony's. She knew her daughter well; most probably she had chosen to elope with someone. She would be capable of doing it and she had said something about wanting to escape all that surrounded her. She could not forget that Peony had the daring to plan an elopement with An Tonien; the possibility was not ruled out that he had something to do with her disappearance.

"What makes you think that Peony will return safe?" asked the father.

"I have consulted the oracles at the Paosuta Temple. The omens are good."

"You don't believe that she might have been kidnaped by the underworld for immoral purposes?"

"I don't. They kidnap orphans or young girls away from home. A woman does not fall into their traps unless she wants to. Not Peony. And she can take care of herself. If the kidnapers are men, she can make them do anything she likes."

"You do not know the Red-and-Green gangs. They do it for revenge, for money, for anything."

"Then you do not know your own daughter. If she disappeared, it was because she wanted to."

The father sighed with irritation. "And it would be just like her not to think of us and leave us guessing and worried," he said shaking his head. "And if and when she returns, she will say with the utmost candor, 'Who told you to worry? I can take care of myself.'"

"Of course, I don't know," the mother said. "She could have just gone off with some young, handsome man who caught her temporary fancy. I cannot take my mind off An Tonien.

Since the Shangyuan festival, they had been meeting in hotels. ... And they had planned to elope. ..."

As she developed the full details, the father's face darkened. It was beyond all bounds of his forbearance. He stormed at her: "And you knew all about it and encouraged it, I daresay. You never think of me, do you?—of the honor of our family. I am a father and everybody tries to keep secrets from me. You knew what a scandal it would be if she did elope with another woman's husband! You silly old woman!"

"Now you are blaming me!" the mother flared up. "What did you do to encourage her to talk with you? What did you care about her? All you wanted was to see her married off and disposed of and off your hands. You and your virtue!"

The father gave a hoarse, hollow laugh. "I am ashamed of the word. Women do not believe in virtue any more. I am not so sure that she is my child."

The mother had never heard such an insult in her life. She covered her face with her hands and started to weep. She felt exhausted. "All I want is my daughter back," she moaned. The father stalked out of the house.

It had become a nonsensical squabble between husband and wife—a quarrel that led nowhere, both being irritated and short of temper. The following day, the mother told the father that it would be a simple matter to find out directly or indirectly whether An Tonien was still in town. And objectively considered, it might not be a case of white slave traffic; someone might have done it for revenge—the salt smugglers, for example, or the Feis, or Chin Chu's family—someone who had been hurt by Peony's conduct and wanted to bring her into disgrace. The truth probably lay somewhere in between.

Jasmine received the letter from her parents the day before Mengchia returned from a business trip. She and Mengchia had been preparing to go home anyway. Jasmine had been anxious to visit her parents since her marriage, because she had heard so many rumors about her sister and did not know what was going on in the family. Also, she was pregnant and wanted to make the voyage while it was still easy for her to do so. But Mengchia had been called away to Hankow in May and the trip had been delayed.

She was deeply worried by the letter, for the last she had heard from her mother was before Peony's break with An Tonien. She was completely at sea as to why her sister would suddenly turn up in Kaoyu. Mengchia had told her that they should be ready to go back as soon as he returned to Peking, and that whatever purchases she wanted to make for presents to the relatives and friends should be made while he was away. These she had made already. She had been prepared to return as a proud and happy bride with nothing lacking in her love and pride in her husband, whom she adored even more since their marriage. After all, to be a *hanlin's* wife was in itself an honor few women dared to hope for. Now that the joy of seeing her parents was suddenly darkened by the news about her sister, she was doubly impatient.

"Peony has disappeared," she told Mengchia, the moment he arrived. "We must start as soon as possible. My parents want us to stop at Kaoyu on the way and make inquiries there."

"Is this true?" he gasped, drawing in a deep breath, his eyes dark with shock and fear. "And why at Kaoyu?"

"There is the letter," Jasmine said, and showed it to him.

Mengchia scanned the letter rapidly, with grave, puzzled eyes. Deep concern was in his voice when he asked: "But why was she at Kaoyu?" He rattled the letter, and then covered his face, uttering a low cry of exasperation. "What was she doing there?"

"I do not know and the letter does not say. It says the schoolteacher with whom she was staying suggested that she might have been kidnaped for revenge."

Jasmine saw him plump down on a chair, light a cigarette, and puff at it nervously. His eyes focused somewhere in the distance while he stroked his chin with the back of his hand slowly, methodically. He got up again and paced the room, picked up a paperweight, and rapped it on the table absent-mindedly.

"What are you thinking?" Jasmine asked.

He swung around to his desk chair, threw the paperweight on the table, and said, "I can't believe that Peony was such a fool as to return to Kaoyu, of all places, whatever she was doing there. That is the hotbed of smugglers and the Green-and-Red gangs. She should have known better. You know about the case of Shueh, the Tax Bureau Chief who was executed last autumn. Quite a number of people were involved in it, you remember. Any one of them could have remembered her and would be delighted to see her walk into their trap. She invited trouble for herself."

"You mean that it is a case of kidnaping? What could happen to her?"

"Heaven knows." He paused, buried in thought. He lit another cigarette and blew a few puffs, then crushed the stub in exasperation as he said with evident emotion, "Why did she have to do it?" Then more meditatively, "She was always impulsive. One can never tell what she is going to do next."

"Can we do something to save her before it is too late?" Jasmine saw the misery and concern on his face after the first shock was over.

"If it is a simple case of kidnaping we can. I mean, a simple case of someone kidnaping a girl for sale. It is always the Green-and-Reds. They have a perfect organization and you have to apply pressure at the top. If it is one of the Yangchow salt merchants, the case is more complicated. I have to find out first. I am going out now—never mind lunch."

He got up immediately and went out.

"Where are you going?" Jasmine shouted after him.

"To the Censorate. I shall be back in an hour or so."

When he returned, it was long past noon. Jasmine had had her lunch and sat listening to him over the dining table.

"I have studied all the documents of the salt smuggling case and got all the names of the people involved. The whole staff of the Tax Bureau has been changed and I presume Shueh's family must have left the town. Of course, it could be unrelated to them, and in that case, it would not bother

me so much. We have to find out. But the powerful Yangchow salt merchants are a different story. They have a network
working with the smugglers at sea, covering the harbors and
the coastal islands. . . . A man is coming to see me this afternoon. He is the one who was sent out by the Censorate to
Kaoyu while the case was under investigation. I can get some
information from him about the place. His name is Li Cho."

Li Cho showed up about four o'clock. He was a man of
forty, with a deceptively poised, incommunicative look, and
talked in a slow deliberate tone, never raising his voice. He
was a man who knew many secrets, made his own decisions,
and never talked more than necessary. The Censorate had
sent him on the Kaoyu case not only because of his fine record,
but also because he came from Yangchow. Li was extremely
courteous and wanted to know if he could be of any service.
He listened quietly and thoughtfully as Mengchia outlined
to him the situation and then asked for his opinion.

"What do you think?"

Li bent his head, stroking his chin slowly and meditatively.
"The course of action is clear. What you may have to do
largely depends on who is in back of it. I do not think"—he
pronounced the words explosively one by one—"that it is
the Green-and-Reds. Their headquarters is about three miles
from Yangchow. You mustn't misunderstand. They don't do
things like that. Their leader is a philanthropist—it's a non-
profit organization, if you want to call it that. They rob and
kill and break into prisons when they know someone has been
wronged. Of course, they work with riffraff, too, and many in-
dulge in petty thievery and pickpocketing unwary travelers.
Then the leaders look the other way, on the theory that they
have to make a living. But they are a tight organization with
their own code of honor, subject to the most rigorous discipline. They don't go around kidnaping women. That would be
against their principles. I shall give you the name and address
of the head. His name is Yu Shuchuan, "Gargle at Springs";
they call him Yu Tako, "Big Brother." Yu lives in a beautiful
garden just outside Yangchow and he would be honored to

see you if you go as a friend, not as an official. He is the first man to see. You will find him most generous and obliging, most chivalrous with help and advice."

"What if the Green-and-Reds have nothing to do with it?"

Li bit his lips. He gave a quick, smiling glance and said, "Remember Yang Shunli—the millionaire who was fined a hundred fifty thousand dollars? He got away and bribed two fellows into taking the punishment for him. I think their families got five thousand dollars each, and ten thousand if anything should happen to them." He gave a hoarse laugh. "It could be. As you know, he knew your cousin had the documents. A very sensual man. Used to keep other men's wives and virgins, and let them go after he had tired of them. That is why I think of him. He could say to himself, 'Why shouldn't I have a little fun out of that wench who cost me a hundred fifty thousand dollars?' . . . I tell you he would, if he knew your cousin was in his district, and vulnerable."

"What would you do?"

"Give Yu Big Brother a few days and he'll know all about it. Your cousin disappeared quite recently, didn't she?"

"Must have been a month ago."

"Then Yu would be able to find out. Just give him a few days. If Yang is the man, he will tell you, but I doubt that he would help you. The relationships involved are too subtle, too complex, and Yu Tako would not like to interfere."

"Handle Yang with kid gloves—is that what you mean?"

Slowly Li Cho reached for a cigarette. He seemed to be enjoying the situation. "No," he said. "The mailed fist is what he is afraid of. You can scare the life out of him if you want to. You can bring him to his knees if you let someone pass a friendly word that the Censorate is reopening the case. You just say so. You are not responsible for what you hear. Bring the maximum official pressure you can to bear upon him. I'll bet your cousin will be sent home to you in a sedan chair."

Mengchia thanked him profoundly for the advice. Before Li left, he promised to go home and look up some useful addresses to which Mengchia might go and get helpful information.

Jasmine had been listening behind the library door. When the guest had been shown out, Mengchia returned to find her waiting with an anxious face.

"There is some hope?" she asked briefly.

"Yes," he answered, and added in a drawling, vexed voice, "I still can't see why Peony chose to go to Kaoyu. She should have better sense than that."

"She always has been impulsive."

"I know. I know."

"When can we start? I must write my mother immediately to tell her and relieve her anxiety."

"It will take a day or two to get the necessary information. Anyway, not tomorrow. The earliest will be the day after." He paused as he recalled out loud the junior censor's words, and drummed his fingers and said, "Maximum pressure. You write your mother that we are starting day after tomorrow, and everything will be in control. Say that we will be doing our best. . . . Oh, Peony!" he almost screamed in exasperation.

Mengchia and Jasmine had come to understand and speak of Peony as only loving relatives could. He still thought of her as the most unique girl he had ever known. He understood her as a passionate young woman, capricious, impulsive, unpredictable, and very confused in her search for a lost love. He knew very well that she would prefer younger, handsomer men, especially more muscular young men, and had spurned him because of his age, even though she had hotly denied it. He saw it from her point of view, realizing that he himself would rather sleep with a young girl than an older woman. On this point, Jasmine contradicted him and said that he and her sister had confused passion with love. Jasmine understood him so thoroughly that she was able to stand above jealousy and they were both able to joke about Peony. Just now she was even more concerned about her sister than was Mengchia, who was getting really exasperated with Peony's whims and caprices.

"Don't be angry with her," she said. "We mustn't lose too much time."

"I am not angry. Of course we will do our best. If only she will not do anything rash and remain in good health, I am confident we can save her from the millionaire."

"You talk as if it *is* the millionaire."

"We really don't know. But Li Cho is inclined to think so. He knows the place and he knows Yang. I am going to write a letter to Prince Yi."

"You mean the Military Governor at Hangchow?"

"Exactly. I think I am going to follow the censor's advice. I will get Grand Councilor Chang to write a letter to the Governor of Nanking tomorrow. And I will write a personal letter to Prince Yi. If official pressure is what Yang needs, he is going to get it—and it will be *maximum*."

That evening he sat down at his desk and wrote to Prince Yi. It was a warm letter, semiofficial and semipersonal. He begged him to do his utmost and communicate with the civil governor at Nanking. To exert the utmost pressure he was to say, of course, that the kidnaped person was his own first cousin and, if he considered it appropriate, that she was Prince Yi's own adopted daughter. That should do the trick.

The next morning's mail brought a second letter from Uncle Sueipo, which was more detailed and more factual. Reinforcing the father's plea that they stop at Kaoyu, Uncle Sueipo also added new information. He mentioned having verified that An Tonien was in town and could not possibly have had anything to do with Peony's disappearance. It also said that Peony had planned to elope with the poet, but that the romance had since crashed, and that this might indicate a motive for her sudden disappearance. She had been highly nervous and upset and had told her parents that she wanted to go away and "turn over a new leaf." He believed it was all genuine. That was why she had decided to go to Kaoyu and stay with Mr. and Mrs. Wang, where she had been teaching in his private school. On the whole, the letter gave a better impression of Peony's course of conduct, and assuaged some of Mengchia's annoyance with her.

"I still don't see why she didn't come to us if she wanted to get away from Hangchow," said Jasmine.

"You know why," said Mengchia.

"I don't."

"Her pride. And what is she going to do when we have found her?"

"Come and live with us, of course," answered Jasmine.

Mengchia pursed his lips. He glanced at his wife and admired her for her complete confidence and simplicity of thinking. Jasmine saw the hesitation on his face.

"You are not afraid of her?" she said with a teasing smile.

"Not afraid. But it would be simpler if she didn't come, wouldn't it? Your sister is so unpredictable."

Jasmine kept quiet, not wishing to tread upon his emotional toes.

"Jasmine," he said, "you don't have to worry. I loved your sister once—madly. I soon discovered she was very confused. I am beyond that madness. I did not know her then. I know her now. You speak about bringing her to Peking. You know that ours is a different kind of love. Nothing can come between us. That is the first thing I want to say. The second thing is that if we have to bear the responsibility for her, I would be happy to find her a man as quickly as possible, to put her out of mischief. If what Uncle Sueipo's letter says is true, she has had enough of love affairs already. If she hasn't, then she will create as many scandals here as she did at Hangchow."

Jasmine detected a note of bitterness in Mengchia's voice. How he must have loved her and suffered for her!

"My sister is not as bad as you think. You don't understand her."

"No?" Mengchia added facetiously, "I'll tell you the best thing we can do for her. Choose a young man with a handsome, white, muscular body. Bundle her up blindfolded and send her into a sedan chair and marry her off to him. A nice young man, of course. Next year she will have a baby and be rid of all this nonsense."

"How horrible you are!"

"Don't you think that this is what she really wants?"

"There is some truth in what you say. But you don't have to put it that way. If you object to bringing her to stay with us, we don't have to. Mengchia, please."

Mengchia was mollified. A word of love from Jasmine always had that effect. He made her sit on his desk and gave her a kiss.

"You are impatient with her, aren't you?" she asked.

"Of course, bring her here if you want to. I was merely saying that it will be our duty to help find a young man for her."

She bent and kissed him sweetly. "That sounds better. I know you will always do the best you can for her."

"You know, I ought to be very grateful to your sister," he said, examining and stroking her soft hands.

"For what?" she chuckled.

"For making me meet you."

Then she kissed him again, sweetly as always, not wildly, as Peony had. Jumping down from the desk, she said, "Let's go to bed. We have a lot of things to do tomorrow."

In a way their marriage was almost ideal, like that of Joshui and Paiwei. Of course there was sex in it. But this love of the other sex was so natural in two such personalities that it came through in every word they said to each other, in every touch of the hand, every sound of voice, every discussion of ideas, even in their very differences. How much Peony had missed!

CHAPTER 26

It was terribly hot in Kaoyu. They had left their luggage in the Ride-Stork Hotel in Yangchow, one of the luxury hotels located in a sprawling garden. Sleep was impossible because of the heat and because of the flute and string music that floated up from the garden most of the night. Without letting anyone know, they had come up in a boat, as Mengchia agreed with his wife that it would be more comfortable than traveling by cart or sedan chair. Jasmine had wanted to come along and talk with Mr. and Mrs. Wang and see for herself where Peony lived. She had never realized before how much she loved her sister! Her mind oscillated between the blackest fears and a hope that perhaps by the time they arrived they might find that Peony had returned safe and sound. "What if we find Peony today in Mr. Wang's place?" she asked Mengchia several times.

"I would like to hope so, but I don't."

"What would we say to each other if we found her? She really could have voluntarily disappeared and come back again."

"Possible, but improbable. We shall soon find out."

It was one of those *kuaichuan* ("fast boats") making better than three miles an hour, a shallow light craft, manned by four husky oarsmen. The men had been promised extra tips if they could make it before sundown. The light boat sped along, overtaking the others one by one, coming to near collisions as it shot its way through the crowded traffic. Every time the oars splashed into the water, the boat shuddered with the stamping of the men's feet. Their bare bodies, clothed only in shorts, glistened in the sun. Jasmine's heart was in her mouth whenever she saw an oncoming boat heading straight toward them, but each time they managed to scrape by without a disaster.

"Be careful!" cried Jasmine, as they just missed hitting another sampan.

"Don't be afraid," said one of the young men. "You want to get there before sundown, don't you?" It was a laughing, shouting, and swearing lot of young men reveling in their physical prowess.

Mengchia looked sad and preoccupied. He did not talk much during the voyage. The possibility of seeing Peony again awakened him to the fact of their separation. His mind went back to those first days of meeting Peony on the boat above Taihu, when all of a sudden everything he saw had been touched with new meaning, and of how he had played the game and lost. The echo of that lost love always remained. Life never quite looked the same again for him. Just now, when he saw these bare-backed boatmen, he thought of Fu Nanto, the boxer, and how he must have fascinated Peony. Jasmine saw the distant look in his eyes. When he was like that, she always left him alone.

The boat really seemed to fly along, cutting an arrowhead of waves in that placid current. With every splash of the oars, their bodies lurched backward. Soon they had left Yangchow far behind and reached Fangchia Bridge, where the Canal joined a big body of water. Here the landscape skimmed by with a kaleidoscopic change of blue hills and tree-covered islands connecting the various bodies of water, refreshingly different. Wooden bridges spanned the streams, and here and there little dark red pennants raised on high poles indicated the locations of wineshops and inns among the distant hamlets. It was a rich, variegated country that provided beautiful hide-outs for the smugglers, and excellent avenues of escape from the water police.

A blazing white sky hung overhead, transforming the lake into a solid white glare. Mengchia held a parasol over Jasmine. The heat of the day was relieved by a fresh breeze sweeping across the mountains. The rhythmic motion lulled Jasmine to sleep. They had not slept well the previous night and had got up at five. Still sitting erect, with her hands in her lap, her chin rested on her chest like a tired child's. It amused Mengchia to see his wife's serenity and propriety of manner even in her sleep.

Her profile stood out sharply against the shining sheet of water, and again he was struck by the resemblance to her sister—the same oval face, the same pointed nose, the same well-modeled lips and chin, the same arching forward of her head—even the nape of her neck had the same lovely fullness.

It occurred to him once more that she was a younger, sweeter version of Peony, a Peony purged of her violent and impulsive caprices. How alike and yet how different! Now, even in her sleep, her hands lay in her lap, her cream-and-apricot jacket well buttoned up around the neck, her skirts carefully arranged before she sat down. Jasmine thought of herself as a "madame *hanlin*," and wanted to appear as one; she did not want to disgrace her husband. At home, he had never caught her slouching on a couch, or letting her legs sprawl in Peony's provocative fashion. While she saw and felt a great deal, she was more clear-headed than Peony, always sweet-tempered. She never spoke tactlessly, or out of turn. At their wedding party, everybody had remarked on her sweet serenity and quiet dignity, and did not wonder that the confirmed bachelor had fallen for her. Just now, even as she was napping, she still looked every inch a "madame *hanlin*." She seemed to have one purpose in life: to make him happy and proud of her.

The similarity of the profiles was really extraordinary. Jasmine was to him the Peony that might have been, a Peony faithful and true. Whether she was truly asleep or not, he did not know. He touched her gently on the back, and she opened her eyes with a smile, and saw him looking intently at her.

"What are you thinking?"

"Just looking at you and thinking how you look like your sister from the side."

"Oh, Peony! Where do you think she is now?"

"We really don't know, and shall not know till I see Yu Big Brother. It must be four or five weeks since she disappeared. I should be surprised to find she has returned. If she has not, she may be in real trouble. That is why time is so important."

To their surprise, they made Kaoyu in midafternoon, and told the boatman to wait, since they were going back to Yangchow the next day. They lost no time in finding the address of Mr. Wang.

The Wang house was one of those old stucco houses built
to endure. It had been in the family for generations. There
was a hedgerow at the back, outlining a straggling garden
where Mrs. Wang grew her vegetables. Small back windows
on the top floor overlooked golden fields of ripening wheat.
Mrs. Wang had just finished her chores and was fanning
herself, her fleshy body resting in a chair which she had
placed against the kitchen door to catch whatever breeze was
stirring. Her summer linen jacket was half unbuttoned and
she was thinking to herself what a hot day it was. Now and
then she wiped the perspiration off her brow. Two of her
daughters were married and she was managing the house all
by herself. Two younger children, a boy and a girl, were at
school, and the youngest, who was eight, stayed at home to
keep his mother company. Suddenly Ah-pao ran in, shrieking
at the top of his voice, "Sister Peony has come back!"

Mrs. Wang leaped up and waddled her way out to the
front gate to find an elegantly dressed couple waiting for her.
The boy was grinning from ear to ear and calling "Sister
Peony," and made as if he were going to grab the young
woman's hand.

Jasmine said, "I am not Peony. I am her sister."

The boy let his hand drop slowly. "But you are so like her.
I thought you had come back married."

Mengchia surveyed the middle-aged woman and hastily
explained who he was.

The schoolteacher's wife was overcome with surprise and
apologized for her disgraceful appearance. "Come in," she
said. "It is such a hot day." Turning to her boy she said,
"Quick, run to school and tell your father to come home. Say
Peony's sister and the *hanlin* from Peking have arrived."

Towels and basin were provided for the guests to wash up.
They had just finished the preliminaries when the scholar
Wang came shuffling through the gate in quick, unsteady
steps, a little out of breath. He greeted the guests with a
look of flurried excitement and confusion. The guests stood
up and they bowed to each other.

"I'm sorry to disturb you like this," explained Mengchia. "It is because of my wife's sister. You were kind enough to take care of her."

"Why, I never dreamed of the honor of this visit from you," Wang answered, still looking a bit dazed. "I heard Peony talk so much about you and have had the pleasure of reading some of your books."

They seated themselves, and Mengchia explained that he had come to find out exactly what had happened.

The schoolteacher spoke slowly, with a deliberate gravity appropriate to the occasion. "It happened on May the twenty-eighth. She failed to come home from school at the customary time. We waited all evening. It's only fifteen minutes' walk from school, and she had left her room just as usual. She never said she was going anywhere. The next day we learned that someone had seen her on the river bank. She had come from the outskirts of the town, where the streets stop and there are only a few straggling shops standing back from the bank. Later we were told that there had been an incident in the street. A crowd was standing around watching two men fighting over a peep show. Someone in the crowd had seen her knocked down by a water carrier, drenched, and prostrated on the ground. A young man stepped forward to help her and pull her up, and she was seen walking away assisted by him. For all we know, the whole incident may have been arranged by the unknown young man. That was the last they saw of her. We reported it to the local authorities, but they were unable to turn up any clues. It has been over a month now. I have sent several letters to Hangchow."

The matter touched Mrs. Wang deeply. She spoke in a sad voice, "She is such a sweet girl, like one of my own daughters. She always came home and never went out with any young men. She felt very much at home with us and then this thing happened. I feel so responsible to your parents."

"You don't have to," said Jasmine sweetly. "My parents wrote me that you have been wonderful to her. I want to thank you on behalf of my parents. We came as soon as we could after hearing the news."

"Tell me," said Mengchia. "You know about the smuggling case last year. Is the family of the Chief of Bureau Shueh still here?"

"No. The whole staff has been changed. His family went back to Anhwei after that."

"Do you think she has enemies around here?"

"Why should she? She hardly ever went out after school or knew anybody."

"Did you hear of others who were involved in the case?"

"Quite a few members of the Tax Bureau staff were arrested and questioned. Some singsong girls, too. Peony's husband was involved, too, so I heard. I couldn't see how she had anything to do with it. It's a mystery to all of us."

"Have there been many kidnapings lately?"

"No. There have not been any for years."

Jasmine pressed this question, the one which frightened her the most. "I mean, kidnaping of girls for immoral purposes."

"No, why should anyone do that? There are plenty of girls sold by their parents in famine years. They have to be brought up and trained as singsong artists. There is a regular market for them at Yangchow."

Jasmine drew a sigh of relief, and her shoulders sagged a little.

That night Mengchia invited them to a supper at a restaurant. Having gotten all the information they wanted, they thanked the Wangs profoundly and excused themselves by saying that they were going back to Yangchow early the next day.

The nearer Mengchia came to locating Peony, the more nervous he became. He had been quite calm at Kaoyu. But the meeting with Yu Big Brother, the head of the Green-and-Reds, promised to lead to a break. The first meeting was a courtesy call on Yu in his large garden outside Yangchow. Few men had the chance to meet face to face with this legendary figure. Mengchia found him an offhand, straightforward man of sixty-five, working in his shirt sleeves over a desk piled with papers, with two gold teeth glistening in his mouth. He was quite used to the most polished forms of social intercourse. His hall was decorated with scrolls from many famous writers, and in the garden in front stood a tablet in white stone commemorating his honesty and civic virtues on his sixty-first birthday, with a long list of homage from prominent business and social leaders. This was readily understandable, in view of the fact that his name always headed appeals for public charity and famine relief. These Green-and-Reds may not have lived up to the banner standard of "Loyalty and Righteousness" handed down from the *Shuihu*, a romance celebrating the "Heroes of the Lake" around this region, that society of outlawed men who had banded together to fight corruption and injustice in times of a rapacious government; but at least they had not entirely forgotten these principles. When the docile, defenseless, law-abiding citizens submitted to tyranny, these men of the lakes and rivers rose to defend them. Their sharp code of honor (although, to be sure, it was honor among thieves, as they robbed the rich to give to the poor) and their very efficient net of secret intelligence often made it necessary for government officials to work with them.

Accordingly, Yu Big Brother, ever mindful of courtesy, made a return call. The rank of *hanlin* carried with it an honor that was popularly understood. Yu felt greatly honored by Mengchia's visit. He had said that in a few days he would get the necessary information. Now he had come not only with useful information, but also with an offer of invaluable assistance.

He had walked into the hotel and inquired at the desk for Liang *Hanlin* in the suave, refined manner of the true aristocrat. There was a great deal of bowing and curtsying—it was hard to believe that this gentle old man controlled the life and death of every man in that organization, which covered territory all the way from Shantung down to Shanghai—that his word was law, obeyed without question.

Mengchia ushered him into a private guest room, shutting the door behind them. Over a cup of tea, the elderly chief spoke in a brisk, precise voice, and did not mince words: "I have asked our men to investigate. I have been assured that none of our men was concerned with the disappearance of your cousin-sister. On the other hand, I have reports which lead me to think that there are people who may have wanted to carry her off. Last year when the Censorate sent a man down to investigate the salt smuggling case, some of our men at hotels and singsong houses were helpful. We knew all about it. I understand that your sister was the former Mrs. Fei Tingyen, and that Shueh was aware that when Fei died his diary had fallen into the hands of the Censorate. Shueh had himself sent the diary along with other things to Mrs. Fei. The conclusion is plain."

He showed him a copy of those who were arrested and those who had received various degrees of punishment. His sharp eyes followed Mengchia's as the latter glanced down the paper.

"Does that suggest anything to you?" Yu asked.

"I would rather hear your expert opinion," answered the *hanlin* with great diffidence. The chief seemed to have gone to great pains to make a thorough investigation.

"My men are following up. I have let them know that the matter concerns one of my best friends."

Mengchia rose slightly from his seat in acknowledgment of the compliment.

Yu continued: "I do not know what led your sister to return to Kaoyu. From the time she arrived till the day she disappeared, she is not known, from all reports, to have made friends with any improper characters. As I told you, my men are still trying to find out who did it. I rule out the Tax Bureau chief because he was far away from the scene. I am taking special interest in this matter, not only because you paid me the great honor of coming to me, but also because this is exactly the sort of thing that our 'Loyal and Righteous' comrades have been fighting against, the abuse of power and wealth. On the other hand, I must be perfectly frank with you: I am in a kind of dilemma. The salt smugglers and our men have a tacit understanding to operate each in his own territory. As you are probably aware, we operate on the Grand Canal and the Yangtse, from Hankow down; they operate on the coast. We do not interfere with each other, nor do we fight them. If we assume that it was done by one of their men, I cannot render active assistance. I wish to keep our agreement with them. I am sure you have other means by which to recover your sister, while our intelligence men can supply you with whatever information we have."

Yu spoke clearly and sincerely, in a way that left the impression that he would remember every word he had said. It was well known that his word was as good as a deed. It sounded very encouraging. Mengchia at once expressed his great appreciation for the assistance he was giving. Locating Peony was the first essential step, and then he would know how to proceed from there.

Yu looked at him intently and said, "I want your help."

Mengchia laughed in surprise. "How can you say that? You are really helping me."

"I know I can trust you. But don't breathe a word to the others. I will tell you why, if I enjoy your confidence."

"You do," answered Mengchia, briefly but gravely.

Yu looked around the room and drew his chair closer, and spoke in an increasingly low tone: "I want you to do something. Do as I tell you. Make a courtesy call on the *taotai* magistrate. Spread the world around that the Censorate office is reopening last year's case of salt smuggling."

"Why do you want me to do that?" Mengchia remembered that the censor had suggested the same approach.

"Never mind. Manage to convey the idea that you've got the power to have the case reopened. You do not make an open threat, of course. You just say you've heard it—that furthermore, in your opinion, this is entirely possible. You have just come from Peking. That makes it perfect. You are telling it as a behind-the-scenes story, of course."

"Why particularly the magistrate?"

"He is a friend of the rich salt merchant, Yang Shunli. You remember that he got away with a heavy fine and paid some clerks in his firm to take the punishment in his stead. No doubt, after a year or so, he will bribe again to have the poor fellows released, or the sentences commuted. I know Yang is not above taking women for his pleasure. A number of women have been taken by him and kept in any one of his three villas. We do not interfere because as an organization we do not fight him. But, as I told you, this is the sort of thing our society does not stand for. In this case, I have reason to think that he may quite well have a hand in it."

Mengchia was still quite at sea. "What's the purpose of telling the *taotai* about it?"

"I want the rumor to reach Yang's ears. Yang is pretty close to the local authorities. He has to be. Probably the magistrate will send for him and give him the news as a friend. You are going home with your wife to Hangchow, right?"

"Right," answered Mengchia, amazed at the accuracy of his secret intelligence.

"All the better. Make it natural. You are passing through the city and making a courtesy call. Casually mention that you are looking for your lost sister, and ask for advice. Kaoyu is under the *taotai*'s jurisdiction. You'll appreciate any help he can render. I assume you are stopping here for quite a few days."

"As long as necessary."

"Just as casually bring up last year's case, and say that you have heard what the Censorate is thinking of doing. If the *taotai* does not himself pass the word, there are secretaries in his office who are bound to inform Yang."

"And then?"

"That is all I ask of you. You see Yang is a timid man. All rich men are. I want to badger him, flush him out, and watch his moves. If your sister is in his place, he will do something. Then we will know. In summer he lives in his garden near the Pingshan Hill, beyond the Twenty-four

Bridges. It is a huge place. And inside the garden, there is an inner garden where he lives, surrounded by high walls. Nobody can break into that. That is why I want you to throw a scare into him."

"I am beginning to see the point."

"You must wait for my news. Don't come and see me. I'll send you what news we get. The first thing is to make sure where your cousin-sister is."

In Yu's face, Mengchia saw a man of great vitality and courage and quick decisions. He felt a warm admiration for this man with such outward suavity and gentleness.

When Mengchia had seen Yu Big Brother to the door and bowed good-by, he came back to his room. Jasmine had been waiting.

"What's the news?" she asked anxiously.

Mengchia's face was flushed and nervous.

"Yu thinks it is the salt merchant, the man who sent a representative to Peking to talk with us—you remember?"

"I remember. Where is Peony?"

Mengchia scarcely heard her.

"Where's Peony?" she repeated.

"We do not know yet. I am waiting for news from Yu. He is a wonderful man." He wore a troubled, heavy look as he visualized Peony detained in that rascal's home. His hope was that she might be safe and unharmed. He had a sense of something impending and told his wife, in broken answers to her inquiries, Yu's plan of action and his having to call on the *taotai*.

"I guess that is what I'll have to do. Once we know Peony's whereabouts, I may have to request help from the authorities. I may have to see the Governor at Nanking. Meanwhile, we can do nothing but wait."

"Then we will wait." Jasmine watched him sitting there, burdened with thought. She came and stood behind him and laid her hands on his shoulders. Mengchia's hands caught them and held them tightly. She said comfortingly, "I am as worried as you are. We'll soon know. But it's Yang who will have to do the worrying now. I am sure the Governor can help us."

"Perhaps you are right." He pulled her over to sit on his lap. "While we are waiting for news, I suggest we visit the Twenty-four Bridges. It's supposed to be magnificent—a stretch of rich villas and gardens, a mile long, on the banks of a winding river. Quite fabulous, I am told."

"You go and call on the *taotai* this afternoon. We'll see the Bridges tomorrow," she said with a vivid smile.

"Jasmine, you are wonderful." With a warm kiss, he said, "Now get up. I have things to do."

CHAPTER 27

"Your honor, we have seen your sister," the man whispered as soon as the door had closed. He had called on Mengchia at the hotel with a card from Yu Big Brother. He was a tall, lanky person, with a scar on his left cheek, and his queue was wound up on his head, under a black turban.

Mengchia pulled up a chair and asked him to sit down.

"Where is she?" he asked impatiently.

The man looked around circumspectly. He was slow in answering. "I have come to deliver a message from Big Brother. She is out on one of the islands, down the estuary of the Yangtse. Our men have just returned after tracing her there. We had Yang's residences covered, all three of them. Yesterday morning, one of our groups spotted a covered sedan chair waiting at the gate, outside his big villa at the Pingshan Hill. Our men saw a woman carried out and put in the sedan chair. We are sure it was your sister."

"Was she struggling?"

"No. She had her head bowed all the time until she got into the sedan chair. Then the chair was all covered up and our men followed. She must have been told something, perhaps that they were sending her back to you. Our men followed and saw her put in a boat. At the beach she made a futile struggle to get away and was immediately gagged and carried onto the boat."

Mengchia looked at the man anxiously. "What are they trying to do?"

"It is quite clear. Yang got scared as soon as he heard that you are in town looking for your sister. He knows that you have influence. He is going to shift the blame when your sister is traced. Then he is safe."

"Where is the island?"

"It is one of those small fishermen's islands below Chinkiang. Our men followed with a boat. There were four husky men who carried her ashore."

"Will you wait? I want my wife to hear all this. She is the woman's sister."

When Jasmine came in, she was introduced and listened breathlessly as the man told his story.

"What does Yu Tako think?" she asked.

"Big Brother says it is one of the salt smuggler's gang, working with the pirates at sea. We are to leave her there and not scare them off. It takes half a day going down with the current, and a whole day coming up. It is a small primitive island, absolutely flat, growing out of the estuary. Provided we do not scare them into moving her farther out to sea, it would not take more than thirty or forty men to surround the island and take them by surprise. Big Brother says you will know what to do."

The man delivered his message and stood up to leave. "If there are any further developments, I'll come and let you know."

"Are you sure that we can find her?"

"We have left three men there to keep them covered. If the situation changes, we'll hear about it immediately."

"Tell your chief how grateful I am. I shall not forget what he is doing." He showed the man to the door.

"At last!" said Mengchia, breathing deeply.

"What are we going to do?"

Mengchia took a cigarette, lit it, and inhaled deeply. The

blood drained from his face as he pictured Peony's struggles in the hands of her captors and her present distress. He walked slowly toward the window, paused a minute, and slowly put out the cigarette. Turning around, he said, tense with emotion: "We must be off to Nanking and see the Governor at once. We have no time to lose. If she is moved again by her captors, it may take a fleet to hunt for her along the entire China coast."

Mengchia sat down and wrote a brief note to Yu, thanking him for his help and begging him to send a man to go with him to the Governor. He would need a man to tell the Governor the story and the exact location of the island. He had the letter sent by messenger and came back.

Jasmine looked at him anxiously. Mengchia told her, "You'll have to come along. I can't leave you here alone."

"Of course I am going. The case concerns my sister."

"Most likely the Governor will invite us to stay at his home. As soon as I get an answer from Yu, we'll have to start."

The packing was done. Jasmine took a long time at the dressing table, combing her hair into a pompadour and matching her jewels carefully. Her hands trembled and she did her hair again and again. She tried on a pale blue toile, elaborately embroidered with delicate jasmine designs, and stood looking at herself in the mirror.

"You look marvelous in that," said Mengchia.

"It's my favorite. Shall I put on that pearl or coral set?" she asked.

"Anything will do."

She opened her jewel box and picked out a coral necklace and a pair of earrings with coral pendants, turning her head sideways to look in the mirror.

"How is that? Tell me."

"You are divine. It's not so important. Come on. Hurry up. Yu's man may be here any minute."

"But you say we may be invited to stop at the Governor's house."

Jasmine was always like that. Whenever she went to court

parties, she always wanted to look convincing—to herself and to others—that she was the girl who had captured the heart of a famous writer and a confirmed bachelor.

The Governor's home was in the north of the city, not far from the famous Cockcrow Temple. Governor Chen Taonan was a man of about fifty. Mengchia had not seen him for years, as Chen's posts had always been in the south and southwest. But they had passed the imperial examinations and been made a *chinshih* in the same year, a fact of great importance among scholars; it was a fellowship that lasted a lifetime, as men who had gone through the most crucial moments of their life and triumphed together. As soon as their cards were presented and Governor Chen was informed that Liang *Hanlin* had come with his wife, he instructed them to be shown in to the inner court.

After an exchange of pleasantries, Mengchia produced the letter of Grand Councilor Chang Chih-tung. Governor Chen read it with great formal respect. It was always a favor and a privilege to receive a letter from such a high personage.

"It is very kind of the Grand Councilor to remember me. But, Brother Mengchia, there is no need. You know I would do anything in my power to be of service to you. What is the business he mentions in the letter?"

"It is about my wife's sister." Mengchia described the situation briefly and suggested that the Governor send for Ku, the man who had come with them. When he was received, Ku fell on his knees and remained there until the Governor ordered him to stand up. After asking him the necessary questions, he said to one of his secretaries, "Have this man put up inside my office compound. I shall want his help."

After Ku had withdrawn, the Governor said, "You were extremely wise to have gone to Yu Tako. It is a simple matter now. I shall call upon the Naval Office to furnish the necessary men. Fifty or sixty can go in two boats. I want to make absolutely sure that the culprits do not escape." He sent for his secretary and asked him to send for the Chief of the Naval Office at Nanking, and then turned to Jasmine.

"You must do us the honor of staying with us so that I may have the pleasure of your and your husband's company for a few days." He spoke with great warmth of feeling, and then paid her a subtle compliment. "I hope you received my wedding present, which I sent when I heard that the famous bachelor *hanlin* was finally going to get married. And no wonder, now that I have seen you. We'll celebrate tonight in your honor."

"You are really too kind. I am afraid we are troubling you. We shall depend entirely on your help," replied Jasmine with her usual poise.

"Brother Mengchia has already found out where your sister is. That is usually the most difficult part. I can see that what we have to do is fairly simple. When the naval officer is here, I will give him instructions to have the river watched both up and down, at Chinkiang and Kiangyin. I don't think you have to worry. Escape by water is impossible."

"You don't think there'll be any shooting?" Jasmine asked, with a worried glance at Mengchia.

"Don't worry, don't worry. We shall take good care of your sister. According to this man Ku, there are only half a dozen fishermen's families living on the island. There'll be no shooting unless it is absolutely necessary."

The Governor's wife and two concubines were all present at the dinner that evening. For a moment, Mengchia and Jasmine forgot Peony, as toasts were drunk and the conversation grew lively. The naval officer had been sent for and received his instructions. They had done everything possible. Orders had been sent to keep a sharp watch over river traffic between Chinkiang and Kiangyin, and the naval station at Kaochiao was to be in constant communication with Nanking.

Jasmine and Mengchia were seated at the top in the seats of honor. Jasmine was made to feel very important. The Governor's wife kept talking to her and when she spoke all the ladies listened. She had had no idea how famous her husband was until she heard the Governor's wife complimenting her husband about his books. Somehow the word *hanlin* possessed a magic in Chinese ears; it sounded better than the title of minister or governor because of its implied literary distinction, a dream that all scholars coveted and few achieved.

In the midst of the gay laughter and talk, the chief steward brought in an urgent message that somebody from the Hangchow Office of the Military Governor of the Two Kiangs had arrived. The man was waiting in the reception room at the front. The Governor read the card and passed it to Mengchia.

Mengchia licked his lips, then looked up at Jasmine and said, "It is An Tonien, Secretary to the Military Governor of the Two Kiangs."

Jasmine suppressed a half gasp, and felt the blood rush to her cheeks.

"What is he doing here?" she said.

"Do you know him?" asked the Governor's wife.

"No, I know about him."

The Governor told his steward to say that if it was urgent business, he would be with him in a minute. The steward replied: "He says it is very urgent. He brings a personal letter from the Military Governor."

"Then it must be important," said the Governor. "Have him shown into the parlor inside."

The Governor left the table to see the emissary, and returned after a few minutes to say that An Tonien had brought a letter from Prince Yi.

"It is about your sister," said the Governor to the *hanlin's* wife. "I did not know that your sister was an adopted daughter of the Prince."

Mengchia smiled and answered, "She is. Prince Yi took quite a fancy to her at a clan dinner given for me in Hangchow."

Jasmine was surprised, but with her usual presence of mind, kept it to herself. Her husband had not told her about the adoption. It was the result of a casual suggestion on Mengchia's part in his letter to Prince Yi, as a means by which "maximum pressure" could be exerted. He was gratified that Prince Yi had taken his suggestion seriously.

"Why not ask him to join us?" asked Jasmine, dying to see the man who might have become her brother-in-law.

"He says he has dined and would rather wait. He would prefer, I am sure, to discuss this business in private."

The sumptuous dinner kept coming in, course by course, until Mengchia requested that the host call a halt and give them some congee to finish up with.

After dinner, Jasmine and Mengchia went with the Governor into the reception room to meet An Tonien. The latter was impeccably dressed in a formal cream silk gown and black gauze jacket; he was a few inches taller than Mengchia. When the Governor introduced Mengchia, An Tonien bowed with dignity and cast a swift glance of surprise in Jasmine's direction. She could see the extreme distress and anxiety on his face.

"This is my wife," Mengchia said.

Jasmine stepped forward and they bowed to each other. She liked him immediately. In spite of the grave business he had come to discuss, he was vivacious and was completely natural and at ease in the Governor's presence.

An Tonien was not prepared to meet Jasmine here, and his eyes betrayed evident shock at seeing this elegant young lady who bore such a marked resemblance to Peony.

They seated themselves on luxurious redwood chairs covered with large vermilion satin cushions. Tall blue porcelain vases, two to three feet high, stood on the carpeted floor. Tea was served.

Seated in an easy chair, his knees crossed, a cup in his hand, An Tonien addressed the Governor in a composed, but sad and solemn, voice: "The *shünwu* considers the matter so important that he has asked me to come personally and beg for your help and co-operation."

"As a matter of fact," replied the Governor, "Liang *Hanlin* is a step ahead of you, and we have already been able to locate the *shünwu's* adopted daughter."

"Where is she?" asked An Tonien, his voice rising, although

he was trying to appear composed. He looked from the Governor to Mengchia, and laid the cup aside. Jasmine repressed a smile.

The Governor outlined what was already being done. "The Naval Office is in charge. If you had gone to the *shünwu's* office here, they would have told you that already."

An Tonien felt relieved as he followed the Governor's story intently. He cradled his crossed knees in his hands and spoke again in his ordinary tone.

"I did not know this. My instructions were first to seek your guidance and co-operation and discuss what we should do. If our Naval Office is already taking charge, I can get in touch with them directly. Of course, I shall still come to you for assistance."

"Of course. All the facilities of my office will be placed at your disposal. Where are you staying?"

"As a matter of fact, I have not yet decided. I came here directly and did not realize that I was disturbing you at your dinner."

An Tonien almost felt a sense of guilt. He had persuaded the Military Governor to send him on this mission with the powers of a personal representative. He had begged to come, out of a burning desire to trace Peony, to find her and see her once more. He had been in torture ever since that morning when the boy had died, and she had asked him to let her go. He had refrained from seeing her, or corresponding with her. His mind was a chamber of images and memories of her face, her gestures, her words, her embraces. Day and night the images tortured him, and while he sat at home saying nothing in the evening, his wife thought that he was only grieving for their lost boy. And now he was given this chance to obey a command of his heart while ostensibly serving on official duty. This mission was such a personal thing to him that he felt ashamed to meet Jasmine and Mengchia and be seen by them. His eyes shifted constantly from Mengchia to Jasmine. All three of them felt secret thoughts that they could not, or would not, express. Once or twice he caught Jasmine looking at him with a questioning look, as if she had seen into his deepest heart and purpose. He wondered how much they knew about his affair with Peony. How much could he discuss the matter with them without betraying his personal feelings? His one desire was to find and see Peony alone.

CHAPTER 28

The night was still. The lights on the banks had gone out. A half-moon hung high up in the sky, now and then hidden by broken, fleecy specks of sailing clouds. Moving patches of black shadows crept across the islands, obliterating and then revealing the white shore line.

A stiff midnight breeze was blowing across the Yangtse as Mengchia and An Tonien stood on the prow of the 2,500-ton destroyer, peering into the distance. The *Lunghwa* was one of the small destroyers the infant Chinese navy had stationed between Nanking and Kiangyin. It had steamed down from Nanking that noon and anchored above Kaochiao, about a mile and a half from Yuchun Island. That afternoon, they had surveyed the island through Captain Sha's field glasses, and had clearly seen the fishermen's houses and a long stretch of trees.

Captain Sha considered the choppy water and the dusky moonlight as especially favorable for a night operation. He regarded it as a very minor maneuver and had been entertaining his guests with jokes and drinks all afternoon. The lights on the island had gone out some two hours ago, but he had wanted to have his crew of forty-five men start well after midnight, when the high tides would make their landing and return easier.

The hour had finally come. Mengchia and An Tonien, leaning on the railing, stood tensely, now and then exchanging a word or two. They were the only two men in civilian dress and their gowns flapped noisily in the wind. An Tonien had planned to go down with the boats, anxious to be the first man there when Peony was found.

"I am going down, too," said Mengchia.

"Are you sure you want to? You really don't have to, you know. It might be more comfortable for you to wait here until we bring her to the boat." His tone was clearly reluctant.

"I am sure," answered Mengchia insistently. "She will feel more reassured as soon as she sees me in the party."

"I was only thinking that we may be in the way if they start any shooting. One of us civilians might be enough."

Mengchia laughed it off airily. "I have seen some tougher fighting in my day."

"Of course," An Tonien conceded.

"And I don't believe that any shooting will be necessary."

"Maybe just a shot or two to frighten them from their sleep. I have just talked with Lieutenant Chang. The important thing is to prevent her from being carried away by the pirates."

Mengchia scoffed at any danger of a bloody resistance. "There can't be more than a dozen able-bodied men on the whole island. We'll catch them in their sleep and easily outnumber them. By the way, can you recognize her?"

"I believe I can."

There was an awkward silence.

"Oh, yes. I remember she was working in your home some months ago."

"Yes."

Another awkward pause. An Tonien wished Mengchia wouldn't ask any more questions.

"Can you recognize her voice in the dark?"

"Oh, yes, very well."

"Of course. I just wanted to make sure that you didn't capture a pirate's daughter in the dark by mistake."

"Oh, no, you can be assured of that. You come along then. We will deploy some men to guard the exits from the village and the boats to prevent their escape. I would recommend that you stay a little distance away until I bring her safely to you." An Tonien looked at his watch and said, "Let's go."

In the darkness of the night, three boats were let down from the small destroyer under the command of Lieutenant Chang. The men carried lanterns, bayonets, and pistols. Silently, they took up their places in the boats, Mengchia and An Tonien sitting with the navy Lieutenant. The boats crept forward in the hazy light. The river was choppy and the night was dark, but at close range they could see each other's faces.

At the landing, men with pistols were posted to guard the boats, while the company proceeded silently up the sandy beach. All the lanterns had been extinguished. In the silence of the night, one party went for the smugglers' boats, while the main body stole across the fields toward the village half a mile ahead. Orders had been given not to shoot until positions had been taken up around the village, and then only after a signal was given. The low whine of buoy-markers on the river floated across the midnight air and was heard above the incessant, waspy rush of the surf.

Lieutenant Chang led his men around the village to the south and halted to survey the situation. The pirates' houses stood close together without enclosures, for all outward purposes like any fishing village. A broad road of white sand led to the quay where a few masts were discernible against the white band of the river. Their best chance lay in ambush and surprise, by stationing men around the entrances, and making no noise until the signal was given by the Lieutenant. A separate detachment went off to the east where two or three other houses stood apart on a slight elevation.

"Do not shoot indiscriminately. Our object is to find and recover the captive woman," said the leader. "She answers to the name Peony Liang. Take up your positions and do nothing until I give the signal. Be ready at the doors when they rush out from their houses. Herd all the young girls together. Now get going!"

At the sound of a gunshot, Peony woke up suddenly. It took her a few seconds to realize that something was happening outside. She stole out of her bed and looked across the grilled window. Indistinct cries and shouts came from the center of the village. She saw some dark figures rushing about. There were more gunshots.

Some minutes passed and in the next room she heard a door open, followed by a heavy thud as of someone falling, and then heavy footsteps.

"Don't move," she heard a gruff voice say in the next room. "We are looking for Miss Peony Liang. Where's the woman you captured?"

Peony rushed out to see a sailor in uniform. His face was ruddy in the glow of the lantern he was holding. The sailor came and grabbed her. "Come with me. Don't be scared. You are Miss Liang, aren't you?" Peony allowed the sailor to pull her along with him.

She had no time to think and could not understand what was happening. She had been so unnerved from the experience of the last days that she shuddered and burst into tears. Vaguely she heard the sailor say that it was the navy, come to rescue her.

A whistle blew. More men emerged from the darkness.

"Here, here!" the sailor shouted. "We've found her." His arm was supporting her.

The moon had come out, and she could see men running and scrambling about in all directions.

"Can you walk?" the sailor asked.

"Yes, I can."

She heard a cry from below. "Peony! Peony!" The voice was strangely familiar. A man was coming up at great speed toward her.

"Peony!" the voice repeated.

"I am here," she answered.

In a moment the man appeared whom she least expected to see.

"An Tonien! Is it you?"

Her legs yielded. Her whole body sagged and she fell into his arms and felt hot tears staining her face. It was An Tonien after all.

"You are safe now. I'll explain later. Your cousin Liang *Hanlin* is also here."

"Is it you? Is this true?" She could hardly believe her eyes, as she allowed herself to be literally borne along by An Tonien's strong arms.

When they had reached the center of the village, the operation was almost over. Lanterns crisscrossed the yards. Two men were lying wounded on the ground. Three or four others had been handcuffed. A knot of women and children were cowering in fear at a distance. The men were slowly returning from their assignments.

Peony was aware now that she was among friends. She turned her face toward An Tonien and all the longing of the past few months surged through her, and she clasped him tightly in her arms, covering his face with kisses. She did not see Mengchia, who was standing close by in silence. An Tonien noticed him and said, "Look. Your cousin Liang *Hanlin* is here."

Peony turned. Mengchia was watching her silently but steadily. "Oh, Tako!" she cried. She broke loose, and to his great surprise, threw herself upon him. She broke out into great sobs, crying hysterically despite herself. Trembling inwardly all over, Mengchia's arms encircled her lightly. He was not only extremely embarrassed but he was also sharply reminding himself that Peony did not love him any more. He had lost her even though he had found her now. Why did she throw herself upon him in front of everybody? She raised her head slowly and gazed up at him. There was just enough light for him to see the white oval of her face, and in the depths of her eyes he believed he saw a touch of remorse. She bent her head once more, crying pitifully, and he felt her hot tears wetting his gown. A tumult of conflicting emotions surged through him. Very gently, he raised her head, and his voice was quivering when he said, "Peony, don't cry. We've been searching for you. Jasmine is waiting for you in Nanking."

She raised her head and asked, "Where are we?"

"Not far from Nanking."

He turned and said, "Here's Lieutenant Chang. You should thank him."

She saw the tall, handsome officer, with his white teeth gleaming in the darkness.

"I'm glad we have found you. The whole Chinese navy is at your service." His voice was gruff, but he was staring at her admiringly.

She uttered a word of thanks for all their help.

"Are we all ready?" the Lieutenant shouted. He told one of the men to give a whistle for the party at the quay to assemble for return. Turning to the lovely feminine figure in her white pajamas, he said with a laugh, "Can you walk? Our men will be very glad to carry you piggyback, you know. We neglected to bring a sedan chair along for you."

"I can walk, thank you."

The party started to move off. One of the captives had been wounded in the leg and limped along painfully. Their wives were screaming and wailing, as they saw their men being carried off. Here and there lanterns were winking with red and yellow lights, and the path was crisscrossed with moving shadows. Lieutenant Chang, walking directly ahead, constantly swung his lantern around to illuminate the way for Peony.

An Tonien was walking on her right, Mengchia on her left. She was too dazed to know what to think or what to say. She knew that it would have been more proper for her to hang on to her cousin and ask about home; yet Mengchia was strikingly silent and it was An Tonien's arm that was supporting her. Did Mengchia know, and how much did he know of their love affair? She did not care. She let herself lean on An Tonien more and more. He was telling her that they were going up in a gunboat which would take them back to Nanking.

"How is your wife?" she asked.

"She is at home. Grieving and weeping, thinking of our boy. It is hard for her. I am doing my best. When this thing came up, I had to come away. She was so shocked to hear that you were lost."

Peony felt apologetic and made an effort to talk to her

cousin. She removed her arm from An Tonien's and asked: "How is Jasmine?"

"Very well. She is stopping at the Governor's house." He was a bit frightened to hear himself talking to Peony once more.

"I heard Sister and you were coming down south. Have you seen my parents yet?"

"Not yet. We are going back now to Hangchow with you." Somehow he had made her feel guilty by his reluctance to talk, his lack of warmth and excitement on meeting her.

In the dinghy that was carrying them to the gunboat, she was seated beside him, while An Tonien chattered away with the officer. Her hand touched his back slightly, timidly. He did not move, nor did he even glance at her, but she felt a light quiver as she touched him. He was not looking at her and his jaws were rigid. He shifted his legs nervously.

One by one the captured pirates were shoved up the ladder to the gunboat. The Lieutenant and An Tonien went ahead, and Mengchia lent a hand to assist her up. The Captain, a man from Foochow, invited them to have a cup of tea and refreshments in the officers' room.

"I will be with you in a minute," he added, "as soon as I get the names of our prisoners."

Lieutenant Chang took them to the officers' mess hall. Throwing his cap down, he said, "Be seated. Will you have tea or coffee? We have both."

"Coffee of course," said Mengchia. Mengchia felt more relaxed as soon as they entered the brightly lit room. "I was once on board an English gunboat. They offered me tea. I said I preferred coffee. They didn't understand. They forget that we have tea all the time at home. Besides, coffee is international."

Peony's eyes brightened as she recognized Mengchia's old voice and manner of speaking; he was her cousin, the *hanlin*, again, and whatever he said she found thought-provoking. A feeling of the old Peking days came back to her. Now he was looking straight at her with a searching, questioning look. She

looked away in embarrassment, despite herself. Mengchia saw
a trace of that haunted look in her eyes. She had grown more
sallow and there were dark patches under her eyes. What a
harrowing experience the past month must have been for her!
He said sympathetically, "I hope you were not too frightened
tonight!"

"I was at first, when I heard a gunshot in my sleep. I didn't
know what was going to happen next."

Her eyes narrowed in the bright light of the cabin and she
had an indistinct, tired feeling that she was still in a dream.
An hour ago she was sleeping on a thin mat on a desolate
island in the hands of her captors. Suddenly she had found
herself on a modern gunboat, with both her lovers together.

The Captain came in and said, "The prisoners have been
questioned, and their names taken. Yang is dead. We shall be
starting back for Nanking." He spoke with the happy sense
of a mission accomplished. Then he turned to the pretty captive and said, "I hope you are not too upset. I hear that you
are Prince Yi's adopted daughter."

Peony nodded mechanically, ready to accept anything which
could happen in a dream. Her dubious glance met An
Tonien's.

"That's so," Mengchia said for her benefit.

Peony was acutely conscious of her disheveled appearance.
"Please, Captain, may I wash up?"

"Surely. Follow me." He led her to his room and showed
her the towels and things.

"Have you got a comb?"

"Oh, yes." He gave her a navy jacket and said, "Here, you
may put this on if you feel cold." Then he came out and shut
the door.

Peony hadn't seen a mirror for four or five days. Hastily she
washed her face and combed her hair, studying herself in the
mirror sadly and meditatively, and trying to order the confused thoughts in her mind.

She had reason to be flattered that both old lovers had come
out in search for her. Mengchia was now married. Had he

changed? He had been so silent, so aloof. An Tonien looked much thinner; he must have lost ten pounds since she left him.

She came out again to join them, feeling somewhat refreshed.

The Captain was chatting with them about the fight. He looked up at her and said, "You can have my room for a rest. I shall be on the bridge." He looked at the clock on the wall. "It's past three already. It won't be two hours before daybreak."

When the officer left, the three of them sat talking for a while.

"What's this about my being the adopted daughter of Prince Yi?"

Both tried to answer at once. Then Mengchia said, "I wrote to him and suggested the idea in order to get the Governor's prompt attention."

An Tonien added, "Prince Yi asked me to draft the letter to the Governor. He said I could put it in if I thought it would help. I did."

"How did you find me?"

Mengchia told her, and added, "Thank heaven, it's all over and you are back, safe and unharmed. I must ask the Governor's office to send a wire immediately to your father. You had us worried."

"The Governor's office?"

"Yes. Grand Councilor Chang sent a letter to the Governor of Nanking. And Prince Yi sent Mr. An to trace you. The whole navy was set to rescue you. You really had us worried."

Peony sensed a tone of reproach. She was quick to defend herself. "Was it my fault that I was kidnaped by that brute?"

"I didn't mean it that way, Peony."

"I think we all need a rest," said An Tonien, standing up.

The two men showed her to her room, made sure that she had everything she wanted, and said good night to her. As they walked away, the men looked at each other.

"You have a remarkable cousin-sister," said An Tonien.

"Yes, very remarkable," answered Mengchia.

As they went back to their cabins, they heard the rumble of the engine below and felt the soft vibration of the planked floor; the boat was finally moving.

Mengchia shut the cabin door behind him, quite disconcerted and shaken by the events of the evening. In the past year, he had learned to think of her with a certain remoteness, but it was a remoteness tinged with exquisite pain, like a distorted image, a wrinkled reflection of the true love he had found in Jasmine. Tonight that image was violently disturbed, perhaps because of the sallowness in her cheeks and the sad, haunted look in her eyes. She did not look like an innocent, foolish girl, but like a tragic, mature woman, infinitely more attractive. Then the sight of her in the close embrace of An Tonien had shocked him greatly. He had heard only once of a reference to An Tonien in Jasmine's letters from home. His heart twitched violently again at the mere sound of her voice. All night he had tried to control himself. All ideas he had tried to form about her hardness and capriciousness vanished. He felt the rumble of his old emotions like a gigantic ground swell. Once more, his love for Peony defied all analysis. He felt very weak, and decided to go to sleep. Once more, he stretched out his arms for her in the silence of the night and clutched at dark, gloomy emptiness.

Peony could not sleep. The shower, which she loved, made her feel clean and fresh. As she crept into the Captain's berth and felt the crispness of the clean sheets, she found herself fully awake. Her horrible days in captivity were over. Her head swirled with the excitement of all the sudden events of the night, and the dread of meeting Jasmine again. She thought of Mengchia, who in spite of everything had come to search for her, and above all, of An Tonien. She found the old, familiar hot tears of love bathing her face.

She got out of bed and stood peeping out of the porthole. She could hardly see a thing in the semidarkness except moving indistinct shapes on the bank, and the luminous water, swishing and tossing below.

She stole silently out of the cabin. A small light illuminated the passage which led aft. She opened a door and smelled the sharp, salty air of the sea. The half-moon had sunk toward the horizon, and was now a dirty yellow. Toward the east, a solitary bright star blinked with a golden light. Some faint sparks flying in the wind caught her attention. At the other end of the deck, she could see a dark shape, as of someone leaning on the railing, smoking alone. Whoever it was, she went down the steps, holding firm to the white handrails, and walked toward that dark figure. Hearing her steps, the man turned.

"Peony!" she heard a whisper. The man came forward. It was An Tonien.

"I thought you were asleep," he said as he took her hands and in a quick gesture held her close.

"I can't sleep."

"Nor can I."

"What are you doing here?" she asked, her heart pounding within her, as she felt the sudden warmth of his breath.

"Thinking of you—of us, rather."

Their lips met briefly and then parted.

"I love you so, my Tonien." Her eyes were glistening.

In the semidarkness of the starlight, they looked at each other silently. With his arm around her, they moved toward the railing and looked out to sea. His arm squeezed her hard, and she let her body lean heavily against him, as if searching and wanting to belong to him completely. Instead of looking up at him, her eyes were cast down, watching the phosphorescent glow of the waves lapping below them.

"How did you come to be on this mission?" she said finally.

"I begged for it. I heard what had happened to you when Prince Yi sent for me at the office. The news left me stunned. I had no idea that you had gone to Kaoyu. It was afterward that I went to see your parents and got some details. Prince Yi called me in to show me your cousin's letter. I suggested that someone should come up, if it were his Royal Highness's pleasure to take quick action, and offered to come myself. I also told him that on account of my boy's death, I wanted to get away for a while. I begged him to send me. I knew I had to come. Even if he refused me, I would have asked for leave and come on my own to search for you. . . . He seemed to have a very high regard for you. I said something about you. He asked me if I knew you. I had to tell him . . ."

"What did you say about me?"

"I forget what I said. Something about what I feel about you. I may have shown excitement in my voice. Anyway, the *shünwu* smiled and agreed to send me. I know what I feel." His voice quivered. He could not find words and was breathing hard. After a pause, he said, "You cannot imagine what I went through when you decided we should part. . . . It was hard, very hard . . ."

"Don't you agree that we should?"

"Yes," he said sadly.

There followed a hard, tormenting silence. Then he said, "It was too much. I could not eat. I could not sleep. Sometimes I wished I had never known you. But to know you and then lose you . . ."

When he lighted another cigarette, Peony saw with a shock that he looked much older in the short two months since she had left him. He had sallow cheeks and lines under his eyes which he never had before. It cut her heart. For several moments, she could not speak. Finally she said, "You have changed, Tonien—I mean your face."

"And you know why. The torture I went through since you left me. I was in purgatory." And then he said, almost as if he were speaking to himself, "Peony, once in a generation is a girl like you born."

She gave a low, sad smile as she said, "To most people, I must appear to be a wicked, licentious woman."

An Tonien said, "Yes, to most people. The finer the music, the fewer the people to understand it."

"My father thinks I am crazy. Even Mengchia . . ." She stopped abruptly.

"What about Mengchia? I understand you loved him."

"I don't know what to say. It's so different. Maybe he is bitter. I sensed it while we were in the dinghy. He still loves me, I know, but it's such a personal thing with him. Perhaps I hurt him deeply. He must have felt bitter when I left him."

Then she turned to him and said, in a rueful kind of voice, "Only you understand me. I shall always love you for that."

"What are we going to do?"

She drew herself up and said, "Life is bitter. Let's not make it more so."

The two of them fell silent. At last he said, "I understand what you mean. It has to be so. Let us keep it so. Maybe it's the best thing for us." He laughed bitterly. "My body belongs to my wife, but my soul belongs to you. Let's keep it that way. In that way, it will never change. Do you know what is the greatest tragedy of life?"

"Tell me."

"The greatest tragedy of life is when a great love is killed. God! If you ever stop loving me, please do not let me know. I shall not be able to stand it." He touched her hair gently. "I know that if we elope together, we are bound to find out things about each other and the magic of our love may be killed by the cold frost of a gray day. Perhaps you will find me a very ordinary person, raspy at times, moody at others, my hair not cut the way you like. Maybe it's some very small thing that will change your feeling toward me—perhaps a tooth abscess, a new wrinkle in my forehead, a sallowness in my cheeks. But at least this way, you will never find anything that will destroy your love for me."

It was one of the saddest things she had ever heard.

The tragedy of it was that what he said was so true. She remembered something Mengchia had said when he found that her ardor had cooled toward him; he had said it was like seeing a naughty child drop a jade bowl, crashing it on the floor out of sheer mischief and then walking away from it happily.

"You mean we shall stop seeing each other?" she asked.

"Isn't that what you think, too?"

"Yes. Go back to your wife and think of me." And then she turned her face toward him, and their cheeks rubbed against each other in a fond, endearing gesture, their throats choked with a suffocating pain. Their lips met, tenderly, in quick, short, biting kisses.

At last he said, "If it's destined that we shall meet, we shall meet again. If not, this is the saddest night of my life."

"It is mine, too," she said, her voice quivering in resignation.

"What are you going to do?"

"My An Tonien, let me tell you. Let me keep this love. After what you have said, I can bear it. Go back to your wife; let's not spoil the memory of the one good thing I have done in my life. I shall not wait for destiny. Once I waited for Chin Chu, and the price I had to pay was too much. What you said just now suggests something I can do. I can marry someone; my body shall belong to him but my soul shall belong elsewhere. Though I may live in prison, yet I shall feel free."

"Whom will you marry?"

"It does not matter too much now."

CHAPTER 29

Mengchia woke up about six, after a restless sleep filled with strange dreams. He tried to recall the details, but at first could not. He was only conscious of the happy feeling of being with Peony in an exciting adventure. Whenever he dreamed of Peony, that unique feeling stayed with him all day, making the day seem richer. He vaguely remembered something endless and enormous, dragging on and on, and also something very small. Was it some grains of rice? Yes, he remembered vividly now finding some grains of rice spilled on the floor, and both of them were laughing and happy to find them.

Peony picked up the rice and suddenly vanished. He was greatly astonished, and woke up.

He tried to think, and began to recall the dream, tracing it backward, image after image. They had been in a small fishing craft, going up dangerous rapids and whirling streams. It was a deep, long, winding ravine, seemingly endless as they could not see far ahead. High up on the banks, they heard the cries of prowling wolves and roaring tigers before they emerged upon a vast tract of grasslands in a mountainous country. The bottom of the craft rumbled and scraped against pebbles as the river narrowed and became shallower. Giant boulders stood in tumbledown fashion along the banks, while monkeys screeched in the deep mountains. All of a sudden, they were blocked and could go no farther. Forsaking the craft, they walked up hand in hand. The whole atmosphere was menacing. Strange bird cries and howls of beasts filled the air. There was no road ahead. Then suddenly they saw a man with a tanned face, standing half-naked before them and holding a sheaf of grain in his hand. The man offered the sheaf to Peony. He was saying, "So long as the wooded hills are around, why worry about rice and fuel?"—a folk proverb. Peony bent down to pick up some grains of rice on the floor, and then suddenly vanished.

The dream was interesting enough, most likely brought about by the excitement of last night on the fishing island. But why rice? Mengchia did not believe in the interpretation of dreams. Then suddenly he remembered the oracles of a Buddhist temple. When he had received the news of Peony's disappearance, he had been so shaken with misery and fear for her safety that on the day before their departure he had gone and prayed at a Buddhist temple. In his moment of helplessness and uncertainty, he turned to God. He knelt and prayed a wordless prayer, face to face with the powers that govern our lives, and sought an answer to the mystery. He prayed until his shoulders shook. He wanted to know and cried: "Why? Why? O God, why?" Then he lit the incense, threw the wooden shoes, and drew the divination stick, bearing handwritten oracles in four lines of verse. The oracles said:

> A fishing boat sails roaring rapids in a narrow
> ravine,
> Passing forests infested with tigers and wolves;
> When the mountains close in and the waterway is
> blocked,
> There stands the rice field with ripening corn.

Of course, that was where he had got the idea for the rice in his dream. The words of the oracles, seemingly forgotten, now came out in his dream.

He looked out the porthole and saw that the day was breaking. Houses and whole villages and lines of trees on the bank were parading slowly past. He heard the clinking of cups and saucers in the officers' mess, and decided to get up.

With that vague, pleasurable sensation of having been close to Peony, he got dressed and went to the mess hall. He hoped to see her this morning and have a good talk with her. Last night, the few snaps of talk they had had were far from happy; perhaps he had been shocked to find her in the embrace of An Tonien at the first moment he had caught sight of her after their long separation. It had irritated him all night. But now the magic of the old love was still there. All the pain she had caused him was forgotten. Even last night's brief meeting, where she had showed herself as capricious as ever, seemed only to increase his desire to see her because she was truly herself and nobody else. She was the "unique, unique, unique" Peony.

When he entered the mess hall, a solitary officer was having his breakfast. A boy was standing by to serve. While sipping his coffee, he asked the officer when they would be in Nanking.

"About ten or half past ten, I guess."

His eyes were directed to the door of the captain's room where Peony should be sleeping now.

"You haven't seen her up yet?" he asked the boy.

"No."

He burned with the desire to see her at once. After some hesitancy, he went over to tap at the door. There was no answer. He tapped louder, and still there was no answer. He turned the knob gently and opened it a slit. The berth was empty. He threw the door open. She was not there. Peony, he knew, kept the most unusual hours. Where could she be? He closed the door and came back and sat and brooded.

Soon the officer finished eating and excused himself. After a while, he heard a girl's steps coming down the passage. He thought he had imagined hearing her voice in the cabin occupied by An Tonien; now he knew it had been real enough. The clock on the wall indicated ten past six.

"Peony!" he called softly.

Peony came in, surprised to see him there. She looked very appealing in the navy jacket the Captain had lent her, her face still haggard from her experience of the past days.

"I have been up for an hour," she lied obliquely and defensively.

"Come on, have a cup of coffee. It's good and hot."

"Coffee so early?" she said with surprise, and then sat down with a wan smile. She glanced quickly at him, uncomfortably wondering whether he had seen her coming out of An Tonien's cabin.

The boy poured the coffee. She sipped it slowly, waiting for him to speak. Her quick feminine sense realized at once all that was implied in this situation. She had just said a private good-by to An Tonien after making one of the most important decisions of her life, and at this moment she was flushed and feeling particularly noble, while the pain of that sacrifice still left her head in a blur of conflicts. And now Mengchia was here in person, Mengchia whom she had definitely broken with, but who was now Jasmine's husband.

Peony never lost her presence of mind with men. She always kept quiet when she was sure of herself. She leaned back, threw her head up, and stretched her legs out under the table.

Mengchia said, "I am told we'll be in Nanking about ten. Peony, you have changed."

"Have I?" Remembering what she had said in her farewell letter, she wanted to have an opportunity to explain herself. She was waiting for the right beginning. But all she could say now was, "I guess I have. You cannot imagine what I have gone through. I suppose I look horrible—older."

"No, that is not what I mean," said Mengchia. "More mature, not older. I don't know how to say it. You have changed, and yet you have not. I can see from the pain in your eyes that you must have suffered terribly."

Their eyes met. As she heard Mengchia's voice, without bitterness, without rancor, she overcame that momentary feeling of discomfort. They could talk like old friends. Mengchia, she felt, was still the same—gentle and understanding and still wearing that adoring look when he looked at her. And indeed she felt toward him as toward a member of her family.

Giving a side glance in the direction of the boy, he said, "I want to give you news of our family, of Jasmine and your parents. Shall we go somewhere, to your room or mine?"

"Just as you like. Let's go to your room."

They both got up. He knew Peony was the last person to be bothered about good form.

Back in his cabin, Mengchia pulled up a chair for her, while he seated himself on the bed.

"You are not bitter about my leaving you?" Peony was always direct and straightforward.

Mengchia looked up sharply. "No. I was somewhat surprised. I felt lost, was actually ill for several months. Something had been torn out of me. I never felt the same man again. But not bitter—not any more now. I learned to take it, thanks to Jasmine."

"You love her very much, don't you?"

"Very much."

"That's what I want to hear from you."

"After all, you could not help what you did. You were at least honest to tell me. It's just like you."

"Like me?"

"Yes, you and your impulsive nature, your whims and caprices."

They had known each other, heart to heart, so intimately that they could speak very frankly, as if they were a divorced couple now in a mood of reconciliation. There was no point lying to each other.

Mengchia gave a sigh and murmured, as if to himself, "Remember when we first met in the boat?" and gave a slow meditative chuckle.

An old warmth of feeling, akin to love, returned to Peony as she thought of the torture she herself had suffered from Chin Chu. How Mengchia must have suffered, too. She was overcome with a sense of remorse and pity. She got up from her seat, put out a friendly hand, and said, "Pardon me. I am sorry. . . ." Her eyes were veiled with tears.

With a tremendous effort, Mengchia was able to control himself. He clasped her hand tightly. She was looking down at him with pity.

"Will you forgive me?"

A thirst and a longing which he had suppressed for so long burst out of him. He pulled her toward him and kissed her wildly, as if in that kiss he were burying all the desire of a lifetime.

"How I love you!" he groaned.

Peony shut her eyes in pain. Then she freed herself and said, "Let's never do that again."

"I know. I had to do it. And I shall never forget it."

Peony turned her face away from him now. She said, "Jasmine—I cannot do this to her."

Mengchia was silent.

"Why didn't you ask me to change my surname when we were together?"

"I did not think of it until it was too late. And you didn't, either," he replied.

"Do you regret it?" she asked.

"Do you?"

Both met the question in silence.

"Would you, if we had thought of it?" Mengchia asked.

Peony nodded her head.

Then it was like old times. Peony was looking at him sharply now. "I suppose it is fate. If you ask me why I acted that way and left you, I cannot tell you." His hand was playing with the wisps of hair on her forehead.

She said, "I knew that you loved me more than anything else in the world, and I would have married you if we had thought of *kuochi*. Now it is too late. I have to tell you everything. Now there is An Tonien."

"You love him?"

"Yes, I love him. I cannot lie to you. I will tell you everything because you will understand. I just said good-by to him an hour ago."

"And?"

"We agreed to separate." The words dropped slowly from her lips, like a clinging trickle of molasses.

"You love him very much?"

"He is married, like you. Why must life be so complicated?" She went on, musing aloud. "I hate Hangchow. I feel now that I want to go back to Peking. It's probably the only place for me to go. What do you think? I will be fair to my sister. Can you trust me?"

She leaned back on the bed and covered her face with her hands.

"Please do not make it difficult for me," he said, as he pulled away her hands and kissed away her tears. Smilingly, he made her sit up. "Yes, it will be difficult for me, more than for you," he continued. "Can I be brutally frank with you?"

"Go ahead."

"It will be very difficult. I do not want to do anything to hurt Jasmine."

"Who wants to?" she replied, impatience in her voice.

"She is your own sister. I love her, I need not tell you how much. We both love her."

"Of course. Don't you trust me?" She was always quick to

retort, and answered in a tone implying that she was always right.

"Please, I am speaking about myself. Let me be absolutely frank for once, and I shall not say it again. Just a moment ago, as you were sitting in that chair, do you know how I felt?"

She waited for him to continue.

"Don't blame me if I for once regretted that I did not marry you. There you sat—just yourself, as I had always wanted to see you—the same eyes, the same hands, the same way you spread your legs—the same voice. Nothing can substitute for your voice, or the way you walk. It is you, and you alone, Peony. When I was away from you, I had thought of your impulsive whims and desires and your wild passions, and I had thought of your sister as a purified version of you, a 'Peony minus.' Now I think of you as 'Jasmine plus.' It is that plus which I want, all of you as you are, without the minus. Can you understand what I am trying to say? I do not want to see you minus anything. You alone are Peony. Jasmine is not you. You may be tired of hearing me saying that you are *unique, unique, unique*. There is only one Peony in this world; there cannot be two. That is why I say it is going to be very difficult."

Peony listened and drank in the words like nectar. She shook her head and said, "Please, please, you must not talk like that. Or I shall never go to Peking. I will control myself if you can." She broke off and then said, "I gave you my diary. You have read it?"

"Of course I have."

"Tako, you see I have concealed nothing from you. If you have read my diary and still feel that way about me, then you truly understand me and love me."

"Then you must come to Peking. Jasmine will want you to, I know her. I have yet to find a more sensible girl than your sister. We shall never whisper a word of love again in front of her or behind her back. We will bury it. Agreed?"

"Agreed."

"Then it will make me happy to see you married to some-one."

"You always said that."

"I mean it."

Peony looked at him pensively. "Jasmine said that to me a long time ago. She said that I shouldn't be carrying on with you because I would never want to marry anyone else."

"Yes, I remember coming across that in your diary. I won-der who will be the lucky person."

Peony tossed her head back lazily and sighed. "It is all like a dream. My marriage—Tingyen's death—my meeting you when I was carrying home my husband's body—our nights at Tunglu—Fu Nanto and the rest of them. Then Chin Chu's death—an episode over and done with. And the death of An Tonien's boy . . . the horrible days, indignities of the last few weeks . . ." Her eyes were filled with tears.

"Let's not talk about them. Forget them."

"It's all like a dream, especially last night, finding you and An Tonien. I am sure our dream is not over yet."

Mengchia told her about the dream he had had that morn-ing and concluded, "Do you believe that dreams foretell the future? I do not know what to make of it. You see, the dream fits in with a divination stick I drew at the temple."

"Why, Tako, I never knew you would ever go into a tem-ple!"

"You see, when I learned you had disappeared, perhaps had fallen into evil hands, I felt such panic that I had to go to the temple and pray. I suddenly realized how much you al-ways meant to me deep down. I hadn't known how much I always cared. I tried very hard to suppress it; maybe my pride was hurt. The moment I heard something had happened to you, I knew that all the time it was there, that you had never left my heart, that deep down in my soul you are the only thing I want and need. I was seized with such a helpless dread and misery that I turned to the supernatural against all my habitual beliefs and convictions. Yes, I knelt down before Buddha and wept until my shoulders shook. Then I drew the divination stick.

When mountains close in and the waterway
is blocked,
There stands the rice field with ripening
corn.

What can the last lines mean?"

Peony said, "The first lines seem to correspond to what has happened to me in the past month—the tigers and wolves and the fishing boat. But you really prayed to Buddha?"

"I did. When I feared for you, I prayed till my heart bled."

"Oh, Tako!" Her face came close to his. Recklessly and with her eyes closed, she kissed him warmly, repeatedly, interrupting herself to say, "Allow me—just once more—"

Jasmine was a resplendent and happy bride when she returned to her parents' home. She radiated happiness, and dressed with great care and elegance, so that her *hanlin* husband would be proud of her. Her girl friends came to see her and called her the luckiest girl in the world, and she happily agreed. Her parents were proud of her, but she, in her quiet way, told them not to say anything to make her sister feel out of place or superfluous. They had put up at Uncle Sueipo's house where there was more room, but Peony remained at home. Jasmine spent as much time at home as she could, for that was the purpose of her return to Hangchow. She had so many things to tell them about Peking and the journey home and the visit to Kaoyu. Like a proud young wife, her eyes lit up with a smile when she said, "How Mengchia snores!" She spoke of her husband's regular habits of getting up and working late. It was so good to have a husband to talk about.

They had to accept many dinner invitations, personal and official, given in their honor, and had to give many presents. The costly presents she received made her continually marvel at how highly regarded her husband was everywhere.

Among the dinners was one given by Prince Yi to celebrate

Peony's return. Mengchia wanted to give a party to thank Prince Yi, but the latter insisted that he wanted to have the pleasure. Having done one good turn, he wanted to do another. He had always wanted to make friends with the *hanlin* and really wished very much to see Peony and claim her as his "adopted daughter."

The whole family, including the uncle and aunt, was invited to the Prince's home for dinner, given at his villa on the lake shore. Peony's father was frankly incredulous and could not understand, nor quite follow, the many sudden turns of fortune of his two daughters. He had been an honest, dutiful bank employee all his life, but felt that fate, in the form of his two daughters, was playing all sorts of unexpected tricks on him. He put on his best gown and, almost guilty at how excited he felt, standing very straight, he asked for Jasmine's approval.

"How do I look?"

Jasmine surveyed him and was proud of him. He was in his dark navy blue silk gown which he took out only on rare occasions. It was a little tight as he had put on weight.

"You are wonderful," said Jasmine. "But, Father, you should put on a *makua*."

"Is it formal?"

"No, it's a home party."

"Then I won't."

"But please," said Jasmine. "It shows respect."

The mother said, "How many times do you get invited out by the Military Governor?"

Still reluctant, he nevertheless let them persuade him to put on the overjacket. It was a little frayed at the elbows. He was perspiring already. Jasmine wanted so much to be proud of her father and turned to Mengchia who was looking on: "You have a jacket that will fit. Father can wear it."

The father took it off and said, "Don't make me look ridiculous. I am what I am. What do you think?" he asked Mengchia.

Mengchia was the last one to think that clothes make the man. He replied drolly, "Don't take it seriously. It's a home party. Why isn't Peony ready yet?"

"I'll be ready in a minute," shouted Peony from the next room.

Jasmine went in to look. She saw Peony dressed in her own violet jacket, broad-trimmed in white. It fitted her perfectly, and even the slight droop in her rounded shoulders enhanced the subtle, pleasing perfection of its lines. Peony knew that An Tonien would be there. Like all young ladies, both sisters wanted to appear to be more elegant than they knew they were at home.

"How do I look?" Peony asked her.

"You look divine," Jasmine said with a small gasp. She was always in despair with admiration for her sister's beautiful features, that extra something in her dreamy eyes which so captivated men.

The sisters came out. Jasmine was in her favorite pale blue, embroidered with delicate jasmine blossoms in white. Mengchia drew an inward breath. Peony, in his wife's violet dress, looked so much like Jasmine—but a Jasmine with the magic touch of perfection added. He felt a slight sense of guilt at the thought.

"You are both beautiful," he said. Peony eyed him for a quick second. She could not help feeling a sense of satisfaction at his evident admiration.

There was much toasting at the dinner. First, the Prince toasted Peony as his adopted daughter. An Tonien looked extremely fidgety. The Governor's wife studied the two sisters carefully—particularly Peony—thinking how interesting it was to meet personally the girl who broke up a funeral service. A toast was drunk to the Chinese navy and then a toast to An Tonien for his successful accomplishment of the mission.

"I did nothing, really," said An Tonien, with his customary facetiousness. He was happy and excited in spite of himself. "Brother Mengchia had done all the preliminary work and located Miss Liang. A toast to Brother Mengchia," he almost shouted.

His eyes gleamed in the direction of Peony. Jasmine was tremendously intrigued; she had known from her sister all that was going on between them. It touched her to think that Peony could make such a sacrifice in giving up An Tonien. She nudged her sister and said, "You ought to drink a toast of thanks to Prince Yi—and to Mr. An."

Peony could do no less. She stood up and drank a toast: "Allow me to thank the Governor—and Mr. An." She was looking straight at the Governor, ending with a swift, pained glance at her lover.

Peony in the violet dress was tragically beautiful that evening.

She came home and cried all night. Seeing An Tonien at dinner had made it doubly difficult to give him up; but then she thought of the dead boy Lulu and his sorrowing mother. She knew she could not hurt that poor, bereaved mother.

Peony was tired. She felt as if she were gambling at a table with loaded dice. Somewhere in the invisible spheres, the hand of fate was against her. She thought of all the things that might have been—if Chin Chu had not died; if Mengchia had married her instead of Jasmine, and now, if Lulu had not died, now she would have been able to marry An Tonien, the man who most nearly approached her ideal, who could understand her completely—the man who was the most difficult to forget. Peony had always been an optimist; now she felt sadder and more resigned. There was a great emptiness in her. Probably when she went to Peking, Mengchia and her sister would help to arrange a match for her. But where would she find a man like the exciting and distinguished-looking An Tonien? She had a feeling of missing out somewhere. What was wrong with her?

CHAPTER 30

The leaves at Shishahai were browning and the Coal Hill in the Forbidden City was a riot of red and purple when Mengchia and Jasmine returned to their home in Peking. Jasmine's condition was quite apparent, and after the many entertainments on the way, she was feeling tired.

At Jasmine's insistence, her sister had come up with them.

Peony now lived at Peking in Mengchia's home. She knew the line which must never be crossed and which Mengchia and she had agreed upon. She was happy about it, content in the secret knowledge that Mengchia loved her very deeply. That was enough. The agreement was nobly kept by Mengchia and herself. She had come to adore Mengchia more and more for his strength of character, and some of her old warmth for him returned.

How does one describe such a relationship? Where does adoration end and love begin? No one knows, but Peony found the situation sweet and pleasant. The conventional definition of love had to be accepted. They never kissed, never made love to each other; the mutual awareness, the adoration, the sweet breath of a friendly spirit remained, locked in each of them. And there was her sister, Jasmine. If Jasmine had been distrustful, or spiteful or mean, they would have been driven into a whirl of consuming passion again. Jasmine, level-headed and never confused, knew that they had been lovers, but acted with the same ease with which she accepted her social obligations. She had by her poise, and by her quiet unobtrusive happiness, won the admiration of all her friends. She would act firmly when the situation called for it, but she would not worry about it. She was completely trusting, and in this way strengthened her husband's love for her.

The eastern court was now occupied by the married couple, while Peony lived in the main court. But many times Mengchia and Peony were thrown alone into each other's company. Jasmine was several months pregnant, and felt less inclined to go out. Sometimes she joined them in a drive; sometimes she urged them to go alone. It was more difficult for Mengchia than for Peony. How often his heart pounded and his lips thirsted for a kiss. Peony always said, "No. I do not love you."

It had become a kind of game with them. When Peony was sitting close to him, and their knees touched and when Peony felt ardent, Mengchia would say, "No, I do not love you." Then they would look at each other and smile, and their eyes, their smiles, belied all the words they had spoken. The most Peony indulged in was a touch of his arm, a silent pressure of his hand. In spite of all the torture of not "crossing the line," they felt the strength which comes from silent understanding. And so, at home, when their eyes met, it became easy not to show any emotion: they had achieved a peace that went beyond understanding, and a beauty of relationship that few men and women know.

In the middle of the following February, Jasmine's mother arrived. She had been waiting to come but could not get away until the New Year was over. Jasmine would have her baby in two or three weeks and the mother wanted so much to be there. She did not want to go out and see the city at all; she just wanted to see Jasmine through and help look after her first grandchild. The quiet house came alive with the preparations for the arrival of the baby, the hiring of an extra nurse, and the long evening talks among mother and sisters.

At last the hubbub of the women's chatter was joined by the healthy cry of a newborn baby boy. Peony was as excited as Jasmine and her mother. She at once fell in love with the new baby. All her feminine instincts emerged. He was her first nephew. She looked into the baby's eyes and stroked his cheeks and crooned to him as if he were her own child. For weeks she gave up her solitary walks, which had always meant so much to her. Mengchia stood no competition with the baby. He moved about on the fringe of consciousness of the three women, and if he offered an opinion about the care of the baby, he was laughed out of court and immediately silenced, made to feel like a poacher in the ancient demesne of womanhood.

Seeing how Peony adored the child, the mother said, "How about you? I am waiting."

It was that old, old question, uppermost in the mother's mind. Peony said nothing, but her deepest yearnings stirred within her.

"Mother, of course I want a home of my own, like anybody else."

One day, both sisters were in Jasmine's room. The mother turned to Jasmine, who was resting in bed. "There must be plenty of good scholars in Peking whom Mengchia knows."

"It takes time. We will talk with Mengchia."

Peony tossed the baby in her arms and said, "Don't worry, Mother. I will find a man."

She said it with such ease and daring that the mother and Jasmine could not help smiling.

Mengchia happened to come in.

"What are you laughing about?" he asked, glad to see the family so happy together.

Jasmine answered, "Mother was saying that it was time we should find a man for Sister."

"Of course. I wonder who the lucky one will be. I will have to think about it."

"You will do nothing of the sort," replied Peony with spirit. "I will find a man to marry." She kept cuddling the baby and drawing a finger across his cheek and making little clucking noises with her tongue. "Don't worry. I will find one."

Mengchia was amused. "You talk of finding a man as easily as buying a new pair of shoes."

Peony kept goo-gooing to the baby, speaking the primitive international language of mother love which has never been successfully transcribed and for which any kind of spelling is woefully inadequate. Raising her eyes, she said, "Stop worrying about me."

"Do you perhaps already have a man in mind?"

"No, I have a baby in mind—my baby."

"Sister is crazy," said Jasmine.

Mengchia said that he would be going away to Hankow. The Councilor had sent him to see about the Hanyehping Iron Works, which was the Grand Councilor's own project. He would have to be away at least for a month, perhaps two. Jasmine had her sister's and mother's company, and he did not have to worry.

Peony gave him a look, a significant look, which he could not make out.

Later that night, Jasmine questioned her husband: "What is it? Why did Peony talk like that?"

"Who knows? Perhaps she has already found a man she likes."

Mengchia saw his wife suckling the baby and for a moment he was lost in thought. He rose from the edge of the bed and walked to the window, where he stood for a moment, listening to the fluttering leaves in the dark garden outside.

"Come here," said Jasmine as she buttoned up her pajamas. "Is Sister going to spring another surprise on us, do you think?"

Mengchia shook his head in an appreciative smile. "She might."

"What do you mean?"

"It makes me feel uneasy to hear her talk of finding a man as easily as eating beans. I have an idea . . . " He broke off and went to light a cigarette. "I feel that she is like a quail with tired wings, liable to be ambushed and caught by the first man that comes along."

"I don't believe it."

"She is the most unpredictable creature that I know. She has been hurt, terribly, several times. She never speaks of her experience in Yangchow and I never want to ask."

"That's true. She doesn't want to talk about it—naturally, and I will not ask her, either. But what is she planning to do?"

"Heaven only knows. As I say, she is very much like a quail that has been flushed and badgered a long time and may decide just to sit on the ground, waiting to be captured. I could see it in her whole being when she was playing with the baby. I have a hunch that she will simply take a man that she likes, and it does not take much for her to like a man. She has her ideas about men, you know. Like that boxer."

"I still can't get over the idea that she threw you over and went with that boxer."

"That is exactly it. And I shouldn't be surprised if she has found him and they have met again."

"But he was the man who killed his wife! He is supposed to be in jail."

"It was an accident. He didn't really kill her. He convinced the court and got eighteen months. I had it checked after she left. He may be free now. Look at it this way. He may have a lot of physical appeal for her; so if she likes him and marries him and has her children, what's wrong with that?"

"But this is marriage!"

"What's wrong with marrying a young, strong, healthy, muscular body if she likes him and he makes a normal, sane husband? Anyway, we know too little about him to be able to judge."

"Should I ask her?"

"No. She will tell you when the time comes." Then he added: "This is, of course, just my guess."

Mengchia left a few days later. Peony felt a strange peace of mind. Mengchia was not far wrong about Peony's readiness to marry, to make her nest. The whole range of her emotions played out, she now wanted to settle down, like a bird with tired wings. She wanted a man whom she could like sufficiently to marry, a man who could satisfy her needs as a woman, and who could also provide for her and love her. Her experience with men had taught her many things, but now she knew exactly what she wanted. A simple man, an honest man, young and healthy, and tolerably intelligent. She had never found it difficult to get a man interested in her. The difficulty was in finding a man of fair appearance, good health, and dependable character and income—almost the same qualities that a parent would be looking for in arranging a match for a daughter. It was Mrs. An Tonien's idea of a good business arrangement, she thought ruefully. She wanted, above all, a young man and a strong man to be the father of her children. She was not asking for much.

It was late March. The snow was thawing on the Western Hills. Tiny pink peach blossoms were peeping timidly on black branches over the walls of many residences in the *hutungs*. Outside the West Gate, clusters of these trees stood scattered in the moist spring earth, while thick masses of snow still clung to the roots. At the Tungtan Pailou and outside Tungan Bazaar, many rickshaw pullers had shed their lamb coats, which were filthy with a whole winter's grime. The weather was still crisp, but the more well-to-do men and women were coming out in their new spring coats. Once in a while, someone was seen passing by in a rickshaw, loaded with sprigs of peach blossoms, bringing a message of spring from the mountains.

Peony often took walks alone. She enjoyed coming out to see this gaiety, to hear once more the voices of children playing in the streets, to breathe in the happy, noisy, sun-dry air of Peking. She was not thinking of anything, or looking for anybody. The sky was a crystal-clear blue; the people's houses and the long, low walls of the *hutungs* were a bright cream color, contrasting with the darkish gray of the roofs. These were pure, solid colors, possible only in the clear, dry air. Along Hatamen Street, she would sometimes see a train of camels, coming through the Hatamen Gate, carrying sacks of coal from Mentoukow, an important railway station.

All she needed to be completely happy was company. With Mengchia away, she had the carriage to herself. Jasmine's baby was her world, even though the nurse was on twenty-four-hour duty. The same was true of her mother. Sometimes she took a drive outside the West Gate, or to the still generally deserted Tienchiao area outside Chienmen. It was just not possible to persuade Jasmine to wrap up the baby and come out for a drive; the troubles and fuss involved in taking the baby out for a drive were entirely disproportionate to any possible benefit; and in all likelihood, the mother would be looking after the baby all the way, rather than enjoying the fresh sights of the open air.

More often, Peony took walks alone to the Tungtan Pailou, where she could relive her memories in the wineshop. One characteristic of Peony was that she had no patience for details. She never could remember how long Fu Nanto's prison sentence was, and assumed that he was still in jail. She loved to go out to the wineshop, order a cup of tea, and sit and watch.

The woman at the cashier's desk remembered her. She left her chair and came down to speak to her.

"We haven't see you here in a long time."

Peony looked up with a smile.

"I was down south, and just recently came back."

"You remember your friend?" Peony's eyes lit up. "He is out of jail now. He was here three or four times and inquired about you."

"When did he come out?"

"It's three or four weeks already."

"How does he look? Looks all right?"

The woman gave an arch smile. "He is fine, except he looked so dejected when I told him you hadn't shown up for a year. You wait. He'll come this way again."

Peony's face flushed involuntarily. "When does he come here?"

"Sometimes in the morning, sometimes around now. He orders four ounces of *huatiao* and does not talk to anybody, but sits looking out toward the street, just like you."

"Next time he comes, tell him that I have come back. Tell him he will be sure to find me here. I will come every day about this time."

"He will come."

They chatted about other things and the woman went back to her desk. Peony was keyed up. She wondered how Fu Nanto would look after a year and a half in prison. She grew keenly expectant, hoping to see him arrive any minute. Toward the supper hour, she remembered she must go back. Reluctantly, she stood up and left.

She had not gone a hundred feet and was entering Tsungpu Hutung when she heard someone calling, "Peony! Peony!"

She turned around. Fu Nanto was dashing up the side track, dodging the carts on his way. Peony stood still, watching him run toward her. "Why, it is he!" she thought, and felt good all over. She could hardly contain herself, but waited till he had come clear of the traffic and then wildly waved her hand.

He had come up, stopping just for a second to focus his brilliant eyes on her, as if to make sure he was not dreaming.

His white teeth were gleaming. All at once he took her by both hands.

"I came just as you left. The cashier told me." His voice stuttered and Peony felt his hands quivering.

"Oh, Nanto, Nanto, I am so happy to see you again."

"Are you?"

Peony studied him for a second. There was even a suggestion of a momentary coolness and aloofness in her act of sizing him up. Recovering herself, she said, "Of course. I was hoping you might turn up."

"Let's go back to the wineshop."

"I must go home now. They will be waiting for me. I will come and meet you tomorrow. The whole day, all right?"

"Then I will walk with you."

She let him guide her into Tsungpu Hutung, and listened while he talked. Once more they fell into that jaunty rhythm she knew and remembered so well. He gripped her arm and pressed close to her, knee to knee, as they walked. She had a feeling this man could carry her up in his arms and run.

"Did you think of me while you were in prison?" she asked.

"I thought of nothing else. Now I am free. Nobody can interfere any more."

"No one? Are you sure?"

"No one."

They had turned into the Little Yapao Hutung, that long narrow alleyway. They were alone. He stopped and looked at her for a moment and then held her tightly. He bent his face close to hers, but she fought against her own rising excitement and said, "Please, don't rush me. I haven't seen you for so long."

She stepped back as his hands let go of hers. Their eyes met, and then they fell naturally into step again.

"You are not engaged, I hope?" he asked.

"No."

Once more she felt the pressure of his arm around her, and she leaned her weight against him, while she half walked and half shuffled along. He was such a simple, honest man, she thought. She would not admit that she loved him, but he made her feel warm and protected, and she remembered how they had had such fun together.

Just a few blocks from her house they turned into a big cross street. She noticed an open sewer, and remembering what he had done once before, the naughty thought came into her head to try him again.

"Nanto," she said, "do you love me very much?"

"You know that I do."

"Will you obey me and do everything that I tell you?"

"Of course."

She pointed to the open sewer and cried, "Jump!"

Fu Nanto leaped into the sewer, happily, gracefully, and with a great deal of showmanship.

"See!" he said, standing in the sewer.

Peony broke into a great laugh. Luckily, the sewer was dry. Placing one hand on the ground as a lever, he leaped nimbly out of the ditch.

He embraced her and asked, "Now, will you marry me?"

"I don't know. Look, there's somebody behind you." And she broke away.

CHAPTER 31

The next day, Peony went out early. She told her mother and Jasmine that she had made an appointment with a man. Jasmine watched her. She was dressed in an old cotton print jacket and trousers and had playfully changed her hair-do, letting it down in a pigtail.

"Who is it?" Jasmine asked.

"I can't tell you—I am just going out. And I may be back late."

"When will you be back?" asked her mother, always over-anxious.

"I don't know. I just don't know. If I am back, I am back. If I am not back, don't wait for me for supper. Is that clear?"

"Very clear, Sister," said Jasmine wryly.

The mother still looked on with wondering, watery eyes. Peony said, "Mother, do I have to explain everything? Am I not free?"

"Nobody says you are not free," said her mother. In upper-class families, an unmarried girl would not go out alone unless the mother knew where she was going. But Peony was a widow.

"All right, Mother. It's a man, not a girl that I am going to meet."

"I am not saying anything. But my child, you must not rush. Mengchia will be home soon."

"Mother, I have not even made up my mind."

She walked with quick steps toward the front court and left.

"Now that's queer," said Jasmine. "I saw the flush on her face when she came in last night. At supper she was smiling to herself all the time. She is trying to cover up. And the way she dresses to meet this man! She is up to something, I am sure."

The mother said, "This time I am not going to let her run around and involve herself again. You and I and Mengchia must take care of her. And if she likes the man, we must see him before her father and I will give our consent."

"Mengchia said before he left that she might meet Fu Nanto again."

"Who is Fu Nanto?" Her mother had never heard the name. "Did you ever see him? What is he like?"

"I never saw him. In fact I didn't even know his name until I saw her diary. All I know is that she used to go out and meet this man when she was tired of Mengchia. He is a member of the Shuttlecock Club and a boxer."

"A boxer? What kind of joke is this?"

"I don't know. He landed in jail, but Mengchia thinks he may be out by now."

"In jail for what?" The mother looked horrified.

"For killing his wife. It was an accident, I was told. We never paid any attention until Mengchia learned it in the papers and said he was tried and got eighteen months. He didn't kill her. The wife fell in a scuffle against the sharp post of an iron bed."

"She never told me."

"She wouldn't."

The mother got more and more worried.

"What about his family?" she asked.

"We do not know a thing."

At Tungtan Pailou, Fu Nanto was waiting with a hired carriage. He and Peony caught sight of each other at the same moment, and shouted their greetings. There was such joy on Fu Nanto's face.

Two years ago, they had met often in wineshops, theaters, and outdoors. Now Fu Nanto proposed a drive to the Jade River.

"Whatever you say," answered Peony blithely.

She entered the carriage. When she was seated, she looked at him appraisingly. She really did not know too much about the man. She had not loved and could not love him the way she loved An Tonien and Mengchia. But he had such an honest, direct look and she liked his white teeth and his open, youthful smile, and muscular build. She liked him very much indeed, because she remembered that they had so much fun together. He played the shuttlecock beautifully, he could perform the slow, rhythmic, graceful movements of *taichi* boxing with such beauty and skill. He was always entertaining and full of zest. He could drink and play cards and do magic tricks like a professional. Once she had asked him, "Is there anything you cannot do?" and he had answered: "Two things. I don't smoke opium and do not gamble. That's not for me. Oh, yes," he added as an afterthought, "I cannot read or write—that is, hardly. I can read the bills and the house deeds, and sign my own name. I am not an educated man but I am an honest man."

She had laughed because it was so true. She remembered he was very honest and a bit of a miser in money matters. She knew from the way he counted his change when paying a bill. He took these things very seriously. He would not be cheated, nor would he cheat others. Once he discovered he had been overcharged at a wine restaurant. He was furious, went up to the cashier, and drummed on the desk to have it corrected. On the other hand, he would return the change if he discovered that he had been overpaid five pennies. Today she was determined to find out more about him.

"We'll go out rowing on the Jade River," he told her. "I know a place there, a sort of swimming hole, very beautiful and quiet." (She knew that he loved the open air and outdoors. It was such a pleasant change from meeting with a scholar.) Then he added, "On the way back, I can show you my farm."

"You have a farm?" He was growing more and more interesting to her.

"Yes, I am a farmer. I have a farm near Haitien."

"But I see you in the city all the time."

"I have a shop selling rice and coal balls and kindling inside the West Gate."

"Who lives on the farm? Who took care of it when you were in jail?"

"A nephew of mine, and I have farm help. We have chickens and ducks and geese and six or seven lambs. I want you to see my farm."

"Just your nephew and nobody else in the family?"

"That's right. Now that my wife is dead, I don't go to the farm much."

He placed his large hands on her thighs and squeezed them.

"Did you think of me while you were in jail?" she asked. She was really sizing up this man.

"I thought of nothing else. I dreaded the thought that when I came out, I might not be able to find you. I didn't even have your address."

She leaned back, letting her head roll with the rumble of the carriage, thinking. She felt his hand stealing across her back, and she made a slight movement. To her surprise, she found herself overcome with a feeling of great sadness. When he was about to kiss her, she stirred uneasily and said, "Please don't!"

How was she to be sure that she could love this man? But curiously she liked him, had always liked him. These conflicting thoughts kept her mind busy until they had come out of the West Gate "enclosure," a large circular space surrounded by high city walls, set between two gates for the purpose of trapping the enemy. The highway outside the West Gate, which led to the Summer Palace, was new and broad, planted with willows on both sides. Their carriage rolled past rickshaws and people riding on donkeys. When they were passing Haitien, a prosperous suburb settlement about two miles from the West Gate, he pointed to a spot in the distance and said, "There! That's where my farm is—just a short distance from the village. Come on," he said, taking her hand, "let's get in front."

"Where?" He was always surprising.

"The country is so beautiful. I'll do the driving and let the driver sit inside if he likes. It's so stuffy in here."

Peony chuckled lazily. This man was forever amusing her. He tapped on the window from inside the covered carriage. "Hey, driver, stop."

The driver looked down and saw his face popping out of the window.

"I want you to draw up and stop."

The driver did as he was told, and then Fu Nanto said, "Let me do the driving. You get down. *Kuniang* and I will sit on top."

"Can you drive?"

"You will see."

When they had seated themselves in the driver's seat, Fu Nanto took the reins, clicked, and urged the horse gently forward. Peony felt the gentle breeze brushing her face.

"The view is so different from here," she said.

"Of course. It is like being on horseback—you see the world from a higher level. It is a nice sensation. Do you ride?"

"Of course not."

Expertly, Nanto gave a light tug and the horse went into an easy canter. Then he gave a crack or two of the whip, and the nag obeyed his signals and broke out into a gallop. The long vista of the highway changed swiftly; once in a while, a low-hanging soft willow branch swept across their faces.

Half a mile from Haitien, they saw a long stretch of stone-paved highway. He urged the horse forward with the northerner's cries of *Ta-trr! Worr!* and the horse increased its speed. Nanto was thoroughly enjoying himself.

"Hold onto the handrail," he said, with a broad, exhilarated laugh. "Here, put your left arm around me and hold on. It's not too fast for you?"

"No, you are quite a driver."

Nanto's face beamed, his eyes on the road. There was a peasant with a carrier-load in front. He gave an expert little swerve around the man as he kept on talking. "To think that only a month ago I was sitting in prison. And now I am driving with you!"

Soon they turned off from the main road and struck across the country. He pointed to a tree-covered area three hundred feet ahead and said, "There it is. There are some boats for hire. I love the place."

Peony was no longer thinking about her problems. She fell into Fu Nanto's exuberant mood, enjoying the change.

A long hedgerow some seven feet high lined the bank, hiding the small placid stream behind it.

"The Empress Dowager used to come here. That is why it is so hidden. Now she has the new Summer Palace and the place is open, but very few people know about it."

They had alighted and arrived at the bank. A very long boat station, discolored and decaying, was standing on their right. A dozen boats, with paint peeling off, were tied to the quay.

"Are there fish in it?" Peony asked the lone attendant.

"Not many, and only small ones."

"I love fishing," said Peony.

It was early in the year and they were the only visitors there.

They hired a boat and rowed out. Fu Nanto had taken the oars, and Peony sat opposite him, her pigtail hanging over in front across her shoulder. The boat glided gently along. She took out a cigarette and began to smoke. Now and then a heron rose from the trees and flapped its white wings against the blue sky. Small birds dipped down to the water looking for food, filling the air with their incessant, urgent twitter. She felt immensely happy.

"This is divine," she said, exhaling the smoke luxuriously.

"I wanted to show you what living in the country is like."

"If we can fish here, it will be wonderful."

"Sorry, I had not thought of it. I would have brought the tackle along if I had known. There are only small perch here, six or seven inches long."

"It doesn't matter," said Peony gaily. "It's a wonderful way of spending an afternoon, even if we don't catch any fish. With a book, a package of cigarettes, and a clay stove for making tea, it will be perfect."

"No books for me. Even if I could read, I would sooner look at you than read books. I don't know what is in those books. Just talk, talk, talk, I suppose. Look at this country! Why don't the writers *live* instead of writing?"

Peony was not listening. She was trailing one finger in the water, looking down at the small waves lapping at the side of the boat. Now and then she cast a swift, sideways glance at Fu Nanto and saw him looking back at her with yearning adoration. Her heart felt like an oyster; instead of pounding with love and passion, it wriggled and gave her a ticklish, squirming sensation, by no means unpleasant.

"Tell me, Peony, do you love me? You'll make me the happiest man alive if you say you do."

"I don't know."

"Can you care for me a little, just a little? I will show you my house this afternoon. We could be together living like this every day."

"I wouldn't have come out with you if I didn't like you. Are you proposing to me?"

"What else?" He let the oars drift. "Last night I lay in bed thinking and thinking. I am not an educated man. And you— I suspect you come from a very nice family. Can I hope?"

Peony dared not make up her mind. She said, "I like you— very much. But you must give me time."

"I know. You have to have your parents' consent. Are your parents living?"

"Yes. And I have a brother-in-law, who is the head of the family in Peking."

"Who is your brother-in-law?"

"My sister's husband. He is Liang *Hanlin*. I want to consult him."

The word *hanlin* carried with it a kind of social glamour even for the man in the street who could neither read nor write.

"A *hanlin*, you say?"

"Yes, Liang *Hanlin*. . . . What's the matter?"

Nanto seemed quite put out by this discovery. He remained silent for minutes.

With yeomanlike skill, Fu Nanto used an oar to paddle the boat toward the bank where sedge was growing a foot high above the water. "I know a beautiful spot here," he said. Slowly edging the boat up close, he said, "Come on," and extended a hand. Without a word, he lifted her up in his arms and walked ten or fifteen feet before setting her down on a grass plot. He seemed to know the spot well. It was in the center of a grove of trees and thick underbrush. Glowing in his physical health, he began to strip his jacket and inner jacket off.

Peony was aware of being trapped, yet was fascinated to see his round chest and broad shoulders, and his brown skin gleaming in the sun. He came and seated himself on the grass beside her.

"Don't you feel cold?" she asked weakly.

"No," he replied exultantly. "Not cold at all."

She felt faint inside as she drew a finger admiringly across his chest and arms. His eyes were upon her, and he flexed his biceps with an exuberant, proud laugh, like a peacock instinctively displaying its feathers. His face was lean and handsome and muscular.

"Would you like to see me do some *taichi* boxing for you?"

He threw the jacket down. *Taichi* was really a form of calisthenics, consisting of slow, circular movements and controlled inhaling and exhaling of breath in a well-regulated rhythm. His hands and wrists and arms tense at all moments, he ducked and crouched and straightened and twisted, his legs executing the same graceful, tense, and extremely slow movements in response, with the sinuous grace of a cat. Peony watched him in the sun, twisting his body into a convoluting set of harmonious, pulsing movements. At all moments, the positions of head, neck, arms, and legs were in perfect harmony. Instead of a quick thrust, it was a slow, gradual extending of an arm, and instead of a kick, it was a slow, difficult, poised, and gradual lifting of a leg. Its beauty came entirely from the grace and tension of the slow movements. It might be called a "cat dance."

"How is that?" he asked, coming abruptly to a close, panting slightly.

"It's wonderful," said Peony with a smile.

"It's the best exercise for one's health. I do that every morning at six o'clock. It's got to be done early in the open, to get the full benefit of the morning air."

He lay back and pulled her toward him, and she rested her head on his strong chest; his hand roamed over her, across her back, over her shoulders, up and down and up again in teasing, tickling, and yet soothing strokes. He heard the quickening of her breath.

She raised her head to face him and saw his flashing white teeth. Silently she made up her mind to marry this man.

What the mind could not solve, the body solved by instinct with utter simplicity. Probably courtship and mating have not varied in their essential aspects from the jungle days. Peony could have sung like some old poet now: "His face is like the morning sun and I am pleased with the strength of his loins. I will bear this man a son this day that I may find favor in his eyes." The peacock had won.

Afterward, she said with a glad smile, "Nanto, you were perfect."

"And you, too," he replied.

She took his inner jacket and covered his chest so that he might not catch cold.

"I don't need it," he said.

After a picnic lunch, in which they brewed their tea over a fire built from dry twigs and leaves, they left the place. Peony felt she was satisfied with this simple, honest, entertaining man. She hardly noticed the scenery on the way back, and remained quite pensive.

When they reached Fu Nanto's farm, she was thoroughly delighted with what she saw. The homestead interested her particularly. It consisted of five rooms, in a field of one and a half acres. Honking geese and quacking ducks were running about the place. A few black lambs were grazing by a hedge, tied to a stake by a long rope, so that they would not eat up the vegetables. Fu Nanto explained that this was formerly the house of a eunuch, who had retired after a lifetime of service to a prince's household nearby. It was an ordinary farmhouse, one wing of which was open and used for the storage of hay and fuel. It had not been whitewashed for years and the unpainted woodwork had grown a dry pale brown from the sun and rain.

They returned in late afternoon.

CHAPTER 32

These outings were continued in the following days. Then Peony came down with a sore throat and fever, and had to be confined to bed. She kept Jasmine and her mother guessing, and when the latter pressed her as to whom she was going out with, she always replied, "Don't be impatient, Mother. I have not made up my mind." She had the feeling that her mother and sister might laugh at her for marrying an illiterate farmer. It would be a comedown for Jasmine and her *hanlin* husband to have an illiterate brother-in-law. How was she ever going to explain? It would break the old principle of "family status" (*menhu*). She hoped to explain the matter to her cousin.

Mengchia returned when she was still confined to bed. He had barely settled down when Jasmine said to him with a smile, "Something is happening with Peony."

He looked up sharply.

"She has been going out."

"With whom?"

"She would not tell us. I suspect it is Fu Nanto."

He almost leaped up, then allowed himself a staccato laugh. "I thought so. How clever of me! How do you know?"

"Because of the way she dressed up when she went out, in peasant cotton dress and trousers. What kind of game is she playing? She said once that she had gone out fishing and had watched *taichichuan*, the Boxing of Primeval Unity. So I thought it must be the boxer."

That late afternoon, he sought an opportunity to find out from Peony what she had in mind.

Peony was lying in bed, scantily clad, one leg crooked up, holding a small volume in her hand. The south window was closed, and the light from the back window made her face stand out in profile. She saw him come in and gave a smile of welcome.

"What are you reading in this poor light?"

"The essays of yours. Just browsing for amusement. When I read a few pages of your book, my sore throat seems to disappear."

Mengchia laughed.

"Tako, I want to talk to you," she said.

Mengchia pulled up a chair, almost as a doctor would to a patient in bed. He looked at her intently. She was unsmiling.

"It's something serious," she said. "It's Fu Nanto. I've found him again, and we've met a few times." Then she broke off and sighed deeply.

"Go ahead and tell me."

Without turning her head to face him, she stretched out a hand and grasped Mengchia's. She was staring off into space, her eyes blinking in concentration. Still without looking at him she said, "What would you say if I told you I wanted to marry him?"

"Is that what you want to talk to me about?" He noticed that her voice was a little tired, without enthusiasm.

"Yes. You must tell me."

Mengchia's voice was tender. "You forget that I have not seen this man. You have not told me anything about him."

She turned toward him and finally looked at him. Her voice was more lively when she said, "He wants to marry me. I cannot make up my mind."

"Do you love him? You must tell me honestly."

"I don't know. I like him. He is very honest and honorable and he loves me. When I am with him, I am very happy. Yet—is it not strange?—when I come away, I do not think of him at all—that is, there is nothing of that burning pain and longing when we are apart—not like the way I feel about —never mind—not something very close, very deep, that pulls at your heartstrings. It is not the way I miss—never mind— one whom I care for deep down in my soul. Is it not strange? —these things are so deep that we do not recognize their existence in ourselves?"

Her stream of words was disjointed, incoherent. Several times she came dangerously near to pouring out her deep feelings for Mengchia, but checked herself in time. Her hand was lying in his, and her fingers scratched it lazily.

"You don't have to decide . . ." he said, while he lifted her middle finger and played with it.

"No. I want you to tell me. Should I?"

"You told me that he loves you, that you can be happy when you are with him. I suppose that you know him quite well, I mean intimately. . . ."

Peony relinquished his hand and smiled almost an ashamed smile. "Yes. Physically he is quite handsome. He satisfies me. . . . It's that sometimes I wonder. He told me that he cannot read or write. But he is a very nice person, and I know he will provide well for me. He has a farm at Haitien and a shop inside West Gate. Sometimes I feel I may be risking my happiness to live with this man for life—that I might be making a mistake. I do feel that I can be quite happy with him. We'll have children and I shall have a home. You must tell me. There's my father and mother, too. Do you think I should?"

"I am glad, Peony, that you have told me. Did you say that he is a farmer and has a shop? What kind of shop?"

"Selling rice and coal balls and kindling and ice. Do you think I am crazy? What will Jasmine and mother say?"

Mengchia paused a little to formulate his thought, to try to picture her life with Fu Nanto. "Why, I think it is perfectly all right if you can be happy with him. As far as the family status is concerned, don't think about it. It may be quite a change of life for you."

"I believe I could adjust myself to the change. I am young and healthy. Don't you believe I could?"

Mengchia felt pleased that she placed so much trust in his opinion. She went on saying, "He asked me several times if I could love him and I said 'perhaps'—you know we say these things when we make love—and he asked me if I would marry him and I said 'perhaps.' "

The sounds of these words floated across Mengchia's ears. He was buried in thought; then all of a sudden he remembered the dream he had and the last lines of the divination stick:

> *When the mountains close in and the waterway*
> *is blocked,*
> *There stands the rice field with ripening corn.*

He broke out into a mystifying smile.

"What are you laughing at? You don't approve?"

"Yes, I do." He laughed again.

"What is so amusing?"

"You remember the oracles? Did you say that he is a farmer? If the oracles are true, you are going to marry him. In time, I quite believe you will make adjustments and raise a family of your own and you will be a wife and mother like anybody else. Money, status—they do not mean anything except to the snobs, and you know how I hate snobs."

"You don't mind having a farmer for a brother-in-law?"

"Honestly, I don't. Peony, I want so much for you to be happy. Go ahead and marry him if he is an honest man and loves you. They talk about status. My father was a farmer. That did not prevent me from becoming a *hanlin*. Now I am a *hanlin*, and it should not prevent my son from becoming a farmer again. The farmers, you remember, rank first among the social classes in our national tradition—above the businessmen, the artisans—next only to the scholars. I will tell you a good story. . . ."

He told her the anecdote about a prime minister with a rascal for a son who had threatened to squander his entire fortune. "Look here," the prime minister said to his profligate son, "I am an old man and a prime minister and am still working hard every day. You should be ashamed of yourself." The son replied, "Why should I? My father is a prime minister and my son is a *toatai* at twenty-two. Your father was a farmer and your son a man without character, without ambition and without shame. How can you compare yourself with me? Why shouldn't I play and why shouldn't you work?"

Peony laughed. "So true—so true."

"So your sister married a *hanlin* and you marry a farmer. What is to prevent you from having a farmer for a husband and a *hanlin* for your son?"

"So you approve?"

"I do, if what you tell me is true, that you do like Fu Nanto."

"I think I do." Then she stretched a hand toward him and she yearned to say something. She looked at him and said, "If you approve, then I am content. It's for us, too. I don't want anything to change between us." She squeezed his hand softly.

"Nothing has changed. Nothing will change between us," said Mengchia.

He pressed her hand and rose to tell the news to Jasmine and his mother-in-law.

"It is Fu Nanto, as we thought," he said to his wife.

"Oh, no!" replied Jasmine. She gasped involuntarily.

"Of course we will see the man before we give our consent. He seems to be illiterate, and has a farm and a shop selling coal balls and rice. But she likes him."

Jasmine's eyes grew bigger. "It is so like Sister. Did she say she has decided to marry him?"

"No, she wanted to ask my opinion, and I said if he is an honorable, hard-working man and has a regular income and is of good character and good health, why not?"

The mother did not know what to think. She said, "If he has a good character and is not hare-lipped or pockmarked, I don't mind. And it strikes me as not a bad idea to have a son-in-law who owns a shop selling rice and coal balls. Peony will never be in want of rice or fuel."

Arrangements were made for Mengchia to go to see Fu Nanto and his shop and his small farm at Haitien. Mengchia found that Fu Nanto had a few acres of good land, too, at Tsingho, seven miles north of the city. Mengchia wrote a letter to Peony's father informing him of the proposal and soliciting his consent. The father gave up, thinking that this was the last act of a comedy of his whimsical daughter, with all her crazy ideas. He was to come up in September for the wedding.

In midsummer, Peony wrote a long letter to Paiwei, inviting her and Joshui to attend the wedding and visit Peking.

Dear Paiwei:

You will be happy, I know, to learn that I am going to be married to Fu Nanto the first week of September. I do so want both of you to come up and attend my wedding.

So much has happened since I last saw you. You ask me what I am doing. Outwardly, nothing. I can see you two up on the mountain doing nothing, too, happy to see the spring pass into summer and summer into winter. Nanto is fixing the house at Haitien and having it completely renovated. That is why we have to wait till September.

How do I describe Nanto to you or my feeling toward him? He can barely sign his name, but in every other way is what a young girl would want to find in a husband. He has a good appearance, and a dependable character. Yes, I know I can trust him. My mother says half-jokingly and half in earnest that I shall never be in want of rice and fuel. He sells rice and *coal balls*. Coal balls, I repeat. Is it not glorious? I have complete confidence in him and in his love for me. What more can a girl want?

Jasmine does not seem to approve at all of the match, but that's Jasmine. Mengchia approves. Paiwei, I think I have changed. All my longings and my heartaches are buried, safely locked away within me. You speak of love. Physical love I have and I shall be a mother of many children, I hope. That is now my ideal of happiness. I never want anything else. I ask for no more. How can I explain this to anybody but you?

Mind you, I do not say that I do not love Nanto. He is wonderful to me, and very entertaining at times. Only I cannot feel the frenzy which you know that I have felt in the past. That complete surrender of one soul to another is now beyond me, and I do not wish to reopen the old wounds again. But I do love him, though in a different way, and shall be a good wife to him. Poor Nanto, he is so honest, and he needs me.

I have no regrets. I must tell you about Mengchia. I tell this to you and to nobody else. The other day I went out with him and Nanto to see his farm at Tsingho. He has three acres of wheat fields there and a grove of date trees which he tells me bring in an income of two or three hundred dollars a year. (God, how disjointed my thoughts are!) Well, he stayed in the house talking with his relatives, and Mengchia and I strolled down to the bank. The water was delightfully clear and some mules were plodding along a field across the stream. The sun was slanting toward the horizon and ravens were circling over a clump of trees on our left, against a glorious sky of purple, red, and violet. The sunset was so beautiful that I shed tears despite myself. I felt so sad. I tell you I could not account for those tears, but there I was and Mengchia looked at me with such tenderness in his eyes. We have agreed never to mention the word love between us, nor ever kiss each other. He wants to be faithful to Jasmine and I to Nanto. But he said, "I will never kiss you again, but let me kiss away those tears." And he did, and then he said the old familiar line from Po Chuyi's "Song of Eternal Remorse":

Heaven and earth may perish one day,
But this pain of pains shall never end.

His face was flushed, and we never said a word more. He lent me a hand to help me up and we returned to the farmhouse.

Dear Paiwei, whatever we do and whatever we feel, these memories live with us. Sometimes I feel that the best moments, the true moments of our lives, are the only real ones, while other moments pass and are lost forever because they have no meaning in our souls. The great moments cling to us like molasses—you separate the lumps, but the threads are long and drawn out and clinging. Or they are like music that dies, while the haunting melodies linger in our minds. Would you say that the haunting melodies are real, or the music itself? Certain things are interrupted by the course of events, but their memories remain to haunt us throughout our lives. I shall try to be a good wife to Nanto, but I do not believe I can ever shut out the memories of what I have lived through. They are rich in colors for me, like the intoxicating rose of Chin Chu's love, or the dazzling white flame of An Tonien's, or the lilac-mauve of Mengchia's love for me. In my wedding dress, I shall want to hold a bouquet of lilacs in my hand. I used to love violets. Now I like the softer mauve of lilacs.

I know you will see me a happy bride when you come. Please do come, I beg you. I promise you an excellent dinner of goose from our own farm the first evening of your arrival.

Mengchia told me that great books are written with tears and blood. I believe that this letter of mine is written with my blood and tears.

Yours always,
Peony

ABOUT THE AUTHOR

Lin Yutang's family name is Lin. Nevertheless when people call him "Mr. Yutang," he rather likes it because it is so Chinese. In a nation of ten million Changs and ten million Wangs, naturally such a custom developed. But "Mr. Lin" would also be correct. Born of a Presbyterian minister in 1895 in an inland village on the southeast coat of Fukien, he considers his upbringing in a village in deep mountains had a permanent influence on his character.

He took his degrees from St. John's (Shanghai), Harvard, and Leipzig. He considers he got all his English before coming to Harvard. In the Widener Library he first found himself, first came alive; never saw a Harvard-Yale football match. He was a teacher at Tsinghua University, Peking, in 1916-19; married and went abroad with his wife to study, 1919; studied in the School of Comparative Literature under Bliss Perry and Irving Babbitt at Harvard in 1919-20; worked with the Y.M.C.A. for Chinese laborers at Le Creusot, France, to support himself, 1920-21; studied at Jena and Leipzig, 1921-23; was professor of English at Peking National University, 1923-26; and Dean of Women's Normal College, 1926; was chased out of Peking by the Dog-Meat General in 1926, blacklisted among the radical professors; became Dean of Arts in Amoy University, 1926; joined the Wuhan Nationalist Government as a secretary to the Foreign Ministry at Hankow in the first half of 1927; "liked the Revolution but got tired of the revolutionists." Since the summer of 1927, he has devoted his time entirely to authorship. He was editor of the literary fortnightlies *Lunyu, Jenshienshih,* and *Yuchoufeng,* 1929-35 in Shanghai. Now the only important things to him are his books and his family, including two grandchildren, Niuniu and Didi.

THIS BOOK WAS SET IN

ELECTRA AND POST TITLE MEDIUM TYPES BY

HARRY SWEETMAN TYPESETTING CORPORATION.

IT WAS PRINTED AND BOUND AT

THE PRESS OF THE WORLD PUBLISHING COMPANY.

DESIGN IS BY LARRY KAMP